MOTHERLAND

MOTHERLAND

Tetyana Denford

2020

This is a work of fiction, loosely based on factual events.

All of the characters, organizations, and events portrayed in this novel are either products of the author's imagination or are used to explain real events with some fictitious elements.

Motherland. Copyright © 2020 Tetyana Denford

All rights reserved. This book or any portion thereof may not be reproduced, transmitted, or used in any manner whatsoever without the express written permission of the publisher.

First Printing: 2020

Cover designed by Emir Orucevic

ISBN 9798623392046

Tetyana Denford
Tetyana.Denford@gmail.com
New York, NY

www.tetyanadenford.com

www.instagram.com/tetyanawrites

For Babchya—

You gave me the story of your life so that
I could change the course of my own.

And to the immigrants that are searching for a place on this earth:
may you always know that your stories are our music;
without you, our hearts would never learn how to dance.

During and after the Second World War, millions
of Eastern Europeans migrated to New York,
England, and Australia, to start new lives.

Many lost entire families along the way
and never saw them again.

Melbourne, 1952

Tetyana Denford

Motherland

On a cool afternoon in April on a quiet street, Julia kept her hands in the pockets of her brown threadbare coat and stared at the house. It sat politely at the end of a concrete path, set off from the road, with a sturdy white wood porch that wrapped around the front like a smile. The lamplight in the windows glowed warmly against the darkening haze of the afternoon, and well-dressed people gathered inside.

She straightened her shoulders. In her fingers she held a folded piece of paper, her heart beating in her ears, her breath as thin as the breeze that blew across her legs. She was here now; she couldn't turn back until she'd seen them— it would take her two and a half hours to get back home, and her bus would leave soon. *Love takes courage* her mother used to say to her.

She walked slowly to the door, happy conversations and the smells of a roast dinner hovered in the air as she approached. She knocked once. Then twice and looked down. at her shoes. On the pristine white porch, her shoes looked even more battered than usual.

A woman appeared, dressed in a green silk blouse and full skirt. 'Yes?' The pearls at her ears shone at the edges of her icy blonde hair.

Julia smoothed her dark hair and tucked it behind her ears, revealing a small scar on her jaw. 'Hello. I— 'she faltered, and then cleared her throat. 'Are you Mrs. Douglas?'

'I'm Irene, yes, and you are...?'

'I'm...' she started and shook her head. Her name wouldn't matter. Julia reached into her pocket and retrieved the folded paper, showing it to her. 'I wanted to give you this.' Her hands were shaking.

Irene looked at it quizzically, then back at Julia. 'What is this?'

'I'm sorry, I just… I want to… ' tears filled her eyes as she rose on her tiptoes to see over into the hallway, craning her neck forward and moving closer.

Irene suddenly understood and moved to block her view. 'You can't be here,' she said coolly.

'I know.'

'How did you find this address?'

Julia searched this woman's face. 'Please,' she whispered. 'None of this was my fault. Please, just listen—'

'I don't know what you're trying to say —'

'I was…' Julia interrupted, and then she heard children's laughter echoing in the house. It was *their* laughter, as bright as the sun. Desperation flashed across her eyes.

'I can't have you do this,' the woman's heels clicked as she moved back. 'I don't want to have to call the police. Please leave.'

Julia nodded, tears spilling. 'I understand.' And then, knowing it was her last chance, she suddenly lurched forward, grabbing Irene's soft hand in her own calloused one, crushing the paper into it. 'Just,' she pleaded, her eyes shining with sadness. '*Please* give this to them. Keep it for them. Maybe one day…'

Irene extracted her hand, the paper inside it, it and retreated into the hallway, gripping the door handle. She attempted a smile, but her mouth stiffened. 'You have to leave,' she said a final time before closing the door.

The shadow of Julia's body against the inlaid glass dissipated, little by little, and vanished.

Irene turned the latch and walked down the hallway, slipping the paper into the pocket of her skirt, its rough texture in stark contrast to the smooth cotton. She passed the kitchen and found the dining room, the table filled with children wearing colorful masks, playing games.

One of them, a little boy with scarlet cheeks playfully elbowing his sister, smiled as a cake, alight with candles, was brought to the table. She placed a hand on his dark mop of hair and kissed his cheek as she watched both their faces lean forward towards the flames to blow them out.

'Happy Birthday, my loves.'

Later that evening, the children slept heavily, and the remaining, sweet conversations bubbled out through the dining room, then down the hallway, dissipating quietly up the stairs.

Gold hats littered the polished floor, some with broken elastic straps, and the smell of candles and sugar wafted from the kitchen, mingling with the lilies of Irene's perfume. Voices grew louder as guests prepared to leave, shrugging into fur-trimmed coats and hats, offering handshakes and saying their goodbyes to Bill, politely complaining about how the chilly Australian winter seemed never-ending.

Pale-colored balloons happily bumped against one another as people shifted their feet. Irene had tied each balloon herself, with a long, thin gold ribbon, securing a note on the end of each: *Happy Birthday* said one. *You are 4 today!* said another. *Mummy and Daddy love you both.*

In the square, cream-walled sitting room where the fireplace popped and hissed underneath the mahogany mantle, a row of cards had been carefully erected on the antique sideboard beside, next to the family photos, awards, and heirlooms. Across from the fireplace was a cream fleur-de-lis sofa with oak end tables on either side, and Irene sat, stocking feet tucked under her, two unopened envelopes in her hand.

The first one was from Auntie Sylvia; the other was from Bill's brother Joe. She placed them on her lap and withdrew the paper from her pocket. It was yellowed, as if it had traveled in a storm.

She let the words unravel in front of her.

My babies-

How I miss you. I am sorry I can't be with you, but you must be so happy, with so many gifts to open. The other day, I found the two waxflowers that you pressed into my book for my birthday so long ago, and it made me think of you. Do you remember that day? They have their color still— pale pink and white. They remind me of your faces.

I won't be able to write for a while again, but when I can, I will try, and tell you more. Just remember I love you very much.

Mama

Out in the hallway, the heavy sound of wood as the door closed, a crack in the silence. She fed the letter back into her pocket.

'Well, that's the last of 'em.' Bill looked at his reflection in the glass inlay. He was tired, all of his 48 years now gathered in the stoop of his shoulders and the hollow of his cheeks.

Approaching the sitting room, he saw his wife, motionless, staring down at her lap. The room was warm, but felt oddly hollow and expectant: like the pause before a piece of music.

He cleared his throat. 'So, sweetheart, what'd you think? Was pretty nice, having a few people around. Nice to celebrate. You did really well.'

'Yes.'

'Yes, you liked being a hostess?' He leaned against the doorframe.

'Sure, that's part of it, I guess. It was a great evening,' Irene nodded and looked up, her eyes focusing through him, distant. 'Thank you, darling.' She rested her hands on top of the cards on her lap.

'You okay?'

'Yes, of course. Just a bit emotional about the whole thing, I guess. I'd be grateful for a drink though.'

'Well, I have an idea. How about— '

'Now, please? Thank you.' She smiled sweetly.

He winked, and bowed exaggeratedly, a sandy tuft of hair falling over his eyes. 'Sure, sweetheart. Can do. Be right back.'

As he disappeared past the doorframe, she stood up—a couple smoothly diverging— and delicately padded across the room, cards at her fingertips. She carefully placed Auntie Sylvia and Uncle Joe on the sideboard next to the other sentiments of birthday wishes. *Four years*, she thought gratefully, despite being wary of old wounds.

She turned to look towards the hallway; the balloons were already deflating. She placed her hand in her pocket and withdrew the letter.

And then she walked toward the fire.

Motherland

I'm kissing you now — across the gap of a thousand years.

– Marina Tsvetayeva

Tetyana Denford

Part I
Ukraine to Germany
1940-1946

Tetyana Denford

1

Ukraine, 1940

The wheels of the cart thrummed along the ground, a black silhouette moving across the slate skies, the figure of Julia's sister cut out in black, holding the reigns. They were now hours away from what they had left behind, the unknown ahead of them. The horse followed a steady pace through the tracks of the ones that had gone before them already, and Julia watched, curled under a blanket, as the fading stars moved through the small opening in the canvas that covered her. Night was safest for this type of journey.

She held her coat to her body, the wool too thin for the raw spring cold. She still felt the lingering warmth of her mother's arms around her, and the rosary she had given her lay delicately around her neck.

'Maria?' she called to her sister softly as she clicked the horses onward. 'Can't we just turn back?'

'Keep your voice down.'

'But it's so early- no one will hear us.'

'Russians have taken over the entire village practically, they'll be looking for anyone they can get their hands on, now that they've killed our brothers.' Maria hissed.

Julia sighed exasperatedly.

Maria shrugged. 'Maybe I just don't want to hear your doubts right now. I have enough of my own.'

Julia surrendered to the dark, the memory of what she'd left behind leaving a hollow pain in her chest. They were children abandoning their childhoods, at the mercy of a world they had no control over.

Like a receding tide, it had all shifted suddenly under their feet: the humble farm that sat comfortably in the clean still air, beside the rows of pear and apple trees that stretched across to the river, gilded in the pink of an early morning sun and giving off a soft scent on the breeze; the cows and horses huddled in clouds of breath, standing in silhouette against the wheat fields beyond. This was the hand on her back, and it was being taken away, and she faced her life without direction now. The ashes of burning cities would settle there soon, and the home where Julia had lived for 17 years would be no longer.

The sisters had walked unsteadily from school those final days, before it was closed and students were evacuated by the Russian police: families were hunted, forced out onto the streets holding their belongings in their arms; children clinging to their siblings, frightened eyes bearing silent witness in shop windows. Homes were emptied and strange new tenants took possession, most of them soldiers. Curfews were installed. Some tried to run, and were shot in warning, cries haunting the streets. Neighbors began to distrust each other's alliances, and it affected them all, like an illness, from one family to the next, hushed dinners and secret meetings spent behind closed doors, words of prayer and clasped hands, mourning dead sons and brothers that had had no proper funerals. Thatched farmhouses with kerosene lamps filling small windows with a timid glow in the lush, dark valleys. It was only a matter of time for it all to reach Julia and her family, creeping towards the edges of the farmland that they used to call home. And even still, the uniqueness in Julia was that she found a place in her heart for the beauty in the melancholy, like lullabies sung in minor keys. It was self-preservation.

Julia propped her head onto her duffle, the chalk of her name leaving a dusting of white on her shoulder. Just yesterday morning, she had been singing a beautiful song, and she had been unafraid. Just yesterday afternoon they had learned of their brothers' deaths.

Her eyes stung, and she hummed softly, the clattering of the wheels muffling the melody as she let a memory surround her. Just yesterday, she had been home, in a room where her voice echoed happily. It felt like a lifetime had passed since then.

The cold spring sun streamed through Julia's bedroom window that morning, casting shadow branches on the wood floor. Her voice trilled and meandered in the maudlin tones of the song that her mother and grandmother had taught her, her pale, delicate fingers threaded buttons through the holes in the shirt that was now too small over her teenage body, and her skirts moved with her hips, in awkward rhythm.

    'Mama?' she called out, her dark hair trailing over her brow and down her shoulders in molasses waves. She pulled her tights over her bony knees and fastened the shirt that was now a little tight over her breasts. Her body was tall and strong, womanly but also still coltish, in the sharp angles of her elbows and knees.

    'Yes, little mouse?' Anna replied warmly.

    'Are you making tea? Is Papa out already?' She looked out through the window in her room for him, and thought she saw his silhouette in the distance. 'He's out, I can see him,' she murmured to herself, her breath moistening the glass as she plaited her thick hair.

    Her father always disappeared early, before everyone else, and not entirely because he was grieving the loss of his sons. It was because it was the calm he craved: getting out of bed as the sun was still rising, lacing his boots and walking outside into the thin light, hearing the animals in their pens shift and rustle and breathe in jittery bursts. The farmhouse and the surrounding twenty acres of farmland was given to him by his father when Mikola was 19, shortly before his death: a large, white walled house with worn-wood framed windows and a thatched roof hovering thickly over six rooms within. It sat peacefully on acres of lush green, neatly folded within the valleys on the outskirts of western Ukraine, at the base of the Karpaty mountains. He and Anna had married shortly thereafter, and their five children arrived later than they had anticipated, when Anna had assumed it wasn't in the cards for her to have any children.

    In the spring the smell of crocus and mineral earth filled every breath, mixed with wet hides and animal breath. The rich, dark land, the chernozem-- once so proud and large, now whittled away by a famine and war-- spread generously across slightly obstructed southern views to the river, a small orchard towards the back of the house, and animals that constantly moved in it and around it like a hum: there were small families of cows, twenty sheep, a clutch of hens, a handful of shaggy stallions, a few mares, three dogs, and geese. The air smelled of wet hides and manure and grass. On days where the temperature was warm enough to lie heavy on their skins— and if the wind was attentive to the groves— the air tasted of rain and strawberries.

The crops were meager now, though they were so plentiful long ago. After the great starvation, the Holodomor, the family gave everything they had: vegetables sprinkled in fresh soil, fresh milk, wild blackberries, sweaty fat plums and sticky pears. Now, they lived on what they had stored, and the food cards that they were allowed as part of the occupation. Police checked on them regularly, so they had to be careful.

Julia strode into the kitchen and ran her hands over the heavy wooden table beside her mother, her palms feeling the soft grain of it. The kitchen was warm, open, windows looking out to the fields, decorated with red-embroidered curtains. There was no food set out yet, and she was hungry, and her mouth watered for sugar, and preserves, and sausage. She could imagine it, taste it. Julia reached for the oven, and her mother, without turning around, slapped her hand away.

'Chekai.' Wait. 'It's not ready yet.' Anna crouched in front of the stove, hovering in impatience, and then moving again, keeping busy. The flesh of her arms vibrated as she kneaded dough for a batch of pyrohy, cracking fresh eggs into it, glistening like little suns. Her wiry, greying hair was scraped back off her face to reveal a strong jaw, dark blue eyes and creased, milky skin. Her face had a weariness to it, but her eyes always shone like stars.

The heavy smell of butter and onions dominated the kitchen in a cloud of acidic sweetness. 'Breakfast after your chores,' she groaned. Her back suffered often. 'Your sister will help later, but right now there is only you and your father and I, so we have to work harder.' There was sadness in her voice, as there had been for months. She wiped the table in front of her, clearing a path in the flour to make more dough.

'How is Maria?' Julia walked across the room to get her coat and glanced down at the small closed door across from her own bedroom. Maria had been ill of late, an occurrence in her life that had been common since she was little, and a dry cough that had become almost a pattern of her speech. She was slight. Pale. Her body was always fighting to remain strong. 'Is she still asleep?'

'Yes. She needs her rest.'

Julia held her coat in her hands. 'It has always been this way. Seems as if she has been ill forever.'

'I know,' her mother shrugged and pressed her palms together as if in prayer. 'Bozshe moye.' Dear lord. 'For twenty years. Same as always. Tired.'

'Will she ever get better? Isn't the older sister supposed to teach the younger one of life? Of boys?' Julia blushed and laughed, her roman nose and sharp cheekbones jutting coyly, but then stopped herself as she saw her mother's face. 'Sorry, I just wanted to lighten the air.'

'I know.'

Julia turned, as if looking for an answer past the door, in the bed where her sister lay, imagining her heart beating feebly.

The kettle boiled with a squeal, and Anna was grateful for the interruption.

'Mama…' Julia, now by the door, slid her foot into a boot.

'Hmm?'

'I love you.'

'Little Julia, moya dusha, you are young. Foolish.'

Julia chuckled as she fastened her coat. Her mother still referred to her as her center. Her soul. 'Fortune favors the foolish.' She winked at her mother.

Anna wagged a finger. 'You are impulsive. Be more wary.'

Julia leaned in and kissed her mother's cheek, the soft skin flushing on impact, and then retreated with a smile.

Her mother waved her away with a cloth that sputtered flour off the ends and watched her move to the door. 'Wait…'

'Yes, Mama.'

Anna wiped her hands on her apron and walked over to the heavy wooden dresser that hulked against the wall by the door. On the surface was a deep crack, and on top of it sat a small brown paper parcel, addressed to Kharkiv prison, and wrapped in twine. It smelled of sausage. 'Take this to the post office. But be careful. Keep--'

'Yes, yes I know,' Julia interrupted, tying her scarf around her hair. 'Keep my head down and don't draw attention to myself.'

Anna nodded, ushering her off.

Julia walked into the crisp morning and knew that her mother had longed for the faces of her sons.

2

Uzhorod was in the distance, the sky had bloomed in greys and pinks as the sun rose, and now the corners of Hungary and Poland were at their sides and under their cart as they progressed. The edges of the woods teemed with families on similar journeys, all quiet, none exchanging looks with anyone as they kept their heads down, their belongings on their backs. The flat wood rumbled beneath Julia's hips, rattling her bones, her clothes not nearly enough to pad the space in between. She missed her bed, she missed the smell of her mother's hair, she missed the sound of her mother's knife thudding the wood of the kitchen table as she sliced crisp vegetables, or the scratch of it as she scraped the skin off potatoes. She pulled her coat down further on her hands, covering her fingers.

'Maria?'

'Yes.'

'I want to go home.'

'I know you do.' Her voice was weak, but still brave. 'But there's no home left for us, Julia.' Her voice faltered, even in its whisper. 'We had to leave.'

'I'm hungry. I wonder where that parcel went,' Julia murmured absentmindedly. 'We could have kept it. It smelled delicious.'

'Oh. The one that Mama told you to send to— '

'Yes. The prison.'

'I know. Well, we have enough, for now.'

'We could have kept it,' Julia repeated. 'It's gone. They're gone. And now— '

Maria sighed. 'Stop. We didn't know, Julia. We didn't know then. Now try not to look back. We have enough at our feet.'

Julia's eyes shone like tiny stars in the burgeoning light and she held her hand flat against her coat.

The parcel. She had clutched the it to her chest that day denting the stiff paper with the shape of her hand. She had been tempted to open it, the smell of sausage oil and spices under her nose. Her stomach grumbled at the memory now, her mouth watered.

The path to the post office that day had been as familiar as if it were her own skin, and yet the shaded trees held secrets and fear, the air was peppered with new sounds: unfamiliar trucks, new voices, horses and carts that had a wary urgency. Lviv was once beautiful, full of cafes with people spilling out into the streets, sat at tables, music wafting on the breeze through open windows, the smell of bread and honey and freshly fried sausage. Now, it was haggard and empty, like an old woman that had seen too much pain and had given more of herself than she had. Soldiers didn't care. They took what they needed and left nothing behind.

Her brothers had been ten years older than her. They were her protectors, the ones that made her laugh, the ones that told her to always be strong.

The day of the brothers' arrest, the NKVD splintered and scattered across the field, a broken wave of dark uniforms with silvery buttons glinting in the sunlight. Anna had covered Julia's mouth before she could shout and pushed her and her sister towards the cellar, her father whispering *go go*, behind them. Before she climbed down into the dark room, she saw her brothers appear, standing next to their mother as she pressed her back against the wall, her hands clasped in prayer. Milo, Julia's favorite— the one who had taught her to read, the one who had counted stars with her— stood in his pyjamas with his arm through his mother. He had smiled at Julia before she sunk beneath the earth; she didn't know it would be the last time she saw his face.

The soldiers pounded on the door to open it, demanding Milo and Bohdan leave the house immediately, as they had been tried and convicted of organizing against the government. They were a part of the young resistance, and they were to be sent to prison.

The sisters had huddled out of sight, underneath wooden planks that were covered by a wool rug, clinging to each other and barely breathing, as they heard footsteps above them, the voices growing louder. The glass and metal of family treasures crashed above them, the smell of cigarette smoke lingering as the officers searched the rooms, only to give up and retreat, threatening their return. She would always remember her mother's voice, plaintive and raw. *Please,* she had said. *Please not my babies.*

Soon after, the family began sending parcels to Kharkiv, the prison they had been taken to— it was where most people were interned before they were released or deported. They sent them what rations they had left— cheese, bread, and small pieces of sausage— weekly, without fail, and had done for a year, waiting for news of their release in the form of a list, or a letter; they were a kind of currency in war.

The parcel, in the end, was useless. Julia had posted it, and had walked back home in the sunlight, her thoughts on the day of chores ahead, and her sister's health. Those had been the innocent things she was doing when the letter arrived. They had been with their mother, collecting eggs, when her father had called them inside. She had seen it, sitting delicately in the center of the long kitchen table, black block letters on the front:

MISHIK
STRIY
LVIV OBLAST 82424

There had been no return address. They all watched it on the table as if deciding what to do with it, as if it had a purpose. Worry settled like rain.

Her father had poured a glass of vodka and clenched his teeth around the wood of his pipe as the smoke wafted against his face. He didn't look up at them as they walked up to him, his face was lined and somber, and his hair shone its silver strands in the daylight. He kept a vacant stare at the center of the table, sitting on his chair slightly perched forward as if about to run off.

Her mother had pointed at the glass. 'Starting early?' Julia and her sister had chuckled softly.

He moved the envelope on the table with his fingertips and inhaled sharply.

'Papa what's that?' Julia looked at him, and then at her mother.

'I think he's about to tell us.' Maria rasped. 'Papa? What is it?'

Anna sat down and ran her fingers through her hair. The two girls pulled up a chair on either side and sat down. The air was heavy.

'So. What's this, then?' her mother leaned forward on the table.

'I have a strange feeling.'

'You always have strange feelings.'

'I'm serious.'

'Alright. What's happened then?'

He gestured at the envelope, as if it was a bomb. 'I don't know, but I know I don't want to open this.'

'It's a letter.'

'Yes, but from whom? There's no return.'

She suspected now, and looked at the girls.

'Mama?' Julia's eyes drifted from her father to her mother. Maria took Julia's hand and squeezed hard.

'Oh, well, just open it then, it's a piece of paper.' She spurred him onward with a hand waving it away and then set her teeth and watched as he ripped the thin edge of the envelope, taking care not to damage what was inside. 'No use fearing a piece of paper.'

'Anna.' He stopped, his eyes skimming the words and then drifting to hers.

'Mmm?'

Before he went further, they both went quiet. The world, for a small second, was held in suspension.

Her father read the first line wearily.

'I have seen your boys-- and I felt compelled to write to you.'

It was at this point there was a choice: her could read on and see where this would lead, or, he could close the letter and hide it away and never know; the latter option had a peculiar peace with it. He looked over at Anna, and then at Julia and Maria. Both girls had water in their eyes already.

'Go on.' Anna laced her fingers together.

'I had a son of my own, he died when he was a boy, and I never had a chance to see how his face would be, as a man. You may be wondering how I came to see your boys. You see, I have been working at Kharkiv for the past three years, and I have seen many men, all ages, pass through these doors in my time here, very few surviving. Your boys arrived together, and they were put in the same cell along with three other men. They were afraid

and proud, as most have been, awaiting immediate deportation or release. They had hope and would not silence it. It was dangerous for them…'

Mikola stopped, his throat thick and catching. The smoke seeped out of his mouth and nose in slow rivulets.

'Keep going,' Anna urged. 'Truth is always a necessary pain.'

'…because the struggle only makes the punishment come quickly. And now how do I tell you this, because this will be hard for a parent to hear. Your sons were brave Ukrainian boys. You should be proud.'

'*Were?* I cannot do this.' Mikola swallowed slowly. 'No, Anna.' He folded the letter. Julia walked up to him and embraced him, Maria following behind. 'Oh, Papa,' they whispered, over and over again.

'You must.' It was then that she realized that, despite the death of her sons, she was still a mother, not a widow, but a mother with dead children, and that would never be repaired.

Anna opened the letter and continued.

'I am sorry to tell you that your sons died shortly after they arrived—'

'No! Oh God…' Julia put a hand over her mouth, the color slipping from her cheeks, and Maria held her.

'They were gathered in a group of 25 men, and all were promised their release that morning. They were fed thin soup and bread, and as they walked out past the prison walls, they saw the sun; for though the frost had been thick on the ground, the sky was clear and bright. And they were told to stand against the wall in front of them, and a few men tried to run. I cannot even send you any of their belongings, as the NKVD took everything that was of use and that could be sold. I know that this is not the peace you seek, but as a father myself, I could not spend another day thinking of your hope for their return. May they, and you, find peace with God one day.'

There was no signature at the end, no name to the small white death certificate that they had not been expecting on a day that was sunlit and beautiful. It was the last page of the story of two children that had been loved and lost, their parents and their sisters now sat staring at the walls of a small room that grew larger in their sorrow.

That evening, the sisters fell into a heavy sleep, lulled by grief. Anna and Mikola were free to speak, and they sat at the kitchen table, in the glow of a large kerosene lamp, the remnants of their day scattered on the surface:

the bottle of vodka, glasses, a few plates and half a loaf of bread. No one had been hungry that evening.

'Anna.' Mikola passed a glass back and forth between her hands meditatively.

'Kolya, please.' She spoke through her hands, and then slowly dropped them from her face, looking at him. 'I know what we have to do. Maybe just give me the time to grieve.'

Mikola sat back and nodded, withdrawing his pipe from his shirt pocket, tamping it with his index finger. 'I know,' he said sadly. 'But we don't have time. Don't you see?' He nodded to the letter, still lying on the table. 'What is happening to this family is happening to all families now. The chaos is beginning. Russia has invaded Poland, and they are now clearing us all out— these are not standard arrests. They have cleared the prisons, they will clear the towns, and further.'

'What can we do? Nothing.'

'But there is.' Mikola reached for Anna's hand. She nodded, because she knew what he meant now. Instead of moving her hand to his, she moved her glass towards him, and nodded to the vodka bottle, now half full.

He poured. 'I know, Anushka. This is too much. It's anger and sadness in a dark cloud. It's hovering over all of us.' He moved closer to Anna. 'We're dealing with government, here. It's pointless.' Smoke veiled his face. 'They'll come back for the girls in the next round of deportations. They'll check again. We're on the census. We don't have a choice— we have to save the girls.'

'Choices are dangerous.' She looked at Mikola, and her heart ached. 'Mikola —'

His voice was steady, to hide the pain. 'Bohdan and Milo are dead, so who will be next? Us? We have a farm that is useful to them so they will come back for it one day, and we will be left without any food, or they will shoot us. We are too old to leave now.'

Anna nodded, and ran a palm on her forearm, her lined skin marked with age spots.

Mikola rested his tanned on hers. 'Both Germany and Russia seek out the children, they seek them out to put them to work, to work them to death. The girls can work.' He saw Anna's face settle into worry briefly. 'Even Maria.'

'I'm not sure I can imagine it.'

'What?'

'Seeing them leave.'

'But we cannot watch them die.'

'I know.' Anna took a deep breath and held it, releasing it slowly before she spoke again. 'So. What do we do?'

'Right.' Mikola felt the stubble on his chin and stared up at the ceiling. 'West. West is obvious. I assume it's the safest option. I've heard the alliance is better there—' 'He shrugged, and Anna winced at how helpless he looked.

'Either has danger.'

'We are in the middle of two wars, it seems.' He rubbed his eyes and reached for the vodka; the bottle now almost empty. 'To go East and join the Soviet army would be a short-lived life. They would surely get sent to Siberia and freeze at the edge of the world. Go West, and there would be work there, there is a displaced persons camp in Austria, near Mauthausen. They can stay there until it is all over, and then come back to us.'

There was a creak in the hallway beyond them, and they paused and turned to look, but saw nothing but darkness. The quiet settled again.

Anna continued, downing her vodka, her eyes searching Mikola's. 'Many have gone to Germany already. I've heard that trains leave Kiev and take people there.'

'No, they don't,' Mikola shook his head. 'That's what they want you to believe.'

Anna didn't question it. She trusted his instinct.

Mikola continued. 'I'm not putting our daughters on a train; God knows where they'll end up. They are old enough; we can help prepare them.'

'Aren't the trains to deport the Jews? We're not Jews,' Anna offered weakly. 'At least that.'

Mikola frowned. 'You think God will save us? It doesn't matter now. We have friends that are Jews. This is a war against humanity. We're all the same.' Mikola sighed.

Anna set her teeth and her chest tightened. She clasped his hand, their wedding rings clinking together as their hands met. Mikola saw the sadness in her face and his heart was heavy.

'Let's prepare a horse, a cart, supplies. Maria knows how to ride well, they can both sleep in the covered wagon if they need or stay at a camp along the way.'

'I worry for Maria.' Her voice caught. 'It's as if we are casting them aside.' The thought was devastating. 'But we have to hope that God will protect us.'

Mikola's face darkened. 'You think God has any say in any of this? You think he listens when you pray? God has no part in this.'

'Mikola. It is what we do when we hope and when we mourn. We bring God with us.'

'Anna— '

Mikola raised his index finger, shaking it at her words. 'Sometimes I think our God has betrayed us, Anna.'

'Maybe so,' she walked to him and took his face in her hands: it was so much older than the man she first saw so many years ago, as the slight, shy boy that she had met through friends in a neighboring village. She had seen him surrounded by friends, his unshakeable laugh piercing the air with so much promise. She saw him now, in the tenderness as he looked at her, despite their age.

The metal of her wedding band that had sunk deeper into her skin over time now glinted on his cheek as she looked at him.

'But still, we must pray.'

Julia covered her face with her hands, listening to her sister's thin coughs in the stillness of their room as she sat in her nightgown, the voices of her parents surrounding her in the dark. She slowly tiptoed back to her bed and pinched her nose to prevent the tears. She would pray, as her mother had said. It was the only thing she could do.

3

They were now at the border of Austria, with little food left. They would need to stop soon.

'Why don't you rest,' Maria advised, turning around to see Julia, her eyes staring, hugging her knees and leaning her body against the shallow wagon. 'Try and sleep instead of being curled up in a ball like that.' Maria wondered where they could stop next, as her hands burned from clutching the reins. 'That can't be comfortable.'

It was early afternoon now, and Julia had unhooked the canvas to let her see the road, the skies, and the trees as they moved past. The sun was finally warming their bodies, and Julia stretched her body like a cat, and for a second, she imagined she was in her bed, before she curled up again, drawing her knees to her chest. So far, no one had asked for their papers, and no dark cattle trucks shadowed them. They had finished their scraps of food from the last farm that they had stopped at, where they were lucky enough to get a half a loaf of bread and fresh milk.

'I can't possibly sleep, because it *is* uncomfortable.' Julia growled. 'This is so ridiculous. Don't you think we can turn back?'

Maria fought back tears and was grateful that her back was to her sister. 'Yes, Julia. I feel the same pain that you do, you can't imagine it. But we have no choice. We have to keep on.'

Julia screwed up her face in annoyance. 'It's entirely rotten, this plan, and I am too sad and angry.' She scowled.

The other duffle moved at her feet: the chalk had worn off a bit during the journey, and the surname was now missing an 'IK', so it only said

'MISH'. *Mouse*, in Ukrainian, and the irony of such a sweet word in such circumstances wasn't lost on her. Her mother used to call her that. *Mishka. Little mouse.* Her stomach rumbled with hunger again. She groaned. 'Can't we turn back?' They were still closer to home than they were to anywhere else.

'You can switch with me soon, I'm getting tired.'

Maria tightened her scarf and clicked the horse onward. She'd lost weight in the last two weeks, her collarbones protruded delicately above her chest and she couldn't get rid of a chill that had descended on her lungs, despite the warmth of the sun on her face.

Tall and preternaturally thin, Maria's hair shone with toffee-colored strands of that clung to her shoulders in two thick plaits, swinging as her lean body moved. Her green eyes seemed brighter than usual and pierced above her flushed cheeks, but tinges of grey hinted at her temples and under her gaze. As a baby, she had been sickly, and though she was the oldest, the majority of her childhood had been spent with adults and siblings worrying for her, as she was the sister that would break easily, like precious china. Over time, and many doctors offering tinctures and rest, she'd adjusted to her fragility and proceeded with caution. And then there were days like today, where, despite the thin bones underneath alabaster skin, and despite the cough that permanently took hold of her, her gaze was protective and wonderful, and there was a strength that comforted Julia immensely.

'Yes, okay, fine.' Julia reached for the small tin flask of tea that had settled by her feet. Blessedly, it was still hot, though little was left. 'You need to stop, I think. Your skin is as pale as a scared rabbit.'

'Don't be ridiculous, I will be fine. Who's the older, more capable sister, eh? Should I remind you?' She cleared her throat and it settled into a raspy cough that lingered. She tasted blood. 'I'll tell you when I've had enough.' She laced the reins through her fingers. They felt dry in her gloves. 'We'll stop soon.'

Julia had been guiding the horse and Maria had been asleep when they arrived the following morning in Salzburg, where there was a large displaced persons camp, with rows and rows of what looked like elongated sheds with corrugated tin roofs, that had been left to rot, crowds of people milling about: tired, filthy, lost, wearing all the clothes on their backs. They could stay here.

After a stuttering explanation of needing somewhere to sleep and something to eat in the few German words they knew, they settled in the only space there was left: a small mat in the corner of an abandoned barn at the back of the camp, a kerosene lamp beside. The horse was tethered to the post outside.

That evening, the sisters had been given thin bone broth and stale bread and were now lying facing one another, fully clothed, under a rough woolen blanket, the lamp flickering weak yellow shadows. They could barely make out each other's faces as they spoke. Maria's forehead was damp, and her eyes had a sheen to them. She shivered, and Julia covered her with her half of the blanket.

'Julia? What do you think it will be like?'

'What, exactly? Which part of this ridiculousness shall we try and understand?'

Maria laughed, progressing into another cough, reddish saliva settling on her lip.

'I'm serious.'

'So am I, Maria. And also, you need to rest. We can't understand any of this right now.' Julia watched her sister's face. Something had changed, so she answered her original question. 'Do you mean, our life? Is that what you wonder about?'

'Maybe.'

'No one knows the future. But that's probably for the best.'

'What will become of us?'

'You will be fat and have lots of babies, and I--'

Maria smiled. 'No, no. Where we're going. Ending up.'

'Germany?'

'Yes.'

'How should I know? It's war. No country has rules now.'

'Does it scare you?'

'It does. But it makes me angry.' Julia knew that the anger covered her fear. It was better that way.

'I'm afraid.'

'I know you are.' *So am I.* The tears threatened, because she knew her sister was weakening, so she willed herself to be still.

Maria searched for Julia's hand underneath the layers and Julia was startled at how cold she was.

'Maria, we have many hours to think about it tomorrow, on the way there. We're almost there and then at least we have somewhere to be. Somewhere to be still for a while.' The horses nickered faintly outside.

'I wish you hadn't mentioned that. I don't think I can take getting in that wagon again.'

'Well, we can't stay here.'

'I know. I just…'

'What?'

'I miss home. Maybe this reminds me of home. The small room, just us, this is nice.' Maria's voice grew sparse and thin. She was tired.

'Home feels very far away now.'

'Two days ago, wasn't it? When Mama packed our bags.'

'Yes.'

'You had an apple in your hand, with that knife. I have no idea why I remember that,' Maria laughed feebly and squeezed Julia's fingers. 'It's stuck in my memory, that stupid apple, and that knife. You turn it over and over in your hands like you were about to throw it or throw the knife.'

'Oh yes. Can you imagine if I had?'

'It probably would have helped all of us, to be fair.'

'In what way??'

'A bit of laughter in the sadness, I guess.'

Julia lifted the corner of her mouth. 'I should've kept that knife. It could be useful now.'

Julia remembered that afternoon. She'd come from school and heard her mother's voice in the bedroom and followed it, only to hover in the doorway and watch as she placed clothing and pieces of jewelry in worn leather cases and prepared to send her daughters away. 'These have seen better days, but they'll serve their purpose' Her mother had said as she ran her palm across the top of an old suitcase. She took a small piece of white chalk and wrote the words MISHIK in capitals on both sides. Mark the suitcases, her father had told them. She wiped her palm on her skirts and walked over to the dresser and proceeded to remove two gold brooches, a necklace, two rings and a fur stole that had belonged to her grandmother. This was currency, and the value was priceless: it meant freedom.

'Did you know that Germany offers food and shelter and work? And that you get paid a small wage?'

Julia had responded in silence.

'Here it is so unsafe, a better life for you is far away from here. You have your things from home--' she pointed to the cases--'and you and Maria can help, work, during the war. If we help the Germans, we will be safe. Do you understand?'

She had memorized her mother's face and listened to her words, as if her real sentiments lay beneath glass and she couldn't reach them.

A few pieces of jewelry lay sparkling in her palm. 'These were mine, but I have no use for them, which is why I am giving them to you.'

'And, what use do I have for a gold ring, an amethyst, a gold chain, and a fancy pin, exactly?' Julia palmed an apple from one hand to the other, holding a knife, about to cut it. She wasn't hungry, suddenly.

'Little one— '

'Mama. No.'

'Yes, okay, not so little. *Julia*, then.' She rested her hand on the dresser. 'We need to talk, you and I.' She folded a blanket and placed it in a suitcase.

'About what, exactly? Am I going on holiday?'

She had been angry and scared. She knew what this would be about.

'Julia. Your father and I have watched our friends, and our children's friends, pass through to God, because of war and famine. We have seen families broken, and for what? For the sake of money and politics?' Her eyes were hard and shining. 'This is world we live in. I have lost my sons. I cannot lose my daughters.' She paused. 'It would kill us.'

Julia speared the apple and set it on the dresser. She had watched quietly as her mother pulled things out of drawers: clean skirts, dresses, tights and an extra pair of shoes, all folded and fitted into the case with such care. A small gold byzantine cross on a necklace hidden in the very
front of a shoe. A small gold signet ring with a square diamond in it: it had been her grandfather's. A black and white picture of her parents, taken at Christmas. They stared out solemnly at her, in their dark clothes.

'I know. You are sending us away.'

The words, they reeked of abandon. They felt like daggers. 'Oh, Julia.'

'Mama.'

It was then that Julia had walked over to the bed, sat, and she remembered it even now, giving way under her slim body, and looked at the room around her. The room had felt small and worn and ancient, as if she'd already left her childhood behind.

'I am *not* sending you away. One day, you will have children that you want to protect so much that the world becomes very small and decisions become very important.'

'Will I? And what would I do?' Julia knew this conversation would have an ending that she would need to be brave for.

'You *will* have children, Julia. And you will do what is right for them. Just as we are.'

Her mother raised a scarf to her face and breathed deeply. Clothes that smelled of Julia, of Maria, smelled of home and salt and earth and oil, memories unraveling and ending.

'I know we can do this. I know we can be brave. But it seems so impossible, the thought of it.'

She heard footsteps behind her and a warm hand that settled on her shoulder. It was Maria. She suddenly seemed much older than her twenty-three years.

'We understand, Mama,' Maria spoke evenly. 'And we will be back, as soon as this is all over.'

As if to finish the discussion, her mother had snapped the cases closed, but then as an afterthought, opened one of them and lifted the rosary off her neck. She clutched it in her palm, her fingers marked from the facets of the pale blue stones digging into her flesh, and then placed it in both of the girls' hands, covering them with her own. 'Be brave. I will be with you always.'

Julia looked over at Maria, small and fragile now, her face yellowed by the lamplight, and bit her cheek to stop from crying. *We will be brave, Marioshka.*

Silence. The horses moved outside.

'Maria?'

Maria's eyes opened slowly, carefully, as if the world was suddenly too bright. Julia watched her smile wanly, and then watched as she turned her body, pitched her head forward, and vomited all over the floor, the hay darkening under the bile. And then again.

Julia sat up. 'Oh *bozshe*, are you okay?? What can I do? What's going on?'

Maria groaned and stayed curled over the edge of the mattress. 'I don't know.'

'Is there a doctor in this camp? There is, isn't there? They have them somewhere, *somewhere.*' They'd been in camps previously that had had a doctor, and she prayed that there was one here.

Julia rose and fled the barn, just as Maria rolled onto her other side, moaning and shaking, clutching her knees to her chest.

Julia ran slowly in the dark, her tights sagging and catching on brambles, her eyes adjusting to various shapes of sheds and houses and fences, and paths that led out too far, searching for help.

Julia had seen groups of German and Russian officers in the town square, in the cafes and the bars and the shops, and she knew enough to know the word for *medicine*, *doctor*, and *help*. She wiped her streaming eyes and scanned the sheds, and the makeshift tents. Minutes felt like hours and she walked swiftly and impatiently until her lungs burned and she knocked on doors and pleaded for help for her sister, eventually her voice rising in panic.

'Please! Hilf mir! Kranheit hier!' *Please, help me. Illness here.* No one answered.

When she finally found a doctor who had escaped Kiev with his own family, she explained to him in broken words what she needed, and he walked back with her to the tent, where they found Maria, small and huddled, moaning. Her breaths were shallow, as quiet as whispers, and Julia wondered how she had gotten so ill so quickly.

Had she missed something important? Could they turn back again? She so desperately wanted her mother.

'Maria?'

She wheezed in response.

'I found someone.'

Maria turned her face towards Julia, and her face in the light looked as if the skin had been pulled tight across her skull. Her lips were wet from fresh vomit, as was her hair.

The doctor placed a mask around his face and approached her. 'Miss? I examine you, yes?' He took her wrist in his hand and took her pulse. 'Hmm. Very rapid.' He frowned. 'Your wrist,' he started, and pulled up her sleeve to reveal angry red spots. He leaned over her and spread open the collar of her dress. He found them there as well. 'Is very bad, I see.' He gestured to Julia in reference. 'See here, this very common for many. Typhus. Is what it's called.'

'What does that mean? I don't know what that means, this word you're saying.' She spat her words out, indignant and infuriated at this man who could come to a conclusion so quickly. Aren't there many *many* illnesses that she could have? Surely it couldn't be this easy.

The doctor remained unreasonably calm. 'Typhus is headache, fever, vomiting. It can last for weeks or it can only last days, miss.'

'So, fix her.'

'I cannot. These camps have disease, it is very common.' His hands ran delicately through his hair, fingers uncomfortable in this interrogation.

'I don't understand!' Julia moved him with her arm, small bottles clinked in the bag at his feet. She needed to see Maria more clearly. 'You have medicine in there, can't you *use* it for God's sake?'

'Listen.' He placed a hand on her arm to stop her from shaking. 'Your sister is very ill.'

Stupid man, she felt like taking his mask and shoving it down his throat. 'Well. Yes, I *know* that. But how do I *help* her? She cannot be ill forever!'

The doctor took the mask off his mouth and sighed, chewing the dry skin of his lip. He seemed preoccupied. He'd seen too many of these and there were always so many ways to declare illnesses, depending on the person he had to declare it to.

'There is no way.'

'What do you *mean*? There are always ways.'

'Well, you see, it's a horrible disease.'

'Yes. Diseases are common. We're in a god damn trench, practically, we're all ill.'

'No, I mean, we have no medicine for it, we have not been given vaccines for it.'

'Well, why not?'

He shrugged his shoulders and said the thing that was the only thing that made sense but was incredibly cruel: 'War.'

Julia looked at her sister. She was listless on the bed, eyes closed and sleeping. Her hands were loose by her side and peaceful. She looked like a lost child.

She softened in that moment. 'What do I do, then,' she pleaded, grabbed him by the arm, and then corrected herself, embarrassed at her display. 'Help me. *Help me.* What do I do?'

The doctor was closing the bag that he'd carried with him. 'You can only pray.'

When he left, Julia sat down on the floor next to where Maria lay, and traced the line of her hand, all along the perimeter, and then the circumference of her fingers, and then the wrinkles that gathered around her knuckles. As she was doing this, she imagined that they might be able to leave in the night and progress to Germany and then at least she could have proper medical care. She wondered if she could lift Maria and gently cover her with blankets in the back of the wagon and she thought she could. And maybe tomorrow morning she would be well enough to continue on the journey, and she would promise Maria that she would drive the wagon the entire way there, and she wouldn't have to do anything apart from rest. They would try and steal extra bread from somewhere, or someone, and Julia would explain that it was for her ill sister, and she would slowly get better. Fresh air might do her good.

It would be alright, she thought, and their mother would nod and tell them that that was a good plan and that Maria would recover quickly, because she always had.

Julia watched as Maria's face would grow paler, more still, as the minutes passed.

'Maria.' She stroked the hair that once shone so brightly, now dimmed. 'Marioshka.'

Maria opened her eyes, though feebly, as if in a bright light.

'Do you remember the song?'

'Which…?'

Julia began to hum softly, the words whispered and pure:

Look at the sky, so clear and free,
Come out, come out sweet darling
Though you're weary from work,
Come and spend a moment here with me.

Maria smiled. 'I remember.' And then she closed her eyes and reached for Julia's hand.

And then they were in the fields of their memories, plucking handfuls of old leaves and throwing them into the air like offerings as they laughed and played. Julia spoke of their brothers, and of their childhood together underneath banners of blue skies, and how they would whisper secrets to each other about the world and where its magic lay.

'You know, Mama used to always say that we were mother and daughter, not sisters, remember?' Julia was tired, but she kept on, staring at Maria to see the shallow rise and fall of her chest. And then she remembered. 'Let me show you something.'

There was a picture of them that Julia had found on the table beside her mother's bed, a picture from four years ago, and she'd placed it in her coat pocket the day they left. She found it now, in the pocket of her coat, and withdrew it to show to Maria, but she was already asleep, so she looked at the faces staring out: it was a picture that a friend had taken of the two of them sitting in the fields, hair in plaits, dresses with shortened sleeves for the heat, palms up towards the camera to shield their eyes from the bright sun.

She remembered that it was summer that day, and they had gone flower picking, and that they had made chains out of the wheat and the wildflowers and secured the them in a kind of wreath, *vinok*, with blades of young grass. They wore them that day as they walked slowly home, and then when the wreaths dried and became stiff, they left them in their rooms as reminders of that one-day. She thought of the warm air, and how the insects hummed in the shadows. Their life was nearly what they wanted it to be, then; they'd possessed a sense of wonder still.

Julia took the photo and placed it next to Maria, within the blanket warming her suffering body. She looked at the woman who had promised to take care of her, the woman who was now small and childlike, and squeezed her alabaster hand as it lay limp, listening to her thin breath course through her lungs and gently out of her parted lips. 'We'll be alright,' Julia whispered, and it was one of many times she would utter words that she was dreadfully unsure of.

Maria's eyes flickered faintly, whilst Julia rested her head on the edge of the mattress, and they both fell asleep in the buttery glow of the lamplight.

Julia woke to the sound of gunfire and the all too familiar sounds of tanks on the ground. The walls of the barn vibrated with it.

They had both been asleep until late morning, their arms around one another, and when Julia woke, she had forgotten the events of the previous night. But only temporarily. She saw her sister's face was still, eyes closed, her mouth slack and lips thin. Julia wept silently, and clutched at her, bringing her closer, feeling for any part of warmth that was still there. A part of her wondered if she would wake up, and if this had all been a feeble, feverish dream. Julia's body curled towards her sister and stayed there, not caring of the world around her.

She stayed hidden in the far corner of that barn as the day brightened, her eyes pink and wide, listening as the soldiers approached, bellowing. She heard hurried footsteps and people shuffling outside, waiting to be counted, panic in their voices.

'Raus! Schnell!'

She stayed a moment longer, and then she finally rose as the air outside filled with voices, her face red and swollen, and stood staring at her sister as if giving her the chance to wake up. *Just one more minute. Wake up. Be brave.*

Silence.

'Komm raus, bevor ich schieße!' *All come out before I shoot.*

She looked at the barn door and then back at the loose boards in the wall by where she now stood. She had two choices: she could risk making a run for it, carrying her sister, hiding in the shadows, making a path through the woods... or she could try and survive, and promise to stay alive to see her parents one day, or to have children and a family of her own.

Her hand reached for her scarf and turbaned it around her hair, and she wondered if within this decision, there would be grief either way. And she would have to take that with her, to a place where she might never survive, and the weight of that choice now lay heavy on her slim shoulders.

She did her buttons slowly, one by one, her hands trembling, smoothing the layers of her clothes. She remembered her father's voice as she put her gloves on.

'Papa. Will we see you again?'

'I don't know.'

'Well, all this madness will be over soon, and we will turn back and you and Mama will be here, and it will all be like before, yes?'

'I need you to find your way, no matter what happens. Find the use in the broken things, the courage in the frightening things, and the joy in the sadness. There will always be sadness.'

They were at the door.

Steadying herself, Julia knelt by her sister, so small now. She saw that Maria had worn brown leather shoes; they were practically new. Julia looked down at her own, the battered lip of the sole undone at the front. They would slow her down. She whispered, 'I'm sorry, Marioshka,' and her tears wet the hay as she removed them swiftly and put them in her own duffel. She brushed a lock of hair off Maria's forehead, and told her softly that she loved her. Her eyes creased at the corners and the few tears that came again, made her face shine as she steeled herself.

Julia covered her sister with the still warm blanket that they had both shared, took both of their duffels, and slowly walked through the barn door into the cold, hollow light.

Jetzt! In die Lastwagen!

Her legs trembled as she opened the door and walked into the cold, hollow light, two duffels in her hands. The black cattle truck waited for her.

4

Germany, 1941

On the afternoon of his twenty-second birthday, Henry stepped into his barrack on the far eastern corner of Neumarkt labor camp and emptied his pockets onto his bed. He had a tarnished lighter, cigarettes, a handful of coins, and the train ticket that he'd used to leave home. He was sure he'd made the right choice, despite the distance from everything he'd ever known. He shook his head. It was better this way. He had never remembered a birthday after his mother had died, and so he had been a stranger in his own home, just as he was here.

Henry had arrived in Germany in 1940, having used his own money to buy the train ticket, the rest of his money hidden in the linings of his shoes and sewed into the pockets of his thin wool coat. They'd had an argument the day before he'd left home, and it stung Henry deeply, as his father grew more impatient with a son he didn't understand.

'You just wait,' Ivan's voice had been dark. 'Just wait until you have to understand what direction your life will go, during a war, during hunger, during pain,'— a fresh cigarette, sparks flying, punctuated his words— 'trying to make decisions on life, decisions that no one will warn you about. You just wait until you have to pick up the pieces of a life that you never wanted but had to withstand. You have no idea who I am, son.'

'But I don't *want* to.' Henry had said, and stopped, finding immense power in the moment. 'You don't *make* me want to understand. You don't even try.'

'Correct.'

'But why?' And then his voice had turned soft again. Young.

'Because men don't need to explain themselves to boys. Life is too complicated.'

'So why did you become a father?'

'Stupidity, if you ask me. Love. Nonsense. Feeling as though it was my obligation to your mother. Also…'

Henry had hoped for something kind. 'What?'

'Survival.' Ivan stamped out a cigarette. 'I had no choice but to teach you how to survive. That's what parents do. Survival has nothing to do with love, and everything to do with purpose. Your purpose is to continue my life, and the name I gave you.'

'And what if that's not what I want?'

Ivan looked over at his son, and then away, scanning the fields. He turned back to him. 'So, what is your plan, then? What will you do?'

'The war is on our doorstep. Aren't you afraid?'

'I'm not afraid of anything.'

'I don't want to stay here. There are jobs, there is money, and there is work. Did you know, that I could work in Germany? Not as a laborer but as an officer? My friends have all said— '

'Hironimus. You are so naïve.'

'Am I? I think it's smart to hope for something. And this isn't what I hope for, for my life, Papa.'

His father had softened at the name that his son had only called him as a small child, but only briefly. 'Hope is dangerous, son.'

When his father had turned his back to leave, it was then that Henry saw the first fleeting glimpse, which vanished almost immediately, of a man whose life had stripped him bare. Henry promised himself that day that he would vow never to carry his father's legacy; he could never carry that much pain.

Henry took off his uniform and laid it carefully on the bed, changing into crisp, pale grey shirt and grey trousers, the only other clothes he now owned. There was a small mirror on the wall of his barrack, and as the sun filtered through the room, Henry watched his reflection, cigarette clamped firmly in the side of his mouth, leaving his shirt unbuttoned at the very top. He had been deciding what to do: after his shift of deliveries to the Nazi officers, he was given his papers to leave the camp if he wanted. He could walk into Neumarkt and eat and drink there with the other officers, because his role as an officer would mean he wouldn't need to adhere to the rations that prison workers had. But today, he decided to stay at the camp and meet a friend.

He examined the wavy dark brown hair that was long at the crown and short on the sides, and the way his brown eyes and long lashes shadowed his cheekbones. He ran his long fingers through and swept it back, pausing to flatten his anemic mustache before placing the lighter into his pocket.

'My father's face.' He mused, his flat lips lifting at the corners, but felt nothing.

⤤

The sun was sinking lower still, sitting on the metal tables in the common area, as Henry strode over, clapping Yuri on the back forcefully and sitting down next to him, drawing a cigarette out of a creased packet.

'Well? What's new? What's work been like?' he found a match and sparked it on the edge of his metal chair. He looked at his friend: young man, old body, hair the color of straw, face lined, blue eyes shining under a worried brow.

Yuri lowered his head, shaking it. 'Germans. I mean, doesn't it make you angry?'

'What, exactly?'

'Being...' Yuri paused and looked up, limp hair drooping in front of his left eye. He looked hopeless. 'Here. *Here*. Cattle to the slaughter.'

Henry felt a bead of sweat along his temple and wiped it with his arm, tapping the cigarette packet on the table, turning it over and over in his fingers. 'What else is there? What other options do we have right now?'

He heard the cattle trucks approach in that moment, and saw groups of men, women and some children, piling out in groups and hovering far beyond where he now sat. He watched as they were herded and directed where to stand and when to stay silent.

'Yes, fine, you're right. But *dignity*, that's what I mean.' Yuri wove his fingers together and undid them slowly, over and over. 'Animals. We're animals in here.'

Henry turned back to his friend. 'Dignity doesn't feed us.'

'Since when did you get so philosophical?' Yuri wanted an answer. He was clinging to hope like fistfuls of sand.

Henry rubbed out his cigarette in the table and flicked it away with a finger. 'Look. This won't last forever. Wars aren't forever, nothing is forever. We do what we can with what we have for now, and the only thing we can hope for is to survive this with some hope left.'

'And who the hell left you the cock in charge of the hens?'

'Ha. Well, I know how to manage a situation.' He tapped his index finger to his temple. 'Don't let it get to you.'

'So, this is a--' Yuri stuck his hand in the air between them, cigarette aloft, and circled it as if he were conjuring '-- situation, you say?'

"Mmm.'

'Death is everywhere, Henry. Don't you think we could be next?'

'Make yourself useful then. Play the game.' Exhale of smoke. 'Be smart.'

'About...?'

'About how *you* can make yourself useful to *them*.' Henry looked up and saw a pair of officers striding across. He leaned on his elbows towards Yuri. 'As soon as you look hopeless, weak, useless, they have you.' And he made a fist with his hand and released it. He lit another cigarette and clamped it in the side of his mouth, his trimmed mustache grazing it lightly, as he rested both his hands on his friend's forearm. 'Survival.'

'Sure.' Yuri stood up to leave. 'I'll leave you to it.'

'Wait. Just wait.' He left his hands on his Yuri's arm and his gaze was directed at something across the ground, past the fencing. It was then that he saw her.

He hadn't noticed her before, and now he was curious. The small girl with the faltering, elegant walk seemed familiar. Yes, he knew her. He had known her, and had seen her before, he realized, but couldn't place where. He'd seen her once before (*or was it twice*), as she sat with someone (*her sister? a friend?*). Her hair was careless, thin wisps flying around her face getting caught in her eyelashes and lips. Today she was in her dark uniform with plain skirt that grazed her knee ever so gently, flat black shoes making it easier for her to manage the hours she was expected to be on her feet. Her head was covered in a scarf, and her nose was sharp on her face, softening slightly when she smiled.

Looking at her felt sobering, like cold water in stifling heat. He wanted to see her hands: a ring would tell him more, though she could have hidden it, or sold it. She moved as if she had music at her feet, but her body looked painfully aware that it was in a crowd. She was smiling as she was walking.

Yuri's head turned behind him and he understood as he followed Henry's gaze.

'Yeh, a good girl, that one. Bit plain.' A cat slinked over to Yuri and he kicked it away, distractedly. He leaned in and studied Henry's face. 'Surely you know her. Sister of that kid from school. Milo. Lived on the *selo*, not too far from Stryi.'

Oh, right, Henry thought, and nodded, inhaling his cigarette smoke slowly, squinting as it passed around his lips and dissipated into the air. *Sure. No one of status.* He bristled as he heard the voice of his father in that moment. *Don't waste time with anyone you can't get anything out of,* he would often tell him. He shook it off.

'Well, interesting anyway.' He rubbed out the stub on his boot. He looked at Yuri and smiled. 'We should go.'

Yuri sighed. 'Finally. Thought you'd never let me leave. I have a party to attend,' he said with comedic tone, and loped off, waving his hand in departure. Henry watched his friend, watched the curve of his back tighten his shirt. The boy was a hard laborer. His hands were chapped, his shirt had dust in the creases, mirroring the lines that had gathered around his eyes as he spoke. He was tired, like all of them.

Henry sat staring at the road ahead for a moment-- a road separated by barbed wires and concrete blocks on either side—and wondered where he was. He was hungry, but he was safe.

Yuri's voice suddenly bellowed out in front of him as he walked away. 'Julia! Ey, Julia!', Yuri pointed across the filtering crowds. Henry looked to where he was waving to, and as saw a face in the distance that smiled in recognition as she saw Yuri. She waved back briefly, and then followed Yuri's hand as he gestured to Henry. She stopped waving as their eyes met, and then the crowd closed back in around her like a dream, vanishing.

And then a memory descended on him: a mere seven years ago he had seen Julia, and it was when she had gone to church on Christmas Eve, for their lives had intersected often as they lived only 30 minutes apart as the crow flies, and Lviv was small (small enough where people didn't forget faces). And he had gone with his father, and crowds stood silent and cold to listen to the sermon underneath the vacant stares of the gold icons surrounding them. And he had watched in a daze as she smiled the kind of broad smile that someone does in private, without awareness of others. Her hair surrounded her in a kind of dark halo, beneath her headscarf, her cheeks flushed from the cold, and her body was tall and lean, newly softened into its adulthood, and he felt a kind of longing to walk to her; it caught in his throat and he kept it in his memory as he walked away that night, hoping to see her again.

Henry left the embers from the other cigarettes burning in the ashtray and walked back the way he had come, thinking about her, as he would do every moment until he saw her again.

Julia carried the grief of her sister's ghost with her, like a shadow, as she stood at the brick and iron gates of the labor camp with a few hundred others, two duffels in her hand.

She had placed herself in the lion's mouth: rows of identical grey-hued wooden buildings, made to look like barns; long, narrow houses plain and square. They were squat and wide, and seemed to go in an endless line towards an empty distance. A metal fence wrapped around tall wooden posts— and with what looked like sharp metal teeth adorning the wiry tops— bordered the perimeter as far as she could see, displaying flat, deserted earth; this place looked like it had risen up from the ground just to be used, sucked dry, and eventually swallowed up by the very ground that had given birth to it. The camp was far away from town. It was separated by forest, isolated and vanishing. An afterthought, this life, and it would be extinguished.

'Welcome to Neumarket. One stop before Hell,' a woman spoke as she drifted by, yellowed teeth and sunken eyes. Julia fisted her hands and held them to her sides.

She was shuffled into a group and then into a building to be disrobed, examined, standing in front of concrete walls, bruised orange and brown from rust and paint. Their eyes were stretched open, thumbs prized open their mouths to check teeth and throats. Hair was checked for lice and skin for disease, and then they were to bend forward, exposing their spines to further checks for stability and strength, their body cavities were searched. When she was allowed to dress again, she was given a dark uniform made of stiff cotton that hit at her calves, a blue armband brandishing her as an OST (Eastern Worker), and they all walked to an allocated a building where they would be given their work orders.

'Hey.' A girl in front of her, slim, with thin yellow hair underneath her headscarf whispered to her. 'You see?' she pointed.

'What?' Julia whispered back.

'They are looking at us. Like a zoo.'

Julia followed her gaze and saw a handful of officers stood pointing, wide grins and powerful stances. 'Ey! Hey Mädchen, was guckst du?' *What are you girls looking at.* One of them spat on the ground and turned around.

The girls both turned back, flushed and scared as the officers moved on, and as they parted, Julia caught sight of a man that she'd seen before. Tall. Dark hair. Broad shoulders that seemed too thin for the clothes he wore. He was sat down and they locked eyes, and then the crowd of women moved into the concrete, and she lost him.

A few months later, Julia and Henry sat side by side in the sun on the narrow step by the barrack door one afternoon, the shadow of the SS officer pacing a few hundred feet away. The step wasn't wide enough for two people, and she'd moved closer to him, the worn material of her work dress almost brushing Henry's uniformed arm, her heart pounding. Had they been anywhere else, there would have been a lake nearby, or a field, and a group of friends with a variety of food on a wool blanket, the wheat itching their bare legs. But it was in war, and they did what they could.

'Hello, Henry.'

'We have to stop meeting like this, Julia.' He watched her face, his eyes smiling.

'But I thought you'd asked me to come to see you.'

'It was a joke,' he laughed, a wide smile, his eyebrows raised, and shook his head.

'Oh.'

Henry nodded to one of the officers as he passed by, eyeing the pair. This meeting would be short, today.

'Did you eat enough today?'

Julia's face flushed. 'The same.' She crossed her arms, feeling their thinness.

'Listen, I have some of my rations that I can give you.'

'Henry, I can't keep doing this. It'll get you into trouble.'

'Don't worry about me, I have it easier than you do.'

Julia blushed. 'They'll start wondering why I'm one of the healthier ones,' she looked furtively at him. 'All this special treatment.'

He had been a *Werkschutz*, an elite worker that would oversee production and maintain delivery routes. They were luxuriously free from certain constraints: they were allowed women, extra food from the pantry, and Henry had chosen her, after seeing her daily.

The first few weeks of innocence had turned into companionship: his hand on her shoulder as he passed by her work station, their bodies brushing up against one another as they walked, first accidentally then with purpose, navigating narrow overgrown paths at the perimeter of the camp's east corner, discreetly at night, for that was all she was allowed in his company. He told her of his mother and how he had lost her as a child, and of his father's cold nature, and she felt relief as she unburdened the loss of her sister to him. They uncoiled their pasts and gave them to each other reverently, and then slowly this trust became a kind of love.

They clung to it immediately, because it was all they had. They navigated invisible barriers that separated their stations in that camp: there his dark eyes moved over her face, and she thought of the way her slight body would fit neatly into his.

Henry paused, his eyes scanning the movement of the officers around him. 'Meet me at your shift change,' he whispered. 'I'll have a few things for you. Not a lot, just what you can hide underneath your coat.'

She looked up at him. 'Thank you.'

He looked over at her, his eyes letting the details of her seep into his memory: her hands were scarred, and her nails had been bitten to the quick, her thin arms displayed a burn mark and a bruise hidden amongst a smattering of freckles, like a constellation. Her uniform had a tear in the hem, the blue fabric displaying threads splayed through the dust that had collected on it. Her face was strong, sharp and proud, and, didn't reveal any sort of weakness, and he loved the way she looked at him: with a wary abandon.

She felt complete longing at the feeling of his tall, warm body inches from her slight one. She moved closer, keeping her head down. He offered her a cigarette, and her fingers brushed his as she cupped her hand over the flame, watching the embers glow. She had inhaled, a sputtering cough erupting as the smoke tickled her lungs. She finished half, and stubbed out the ember delicately, saving the other half for later. When it cooled, she placed it in her shoe, and Henry laughed at the remnants of their small lives here. That was simple way it began.

The winter of 1942 was bitter, and Julia and the other workers would layer newspaper and hay within their clothes to stay warm most days; their bones felt as if they would break at every step. After her shift ended and other workers replaced her seat, she quietly navigated the dark path to Henry's barrack, for it had heating, and though it was incredibly risky, the nights she spent with him were worth it. Julia began to spend nights there with increasing regularity, always leaving for her building before the night skies faded into morning. They belonged to, and protected, each other. It was a few years later, just as the war had begun its slow, painful decline that their lives would change forever.

In the winter of 1945, Henry had been sent on delivery orders to a different camp for two months, and when he returned, Julia told him of the pregnancy, as she had begun to show, and her work shifts had begun to take their toll as the population of the camp diminished— the Nazis had begun to evacuate the workers slowly as the Allies approached, and Julia feared the worst. They decided to marry swiftly, holding on to on piece of joy amongst the ruins— they gathered one evening in the back of a barrack that smelled of wet hay and cold concrete, with witnesses that they didn't know, and a dying priest that had recently finished his metal-polishing shift. Henry had worn the suit jacket that he'd stolen, his hair freshly wetted and finger-brushed, and Julia had nothing apart from her dark uniform, but she removed her arm band before placing her arm through Henry's. Maria's shoes were at her feet, and her mother's rosary in her pocket. Henry left, and the sirens announced the workday two hours later.

Their daughter was born soon after, in the spring of 1946, on a lonely bed in the medical barrack, next to a disused brick furnace, with the help of a kind midwife whom Julia had shared a wooden bunk with. Henry had been transferred to another camp, so it was three months later, upon evacuation, that he would finally meet this girl, his daughter, with bright eyes and a doughy round face. He had asked Julia what she'd named her, as he placed his broad hand on the baby's head, his eyes filling with tears at the soft, warm skin underneath his own.

'Meet your little Slava,' she smiled. *Glory,* in Ukrainian.

5

When the liberations slowly tapered off in the summer of 1946, Julia and Henry, along with seven million prisoners and forced laborers left Germany, most travelling slowly West, without families or homes to come back to, as the East threatened more oppression.

The new family had taken their belongings, wrapped Slava in a partially torn blanket that had been discarded in one of the barracks, and ventured into town, hoping to find a house to stay in temporarily, rent that they could afford, from the little money Henry had saved from the jobs that he'd had for the army. Deutchmark was worth something now, for a short time at least, before the economy collapsed again, and they'd had saved their rations to take with them.

Neumarkt looked partially deserted, but was coming to life in fits and starts, with shops opening their windows and roads empty of military vehicles. It would be dangerous for them to stay in an empty house that would most likely be occupied by the Russian military soon, so they wandered off the main street and wound their way towards a group of houses on the Caritasstraße until finally finding a tiny room to rent. It was at the back of a small house with an orange, pyramid-shaped roof on the and a narrow door with one window beside it, owned by an old woman by the name of Helen Wasser— a seamstress with a small shop in the middle of town. It had not survived the war, and most of it had been looted, but her spirit remained. She was short, her grey hair cut sharply to meet her jaw and always tied back with black hairpins, thin glasses perched on her small nose, her wide face welcoming and curious. She was kind to them and gave them the room that once belonged to her son, who had died in the war, and encouraged them to use the kitchen as if it were their own. 'Warm food is almost as important as kindness', she would say. 'Nourishment within a heart comes in many ways.' It made the family feel safer than they had in years.

It was late January, and Henry was rubbing his cold, dry hands together, reaching for the kettle in the kitchen, as Helen had gone out for the morning, and had left them eggs, bread, and a tin with coffee in it. He pulled his clothes to his body. Everyone was dressed in so many thin layers, heavy woolen socks.

'Julia.' There was affection in his voice, as Henry watched her feed Slava dangling her legs off a highchair at the small kitchen table. He made a face at Slava, and she squealed her response, reaching for him.

'Ach,' Julia had been peeling a freshly boiled egg, and winced as it burned the tips of her fingers. She rolled her eyes and smiled at the two of them. 'Stop distracting her, she needs to eat.' Henry became serious again, and Julia directed him. 'Yes, go ahead, I'm listening,' she answered as she broke the egg apart.

Henry sat down across from them. 'Well, I think we need to talk about what is going to happen to us. Germany is falling apart, and now the Russians will come back in. Reparations. A new Germany. It's going to be for us like it was ten years ago, back home. He folded his arms across his chest, waiting. 'We cannot stay here, Julia.'

Slava squealed, wanting attention from the two adults who suddenly weren't looking at her. Henry stroked her head absentmindedly, as he watched Julia's face for a reaction.

Julia put her head in her hands, and then moved them to her lap. Her head moved slowly back and forth. She looked defeated. 'Henry, I really wish you'd just left this morning, just done something else with the time you have, instead of hovering. Worrying. She looked up. 'I can't think about another move. Can we please discuss this later?'

He folded his hands and leaned on the table. 'Alright, when exactly, because I'm the one that has to think ahead for the three of us' Sensing a barrier between them, he softened. He knew this would be difficult. 'We can't live here forever and pretend to play happy family.'

'Why not?'

'Do you really think that Russia coming back here is a good thing for us?'

Julia shrugged. 'Well— '

'I need you to think back. To the arrests. To the lists. To everything that we left behind. You and I will be on those lists still. Do you want to relive that?' He looked over at Slava, and back at Julia. 'We have to find somewhere where we can stay. Build a life.'

Julia looked past him into the small room. The rust-colored paint had faded on the crumbling plaster walls, the wooden cot was pushed up against the unmade bed which was then pushed up against the wall, and the window was too small to let any decent amount of light in. It felt like a rabbit warren.

She looked back up at him, her voice even and calm. 'We can't go back home.'

'No, Julia.'

He leaned closer to her.

'Listen, we've talked about this before. We can't go back to a country that is under Soviet rule again. It's too restricted, violent, unsure.'

He reached into his pocket and withdrew a folded piece of newspaper from his pocket, which looked like it had been in there for weeks. He flattened it on the table and pointed at one of the articles. 'Here,' he said, boldly. '*Here* is where our new plan is.' The small print had strayed and smudged a bit, but Julia could make out the words where his index finger rested: **MIGRANTS NEEDED** and **WORK THE LAND AND RECEIVE YOUR OWN**.

Julia knew what he spoke of— she had heard it on the small kitchen radio over the last month. News of countries accepting the overspill of refugees from war-torn countries. The United Nations had sanctioned it, and handfuls of countries had opened their doors.

Henry lit a cigarette. 'It is money. Freedom from this,' he gestured excitedly, the smoke floating to the four walls surrounding them, smoke disappearing into the air. 'It is a way for us to leave this collapsing Europe and start a new life for ourselves.' He let out a stream of smoke. 'Julia, there is nothing left for us, here.'

She hesitated and looked at Slava. She smoothed her palm over her daughter's head and suddenly felt her own mother's hand on her cheek. 'But what about me? What am I supposed to do?'

'What do you mean?'

'A new country? Again?' She leaned back and looked up at the ceiling. 'I feel that if I move again, I might collapse.'

'I know. But we can do this. I know we can. We have to.' Henry reached out for Slava's warm little hands, and then reached out for Julia, his hand open, waiting for hers. An agreement.

Julia was torn, for where she belonged was with them, this was her family now, but her heart yearned for the miles beyond, still.

'I feel you're right but also, I feel so angry.' She frowned, and his hand retreated back to his lap. 'It's not only about you and what you need. We only just survived one event in our lives, is it possible to survive yet another?'

He bristled. 'So, you want to stay here, then? And do what? Constantly live with one eye on the shadows?' He sighed, stubbing out his cigarette and reaching for another.

'I don't know. Maybe Germany will get better over time.'

Henry snapped his lighter closed. 'Julia, did you even ask me where we can go? Where we could work and live and actually receive our own house and land?'

'I'm not sure I want to.'

'Australia.'

Julia's eyes widened. 'Isn't that somewhere on the other side of the world?'

'Yes. But—' he counted on his fingers. '—They're offering paid work, our own house, our own land to farm, and after three years, we become citizens there.'

Julia smiled weakly at his eagerness. 'Henry, it's a world away from what we know. I feel that I can't keep re-packing our bags, hoping we stay somewhere long enough for it to feel like home.' Her face was a mix of exhaustion and understanding as she looked at him, hoping she'd be heard, despite knowing that he was right.

He was done with being patient. 'You're being selfish.'

Julia wiped Slava's mouth and picked her up from the chair and placed her down with a small stuffed rabbit. She stood with her arms at her side, which gave her the space for an argument. 'No. I'm telling you how I feel.'

Henry's face darkened. 'What about how *I* feel? I made a promise to take care of you, and now you're saying I'm *selfish*?'

'It takes two people to make a decision, Henry. Two people to make a child and create a life and a family.'

'Which is exactly my point. We have to be together in this.'

'I don't think I can move again. I don't know if I have it in me.'

'Julia, please listen.' He came to her and grabbed her by both arms, his fingers digging into her flesh, making her wince. 'We can't stay.'

Julia wrenched out of his grip and sat back down in defeat, rubbing her arms. 'What do you want me to say, then?'

Henry placed his hands in his pockets. 'Maybe we need the space to let it settle. We have two months to make this decision, but the train leaves then, so we have to put ourselves on the list.'

'Train?'

'Yes, from Munich station. Trucks are taking people there, and then from Munich, we go to Acerra, Italy.'

Julia lifted her mouth in a smile. 'As if we're travelling the earth.'

Henry smiled, sensing that she would come around. 'But then, from Italy, we make the trip to Australia on a boat.' He put a hat on, ready to leave. 'A boat, with food, and a view of the sea, and maybe even a cabin to sleep comfortably.'

Julia nodded. 'Alright. Let's give ourselves time to think.'

Henry walked out, not saying where he was going, but he left without a glance backward. He knew he'd been hard on her. But he couldn't face another day looking over his shoulder, wondering about an uncertainty that was out of his control. Plans. He needed plans.

Julia cleared the plates off the table and stood at the sink untying her apron. The floor beneath her feet felt unsteady, it was shifting undetectably at first, and then she felt as if she were falling through. Drifting. Needing an anchor when there was none. She looked through the small window next to the door and stared out onto the street. Rows of small houses huddled together, quietly; the streets empty apart from a few Russian military jeeps. Maybe Henry was right.

That afternoon, Julia was outside, the laundry line heavy with sheets snapping in the wind. Slava was at her feet.

She heard a sound behind her, the footsteps were slow, deliberate. Julia turned, expecting to see Henry, as he hadn't yet come home. But it was Helen. She smiled and walked towards the older woman and kissed her papery cheek.

'Hallo Madame Helen! Schön dich zu sehen!' *Nice to see you.* Julia was reminded of her mother, and her voice was plump with affection.

'Julia, it is nice to see you outside with the baby.' She looked at Slava. 'So German looking, all that blonde hair and pale skin.' She chuckled softly and looked at both the woman and the child. 'What an odd pair you are, and yet so matched. Dark and light.'

Helen's thick embroidered blouse erupted in waves on her arms, tucked into her full skirts, hands in pockets, with thick ankles stuffed into leather shoes. Her glasses were on top of her grey hair, her skin soft and clear on her face, underneath a chaotic sparse white bun threatening to unravel in a shock down the nape of her neck.

'Your German is getting good, yes?' She looked down and smiled at Slava looking up at her. 'And your little one is very happy today, I see.' She pointed up at the sky. 'Grey clouds hiding the sun- maybe a good omen, with
the sun coming out, good things to come, no?'

Julia placed the clothespins in her pocket and looked up, squinting, the sky still bright despite the grey. 'Well, yes, maybe. Who's to know.'

Helen grabbed her arm affectionately and squeezed. Julia tensed as the bruises on her arms were still tender from the other evening. 'You seem sad. And your arm so thin. Come. Some tea.' Helen gestured for her to follow. Julia hoisted Slava onto her hip and went inside.

Helen moved around her house as if it were larger than it was, her full skirt and the way she gestured as she spoke with life and color. It was the prerogative of the owner, it seemed, to know how to use the spaces, despite there being little. Julia would remember this always. She studied it, this kind of rooted energy.

Helen smoothed the front of her dress and reached into the

cupboard for a tin of tea leaves, withdrew two cups and saucers, and placed the kettle on the stove.

'Now. What is it?' She sat down and nodded for Julia to join her.

'Oh, Helen, it's nothing.'

'*Not* nothing, Julia. I know your face by now. You speak even without saying anything. Your eyes are sad.'

Julia ached suddenly, for only a mother would say that. She fought the tightness in her throat. 'Henry said he thinks we should leave. Leave here, find somewhere else to live, to work. Ridiculous.' She looked down at Slava, happily rattling a few clothespins on the tile floor. 'I'm so tired, Helen.'

'Yes, that I understand. We are all so tired.' Her hands rested on the table, fingers mildly bowed and arthritic, blue veins running like rivers underneath milky skin. "But, Julia. Think to yourself. Why is it so foolish? Staying *here* would be foolish. Look at how much it is changing already. The rules are always changing for all of us. It is quiet now, but for how long?' Helen's eyes grew intent. 'Why do you not trust him?'

'I do.'

'Well then.'

The kettle boiled, and she left the unanswered words to hover. Julia watched Slava gum the clothespins, and Helen poured the tea delicately and brought the cups to the table.

'Oh, no. That won't do, little one.' She withdrew a biscuit from a small metal box for Slava and took the clothespin from her chubby fingers. 'Trust him, Julia.'

Julia sipped the hot tea and placed it on the table. 'Well, yes, but I think—'

'He hopes for the best for you both, I imagine. You know, when Martyn was alive—'

Julia smiled. Helen spoke of Martyn often. They had never had children, though they had tried and failed. They lived a quiet life and then Martyn was recruited to be a soldier in the German army during the first world war, and he had been young when he left; they had only been married for two years.

'—he made the brave choices that I could not. He encouraged me to live in his absence. He guided us both when the world felt as if it were on the edge of insanity.'

'I don't know, Helen. This is what I struggle with. How am I supposed to know? What about me?'

'But you are one and the same, now, Julia. You are a family. You are not alone anymore.'

'What if something happens? What if I have nothing left, and all of this has been a struggle for nothing?'

Helen placed her hand on Julia's; cool smooth skin atop her own warm skin. 'Julia. There will always be tragedy and sadness. You cannot spend time thinking about what might happen. You must make choices and sacrifices for the ones you love. It is part of life. It is part of being a woman, and a mother.'

The steam dissipated and the tea grew cold as their thoughts filled the room.

That evening, after Henry had returned, and when the house had finally settled into its quiet and Slava lay sleeping, the couple sat and listened to the faint strains of a radio broadcast filtering through the walls from the other room where Helen lay in her room. On the center of the small wooden table were two very small glasses of sweet wine, poured from a dusty bottle that Helen had found earlier in a drawer in her room ('take some, it would be sensible for you both to enjoy something').

There were two kerosene lamps in either corner of the room, flickering a ghostly orange light. Julia had undone the plaits in her hair, and it lay across her back and down her shoulders in a way that made Henry ache with a peculiar kind of sadness: a sadness that only existed when loving someone.

She didn't notice him watching her, for she was looking down at the newspaper clipping that had stayed in the same spot since this morning's argument. She smoothed it down with her long fingers and he noticed she'd been biting the skin by her nails. She spoke first.

'Australia. Are you certain?'

He paused briefly, for his answer would never be as clear out loud, as he heard it in his head. 'Well, we have to try. At least try.'

Julia stood up and moved towards him, stopping next to his chair.

He looked up at her and noticed that the skin around her eyes was a faint red, swollen, as if the tears had long dried, but the sadness remained. She bent down and turned his face to hers, and gently, quietly, kissed him, and then drew back, and then kissed him again, lingering long enough this time to make it mean something.

She turned and padded to their bed, Henry following behind.

6

Munich

Munich train station was teeming and vibrating with groups of people-- so many more than they saw in Neumarkt-- like ants on a piece of food. There were covered wagons, train cars, military vehicles, police officers, families, soldiers. The station itself had a grand main 'hall', an impressive stone structure that stood in the middle of the forecourt, but as it was with other buildings after the second world war, it was being reconstructed from bombing damage. It stood proudly with parts crumbling and defaced, and yet still looked taller than it was; grandeur in the face of humility.

One-hundred and fifty-three kilometers. Two hours of road. Julia looked out of the back of the truck, trying to see through the gaps of people's legs. It was early afternoon, and grey skies offered no indulgence of view. All she saw was a shrinking horizon, familiar landmarks that were moving out of her reach and changing into something new. Eventually, the roads underneath their bodies started changing from grit to a smoother, more sympathetic terrain. The air felt brisk and efficient, as if its sole purpose was to push them faster towards their destination. *Keep looking up,* she told herself. She clutched Slava to her side, feeling a tightness in the center of her chest.

The trucks pulled up and stopped abruptly, ordering everyone off. Julia held Slava as she shuffled off the back onto the ground, and looked back around, making sure Henry was there, with their cases. Everyone stood in groups, looking left and right, listening for direction. A command. Pointing. Shouting. Henry and Julia deduced quickly that they were to form a queue and walk towards the 6 train carriages that were to take them to Naples. The trip would take eleven hours.

'Henry, will there be food on the train? I'm so very hungry. I only have the bread that I took in my bag, from Helen's, from earlier.' Thinking about food just made it worse, she didn't want to think about it.

'I don't know, don't expect it. Just ration what you have.'

'Okay.' She thought the best thing was to save the bread for Slava. She felt her breasts instinctively and realized she could still feed her as long as she had enough water for herself, so they might be alright for a while. She looked over at Slava, happily clutching her battered grey rabbit, now missing an eye, its legs dangling comically.

No one spoke, though glances said more than enough about how similar they all were. Not speaking felt like the last shred of privacy that one could keep; they had their own secrets and musings and fantasies of elsewhere to rely on. Julia leaned on Henry's arm, clinging tightly to avoid being separated.

Acerra was a small town on the edge of western Italy and would be the final edge of land under their feet before they boarded the boat to take them to Australia.

It was dark when they arrived at the station, finally rumbling to a steaming, squealing stop. The few lamps dotting the station building looked like small, phosphorescent balloons. It was one o'clock in the morning, and Slava was asleep on Julia's shoulder; Henry was leaning out of an open window, smoking, the smoke clouds mixing with his icy breath in the air. He had been in this position for the last two hours, unable to sleep.

Julia braced herself for shouting, the panic, the worry. She had been used to it for so long. But none of it came. When the doors opened and kind Italian voices waited patiently and reminded everyone to stay together, Julia almost wept with relief.

Yawns mixed with the shuffling of tired feet and bodies spilling out onto the platform. The night makes years out of mere moments, and tonight stretched like a dream with no end and no beginning, but soon, everyone was directed into lines and directed with torches to walk a mile towards small stone houses that stretched in many rows. Julia scanned the faces around her, and behind her: men carrying bags, sleepy children burying their faces into their mothers' necks, old men and women huddling in groups like children. She heard conversations peppered with '...Where we go now?' and '...Where do we sleep?' and '...Is there food?'

Men were separated from the women and children, but not for any other reason other than medical exams and modesty. But there was no threat in it, and because Julia felt safe, she adjusted.

'Henry, where will I find you tomorrow?' She searched his face for answers as he separated with groups of other men, filtering from the crowd.

'The line for food? I'm not sure, but I am guessing that during the day, we can be together, and at night, we sleep separately.' He nodded respectfully at one of the Italian volunteers, and he walked over in response, overhearing the conversation.

He clapped a hand on his back. 'Name?'

Henry looked at Julia and back at the man standing in front of him. 'Hironimus.'

'Dio! That's a tough one!' he laughed, black curls falling on his tanned face. His teeth were stained from nicotine. 'Tell me an easier name.'

Henry smiled. 'Henry.'

'Much better, eh?' He curved his body as he lit a cigarette and straightened again. 'You all sleep in separate camps, eh?' He pointed to the rows of stone houses with flat roofs, divided by a long building in the center. He pointed to the center building. 'Those are toilets.' He looked down at Slava, clinging to Julia, and pinched his nose, grimacing. 'Whew! Very smelly!' Slava laughed shyly.

He took a drag on his cigarette. 'Daytime, you can go and walk to the beach. Takes a little while, but the weather has been nice for it.'

'And, food?' Julia interrupted.

'Meh. Food is terrible. Not much.' He shrugged. 'War, eh? But. Not too long until the ship comes.' He smiled and clamped the cigarette in the corner of his mouth, his hand outstretched. 'My name is Angelo.' Before he walked off, he leaned towards Slava again and whispered. 'Means 'angel'.'

In the morning, Julia looked around at where she had slept: rows of cots with thin blankets, cups and saucers next to the beds, to use for food later. Cases and duffels were piled in a corner. The walls were cold and damp, but not unpleasantly so. Bodies moved, slowly waking, and mothers hushed their children back to sleep in their embrace.

Julia walked outside of the barracks in the quiet morning, the sun peeking through the grey. There were rows of brick houses that had been designed to look intimidating in their hardness, but they were small and ugly in size, with small steel-barred windows and each building with a square concrete slab as a step in front of the door. They had corrugated steel roofs, undulating and silver in the yellow light as the sun rose behind them. They looked recently abandoned of their previous inhabitants, and Julia wondered where they'd gone.

The air was damp and mild, and the ground was thirsty, and high metal fences surrounded the compound, though they weren't electrified, and they didn't have those metal barbs at the top. The air smelled different, not better or worse, but less rigid and more substance to the breaths, more humidity, more of a mouthful for the lungs, and it tasted faintly of the sea. Slava would be awake soon, so she slowly walked back into the barrack, stopping at the doorway only to listen to the heavy breathing so many tired souls. Slava wriggled, pushed her face into the bed, let out a yawn and stretched her arms toward Julia.

A figure in the door appeared.

'Prima colazione!' *Breakfast.*

Lines of people streamed out of the barracks, faces curious, some even breaking into smiles. They all followed their guides to the main building where they would stand with their bowls in outstretched arms. Julia wondered if she would see Henry there. There were no tables, no chairs, just queues of hungry people and smells of bread and broth mixing with the smell of soil, petrol, and chlorine hovering over it all. It was because of the toilets: they were in a separate building in the middle of the empty yard, and were doused occasionally with large buckets of disinfectant, the smell permeating the top layers of air with a sharp, acidic pong. It didn't matter. There was food. It's all anyone cared about.

Julia looked down at her bowl: two slices of bread sitting on top of thin porridge. A piece of ham. She took the cup of weak tea and the both of them slowly shuffled a few feet away from the line and sat down on the ground.

'Mama?'

Slava pointed at the bowl.

Julia ripped off small pieces of bread and ham and watched as her daughter ate happily. And then, separating himself from the line was Henry, and she saw his familiar walk, and watched as he approached them both, his shoulders softening with gratefulness.

Three weeks had passed.

Julia packed the last few things into the same worn duffle that had lived through too many wars. The chalk had faded, and the thick canvas was scarred with the paths she'd traveled. She remembered her mother, in their last moments together, as she balanced on her knees and folded Slava's pinafore. The stitching had come undone on the hem and she wondered if she had time to fix it, and that detail then led to Julia searching for a needle and thread, and that led to her searching through pockets of dresses and coats and then to a pocket that had a picture in it. It was a picture of her parents: the one given to her by her mother, on her departure so many years ago. She turned it over and re-read the message on the back; she had read it from time to time these last years, as a kind of reminder of where she had come from, and how strong she had become.

> *May this picture be a lasting memory of us,*
> *forever in your heart. Love, Mama.*

She pressed the photograph to her chest and then slipped it inside the duffle, with Slava's toy rabbit on top, then a blanket. She brought it up to her face and smelled the sweetness of Slava's skin that clung to it, and she realized that the pain and nostalgia she was feeling was of motherhood: her mother had felt it, and so had her mother before her.

It had been raining all day, and Slava was napping on the mattress on the floor, a single sheet wrapped around her fat thighs. The doorway to the building was open, and the air felt heavy, the tin of the corrugated roof added a metallic taste as Julia inhaled deeply. Henry had arranged for them to have a space on the next ship out to Australia. March 31. That was tomorrow.

She stood up to reach for one of the other cases, and her stomach suddenly cramped intensely, and the ground started to spin, and her breath caught in her throat. She held onto the edge of the bed feebly, and just before she fell back, before the spinning became too much and before her head hit the floor, she looked over at Slava, still sleeping. And then, black.

❧

Have I been asleep for long?

Her eyes fluttered but didn't open yet. It was pleasant, this feeling. It felt weightless, as if within a dream that lay heavy on her body. Then, a hardness underneath her hips.

Why am I on the floor?

She heard a cry. It was Slava.

She rolled over onto her other side and lay there for another minute. The heaviness was leaving her, and she was waking more, and then her eyes opened at the sound of another cry. And then she felt her body stiffen, her stomach muscles tightening in a knotted nausea. She grimaced and curled onto her side, waiting for the pain to subside.

She noticed the unevenness of the floor: it had faded and bowed with footsteps over time and smelled of old varnish. There was no urgency to tend to Slava just yet; she was protected by pillows around her on the bed in a sort of cushioned fortress. The pain subsided for a moment. Perhaps she'd not eaten enough, but she wasn't particularly hungry.   Julia stretched out and felt her spine expand deliciously. And then her stomach contorted again, in a hot new burst of pain. Nerves, probably. Anticipation. She waited for it to dissipate.

Slava peeked over her barrier, punching it with a doughy fist, exclaiming 'Mama!', and then falling back onto the bed, in a flurry of legs and giggles.

Outside, the entire camp was buzzing with energy, bodies of families milling about with a focused urgency, but no panic. The air had the faintest smell of salt, and it wafted on the air so gently; it reminded her of a dream she'd had about the sea. Or maybe it was the chlorine from the toilet block again. Julia moved slowly, her thoughts ahead of her, running rampant in last-minute questions about where they would live, what would they wear, where exactly they were headed, and more importantly, why she felt so ill.

For the last few days, the camp had reunited the families in preparation for the journey elsewhere, and it was now that Henry freely walked in, his energy abrupt, opening the door and surveying the room before approaching Julia. He had yellowed papers in his hand, and he was fluttering them with excitement and apprehension. In his excitement, he failed to notice that his wife was on the floor.

He dropped down to his knees and placed his hands underneath her, lifting her up, reading her face. 'OH *bozshe*, what's going on with you?'

'I fainted.'

He looked more intently at her. The blood had drained from her cheeks.

'Oh, are you alright?'

Julia pinched her cheeks to bring back the color. 'I think so. Yes. Fine.' She clasped her hands in front of her stomach and suddenly a new thought entered her mind as she looked at him, but it quickly vanished.

'Right. So, tomorrow. We're ready?' He looked over at Slava, and back at Julia. 'Well?'

'Yes, but...' Julia started, wanting the questions in her head to tumble out like coins onto the ground. She wanted him to pick them up and answer them and give them to her and make her feel certain again. She wanted him to make her feel safe.

'What?'

'No, nothing. Yes, we're ready.'

He picked up Slava and brought her to his chest triumphantly: a father feeling like a man, having a conversation with his family about the life they would have. He cooed at her and his answers came rapidly as if shutting out the doubt that they all felt creeping forward: 'It'll be fine. Australia is warm. They have plans for us, we'll have a house. You'll be able to find work when Slava starts school.'

Henry turned to walk away, but then turned back to Julia. 'We will be fine, Julia.' And then walked towards the door and out into the light with their daughter, leaving Julia standing there, their life quite literally at her feet.

'Fine, yes. Fine.' she whispered again, to no one in particular.

'Mama! Papa! *Lotka*!' Slava pointed. The ship that loomed at the harbor was bigger than anything Julia had ever seen in her entire life. The sound of hollow, creaking, cavernous metal settling in the dock rang in her ears and reverberated around her.

She looked up at it, tenting her hand over her eyes. The ship was bold and dark, in contrast to the bright sky behind it, the blue water sitting below it, the bulk of metal splitting the surface of the water like a knife. She looked around at everyone else, wondering if they'd had the same thoughts, and were also in awe of what was before them, and they seemed to be: groups of people standing and waiting with bags, with children, all looking up, hopeful.

Big white block letters branded the boat's flank: GENERAL STUART HEINTZELMAN 159. Julia wondered who it was, this German, that had been so important, to have had something this big named after him. What had he done, and how many had sacrificed their lives, possibly, for this man? And yet, the irony of the fact that this ship would bring them away from war, was not lost on her— a German ship that would take them to freedom. And she was finally ready to give over to it.

There were passengers already walking onto the boat; from where, she had no idea. Some looked to be dressed nicely, looking like they had money to spare. Julia held onto Slava's hand tightly. The ramp started lowering.

'Hey!' the family turned and saw Angelo, loping across to them, his hands behind his back, his shirt with stains and sweat marking it. 'I thought I would say arrivederci, eh?' Slava stood by him. She had now grown comfortable around the 'nice man with smoky face'. 'Can you say it, little Slava? The word for good-bye?'

Slava shook her head.

'Well, in that case, I cannot give you the present. Ah well.' He pretended to turn away.

'Aree-dechee.' Henry chuckled, watching the scene. Julia's face creased, grateful that a kind man would make Slava smile. Perhaps creating a memory for her amongst the chaos.

'Perfetto!' Angelo bellowed, and moved his hand from behind his back, revealing a bright, round orange, as bright as anything Slava had ever seen.

Slava gasped and looked up at Julia. 'Mama can I have it?'

Angelo straightened up to face Julia and Henry. 'My nonna has an orchard, and the most beautiful orange tree that I remember as a child. It was a happy memory, having my first orange. I think it will be her first one, yes?'

Julia nodded.

'Well, then.' He stuck out his hand and Henry shook it. 'Good luck.'

Before Henry could say anything, Angelo walked off with a smile and a wave, Slava clutching the orange like a jewel, holding it to her face and smelling it with utter joy.

'Cargo! Cargo section!' Directions in the chaos, shouting to create mass order.

Would have been nice to be in a little cabin with linens and a dresser, and a seat by a window, Julia thought, as she passed by tables set with linens and lamps and china plates.

Walking through into the lower section of the ship, it was as if they were all being hidden away. The family were ushered into a small storage room with a tiny port hole and a mattress on the floor for all of them to share. The ship creaked and moaned as more people loaded into its spaces. Henry sat on the floor, his back against the metal of the ship, looking at Julia, and placed a hand around her waist.

'You feel strange?' He knew her face so well now.

She nodded. 'Feel a bit tired.'

'Aren't we all.' He leaned his head back and closed his eyes. The smell of the orange was filling the room, Slava's hands sticky with it.

The door, ramp, gangplank, whatever it was called for she'd heard too many words today and couldn't remember, was being pulled up. The small hatch was closing. Julia watched through the small, red-painted porthole, her tiny circle of a window like a changing portrait of a strange world and watched as the sandy coast became smaller and smaller until the harbor slowly became smaller and the blue of the sea overtook it. She thought was almost more beautiful, in this way, as blue of the sea met the pale horizon of the sky, and this was a salve to mend her broken story and make it whole again.

Julia prodded Henry.

'I need some air; can you keep an eye on Slava?'

'You just need some rest.' He placed an arm around her shoulders, and she was grateful for the safety of his embrace.

She was restless. 'Sure. Maybe I'm just hungry.' She felt her stomach contract, and then a warmth between her legs. She stood up, her cheeks flushing suddenly.

Henry cocked his head to the side. 'There's food: black bread, some soup made out of potatoes. Maybe even sausage.'

The thought made her want to wretch.

She shook her head. 'No, no. I just need air.' She started walking away, impatiently. It was starting again. She winced at the pain.

'Okay, I'll be here.'

Julia made sure she remembered exactly where he was as she left, trying to push her way around and through groups of people as her stomach began to cramp again, this time in quick succession. When she finally, slowly, climbed the last flight of stairs and found the doorway to the long flat walkway above, she walked out and carefully gripped the railing that traveled the perimeter of the ship. It was extraordinary, how the world looked here, and it was the first time she'd ever seen the sea, and it was not at all as she imagined it. She breathed deeply and gratefully and then prepared for another fresh burst of pain and looked out onto the vast emptiness of sea in front of her as blood from the failing pregnancy slowly traveled down her thighs, staining her legs underneath her skirts.

Afterwards, when she had found a toilet room and silently mourned what could not be, she used salt water from a filthy basin to dry the marks on her legs and tore a piece of the inside of her skirt to finish the process, and then a bit more to soak the tears off her cheeks—though they kept falling faster than she could catch them— and erase the story that had been, and was now no longer. And then, aching still, she carefully walked back to her husband and daughter. He placed his arm around her, and she pressed her face against his chest, hearing Slava's breath become even as she fell asleep on the mattress, the orange peel in her slack hand.

They were once again a family of three.

The next six weeks they were all moving: the ship, the people on the ship, the sky and sea surrounding them. And yet, they were standing in one space, in one place, and given time to unfurl themselves for a time.

The first-class cabins were on the upper deck, the wide wood circling the entirety of the ship and secured with heavy steel poles and railings. There were lifeboats piled up and tied close to the bow of the ship, a German flag snapping its colors at the stern. People were segregated by class— first, second, third and cargo—, there was a hall in the center of the ship that served food to everyone but first class (first class had linens and fine crystal and silk-backed mahogany chairs), and there was also a small pool of fresh water where everyone was allowed to swim at marked times (first-class always went before everyone else). Julia and Henry occasionally walked the length of the ship, arm and arm and holding Slava's hand as other families would, talking as the sea air blew across their faces, people-watching, having polite conversations with other immigrants that were emigrating to Australia. They shared food with other families, and watched each other's children play games on the wooden decks. Some evenings there would be glasses filled with rum and card-games in the lower-class cabins, which helped pass the time and made them feel as if they were on an adventure to discover new lands and live in long-awaited freedom.

Occasionally, Henry and Julia sat and looked at the stars, Henry teaching her the constellations that he had learned about in school, pointing his finger to the sky and outlining the shapes of Aries, or Orion, and Julia would ask him how he had remembered all of these strange names and figures. He was a wonder, to her, in those moments and revealed much of the quiet man he had always been.

The ship worked its way peacefully along the length of the Suez, around the corners of India, on the edge of Singapore, and then down towards the southern coast of Australia, stopping at various ports. A few days before it arrived in Melbourne, where the Bonegilla detention center would be to receive them all, Henry and Julia sat one evening on the middle deck, after a dinner of boiled potatoes, ham and vegetable broth. Slava was sleeping in their cabin already. They were imagining what their life would be like; the newness of the idea was exhilarating.

'I think the house will be small, but sweet. Like a little version of my childhood home.' She paused, confirming that detail. 'With a garden. And an apple tree, for Slava to climb.' Suddenly, Julia was young. Younger than her twenty-four years, and her memories flooded her head. But they didn't make her mourn her past— they made her want to recreate it, somehow. Indulge in the celebration of it.

She continued. 'Also, *tsvity*. Wildflowers. I love them. Or anything pink and white.'

'Orchids.' Henry had read that orchids were a relatively easy import, the seeds arriving from farms in Fiji that spanned acres; they were a rarity, and only afforded by the wealthy, in Europe. It reminded him of his childhood, and his mother; it was one of the only things that remained in her room after she had died.

'Why orchids?' Julia had never heard of Henry having any bit of nostalgia about something so delicate. Or anything much, really.

The warm air moved strands of his hair across his forehead as he spoke. 'My mother loved orchids. She would have them in her room, and I remember they were the darkest, blackest purple color… Maybe we can have orchids, somehow.'

'Oh, a greenhouse, you mean.' Julia nodded. 'That's a lovely idea.'

Henry stood at up and leaned on the railing. 'Listen, I think it'll be small, but we will make it as we want it to be, this new life.'

'Yes, probably. I think you're right.'

Henry turned slowly to her in comical shock. '*Yulia Rudnick.*' Julia smiled as the Ukrainian sounds rolled off his lips and he said her full name. 'Did I hear that right?' He heard the contentment in her voice, and he saw the way her arms rested on the arms of the wooden chair, as if she had opened herself up to the night air. 'I never thought I would hear you say that.'

Julia laughed. 'Don't get used to it.' She slipped her feet out of her shoes and sighed at how good it felt. 'I think we will have chickens. And cows.'

'My little farm girl.' Henry turned back to the black of the sea, the moonlight in small shards on the surface of the water. He smiled at the thought of Julia on a farm, Slava growing taller, stronger, under the gaze of a sibling or two. He thought of stability, and security, and not once did he long for where he had come from.

Julia interrupted his thoughts with another question. 'What do you think cane cutting will be like?'

Henry gritted his teeth. 'Hard labor.' He reached into his pocket and felt for a cigarette. 'I've spoken to some of the men on the ship. They've told me it will be hard; I really don't know.' The flame burned the edge and the red glow added to the starlight. 'Hard work doesn't scare me.' He squinted as the smoke curled by his eyes.

'Nothing scares you.' Julia's face shone in the moonlight as she tapped his leg gently with her bare foot. 'You seem to be made of granite.'

He turned to face her and leaned back against the railing. 'Ahh, and maybe you are made of dreams. Always dreaming. Imagining. Believing.'

'That's very true. But dreams vanish. Granite stays.'

Henry smiled and shook his head. 'Both are strong.' He inhaled on his cigarette and let the smoke fade and curl out of his mouth lazily. 'But both have a breaking point.' He walked over and sat down next to her.

Julia leaned over and kissed his cheek and sat back in her chair, looking up at the stars. 'I don't think I could imagine us breaking.'

Henry reached for her hand. 'I don't think I would want to.'

Julia remembered her mother telling her once that 'secrets are like promises; both are thin, both fragile.' Julia and Henry's promises to each other felt quiet, and understood, and felt heavy on their shoulders. There was an unknown that they would be stepping into, and their promises took valuable space in their hearts. They held onto it dearly.

But sometimes, through even the most generous of efforts, it can all be broken.

What is true, belongs only to me.

– Seneca

Part II

Australia
1947-1955

7

Stratford, 1947

They had arrived, the vastness of the land before them, houses littered across the dust like lifeless animals, or statues. Their faces were wide and open, like children taking in a new world. They had no idea what they were about to do, or see, clutching their possessions to their bodies.

'Oh, Henry. My God. We're in the middle of nowhere.'

Twenty miles outside of Stratford, Julia stood, wide-eyed, staring at the small white house with the pitched roof and shingled sides sat serenely on thirty acres of alternately green and arid land; mostly flat and nondescript save for rows of farmhouses dotted in a line on uneven grassy parcels, bundles of tall trees and thrusts of grass decorating their sides. They all had screened windows and two wooden steps leading up to the front doors, and they seemed friendly and small, if a bit lonely in the vastness of the landscape.

When the family first arrived in Australia, they, like most immigrants that had filtered out from war-torn countries, were one of thousands of on Australia's teeming, wide open shores, looking for work to make a better life for themselves and their families. It was at least a two-year indentured service, which culminated with a small parcel of land and automatic Australian citizenship. This was the new life that awaited them, 2,758 kilometers from the detention center in Bonegilla and a world away from the countries they had once called home.

POPULATE OR PERISH! The slogan had greeted them everywhere, on propaganda posters plastering shop windows and street lamps, painted on wagons and printed on milk cartons, and it shouted out at them as they drove past in the truck that would transport them from the train station to the house that would begin their life here. It seemed to be a noble act almost— come here and cultivate our land, and we will offer you the world. Try your hardest, and you shall be rewarded. It was a sermon of hope. It took them an entire solid day and a bit more, to get to Stratford, pitched neatly into the north-eastern most part of Australia, tucked away amongst barren plains and borderless outskirts, it was quaint, and had quaint people.

There was sheen to the landscape, most likely because of recent rains at the end of the wet season. In the distance, the cane fields dominated the bottom half of the property, standing twice as tall as the tallest man Julia had ever seen. It was more land than she could imagine having, and yet she immediately thought of her father standing next to her, his strong arms crossed over his chest and a capable glint in his eye. *You can do this*, he'd say, and she would smile and lean her head on his shoulder and smell the tobacco on his clothes and the sweat on his brow.

After being in the detention center for a few months, they had learned that the Avon River bordered Stratford, which in turn fed into the Barron river, which snaked around and nestled on the outskirts of the suburb of Cairns. There were the things that afforded them the convenience of a structured life: a post office, an airport, food stores, quaint little cafes, a hospital, a school, and a reliable bus service. But from where Julia stood, she may as well have been on the moon. Not much was visible, most things farther than a 10-minute walk, westward, which would require taking the bus from the stop that lay at the end of the long path to the farmhouses on the outskirts.

Henry stood next to her now, and she didn't lean on him. Instead, Julia covered her mouth in shock, her feet rooted to the ground in front of this house.

'We are living *here?*' She squinted at the houses in view, and then at the one they would live in, and then her eyes widened comedically. 'Who, what… I mean… how??'

She turned around on herself slowly, taking in the vastness of where they were, and then back to the house.

It was timber framed with a soft A-shaped sloping roof and wooden stilts (apparently protection from flooding and insects) that Slava found terribly funny ('leg! *Leg, Mama!*') with an outhouse to the back of it. There was nothing else, as basic as could be, and very apparent that this was theirs to make into something bigger than it was.

The couple stood next to each other in silence.

'Come on,' Henry encouraged. 'It's our own, at least.'

'Well. *Not* what I imagined.' Julia's right hand made the sign of the cross in front of her chest, and then copied what Slava had said, her hands splayed out: 'It has *legs*!' She pointed at the stilts underneath, rising a few feet off the ground. 'A house on legs, Henry.' She watched as he broke into a low laugh.

'I understand. But, remember how we imagined it?' He pointed at the far-right corner of the field, towards a withered wooden fence with two chicken coops and a stable. 'You could make a fine garden, I imagine. There's also space in the back as well. You'd probably have to clear it.'

Julia cocked her eyebrow at him.

'*We* would clear it.'

'Henry, it's a lot of work— '

'Come on. It can be good.'

'You're very positive about all this.'

Henry placed his hands up as if he were admiring a work of art, or gesturing at a palace that didn't exist yet, and he spoke of things that he had only briefly learned in his childhood, with his father. *We can build a greenhouse here, in this far corner, and then maybe we can have a small farm, and then a garden out towards the back.*

Henry put his hand on her shoulder and felt it soften under his touch. 'We have to be patient. Also, now that we're here…' and he looked down at her stomach and looked back at her, raising an eyebrow.

Julia laughed and pushed his hand off. 'Oh, so *now* you see that as a good idea, do you? With everything else we have to undertake?'

He kissed her cheek, and she felt the sharpness of his cheeks.

'Mama! Mama, Papa!' Slava was back behind the house and they followed her voice. A discovery: a dark blue, rusted bicycle, as if someone was inviting them in, to explore.

Henry inspected the sad little two-wheeled thing. The metal was still solid, but the paint had worn, and orange rust had settled on it. 'Guess that's mine, for now. but we'll save some money and get a car somehow. Maybe tomorrow we can take the bus to the city and find food. See where we are, and how we do things in this new world.'

'*We* will take the bus and explore.'

Julia walked ahead, following Slava. 'Wait for me. I'll help you up the stairs. Let's go see our new house.'

That evening, Henry was gentle and attentive over dinner, however sparse it was. They were finishing the last of their rations that they had brought with them from the camp (small pieces of sausage, a half pint of milk, bread and weak tea in a tin flask) at the small wooden table in the sitting room next to the kitchen.

There were shelves behind them, and windows above the sink basin, and also was a kettle that boiled suspended over a wood burner, a few kerosene lamps, a few chairs, and two beds. There were shelves behind them and a window on the other side, and beyond the kitchen there were two square rooms; the footprint of the house was a tidy rectangle split into inhabitable parts. They ate, and sipped their tea, and Henry touched Julia's hand across the table as they spoke.

After she'd put Slava to bed, and Henry had gone to sit on the step to smoke, she went into their bedroom and sat down on the bed, their two cases at her feet, up against the wall. It took her a few moments to realize that there was no mirror, only a frame, and all she thought was of the luxury of owning a mirror one day. She craved the familiarity of her own face and proceeded to trace it with a fingertip: the long slight arch of her forehead, the soft indentation of her temple and down to the cheekbones that had been so prominent ever since she was a child. She traced the aquiline profile of her nose, across the soft skin of her cheeks, down to her lips that had grown dry, the skin flaking. She went down the curve of her chin and then down her neck, the lines there creasing as she bent her head to the side and let her thick plait of her fall across. She then began to unplait it one wave at a time, the dust from travel released from each bend, and ran her fingers through the length, finally shuddering it to life again.

The next few weeks, Julia woke early, her familiar restlessness a result of sleeping somewhere new. She walked into the small kitchen, trying to remember where everything was: cold box, oven, plates and bowls on a narrow counter in front of a window; a steel kettle. A water flask propped up against the cupboard. It was starting to get light out, and Henry would be up soon. These new, long, strange days were a new rhythm: seemed as if she wore a path into the floorboards of the house; her gait was the same.

She lit the fire and put the kettle above it, fumbling in the cupboards for the tin of coffee she had bought in Stratford the day before. The bread was in the cupboard where things now lived temporarily until they found their permanent home: bags of rice, flour, barley, a jar of oatmeal, a jar of sugar, and six fresh eggs. Milk and butter, apples, bacon bones and sausages were in the cool box by the window, and a large bowl of pea shoots, carrots, potatoes, beets and lettuce were on the kitchen table waiting to be used for soup.

Julia moved to the cool box and found two slices of ham from dinner a few days ago and took that to the counter and placed it between two fresh slices of bread, wrapping it in wax paper for Henry's lunch that day. She would fill his flask with coffee and another one with water and place it all in the canvas bag by the door.

Cane cutters were brutal, determined and hardy, generally working in 'gangs' of six to eight, roughly fifty hours a week; days beginning at dawn and ending fourteen hours later. Gritty, unpleasant and occasionally deadly work, out in the open in all weathers, existing with snakes, rats and other vermin that carried the risk of disease. It was hot, back breaking and only attractive because of the kind of money earned. Blood and sweat money. *Stoop, chop, straighten, top. Stoop, chop, straighten, top.* It was a rhythm that developed over the course of the day; hunched over fields of green, stopping only every few hours to pause, drink from the flask of water at their hip, smoke. Repeat. The more cane, the more money, and more money meant a sense of freedom that ultimately was priceless to all of them.

And then there was the smoke: thick black sticky smoke that clung to clothes and skin like hot molasses. To get rid of snakes, rats and trash, cane was burnt before harvesting. The sugar syrup, disintegrating from the flames, would start to ooze and bubble, making it sticky to handle; the cutters more often than not would end up being covered head to toe in soot and sweat. Some cutters wore a bracelet of flannel around their wrists to stop the sweat running down their arms into their hands. It was quite literally back-breaking work, bent in half for twelve hours a day, hacking away at the sturdy stalks of cane with heavy, hook-ended flat blades.

The kettle boiled, and she heard Henry move in the room beyond. Julia watched as the plumes of smoke rose from the small fires ushering in the dawn; the horizon of cane would slowly diminish over the course of the day. Julia's role mirrored all the other immigrant settlers and farm. She turned and saw his square frame looming in the doorway now, as it would do at seven o'clock that evening, or even later still, only his teeth showing through the soot on his face.

'Tea?'

He nodded. 'Please.' He laced his boots and prepared for the morning, a canvas bag at the door, his thin jacket on the chair. She watched him as he checked his chest pockets for cigarettes, two taps with his palm on the left, and then his hands would run through his hair briefly. She observed him as if memorizing the words of a song. Marriage felt like that.

'Henry.'

'Yes?'

'Do you think we have time to…' she strode up to him and put her hands around him, clasping them at his back, looking up at him with a smile.

And just then Slava cried out, and it broke the thought, and Julia blushed at her boldness and knew it wasn't the right time. She began to walk away. 'Never mind.'

He strode up to her, the steam of the kettle like a halo surrounding her, and slipped his arm around her waist, bringing her back into his embrace. She closed her eyes and smelled the warm, sweet scent of burnt sugar on his skin as she kissed him.

8

'Hello? What's all the fuss about? What's the noise for?', a rough voice bellowed as the door creaked open. Julia had passed this particular house before, the one with the flowers outside the door, and the large garden out the back. But had never seen anyone, and now the voice jarred her. She couldn't judge if it was upset or teasing.

Minutes earlier, Julia had been standing at the kitchen window when she saw Slava vanish, her grey cotton shorts moving in rhythm with her white-blonde shock of hair, and then a faint giggle as she flew out of sight. Julia had been clearing lunch and all of a sudden, she was gone. She knew she would have to go after her, and it made her nervous: she knew very few people that worked the fields and lived in the modest houses beside her, and now, walking out by herself shouting her daughter's name, had made her feel exposed.

She had walked out the door into the sun and muttered to herself. 'God damn, this child will be the end of me.' It felt like a sentence, having a two-year old. She struggled knowing when to let her run free and when to snatch her by the wrist and relay her disapproval. And it had only been her acting as both parents, recently, for Henry had been absent ever since he'd started work— coming home in an absolute state, nothing left of him. His face gaunt, his hands displaying new blisters that had layered over his old calloused ones. He had no sense of place or identity or loyalty to anything other than the fact that he was shackled to this life temporarily and he had a bed to lay his head on. There were no conversations, no fleeting sense of contentment, no laughter or stolen moments looking up at the sky, just a few (more) cigarettes after dinner and then again before bed, and then he would sleep like a weary child, before the next morning where his whole narrative would start again.

'Slava?? Slava!' She couldn't see her. She couldn't hear her. She wiped her hands on her apron and called for her daughter, and then suddenly she saw her appear again like a sprite, with a naked chest, shining hair long around her shoulders and her shorts now filthy with dirt from the back garden.

'Look at the *state* of you, you ridiculous thing!' Julia lifted up her hands in protest, and crouched down to grab her, lifting her up in her arms. 'You must not run away like that, there are spiders under these houses,' and she buried her face in the child's neck, blowing raspberries.

It was then that he had called out to her, as Julia stood up, her hair wild around her face, her face shining from sweat, her shirt open at the neck, exposing freckled skin. 'Eh? Whose creating all this chaos?'

Julia turned around and recognized the muscular build and square features of Iliya. She smiled politely. She'd seen him before, but then again, she'd seen many of the same people in this strange cross section of space, and she'd always kept herself to herself. She often saw him with Henry, they had a banter, they worked together, and she saw both tall men stand together occasionally, talking about something that she didn't care to ask about. She walked out from behind the house and stood on the dirt road that ran perpendicular, looking up at him standing in the doorway. He had light brown hair that was lighter still at the sides of his head, by his temples, and the skin on his face had browned a dark olive on his cheeks, nose, and forehead. He was leaning against the frame, holding what looked like a cane knife. She squinted up at him, not because of any brightness, but because she didn't particularly know him well, and wanted to do something to affect confusion.

'Oh, hello. Iliya, yes?'
'Yes, and you're…'
'Julia.'
'Yes. Henry's wife.'
'Julia,' she corrected him, flattening her lips.
'Yes, yes. I know you, I think. You live down there.' He waved his hand towards the house, ten down along the path.'
'Yes. How do you—'

'—Henry. I know your husband. Everyone knows everything and everyone here, after a while.' When he spoke, his mouth moved languidly, as if he wasn't in a hurry anywhere. He folded his arms.

'Ah. Yes. And you… live…?

He moved his head, gesturing to the door. 'Here. My wife is called Elina. She works at the small bookshop in Stratford.'

'Oh, yes, I do know her. Or, I have seen her before.' Julia knew her. Elina was tall like a reed, quiet, and held herself proudly and coolly. Beautiful gold hair like burnt honey.

Iliya turned around as if reminding himself where he was. 'We have just recently arrived here, just six months ago, though sometimes I think life here isn't all that better from living— 'He pointed with his knife, and Julia's eyes followed, across the fields to where faint line of sugarcane divided the sky. 'Over there.'

'Oh?'

'War. Well, at least no war, for now. But still too many Russians in Poland for my liking.' He dropped his shoulders in a kind of resignation. 'We all have the same stories.'

'Well, that's true, yes.' her smile came quickly, and surprised her. 'Anyway, sorry about the shouting, that's my daughter, Slava. She's a bit…' she didn't know why she was apologizing for her, but there it was. '...too much.'

'Well, we don't have children.'

'Oh.'

'Probably for the best.' He leaned against the frame and hooked his thumbs into his belt loops.

Julia blushed. 'Ah. Well, they *are* a challenge.'

'I'll take your word for it.' He waved at Slava, and she stuck her tongue out. 'She's quite sweet. Precocious.'

Julia sensed the natural end of their banter, and used the space to gather herself, taking Slava by the hand.

'Okay, well, nice to talk to you, 'and he nodded back to her, and moved as if to walk back into the house, and she turned to walk away. She knew he was watching her because she didn't hear the door close, and she was only mildly uncomfortable about it. She spent the next 10 minutes of the walk back to the house letting her mind wander a bit, thinking about how he ended up here, and what he and his wife were like, behind closed doors.

'Let's go, we have to cook dinner for Papa, yes?' her pace quickened.

That evening, after dinner, Henry was sat with Slava on the bed, and Julia watched as he read to her, her blonde hair splayed out on his chest as she leaned against him and watched his index finger follow along to the words. It was the only book she had, and it was about a mitten that had gotten lost in a forest, and each of the animals that found it, tried to find shelter in the fur-lining within, until there were so many that wanted it for themselves, and the glove became too strained to contain them all, and it burst, leaving all of them to try and find homes for themselves in the cold winter.

'Papa?'

'Yes, love.'

'Where they go?'

'They will find a home, rabbit.' The name for her grew out of her habit as a baby to gum a carrot when she was teething. "Besides, they have each other to keep warm.'

She buried her head into his chest, and he kissed her softly.

Julia walked off back into the kitchen and sat down, retrieving a pencil and a piece of white paper from the shelf behind her. Recently, she'd begun to forge a comfortable habit, in a sort of diary written to herself, and letters that she would never send, all kept aside once they were done, maybe as comfort to her. Tonight, she wanted to write to Maria.

My Marioshka,

I still see your face. It has never left me. Oh, how I imagined my life so differently, and without you, sometimes it doesn't make any sense. Henry is working many hours now, in the cane fields, and it is hard on him, he seems like a different man. Tired. Impatient. Silent. He smokes heavily, and his body is thin. He has started saying that he wants to build a greenhouse- a glass one- in the small square of garden out at the front of the house. And maybe that would be good for him; maybe the quiet hours doing something he loves would help him find life here. I have started a small garden in the back of the house, and we now have a small collection of chickens, as well as a few cows that we've inherited from an elderly neighbor. As for little Slava-- I wish you could see her- she is two and a half now, and though my love for her is deeper than anything I have ever felt.

Truthfully, I have such sadness sometimes, and Henry finds it difficult to understand, because these are things that men cannot have time for-- the luxury of feeling, I think. And yet I wish I could tell him how to help me, and maybe that would help us feel closer in some way. And maybe part of it lies in the fact that we keep trying for children and nothing seems to happen. I do hope it will, one day. The noise of children would make this life a little bit brighter, maybe. Anyway, I wanted to tell you how much I love you, and I wish so much that you were with me.

Love, Yulia

Slava padded out of the room and came over to Julia, burying her face into her skirts.

'Tired, rabbit?'

Julia folded the letter in half, and then into a quarter, then left it resting under a cup, as she brought Slava up into her arms, and carried her into the other room, as Henry walked past them to go outside. Julia placed Slava into her bed, tucked the thin sheet around her small body, and then sat down, the edge of the mattress softening under her.

'Shall we sing a lullaby?' Slava nodded sleepily.

Julia turned the lamp down to a flicker and began to sing the notes to a song that she knew instinctively: a minor-toned, beautiful song that her mother used to sing to her, about love and beauty and death and sweetness.

The moon has gone,
The sun is in its keep,
Slava wants to sleep.
Sleep my dear, sleep,
Close your eyes sweet,
And I'll tell you a story deep.

In the bedroom there was a window, a little square one divided into four panels that looked out onto the small back garden, and though it was dark, Julia stared into the night as she sang:

And once there was
An extraordinary war,
And it lasted for many years;
A cat ate the Prince

A hound ate the Knight
And a mouse left the Princess in tears.

Slava slowly fell asleep to the comforting rhythm of her mother's voice, her tones drifting with softness and care, and landing delicately on the words of the song:

And in the end,
The prince was made of chocolate,
The princess was made of sugar,
And the knight was made of sweet biscuit,
So, none of them suffered.

➤

She'd just closed the door to the bedroom when she saw Henry pick up the letter. 'What's this?' He turned it over in his hand, a cigarette burning in the other. He started to open it.

'No, please don't.' Julia walked towards him, after leaving the dark of Slava's room, and took it out of his hands. 'It's just for me.'

'Oh. Why are you embarrassed by it?' He watched as her eyes revealed more than she cared to.

'It's just nothing. I wrote a letter.'

'For whom?'

'For my sister. For me.'

'Could you write to your parents instead? Would it make you feel better?'

'I should. But there is so much to say. Old wounds, I guess.'

Henry leaned towards her, resting his face on his palm. 'I have them too, you know.' And then leaned back in his chair, having laid the gift of honesty at her feet. 'To this day, I wonder what would have happened to me had she still been alive.' And another cigarette passed through his fingers as the old one dimmed, the metal tray full of dying embers. 'Do you fear for them? What if you sent it?' he prodded.

'Yes. I fear that if I write, it would be a kind of beacon, somehow. As if a trail of my tears would be traced back to them and end in their deaths.'

Her honesty felt like a hole in her chest that would never heal. Henry's questions were necessary— two people should reveal their pain to the other— but it revealed her scars. She looked up at him and realized that he'd placed his hand in the middle of the table, to reach for hers, but had stopped and waited for her; he understood her pain.

Julia suddenly felt uneasy, so she stood up, shaking off the maudlin as if an uncomfortable coat, and immediately started telling Henry about today, about Slava being overbearing and riotous, and how she had been outside most of the day, her shock of golden hair, thin as gossamer, disappearing in and amongst the wild grass and brush, like some indigenous, white-eyed animal.

She'd told Henry that she'd been down the path and seen the other houses, after she and Slava had gone for a walk, and that she'd seen Iliya come out and say a polite hello. She asked what he knew about him.

'Ah yes, that's Iliya. Good man. Keep to themselves, he and his wife, mostly. He works with me, he's in my cutting group. Why do you ask?' Henry leaned back in his chair.

'Just curious, I guess. I see him sometimes, when I'm out with Slava. He's from Poland?'

'Yes. Lublin. They had a tough time during the deportations.'

'I can imagine. We probably have such similar pasts.'

'Don't know much about him really,' he exhaled and leaned forward to inspect a burn on his hand and a cut on his arm, both of which were difficult to see through the soot. 'He's out with us most days, he does contract work on other things, I think. Contract work pays better, but you get moved all over the place.'

'You feel sorry for him,' Henry laughed. 'You like stray animals.'

'What? No, no. Just curious that's all,' she waved her hands as if brushing off the comment.

'Well, maybe we can invite them round for dinner one evening?' Henry looked over at her, a wan look crossing his face. 'What do you think?' He saw that she was off in a thought.

'Julia?'

'Yes?'

'Dinner? You didn't say anything.'

'Oh, sorry, yes sure. That would be nice. If you want to.'

She walked softly into the bedroom, still in thought, and fell asleep listening to him lighting another cigarette. The night drew in and began the orchestra sounds of cricket-song and a child's steady breathing.

9

'Why?' It was Slava's favorite word lately. *Why*, along with, *Mama*.
'We're having dinner, sertseh.' *Sweetheart.*
'Why?'
Slava peered out from under a clean bed sheet in the other room, having fashioned it into a sort of limp tent, hanging between the dresser drawers and the bed, and proceeded to pull it off and onto her shoulders, wrapping it around her and dragging it behind her like a train. She pointed at the kitchen counter. 'Chicken.'

'Yes. For dinner.' Julia massaged the skin with a small cub of butter, her fingers shining from it.

Slava pointed at the broom in the corner and the glasses set out on the table. 'Why?' Her blue eyes were the color of the sea and they glittered mischievously.

Julia plunged her hands into a bowl of soap and water. 'A nice man and a young lady are coming for dinner. A friend of Papa's.'

She started peeling fresh potatoes and carrots, having rinsed off the soil from their garden. Her thoughts ran nervously over menial tasks: *Sweep the floor. Pluck the chicken. Wash the kitchen table. Tidy the rooms. Curl my hair.*

'Why?'

'Because it is nice to have people for dinner.' Julia's voice grew firm to prevent any further questions, and she kept talking. 'And sometimes, having people to come and visit makes me feel less lonely.' She scraped the edge of the knife along the carrot and stopped. She hadn't expected to say that, but there it was.

'Mama, sad?' Slava held the sheet and walked regally, her dusty grey rabbit in her hands.

'Listen, *please* just let me do what I need to, okay?' Julia's voice was stern.

She saw Slava's face scowl at the reprimand, and she softened. 'Oh, you're such a lovely nuisance though,' and ran over to her to grab her face and plant a kiss on her forehead. She still had a carrot in her hand and showed it to Slava. 'Here, rabbit. Now, Mama has to get busy with the dinner.'

That evening, the sky turned a bitter orange, touching the flatlands farther than the eye could reach. It looked a bit like the sky Julia used to see seeping through her bedroom window. And the memories creeped in as she leaned against the kitchen table and inhaled the smell of the meat crisping in the oven and the onions simmering in salty oil. The smells were *home* to her. Nothing else managed to affect her in the way that this did.

'Mama, hungry!'

She opened her eyes and started cutting the carrots into chunks. 'Slava, just wait. Soon, dinner is soon.' She pushed a few bits of paper and pencils across the table (a little too forcefully, to make a point) across to Slava. 'There. Draw. A nice picture please.'

It was evening and the sunset had passed, and the sky was black, and neither of the men had come back yet. The food was settling, warm in the oven, and the table set with simple plates and cutlery, nothing pretty because no one could afford anything expensive and delicate.

Slava was perched on her chair, drawing circles with jagged lines all through them, talking to herself. 'No! No more room in the mitten, it will break! It will break and then…'

The door squealed open. *Must oil that, what a horrible sound*, Julia thought.

And then there were three smiling figures in the doorway. Slava squealed 'Papa!' and dropped her pencil and ran to the door.

'Julia, this is Iliya, is dinner ready? Smells like you've actually gone to some effort.'

Julia looked at Henry, her eyes sharp at the unnecessary comment. He smiled in response and winked. She smoothed her skirt and stood up, walked over with her thin pale hand outstretched. Now that he was closer to her, she could see him more clearly: He was tall and straight-- taller than her (most men were, as she was only slight and just shy of five and a half feet), and he was almost as tall as Henry. His was narrow and his hair slightly wild in its curl, and his eyes were bright blue and almond-shaped, his smile genuine yet inaccessible. There were small creases by his temples and the corners of his mouth, which meant that he was older than 30. 35, maybe? His shirt hung on him disinterestedly, like crisp paper.

'Hello, Julia,' he smiled and took her hand lazily, hers disappearing in his weighted grip. His eyes looked at her intensely underneath careless hair.

'Nice to see you again,' She withdrew swiftly, cheeks flushing already.

He gestured to the woman standing beside him, very thin, with bright eyes, her honeyed hair cascading in waves onto her shoulders, the freckles on her nose moving as she smiled. 'This is my wife, Elina.'

She produced a slim hand. 'Hello Julia. Thank you for having us.'

'Yes of course,' Julia returned, feeling suddenly conscious of her nerves. 'We don't do this often, and it's nice to meet new people.' And then she excused herself, mumbling something about the dinner, and walked back towards the oven.

Henry and Iliya took their jackets off and laid them on the backs of the chairs, wiping their sooty hands on them in the process, whilst Elina took a seat and spoke to Slava animatedly.

'Are you hungry, little one?'

'Yes!'

'How old are you, then?'

Slava looked slightly confused and splayed both chubby hands out to her. 'Four.'

'That's a *very* grown up lady, I think.' Elina placed her head in her palm, resting her elbow on the table. 'Or are you a princess?'

'I am a princess.' Slava said matter-of-factly.

Julia turned and saw Elina's face as she spoke to Slava and was the only one in that room that could sense her longing.

'I think you are a beautiful princess,' Elina said, smiling. 'Your Mama is lucky.' Elina stood up, breaking herself off from the conversation. 'Well, something smells delicious.' She turned to Julia. 'Do you need help? Because—' she gestured to the front door and the men outside with their cigarettes, chatting about their day as they waited to be served: thin arms expressive and agitated. '—obviously the men are preoccupied with righting the world's wrongs.'

Julia was grateful for her kind tone. 'Well, isn't that always the case? Men will fix things? We all know that isn't true.'

Elina laughed, and it sounded like clear water. 'Yes, agreed. I think you and I understand each other.'

Julia took the plates out of the cupboard and handed them to Elina. 'Do you have children?'

'No. Not yet, anyway.' She looked over at Slava. 'Maybe one day,' she smiled and took the plates to the table.

'Well, in time. God has funny plans.' Julia brought the knives and forks to the table.

'Iliya has other plans, maybe. War has been hard on him,' Elina shrugged.

Just then, the door opened. 'Right,' Henry clapped his hands together. 'Let's sit.'

Iliya reached into the pocket of his coat as Julia began to spoon the potatoes and carrots onto plates. 'Just a minute, I brought something,' and he removed a small flask of vodka from his bag that he'd brought with him and set it on the table triumphantly. 'In thanks.'

'Oh, goodness,' Elina groaned and put her fork down. 'You and your vodka.' She winked at Julia.

'And you and your controlling. Let me be.'

'So serious, husband,' Elina laughed. 'Always very serious about the vodka.' She placed a hand on his shoulder, and he bristled, but smiled regardless, and Henry interrupted.

'This is much appreciated. Let's pray that we always have such good fortune.'

They all prayed in a cursory way, all hungry and impatient and discarding the 'Amen' quickly so that they could keep serving themselves. Julia reached for the vodka and sighed happily. She turned to Iliya, the glasses clinking as she moved the vodka to the center of the table. 'So, what is your story, then, you two?'

She spooned out the potatoes for Slava, and then passed them to Elina, and everyone's hands were reaching and mingling, the food glistening on chipped plates. *Someday it would be nice to have good plates*, she thought.

'She's a curious one, Henry!' Iliya clapped his hand on Henry's shoulder like a brother. Julia was embarrassed and instantly silenced, focusing on chicken legs and boiled carrots and carefully cutting up Slava's food. The warmth of the alcohol radiated through her.

Elina leaned over to Julia. 'Don't mind him. He likes to tease.' She winked.

In between mouthfuls, he and Elina provided information.

'...No, we have no family anymore. I came out here from Poland, Elina was in a school in Krakow when I met her, a bit like you all...'

'...Iliya was looking for work. My family made it to New York...'

'...More potatoes please? Thank you... Yes, I had a sister, she was a twin. The other twin, a boy, died from illness when he was 2...'

'...No, I don't know what he died of... well, my sister...'

Iliya hesitated and placed his fork down.

'My sister and my parents were deported to the gulag. I hid in the attic of my parents' bakery. They never found me.'

Henry grunted in a kind of sympathy, poured Iliya a small vodka, and looked at Julia, watching her reaction. He lit a cigarette.

'We were some of the first Polish Jews to be rounded up,' Elina rested her hand on Iliya's arm. 'I was in school and when it was closed down, I was enlisted to work in the ghetto, embroidering linen napkins and tablecloths for the Nazis.'

'And how did you find each other?' Julia asked.

'He and I knew each other through school friends, and when I saw him one night trying to find his way to the shop for food, I took care of him for a time, before— '

'Before I was thrown into a passenger train and shipped to a sub-camp.'

'Which one?'

'Placzow.'

'Placzow wasn't one of the death camps, right?'

'No. But it may as well have been. Even on the train ride there, I saw starving bodies collapsing at my feet. It was torture.'

Julia turned to Elina. 'And you? Were you ever sent out of the ghetto?'

'Well, yes of course. I thought I could hide, but they would do roll call, and if they found me, I would have been shot on sight.' She sighed heavily. 'I was shipped to Soldau. And you, Julia?'

'We were at Neumarkt.'

Elina nodded. 'I had two school friends that ended up there. They died just before liberation.'

'Mama? Mama finished. Finished!' Slava proclaimed, jarring the quiet.

'Okay, Slava, you may leave.' She wiped dried potato off her cheek.

'If you will excuse me.' Julia shot up and followed her into the bedroom, steadying herself on the dresser. Her reflection in the mirror was white, probably more so against her dark dress.

She gripped the edge of the dresser.

'Mama? What's happening? ', Henry called after her, exasperated.

'Nothing. I'm fine.'

And then she walked back in as if nothing had happened.

After Slava was asleep, Julia took her place back at the table, sitting quietly, smiling when the conversation required it. She played the good wife, piled the dishes in the sink and afterwards served *medivnik*--honeyed bread-- for dessert, with bitter coffee.

'Julia?' Iliya leaned forward on his elbow, his eyes sleepy from alcohol, and yet still like a man who knew exactly where he was and what he was doing. 'What's your story? How did you end up here?'

'Ah, well. Not that interesting, really.'

'Iliya, stop, maybe she— '

He put up his hand. 'No, I'm interested. Everyone has a story to tell,' he leaned back in his chair. 'And I'd like to hear this quiet creature with the dark hair.' Elina blushed and flattened her lips. Henry looked over at Iliya, and then at Julia.

Before she could speak, Henry intervened. 'It's all the same, we all have the same story Iliya: we're born into war, we live our way out of it, we have children, then we die, and hope God forgives us for our trespasses.'

'Child,' Julia corrected in monotone.

'Eh?' Henry poured another vodka.

Julia smiled and shook her head, a sign for him to ignore her.

And in that silence, he may have understood, but she wasn't sure.

Elina continued on. 'Well, Iliya, I lived on a big farm with my family, and then my brothers were arrested...'

'They were activists,' Henry interrupted, nodding.

'Weren't we all, at the time.' Iliya smiled sadly.

'Yes, well...' She continued, her eyes pricking with tears. '...They were arrested, and I never saw them again, and then I left home with my sister, Maria, and then...'

'And, where is she?'

'Too fragile for this earth. She became very ill.'

'Ah. I'm sorry.'

'The soldiers came and rounded me up at the migrant camp. All of us that were there, were thrown into cattle trucks. Only the strong ones. They left the old, and the children, behind.

'And then, there I was in Germany.'

'You must have been so lost,' Elina said, her voice sounding wounded.

'I don't remember anymore. I wasn't allowed to feel anything. And then I meet Henry.' Julia smiled, and turned to her husband. 'We had known each other back in Ukraine... in the same circles,'

'Never in the same circles,' he interrupted, turning to Iliya, using his hands to measure the degree of importance. He immediately regretted his tone when he saw her wilt. 'Well, we knew of each other, anyway.'

Iliya nodded. Julia waited for her turn to speak, but then it was Henry that continued the story for her.

'We had Slava, and then we knew that Neumarkt wasn't the place for us to raise a family, so we—well, *I*—decided to leave for Australia. So, here we are.' He stubbed out his cigarette, the bitterness of the coffee smell mixing with the burning embers.

Iliya stared unflinchingly at Julia, his eyes bright in the glow of the lamplight, and she caught his eye, connecting only for a second, then turned back to examine a gouge in the wooden table underneath her fingers. She kept picking at the wound in the wood, scraping her nail into it, grateful for the distraction. Elina blushed and cleared her throat awkwardly.

'Hmm.' Iliya drummed his fingers lightly on the table. 'What a story.' He turned to Henry. 'And you, a traitor, eh?'

Henry flinched. 'That better be a joke. I earned my way out of that hell. I didn't kill anyone.'

Iliya waved a hand dismissively. 'Hey, hey, calm down. I was just teasing. We all had to do what we needed to survive. Life brings too many complications to be rational.'

He turned to Julia, observing her as if he was examining her, trying to figure out what to do with her, or what to say, or what she was thinking about the evening in its entirety. She wasn't sure if it was out of pity or curiosity but either way it made the side of her face burn without even lifting her head up. 'A toast!', he suddenly said.

Henry raised his glass. 'Again? What more could we celebrate?'

Julia and Elina lifted their glasses.

'To new friends.' Iliya smiled broadly, looking around the table and finishing on Julia before downing his drink.

*

The end of the evening descended into simmering laughter and as the glasses emptied and the plates had been cleared, Henry stood up, his chair scraping the floor. 'Well, that was plenty of food and drink, and I think this should be a ritual, maybe. Dinners like this.' He looked around the table. Julia looked at Elina and smiled. 'We have discovered a friendship here, in this bowl of dust.' He laughed lazily and put his hands in his pockets. 'We are lucky.'

Iliya took his lead, and stood up, walking over to Julia. His fingers lightly touched her shoulder. 'Thank you. Dinner was lovely. Chicken slightly overcooked but…' he shrugged and laughed. Julia shot him a look at the cheek of it, eyes flashing and mildly amused. Iliya laughed. 'Just a joke. It was delicious, of course. As was the company.'

Elina straightened in her chair and stood up to grab her coat. Iliya turned to Henry, clapping him on the shoulder. 'Good to meet your family. You're a lucky man.' Henry squinted at the comment and thought that Iliya acted young. H *was* young, after all. And he let it go. 'I am. Yes.' He responded.' Iliya reached over to the table and grabbed a remaining glass that had two fingers of vodka left in it and swallowed it all. He smelled of stale sweat, and soap, and cigarettes.

Elina walked over to Julia, her coat in her hands. 'It was so lovely to meet you- can we do this again? Maybe just you and I?'

Julia touched her arm delicately. 'I would like that.'

⋗

'Well, that wasn't too bad?' Henry had changed into a cotton shirt and soft trousers for bed, and washed his face, his hair damp after he ran his hands through it. He walked over to Julia, still dressed, sitting at the table in a daze.

'Hey.' He moved her chair back as she still sat in it, with a bit of force, so that it faced him, and stood in front of her, his knees moving her legs slightly apart.

Julia looked up at him. 'It was. I'm just tired.'
'You look like you're thinking.'
'You know me well.'
'Is it because the chicken was burnt?'
'It wasn't burnt!' Julia laughed. 'It was perfectly fine.'
'Yes, apparently it was *delicious, of course.*' Henry mocked Iliya's tone.
'Oh, stop it.' Julia smirked. Henry acted protective when he was drunk. Some would call it jealous. 'He was being nice.'
'Sure, he was.'
'Don't be like this.' He was careless when he drank.

He reached over and touched her shoulder, his hand running down the front of her shirt. 'Like what?'

Julia moved his legs aside and placed hers back together sharply, annoyed. 'Henry, you *know* I don't know anyone here, I am trying my best, and it was good to meet new people.' Her head dropped to the side, still looking at him. His eyes were dark. Heavy. His languid body moved confidently around her.

He leaned in towards her, his hands gripping the arms of her chair. With one hand, fed a few buttons out of their holes, at the top of her dress. Her distractedness didn't register on his face; and how could it, as he wasn't looking at her. 'Hey. I am protective of you.' He was breathing heavily. 'What's wrong with that?' He searched her eyes.

Julia knew he longed for her, but she felt like a possession in that moment. She performed, she was beautiful, and the attention destabilized Henry; it diminished his power in some way. Her strength was being aware of it. 'Nothing is wrong with that. Protecting me is good. But sometimes—' Julia shrugged, '—I don't need it.'

He hung his head down, lazily and then buried his face into her neck. 'Come on.'

He took her by the wrist, gently at first, and then firmly pulling her up from the chair, and with that momentum, guided her into the dark beyond them as she wrapped her arms around his waist, stumbling into him.

10

It was on a morning, a few months later, that Julia had seen Iliya again, and the meeting had peaked more of her curiosity.

She had taken Slava to Stratford, to the butchers, then to the park to get some ice cream, and had stopped off at the bookshop to say hello to Elina. When they'd gotten off at the stop, Slava ran off down the path ahead, her little legs carrying her farther than Julia could chase her since she was carrying two shopping bags. She saw a figure approaching her from a distance, and then recognized the voice.

'That way!' Iliya shouted, hooking his thumb to the road behind him, wagging his finger in mock admonishment, his smile bright.

'I *know!* I see her!'

Iliya was walking towards the bus station, and as they neared each other their voices changed to a normal tone. Julia shook her head. 'Why is it, that you always catch me when my child is out of my reach?'

He stopped a few feet away from her. 'I seem to attract the wildness.'

Julia threw her hands up and rolled her eyes, then looked down the path. She saw the flurry of blonde hair, playing, so she turned back to Iliya.

'Where does she get it from, I wonder? I bet that is from you, but you choose not to reveal it to people.' Iliya rolled up his sleeves. His thin blue shirt billowed in the breeze and his hair flopped to one side, revealing the side of his neck. It felt somehow provocative, that bit of skin.

Julia felt her cheeks grow warm. 'You should talk.'

Iliya's eyes darkened ever so slightly. 'Eh? Has my wild reputation been in the wives' gossip circles?'

'That wife of yours is a saint.' Julia knew more about Iliya than he realized, and maybe she had spoken out of turn just now. Elina had confided in her about how his moods would change like a light switch sometimes, and how she was wary of him, yet making excuses for him, as she loved him. It intrigued Julia.

'Oh, you think so, do you?' he teased with a sharpness.

It was a simple comment, but it made Julia feel for her friend. Women were taught to endure their husbands; it bothered her. She noticed now that he was carrying a rucksack, and he was close enough to her now that she smelled soap, as if he'd just had a shower. 'Where are you off to? How do you get to take the day off?'

Iliya paused and adjusted his bag, as if he was looking for an answer that would satisfy her. 'My back, you see— it has too much pain. Today is not a day for being out there,' he pointed at the hot fields beyond them. 'I take the time when I need to.'

Julia squinted. She'd never seen or heard him complain before. 'You seem perfectly fine now.'

'Oh, it's better,' he adjusted the strap of his bag. 'Comes and goes, really.'

'Well, isn't that convenient.' Julia raised an eyebrow.

'Skeptical?' Iliya snapped, and then recovered quickly.

Julia ignored it. 'Well, who am I to judge. But it's not as if you're an old man. You're the same age as I am.'

'Listen, I do what I want. And with a wife like Elina, I don't need to worry so much about work. Lucky me.' He shifted his feet, marking his place confidently.

Julia turned and called to Slava again, cupping her hands around her mouth, and saw her in the distance coming towards her. She put her hands on her hips and focused her attention on Iliya.

'Well, Henry doesn't get that same luxury. But we are happy. All my time is spent here, and his is spent—' she looked at the cane fields '— there. And it's enough for me.' Julia smiled because at first, she said to just to defend herself, for no reason. But then she felt it; she meant it and was pleased that she felt warm at the admission.

'You're a curious one.' He was watching her again with that intensity, like she was under a microscope.

'In what way?'

'Dark, but light. A contradiction. Like a secret that's out in the open, meant to be discovered.'

Julia laughed. 'Iliya, I think the heat has gotten to your brain.' Slava arrived and pulled on Julia's skirts. 'Off to your business then, or wherever it is you're going. I'm to mine.'

He's a good man, your Henry,' Iliya struck a match to a cigarette and exhaled, walking away, the dirt forming clouds at his heels.

Julia nodded. Iliya and Elina had been to the house once a week regularly, and it was a surprisingly normal and familiar energy that developed between all of them. Playful. Open. Teasing. She felt maternal around him, but also interested. Electrified. Wary.

The following afternoon, Slava was in Marta's garden, playing with a kitten, and Julia was folding laundry, occasionally looking in the mirror, gently prodding a yellow bruise that was almost healed. It was on her upper arm, where he grabbed her one day, shoving her out of the way because he had to leave for work. He had apologized immediately after, but it was cursory. *He is a good man, your Henry.* She winced. It had been the morning after an argument. It was fine. She was fine. Slava didn't see much of it, so that was a silver lining. Julia felt swollen and tearful. So what, if he took his anger and frustration out on her? It was normal. It was *normal*, she repeated to herself, stroking the yellow bruise, outlining the faint green edges that had faded into new skin.

She walked into the kitchen. The burners were off, the small radio that they owned was turned off. The house was beautifully quiet. She opened the front door slowly and closed it behind her. She walked absentmindedly, slowly, down the front steps, not entirely sure where she would walk to. She just needed some kind of escape.

She went to Olya's house, knocked on the door. No answer. Perhaps she had gone into town. Disappointed, she sulked back down the stairs and sat down on the bottom step, looking past the houses down the road to the end.

Was it odd to want to see Iliya? Was he even there? Probably not.

She smiled at the thought of his mischievous face.

    She stood up, walked farther down the road, to Oleg and Yara's house. Knocked on the door. No answer. *Had everyone left?* She was stuck. Back down the steps again. She looked back at her house, walked past it back to Marta's house, scooped Slava up and attached her to her hips, then walked back down the path. *Oh, just keep going. Stop being pathetic, it's not like you're doing anything wrong,* she reassured herself.

    She walked to the very last house, up the one creaking step. Three knocks. Silence. She turned around. *Bad idea.* She turned back to face the door and knocked again. Nothing save for the wind through the trees beside her.

    She looked to the right, and then to the left, and then rationalized that this was a friend, and she was visiting a friend, and wouldn't it be nice if she waited for that friend? Or at least brought something with her for that friend? She looked down at her empty hands and disregarded that one detail. She turned the small handle of the door and wondered if it would open for her. It did. *Mama?* Slava asked curiously. *Shhh,* Julia replied. *We've come to see a friend.*

    And then she was inside, and the door quietly closed behind her, and she walked into someone else's life that was displayed in pictures on the walls, a tattered yellow sofa that had a small woolen blanket on it, and a tin coffee pot with wildflowers in it. There was a cream wool rug on the floor, a *kilim*, with red, green, and black patterns woven into it, and there was a small cracked mirror on the wall beside where Julia stood. She sensed a female presence in this house, for it felt known to her. Familiar. Soft.

    The door swung open abruptly, she spun around.

    'Hey! What are you doing here...?' Elina stood with her hand still on the door handle, a fistful of flowers in her hand, the light behind her, amplifying her hair. 'I thought I heard the door open—' she placed the flowers down by the door and came up to Julia, her hands dark with fresh soil. '— didn't realize it would be you.' She looked at Slava standing next to Julia's calves. 'Hello little miss, nice to see you again.'

    Julia backed away, embarrassed. 'I am so sorry; I was just looking for— '

    'Me, I should hope.'

    'Yes, of course, I just wanted to see if there was anyone around. There are only so many loaves of bread I can bake and eggs to collect.'

Elina smiled. 'Of course. Tea? Come let's sit outside.' Slava ran ahead of them.

'Yes please.' She suddenly felt awkward, like she'd interrupted a couple's conversation. 'Slava is asleep, and I went for a walk and thought I would check in on you, and...' her cheeks and neck turned scarlet as she fumbled an excuse. She looked around, trying to maintain some kind of productive stance.'...and I thought I would look, and the door was open and, sorry! Sorry, it's an odd day, I just had no one to talk to.'

'No, no, don't be silly, I understand. Do you want to come in?' And then she laughed as he realized what she'd said. 'And, well, here you are! Well. Never mind. You're here now.'

'Thank you. I'll stay for a minute.'

She closed the door behind him and walked past her to a basin of water to wash her hands. Julia sat on a wooden chair. It squeaked and settled under her.

'Where's Iliya?'

Elina laughed. 'Why would you want to know? Isn't he enough of a bore at dinner?' She turned and dried her hands. 'We keep company with people who have similar stories, don't we.' She narrowed her eyes, observing. 'So, what's happening. You look like a dog without its owner.'

Both laughed at the sadness of that comment. Julia's back relaxed into the chair.

Elina walked over to her and sat down on the chair across from her, placing the tea on the table between them.

'I must keep an eye on the time,' Julia warned. 'Slava will be waking up soon.'

'Yes, of course. So. How are you, Julia.'

'Happy. Just a bit lonely sometimes I guess.'

'Ahhh, welcome to life here,' Elina laughed. 'We all survive the best way we can.'

'The space, however, the quiet, is wonderful compared to…'

'Compared to what we've all been through?'

Julia nodded. Elina cocked her head to the side. 'Well, what a God-awful comparison *that* is.' They both burst out laughing, and Elina gestured to the back of the house. 'Come.'

The garden was a large postage stamp of green, with two metal chairs and a rusty metal-latticed table, a wooden bench to one corner and rows of green leaves poking through the soil on one side. On the other, a little woven fence with rows of yellow and orange flowers climbing up to the top. Next to it was a tomato plant, its bright green vines and dark red globes secured to wooden posts, and across from that, a washing line with a few sheets snapping in the breeze. Julia took a deep breath and closed her eyes. It smelled of mineral and bright green and hot perfume and soap. She heard the rustle of leaves and distant brushing of long grass. It smelled of her childhood.

'Here,' Elina brought a teapot and two cups and sat down across from her. 'It's lovely out here, isn't it?'

Julia sipped her tea. Fresh mint leaves. 'Elina, this wonderful. Thank you.'

'For what?'

'Tea isn't that difficult, Julia.'

'No,' Julia chuckled. 'For being a friend without complications.'

Elina rolled her eyes. 'Don't be silly. We all need a friend sometimes. Isn't that how we find our strength? Leaning on others?'

Julia folded her hands in her lap, covering the bruise that she suddenly realized was exposed, her face reddening.

Elina noticed. 'Don't worry.' She turned away to look across at the fields, and the trees to the left of them, and not at Julia.

'Worry about what?'

She turned back. 'The things you try to hide, and the things that you can't.'

Julia nodded and looked away. 'Life can be confusing sometimes.'

'That's to be expected. Are you happy?'

'Yes. But sometimes, I want more.'

'Don't we all. 'The sheets snapped crisply. 'Children?'

Julia shifted in her seat and placed her hands in her lap. 'Well, yes. Maybe a bit of everything.'

Elina nodded. 'Not a little too much, then.'

Julia laughed. 'Well, maybe I *am* asking for a lot.'

Elina took a fistful of her hair and brought it up off her neck, fanning her neck with the other hand, looking at the garden. 'I know that feeling. I understand it.'

'Are you happy?'

'Yes. For the most part. But it's not without a certain amount of ignoring things.'

'Like what?'

'Oh, it's not even something to discuss in detail, but let's just say that Iliya is tricky, has an itchy eye.' Julia frowned, and Elina clarified. 'He wanders.'

Julia understood. 'His charm.'

'Quite.' Elina took a spoon and dipped it in a pot of raw honey that sat on the table, spun it around itself, and then brought it over her tea, watching as the glistening strands worked their way down into the cup.

'They are all confused in some way, I suspect. Just like us.'

'Probably worse.' She stirred the spoon and let it rest. 'Women are incredibly strong. But we reveal our weakness to each other, not to them.'

'They don't reveal a damn thing,' Julia took a sip of tea and brought the cup back to the saucer. 'We bring it out in them. So, it is up to us—'

'—To be strong,' Elina finished for her.

'Absolutely. It is one of the best things about being a woman. Perseverance and sacrifice.' She reached over and placed her hand on Julia's. 'Which is why you should never feel sorry for needing friends, yes? We need one another.' She removed her hand and curled it around her teacup.

A cluster of birds flew out of a tree, beating their wings against the leaves. When Elina began to speak, there was a wildness in her eyes matched the thoughts that suddenly unraveled into the space between them. 'I found him those many years ago, when he was lost. I saved him, and took him in, and gave him what I could. I became his mother, his sister, his lover. I was the only person he had. And yet, instead of openness because of our past, it's as if we hide from each other in plain day.' She looked into Julia's eyes, her own eyes calm and even, as if she'd thought about these things her entire life and knew how to understand them. 'Sometimes I feel as though I'll burst, and yet, I have trained myself to let it go.'

Julia felt a peculiar strength blossom in her story. 'I imagine it must be difficult.'

Elina leaned on her elbow, her head delicately perched in her fingers, with a crooked smile. 'It is. But we sacrifice and we persevere. And look how strong we are.'

'She's three? My goodness, she's very tall for three.' Elina watched as Slava clutched a pencil, her tongue out in concentration at the paper. Her little body perched sweetly on the edge of the chair.

'Yes,' Julia nodded placing her hands on her lap and smoothed her skirts over her stomach. She ached for the recent loss, but when she looked over at Slava, she reminded herself to be patient. 'She is tall, like Henry.'

Elina wore a simple cotton dress the color of butter, and flat shoes. She always looked beautiful, despite limited options. Her hair shone, and her cheeks looked flushed and coy under her freckles. Julia envied that.

'How are you both?' It was uncommon for even close friends to ask such questions, but for them, it felt normal.

Julia explained her frustration with Henry but apologized for revealing such intimate details of their marriage. She had no one that she could trust, and over the last few months, Elina had become a confidante, friend, and advisor. The friendship had centered Julia.

Her thin arm reached across. 'Oh, sweet Julia. I do think they are all like this, these stupid, arrogant men. Or maybe we picked the best of them. Lucky us, eh?' She smiled, but it looked more like a wince. 'Listen, our men have been through so much. They have a temper. It's absolutely normal. Nothing to get upset about.'

'But he has never been that way with me, at least not when we met, *that* I'm certain of.' Julia straightened in her chair. 'And he can be very sweet, and he works so hard.'

Elina withdrew her hand and placed it on her lap. 'Well, yes, I can sense that. But war changes people. Look at Iliya.'

'Can you tell me?' Julia had begun to learn more about him and was curious.

'Too much pain, in here.' Elina pointed to her temple. 'He gets angry often. He wants to control his life, and me I imagine, and likes things to be a certain way. His temper is explosive. Impulsive.' She shrugged. 'But, like all the others I imagine, he loves strongly.'

'The past is strong in his memory then. It's a hard battle.'

'Yes.'

Julia nodded. 'I know how he feels.'

Elina cocked her head in sympathy. 'Oh, Julia. We *all* have such strange beginnings. Stringing together our lives with little bits of hope.'

Julia glanced at Slava, happily occupied. 'Elina, can I tell you something?'

'Of course.'

Julia tread carefully. *She would reveal a weakness, and she felt somehow that it would risk something in herself. She would remember this, in the future. She would remember how she laid herself bare, and that this could give someone power over her. But at the time, it felt right.*

'I lost one.'

'I don't understand.'

'I... was pregnant, and then...'

Elina covered her mouth with her hand. 'Oh God, Julia. How far along?'

'Two months, I think.' Julia smiled through her tears, reaching for strength. 'I'm alright now.'

Elina reached for her hand and squeezed it. 'Does Henry know?'

'He does. *This* one.'

Elina knew exactly what Julia meant, and her expression withered. 'Oh, Julia. I'm so sorry. Were there many?'

'Two before. He was kind. Understanding.'

'You're lucky.'

'Sometimes.' Julia sighed. 'It's never always perfect, is it.' She sipped her coffee. 'What about you? Have you ever—'

Elina shook her head, looking down at her wedding band and fingered the smooth metal. 'No, it's never happened. Never even stuck, so to speak. Not meant to be.' She looked up. 'And I had thought it would, standing in your kitchen that evening when we met, that it might.'

'I remember that.' Julia put her hand on top of Elina's smiling at the memory. 'But it *could*, no? Life happens in strange ways.'

Elina smiled sadly. 'No, I don't think it will. We've been to the doctors, and I am not sure how they can detect these kinds of things, but the doctor said it is common for the woman not to be able to carry. I suspect it's me.'

The waitress came by to clear their coffees, and the women nodded a silent thank you. She was about to speak and then thought better of it, seeing their faces.

Elina continued, lowering her voice. 'When Iliya is drunk, he reminds me as much. Says I am like a lame horse— pretty to look at, but useless.' She pushed a lock of hair off her forehead and looked at Julia. "Funny, right?'

'No, Elina. That's not. That's terrible.'

Elina threw her hands up. 'Well, such is life. We must abide and be happy with what we've been given. Make the best of it.' She winked at Julia, her standard way of protecting herself. But her eyes showed a kind of defeat.

'Maybe one day, Elina. You are young. You have plenty of time.'

'I am not. Twenty-five is not young.' She smoothed her hair and brushed a lock of it behind her ear. Anyway. You are very lucky.'

'In what way?'

'It's happened once. It can easily happen again, despite the losses.' Elina looked up, straight into Julia's eyes. 'It *will* happen again. You will be a mother. I just know it.' She looked over at Slava, her hair done in two shining braids resting on her shoulders.

'Slava, can you tell Elina what you're drawing?' Julia rested her hand on her small had.

'Heart,' Slava looked up at Julia, and then Elina. 'For you.' She handed over the small piece of paper, a muted pink heart scrawled on it in messy, bold strokes.

'Thank you,' Elina smiled, her eyes watering, and looked over at Julia. 'Maybe one day.'

When they parted, and Julia glided over the front steps of the house and walked home, she kept her hands folded across her chest as she walked, heavy with new thoughts. She and Elina had secrets, *hiding in plain day*. It emboldened her and also undid her, knowing that such strength existed in these kinds of revelations. Elina had given up her life to save someone, and she compromised who she was to create a stable life. Was that enough for her? Was any of it enough for them all? It posed a few questions for Julia that she couldn't answer.

That evening as she sat with Slava, her arms around her sweat-sticky sleepy body, reading a story but not really listening to the words; her thoughts were on the things that had been stirred up from the afternoon, like silt in the sea.

When Henry came home that evening, she threaded her arms through his, and around his waist, and reached her face up to his, testing to see what would settle back down.

11

It was a month later that Julia's knees stung from the gravel and dry grass digging into her flesh, so she slid onto her backside, finishing what she had started. She was tending to the past, positioning a small row of white stones into the shape of a cross. 'I'm sorry,' she whispered as the soft ground collected under her nails.

The loss had happened early, and had been brief this time, and the pain hadn't been too great. This time Henry knew what was happening to her, though she didn't tell him about the ones before. *Maybe we should stop trying*, he had said to her, when he found her standing by the outhouse in the semi-darkness, waiting for him, leaning against the corroded wooden side with her arms folded. *Maybe we should just persevere. Keep trying*, she had replied, and he held her, confused as to what he could have done, or even what he could do now.

Today, in the full hot sun of the afternoon, she needed to remember; she needed to remember in order to someday forget.

As she sat and watched Slava dart into and out of her periphery, Julia was slowly realizing that it was Slava that was teaching her—the impact of her physical and emotional presence, and the fact that she craved her was a gift that Julia was grateful for, and wanted more of. This childhood was an anchor for all of them now, and for Julia especially, and she craved to be surrounded by children, a table full of voices, as though transporting herself back to Lviv. The way her mother's skin would smell of salt and spices and oil, the air thick with onions and mushrooms and dough and flour rising; these are the things that mothers create for their children:

sensory memories that are permanently etched. And within that, lay the foundation of love.

※

Henry came home early enough for the light to still be settling on the fields, and to have dinner with Slava, which pleased them all. They craved the smell of him, the stale, sweetness of smoke like he'd been forged in a fire. That was their security.

'Papa! Papa…!' Slava tapped him incessantly on the arm, her voice almost at shouting level.

He kissed her and waved her off. 'Slava, stop being so loud. What? What do you want to say that's so important, hmmm?'

'I climbed a tree!'

He splayed his hands exaggeratedly. 'The whole thing?'

'The bottom!'

'Keep practicing, that's not terribly high,' he teased, tousling her hair.

'Henry, don't be mean.' Julia looked over at Slava now nibbling on her peas, one by one, pinching them between her fingers.

Henry looked at Julia, scowling. 'What's with you today?'

Julia glared. She had two choices: she could either reply or stay silent. Her reply would be met with a withering comment, the conversation would be a cyclical battle that she would inevitably lose, and that was the dynamic that he often favored. So, she stayed silent, as she had done lately. She didn't know what to expect when he came home, and there was no point in battling him.

Dinner finished in a productive silence. Julia thumbed the broken edge of a glass and Henry finished a second helping of potatoes, scraping the plate. He stepped outside for a cigarette.

'Shall I put her to bed, then?' Julia threw over her shoulder as she tidied the plates away.

Silence.

Later, she read to Slava. She made bedtime long and protracted, and she had invented a story about an evil queen who put a curse on a village, and the curse was that anytime someone was unkind, they would turn into a toad. It felt good to smile.

'... and then--' she wrinkled her nose and put her face in front of Slava's-- 'there was a village full of horrible, smelly toads!'

Slava grimaced. 'Eww Mama! How could the curse be broken?'

Julia gripped her tightly, her hands moving her silky hair off her face. 'Oh, love. Only true love can break any curse. And true love is always the best kind.' She kissed her.

Henry appeared in the doorway, his hands in his pockets. 'Hit a nerve, did I?' And he disappeared again.

In half an hour, Slava was asleep, and Julia walked out of the bedroom.

'What exactly is your problem tonight?', Henry immediately challenged when he saw her. He was sat on the couch skimming a newspaper, holding a cup of tea, milky white.

Julia placed her hands on her hips. 'Well, your words hurt me sometimes.'

'What?? Since when did you stop having a sense of humor?'

'That's not fair. You only see the things you want to see; hear the things you want to hear.' Julia sat down heavily on a chair opposite. 'It's as if you only see *some* of us and I feel invisible. I imagine that you're overworked...'

Henry interrupted, raising his hand to stop her. 'This makes absolutely no sense, you sound crazy.'

'Well, you asked me what was wrong--'

'And I was hoping you'd say something a little bit more constructive rather than pointing at the ways that I'm failing you.'

Julia stood up, and he motioned her to sit back down. 'Please.' She remained.

He lit a cigarette. 'You think I'm overworked.'

Julia nodded.

He exhaled a plume of smoke. 'Yes, how about that, then? I'm trying my best and some days are better than others, do you ever notice that? I love you, but what do you want from me?' he brought his open palms out, cigarette bobbing in the corner of his mouth. 'What exactly do I have? I find pleasure in drink, in smoking, and occasionally, *only occasionally mind you*,' he pinched the cigarette between his fingers and pointed it, 'laying with you. And even *that* has something to be desired.' He delivered the words in such a protracted and measured way, it made them sting so much more. It was vicious. Her body tensed as she sat in her spot, silent.

He continued. 'You think I wanted any of this? But I'm doing the right thing, aren't I? Why can't you understand that?'

She raised her hand up. She'd had enough.

'But I *do* understand. But as much as you need me to listen to you, I need you to listen to me, and what I want and who I am. I am equally found and lost here.' Her voice was removed, as if a light had gone out of her. 'How do you think I feel, being the quiet little wife married to a self-important man, sitting at home taking care of the child that he barely sees? I'm doing the right thing, aren't *I*?'

He stood up and walked over to her, grabbing both of her shoulders and willing himself not to shake her. 'Yes, we are both struggling, but we have it better than most. We left Germany with a promise—' he set his teeth at that word, '—a *promise*, to each other, to try and build a life together which is what we are doing. You cannot run back to the broken walls and empty rooms of your memories. This is what marriage is. *This*. It's a promise to stay.'

She nodded. There was something to be said for perseverance. Elina had said that to her. It couldn't just be about love.

They went to bed that night in a separate stony silence, but eventually reached for each other and found a quiet acceptance. Of course, Julia loved him, because he was her husband, but she understood that the desire she had was not for him, it was for her own happiness.

The next morning, Julia had gotten up before dawn, packing Henry's lunch and boiling two eggs and cutting fresh bread for breakfast. The smell of bitter coffee filled the room. It was up to her, she thought. Her own strength would grow in her head and be turned over and over again like dough.

His shirt crackled under the stiff cotton of his jacket as he threw it on his shoulders.

'I'm not coming home tonight.' His voice had a finality in it that made her ache with apologies.

'Why?' *I've failed*, was her instant thought. And then she reprimanded herself silently. She couldn't keep doing that, it diminished her.

'The cutters' camp is easier for me to sleep in after finishing work. Plus, I may get extra time in today so that I can get more money.' He set about putting a small sandwich in his bag, not looking at her.

'Okay, I understand.' Slava started to rustle in the other room, murmuring half-asleep noises.

He straightened up, looking at her. 'Julia, I may stay a couple days, I don't know. I just…'

'What?

His face looked as if he would soften to her, and make amends, and tell them to try again and forget about what had happened, and she wished he would. But he didn't. 'It feels confusing right now, this…' -- he gestured to the space between them—'*this*, whatever it is.'

She grabbed his arm and came closer. 'Running away isn't the solution, Henry. Sometimes we have to try harder to see it through.' He dropped her hands. 'Is it because we haven't been able to have children?'

'No. But maybe space is something where you and I can figure out a new way of doing things. Everyone has tricky moments.'

'Sure.' She stared at him.

'Besides, the more shifts I work the more money for us.'

'Gold in the dirt.' It was an expression that her father had used.

He smiled weakly. 'That's a way of thinking about it.'

He turned on his heel, and walked out of the house, his steps fading away, increasing the distance between them for now. Slava woke finally, and then Julia would have to get on with her day. But she couldn't move, still. Her feet clung to the floor in front of the door, she was looking out towards the pink sky, watching it turn to blue, starting the book of her day. Turning the page.

'Breakfast?' Slava pulled on her wrist, delicate hands with a strong grip.

'Yes, yes.'

A week had passed, and they hadn't spoken in what seemed like years. Henry stayed in the cutters' camp, the single men's refuge. It was food, and a bed, and peace, and that's all he wanted, to be removed from a home where he felt like a stranger. When he'd arrived, the current shift of cutters were crouched in front of a row of freshly cut cane, a line of their bare chests covered in sweat and grit, dark against the bright green behind them.

He leaned his bicycle against the barrack, its metal scraping against the wall.

'Jesus, you look like someone dragged you off the cross, ha!' An older cutter that had come from Italy was sitting on a metal chair across the large room, chain smoking. He had a scar on his tanned, thin cheek and his black hair was matted from sweat and pushed back off his forehead.

Henry dragged his tall body under the frame as he walked in and dropped a small canvas bag on a cot. 'Wife and kids driving me to drink.' The wind blew through the door, bringing with it the familiar smell of sugar smoke, mingling with the sweat and stale body odor of the men who had been living here for days, some for weeks and months. The thin wood echoed with their grumbling.

Another man, laying in the corner on a cot picking dried sugar from his nails, groaned. 'Who'd have them anyway, honestly. Though, I wouldn't mind a few here and there. Your wife, the dark one, right? Very nice.' Henry's eyes flashed in response and a few other cutters walked in, laughed at hearing the tail end of the conversation as they dropped their belongings and lit cigarettes.

'...Who's this?'

'...Women.'

'...Which one?'

'All of them.' They all laughed and nodded their heads.

'... Henry's one.' A blonde Polish man, broad and short, pointed, cigarette in hand. 'She's a good one.'

Henry sat down heavily. 'Alright, that's enough. Do we really need to do this?' He emptied his back onto his cot. Bread, water in a dented hipflask, some sausage, a clean shirt, cigarettes, and a deck of cards wrapped in twine. 'They're exhausting.'

A tall, lean Russian laughed, exposing a gold tooth at the side of his mouth. 'Ah! I agree! Can't be bothered. Who has the energy? We're all barely alive here.' He flexed his arm, the wiry muscle wrapped around the bone. He had a dog's body, ribs protruding. 'Look! How handsome I used to be and now, I look like a stalk of wheat!'

Henry leaned back on the bed, propping himself up on his elbow. 'Alive. Just.'

The Italian threw an empty cigarette pack at him, teasing. 'Fool, don't be so down. They're great to look at though, not like those fat old *babushkas* that make—and eat—pies all day.'

'You could always see what's on display in town, you know,' The Russian winked.

The Polish man groaned. 'Who has the time? We are here for long days and short nights, and every day the same.'

'Listen,' Henry sighed. 'It's not helpful, any of this.' He needed a drink. He needed to feel something more than duty, though his father's voice rang again in his head, and he would probably shake it in disgust at the son he had raised to be what, a farmer? He was a disappointment to the man who raised him and the woman he had loved once (and did, still, he knew it). 'I need to rest.'

Henry closed his eyes. Another day settled and the humid night closed in and he was sleeping next to men who were lost, and as his breath became shallow, he realized he was one of them.

❦

One of the things, the very few things, Julia enjoyed about life here, is not being overlooked, and she appreciated the beauty in the space finally: it was the space beyond the farmhouses, beyond the cane fields and flat skies where she could reach a world where her parents still were, thinking about her. Being outside in the small garden, hearing the *shushhh* of the trees and the grass as they swayed in the cool breeze before the coming rains soaked the grasses and left a sweet residue on their skin.

Julia felt that she would finally write to them, because it was safe to, now, and her heart swelled with love that she hadn't let herself feel for seven years. She had so much to tell them, and much that she could not, and she wondered how long it would take for her words to reach them.

That evening, after dinner, Julia sat with Slava on her lap, her arms around her, reading her a story, but impatiently waiting for her to fall asleep so she could sit in peaceful silence and write.

'Mama, sing please?' Slava traced the freckles on Julia's arm absentmindedly, the dark hairs standing up as she went against them with her fingers.

'Yes, love.' And she sang softly as she rolled her body softly into bed:

Dream passes by the window,
And Sleep, by the light.
Then Dream asks Sleep:
'Where should we rest tonight?'
Where the cottage is warm,
Where the child is small,
There we will go,
And rock the child and all,
And there we will sleep,
and will sing to the child:
Sleep, sleep, my little dove,
Gentle and mild.

'Slava? Slava....' Julia whispered softly; her voice still raspy with the remnants of the melody. Slava's eyes were closed, a halo of soft hair on her pillow.

She tiptoed towards the door, turned off the light and stood in shadow, listening to the faint, shallow breaths. She walked to the kitchen, by the small window that looked out onto the rain soaking the sugarcane, and sat down to write a letter that she would finally send.

Mama, Papa—
In the absence of you seeing my face and judging for yourselves, I will tell you that I am the same, for the most part: I am healthy, and I am living in Australia with my husband, Hironimus. You may remember him, as he lived in Striy. Rudnick. Papa may have known his father, Ivan.
After we left, Maria and I struggled to continue on, after stopping in a migrant camp in Austria

Julia put the pen down. She decided, resolutely, that she would not tell them. It would be too great a burden to bear, and sometimes a lie is better.

> *but we made it eventually to Neumarkt. Winters were cold, and there was not much food. It was incredibly hard. I worked as a seamstress. Others were metal polishers. I didn't think I would survive the long days. I slept three across, on the hard ground in one of the buildings. We had a woman in our group, Lina, who would pray every night, and I prayed with her.*
>
> *When I met Henry, I was happy again. I did not hope to find anything like love, but it was there, and I am so grateful that we survived.*
>
> *We left there after the war ended, and we are now in Australia with our daughter, Slava. You would love her immediately*
>
> *I am happy with my life, I do not want you to worry, but I do often wonder what could have been.*
>
> *With love to you and Papa,*
> *Yulia*

Julia folded the finished letter but before she could find an envelope, she heard footsteps at the door, followed by a knock.

12

She turned around and saw Iliya. Behind him, the sky was so dark so that the edges of the trees were barely visible against the sky and the sky and ground were the same.

She walked up to the door, and as she opened it, it squealed, and then the wind blew across, clearing the paper off the table and onto the floor. She reminded herself to pick it up later, and to fix the squeal with some oil.

She held onto the doorframe and welcomed him in. 'What on earth are you doing here?'

He leaned forward and caught his stance, faltering a bit. 'Where's Slava?'

'What? Sleeping. It's late.' She shifted on her feet.

'Hmm. Where's Henry?'

'Camp.'

Iliya raised his eyebrows.

'Long story,' Julia replied. She looked down at her bare feet and suddenly felt a chill.

'Argument?'

'Typical things.'

Iliya nodded, running his hand through his black hair, revealing his sun-mottled forehead. Julia's smile was wide, suddenly. She appreciated the company.

'How is Elina?'

'Yes yes, all good. She was with some girlfriends at dinner, I suspect she'll be home soon.' He shrugged. 'I was supposed to meet a few of my friends as well, but, I didn't, in the end. Told her I might see Henry.' He cracked his knuckles. 'Much better idea.'

'Ah, well.' She ran her fingertips over the edge of the door. 'Can I help you, then?'

Iliya stood tall suddenly, remembering himself. 'Oh, yes actually. I needed something from Henry.' He waited, his hands in his pockets, filling the doorway with his height. Julia wondered if she was supposed to invite him in.

'Ah. Well...' Julia shrugged at her husband's absence.

'No, how awkward. Sorry. I just thought that he'd be here.' And then Iliya moved a foot back off the step as if presenting an exit, and Julia felt suddenly apologetic, so she extended the conversation.

'Actually--'

'Yes?' He leaned forward.

'A cup of tea?'

'That'd be nice.' Iliya's tanned face softened into a boyish grin.

Julia pushed her forearm into the door and gestured for him to come in. She smelled the alcohol on his body as he passed by her.

'I don't suppose you have anything to eat?' He strode in comfortably, shedding his coat onto a chair and relaxing into a sofa. 'Elina is terrible at stocking the cupboards.' He finally noticed where he was sitting and patted the cushion under him. 'This new?'

Julia struck a match and put the kettle to boil. 'Henry bought it from a small charity shop in Stratford. The one on King Road, not far from the—'

'— right, yes. The shop that sells ice cream.'

'Hmm. And he brought it home in the...?'

'Car. Had to leave the back open completely.' She laughed.

When the kettle had boiled, she poured the tea and let the leaves steep, drowning them with a spoon repeatedly if they bobbed back up. She felt him staring at her.

'Car. That's nice.' He lit a cigarette and she noticed that he swayed a little, despite the fact that he was sitting down. 'We don't have a car. Elina prefers to spend money at the hairdresser.'

Julia smiled and pictured Elina's shining hair being manipulated into waves of gold, framing her freckled face. She thought her beautiful; the light to her dark.

'It's very useful- though the color is, well, 'muddy' is the best way to describe it.' She laughed. Three months ago, she had discovered that Henry had saved up enough money to buy them a car, and when he rattled home in it (she heard him on the road before she saw him), she'd wondered then if she had made a mistake. Not because of the car, or the color of it, but because it was a sort of an ordinary thing, a car, or maybe even a bit bourgeois, she felt. But he was proud and happy as he stepped around it and gestured for her to come out and have a look, as his arm swept across the length of it, long and wide with low seats and a profile reminiscent of a boat. 'It serves its purpose, that rusty old thing.'

She brought over his cup, and then sat down on the chair across from the couch, her hands folded across her chest as she let her own tea darken. There seemed to be no urgency with Iliya tonight, and the energy felt neither electric nor still. She would later recall that nothing felt wrong about it, it was a friend whom she could talk to, and he to her; they were friends with similar pasts.

'So. Julia. What is this business with the husband?'

'Did you know that male geese hover over their nest whilst female geese sit on their eggs?'

'Eh?'

Julia threw her head back, giggling at the impulse to share this piece of useless information. 'Oh, Iliya. I don't want to talk about Henry, I want to talk about useless things.'

'No idea how to respond to that kind of diversion except to drink my tea and look at you strangely.' Iliya winked. 'You're a strange creature.'

'Strange. Yes. For me it has been a strange couple of weeks, if I'm honest.'

'We all have strange days here.' He cocked his head towards the fields. 'Some days you can go mad from the day-after-day of it all.'

'See, I don't mind that. My life has been *too* full of days where things have been too heavy to bear. Here, I feel calm. Silent. I just want to *be.*'

She sipped her hot tea and placed it back on the table.

'Thing is, I love having someone to talk to,' she focused at a pane of glass across the room that had a crack in it. 'My burdens feel lighter when someone else listens. I'm sure you feel the same…?' Iliya was lighting a cigarette and she felt embarrassed suddenly. 'Ah, I've said too much. Never mind.'

She was fidgeting at the admission, her legs crossed firmly, her back pressed into the corner chair.

'No! This is of course excellent. You— 'he pointed a finger at her '— need someone to talk to. And I— 'he pointed to his chest '— do as well.' He lit the cigarette and watched the smoke tendrils rise.

'But you have Elina.'

'Elina, yes.' He nodded. 'She's… well.' He exhaled smoke. 'Everyone has their stories, no?'

'The connection.' Iliya leaned forward off the edge of his seat toward Julia. His eyes looked heavy. 'Do you understand? You, strange creature, have a story that I understand. A good connection.' He leaned back again, his head resting on the back of the sofa.

He didn't apologize for the way he threw his arrogance around, and it was very much a young man's prerogative. It was so different to Henry: Henry was caring of course, but he held his cards close, and in many ways, despite the differences in their marriage, it did inform how Julia operated as a result; she always felt aware of herself around him.

Julia stood up and walked to the window by the kitchen.

'Do you think of your family often? Do you wonder about them?'

'No, not really.'

'Why?' She knew why, before she asked the question.

'Because I can't do it- I can't remember her without being angry.'

'I can understand that.'

'What were they like?'

'Kind. Hard-working. Patient. My sister was deliciously funny. Silly. Long hair, the color of hay. Always messy. Big green eyes. She hated being wrong. Always liked to win. She took care of me.' His voice trailed off.

'Do you remember the last time you saw her? What she looked like?'

There was silence at first, and then the sharpness of match striking the side of its box. He lit a cigarette and inhaled deeply, the smoke teasing its way around and into his mouth and out through his nostrils.

'Yes. We'd had a fight. We were children. Playing and then fighting. And then I saw fear. The last thing I saw in her face was fear. I thought she'd hide, just like me, but she didn't follow. I think I remember her telling me that she would find me.' His eyes closed, as if exorcising the memory.

'That was the last time I saw her.'

Julia never asked Henry too much about his family. Partly because he didn't like talking about it very much in general, but mostly because she'd suspected a hidden anger that was too easily accessible if he talked about his father. He had left his father to find a better life, and now he's a father who never sees his family, despite his efforts. He didn't talk. He drank. He read. He smoked. He hit. But he loved, and she loved him despite knowing the darkness. She understood why, as much as she was frustrated by it, and so she kept a fair distance from those kinds of questions.

She walked back to her chair and sat down, folding her hands on her knees.

'Life doesn't feel real, sometimes, I think. It feels like a collection of memories and photographs and tears. But it won't always be this way, I'm sure of it.'

'Yes,' he nodded. 'You're probably right.' And when he opened his eyes to look at her, something had changed. His face was set and his eyes rigid and focused, as if he had made a decision that Julia knew nothing about.

'Listen, it's late,' Julia started, getting up to go and check on Slava. 'Another day tomorrow, and may we live to see it, and the next after that.'

'Hope for another day- a very good outlook, sweet Julia.'

Julia blushed at the word *sweet*.

He walked towards the door, but Julia didn't notice that he left his jacket, because she had peered around the corner to see if Slava's door was closed. It was, and the sounds from her room were of deep, contented breathing. When she turned around, Iliya was leaning against the door, watching her. Arms folded.

'Or, maybe a bit longer.'

'Ha... oh, I suspect that we've nothing left to talk about.' Julia's hands were moist, and she placed them in her pockets. 'Besides, Elina will think you'd gotten lost out there--' Julia gestured to the dark fields beyond them.

'Elina knows I've come to talk to Henry.'

'Ah, well. I can tell him--'

'She already has one eye on you.'

'What?'

'Oh, that is typical Elina. Always wary of the world around her.' He pressed his palm behind him to make sure the door was shut and moved towards Julia. 'She spends too much time thinking.'

The room suddenly felt electric- Julia stood in the quiet, wondering if she should move, or stay still. If he would move towards her if she did. If he could hear how shallow her breath was, and how loud her heart.

'Listen, Julia,' and he walked to her languidly, as if he knew exactly what he was doing. She withdrew her hands and folded her arms across her chest, moving away from him slightly.

'Please, Iliya.'

'Please what?' He stopped and smiled.

But he was beautiful, she thought, completely contradicting herself. *Was it so wrong to think that?* She couldn't catch her breath.

'You're suddenly making me uncomfortable.'

And then he moved to her again, echoing her, circling her, and she moved back, an awkward dance, with her backing towards the wall. His palm found the wall behind her and he leaned in, his shoulder blocking her, his other hand gently on her arm, his palm warm on her skin. She was in the middle of fear and longing, and she wasn't sure which would win out, and she closed her eyes.

'Don't you think...,' His face was inches from her own, his nose on her cheek, and he spoke to her quietly, looking down, as if sharing a secret. '... that we both share loneliness? Isn't this what it has all been about?'

'But you're my friend, Iliya.' Her voice wavered, her trust thinning. She opened her eyes and looked at him: his eyes creased at the corners as he smiled, his face purposeful as he looked at her, examined her, his grip firmer on her arm now. She felt nervous, both out of fear and out of curiosity. 'Please.' It felt wrong, but it wasn't unpleasant, and in her confusion, she couldn't find the words. All she could say was *please*.

'Friends give each other what the other needs, surely.' His breath smelled of sweet alcohol and the bitter burn of stale cigarettes.

When Julia tried to reply, he held her jaw in place with a wide, calloused hand, and covered her open mouth with his own, the hard metal of his belt buckle the only sound in the room.

13

New York, 1974

A small rectangular desk clock splayed its thin black hands and ticked regularly, finally settling at the seven; it was the only sound in the room as Julia held her breath, folded the paper that she'd held in her hand and placed it in the drawer, pushing it to the far back. She needed to finish getting ready, and this had delayed her. A tear had collected in her eye, and she dabbed it with her palm, leaving no trace of it.

She called out to the other room, Henry was already dressed and waiting. 'Slava is meeting us here first, and then we'll all take a taxi to the restaurant, yes? Or maybe we should walk? We have to leave in a few minutes.'

Julia walked over to the mirror of the dressing table and retrieved a small gold earring and clipped it to her ear, clutching its matching pair delicately in her hand. She placed the other, and then undid the silver casing of a lipstick and ran it across her mouth in a line of dark pink. 'Do you have a card?' As she moved, the square window opposite reflected her shape against the night and the brick buildings beyond, the angles of her arms and curve of her back displayed in a sheer, ghostly light.

'Do we need one?' Henry's voice called out from the other room, and she heard the clear thin sound as he retrieved a glass, then filled it. Whiskey, most likely. The soles of his dress shoes like sandpaper on the kitchen tiles as he walked, then echoed thickly on the wood floor that stretched from the living area and led to the bedroom where Julia was. He held his glass to his chest, and she saw that his tie was hanging limply under his collar, both undone, a pack of cigarettes peeking out of the breast pocket of his jacket.

'Actually, no. No card. She doesn't like being reminded how old she is.' Julia smiled. 'Our daughter is nothing if not stubborn.' She opened the square black jewelry box that was in front of her and took out a thin gold chain that boasted a small byzantine cross. She fingered the worn clasp and placed it on her neck; it was one of the only items left from what her mother had given her that one night, so long ago.

'Sounds like she inherited that.' He sipped his drink and the ice hit the glass sharply as he watched for her response.

Julia moved her chair back, the scrape of the wood on the floor interrupting him. 'I think I'll need stockings tonight.' Henry grew quiet at her reply. The cream silk of her blouse gently sagged into the waistband of her green wool skirt, draping just past her knees. It was March, but the streets were faintly dusted with the kind of icing sugar snow from her childhood, in a sudden snap of cold that no one had anticipated. She imagined clouds of cold breath erupting as people greeted each other outside the entrances of theaters and bars, the air resounding with the sound of yellow taxicabs bleating in impatience to bring cold bodies from one warm place to the next. She thought of how familiar it all was now, the noise and the color: red streetlights, glittering signs that spelled out names of theaters, grey clouds of steam from the manhole covers and the strains of music seeping out of restaurant windows. There was a safety, here, but her memories took her so very far from the path under her feet now. She longed, only a little, for the ground to soften just a little; to give into her toes and let her feel the ground.

She moved, looking at her reflection long enough to be pleased that she had left her hair down, sitting on her shoulders, as she used to when she was young and had no additional adornments.

'Henry,' She stopped in front of him, lifting his tie towards her and pulling it taught. 'I've lived so many lifetimes in my years.' She looped the slick material smoothly under, over, and through her fingers.

'We both have.'

'Stubbornness equals survival.'

'Or maybe avoidance.'

The shadows under his eyes revealed a kind of faded pain that she knew he carried with him as a constant companion. He sipped from his glass awkwardly; her hands were still securing his tie. His gaze never left her face.

Julia tightened the knot and a moment of helplessness flashed across her face as she looked at the man who had been the cause of it. His once dark hair, now littered with bits of grey, framed his handsome face, the stubble scattered softly on his cheeks. They divided the burden of their secret equally between them. And they loved each other still, regardless.

He lowered his drink and it hung at his fingertips by his side. 'Julia…'

Julia placed a palm on his chest gently and smiled up at him. 'Don't, Henry.'

'Why?'

'Too much pain.'

The doorbell pinged and then a rap at the door. Julia stepped around Henry, and as she walked to the door, she undid her clenched fists and reached for her coat.

14

Stratford, 1948

It was the next evening that Henry finally came home, and the day felt like a month, as she recounted every detail of what had happened twenty-four hours earlier.

She had thought of him after Iliya had left, and she thought of him still as she barely slept that night, and as the sun rose the next morning, and shed its milky light on the farmhouse and the quiet garden, she thought of him still. She had made Slava breakfast, had taken her to play in the park by the Avon in Stratford, and later that afternoon back at the house, she placed the dirt-stained clothes in a tub of soap and water to soak and heated some water for the bath, so that she could clean her little body, as she was covered in sand and crumbs and sticky stains of ice cream. She'd scraped the skin and earth off the freshly collected potatoes, made dinner, read a story-- all with a kind of distant banality, as she thought of Henry. All she wished was to see his face to remember who she was.

Slava was finally asleep. The house was quiet. Julia looked down at her hands: they were thin. Pale. Her nails were worn to the quick and had dirt under them, her skin was dry. Her dinner sat, untouched, and she stared at the door. There was no feeling of sadness, nor happiness, just a stillness.

She waited, and feared, Henry's shadow to fill the space. She imagined his body gliding off his bicycle in the semi-darkness, walking up the path towards the door. The door that she never had fixed, in the end.

The sound of it rattled her now; it felt like a scar. She touched her face. It was still there, she realized, and she stood up, walking over to the bedroom to peer at her reflection in the small round mirror on the dresser. Her face was pale, her hair had lost its wave and sat lifeless at her back. Her lip was swollen and there was a red, angry scar on her jaw. She moved in the lamplight and pinched her cheeks and bit her lip to bring the color back. Would he notice? She opened the drawer at her fingertips and found a powder compact, hardly used, and dabbed a bit of powder, camouflaging the red mark. She practiced a smile. *Hello Henry*, she imagined saying. *Things have been as they should be.*

And then she heard it. The gravel shifted and crunched outside. She walked back to the kitchen and stood in the middle of the room, waiting.

His slow footsteps passed by the door, to the side of the house. She turned her head slightly as she listened to the familiar sound, as he walked into the garden to clean his hands in the washbasin. She heard the water slosh delicately, heard him clear his throat. She heard the scrape of the lighter and smelled the cigarette smoke. She sat down at the table.

He opened the door and her chest felt suddenly tight, as if she were underwater. She breathed slowly, methodically; her eyes suddenly wet. She wiped them quickly with her palm before he could notice.

He dried his hands on his shirt, removed his jacket, and left it on the couch as he walked over to the table, sitting down in front of the plate of food. He prodded it; it was cold. He looked at Julia.

'Thank you.' He rolled up his sleeves. 'Oh, wait. Is this yours? Have you eaten?'

She stared at his face, searching his eyes. She smiled stiffly. 'No.'

'Why not?'

'Not hungry.'

Henry frowned. 'Oh. Why not?'

'Because I wasn't hungry.' she snapped back, instantly regretting it.

'Hey, I'm only asking.'

'I know. I just don't understand, sometimes.'

'What don't you understand?' Henry was tired, hungry, and now this conversation was leading to nowhere.

'I don't know.' Julia shook her head as if to wake herself. 'Never mind.'

He picked up the fork and started to eat. 'I can still eat this, though.

Is that alright? Is there anymore?'

She shrugged, exasperated. 'Look for yourself.'

He narrowed his eyes.

Julia sighed. 'Yes, there is a bit more left.' Each word was a lie. Each word felt painful as it drifted out of her mouth.

She looked down at the table as he ate, every once in a while, looking up, and his face would meet hers, and he would attempt a smile, and she in return, and then the cycle began again. When he finished and walked outside to check on the progress of the greenhouse and the new orchids that he had planted. She followed him, hovering a few feet away until he noticed her. He turned around.

'Julia?'

'Henry, I....' She clasped her hands together in front of her skirt, squeezing tightly. She squeezed harder, the blood draining from her fingertips. She just needed the strength to tell him, to tell him everything that sat in a ball at the base of her throat. 'I just... I wanted to tell you, that...'

He waited, the quiet of the dark behind him, the ember of the cigarette glowing like a star.

'... that I was sorry.' She continued. It was only part of the truth. It was all she would say for now.

He stamped out his cigarette and walked over to her, confused, but assumed it was an admission of her mood. Henry knew her to be like this occasionally: lost in her thoughts, too much thinking, finding her own stillness and strength.

'Hey, hey.' He put his arms around her, his warm body enveloping hers. She smelled the smoke clinging to his clothes. She began to cry silently, the girl with skin so soft and bones so delicate, folded into the arms of a man who loved her. 'Don't worry. I know things are difficult right now. We'll be alright.' He leaned back to look at her closely and pushed her hair back off her face. That's when he saw it.

'Hey, what's this?' He ran a fingertip on her jaw.

Julia covered it with her hand. 'Oh, that's Slava being a tornado again,' she smiled painfully. 'Ran straight into me. Fell headfirst into me as I sat with her in the garden.'

'Hmm.' Henry moved her hair back over her hand that still rested on her face. 'Love can be a bit a violent,' he smiled and laughed. Julia leaned back into his arms and closed her eyes, her heart tightening like a fist.

15

When she remembered that night, the memories rushed at her like knives, scattered and sharp and searching for weakness. She fought to forget, but the more she fought the more they pressed into her: she felt and saw him everywhere. And that was her prolonged punishment, though the physical effects had worn off.

Already a month had passed in painful, crawling minutes. The unfortunate result of harboring a secret is that it forces you to pay attention to the details; you are forced to remember how you were *before*, and then how you were *after*, and these two worlds had entirely different colors and shapes, and even tastes. The way Henry touched her felt different, the food she ate was tasteless and occasionally, she didn't eat at all. Julia floated in a kind of wan acceptance of her life in these two states of being, but then a silent irrational anger wishing that her husband had never existed would suddenly erupt in absolute clarity. *None of this was Henry's fault*, she had to remind herself.

She tried to seek solace in the mundane: she walked with Slava to the bus stop and took her into town—seven stops, like always, and seven stops back. She would visit the butcher and distantly ask for a five-inch square of meat that bled onto the parchment. She took Slava to the park to feel the breezes off the Avon on their faces. She would smile coolly at women who had bright red lips and delicate hats and dresses, and she would adjust her skirts and pat down her shirt, glancing at Slava to see if she'd tied her hair back properly, for beautiful hair displayed a certain kind of status (of which they had none). She watched, removed, as the days passed on their parcel of land, hours and minutes marked by mealtimes, sleep, sunrises and sunsets, and she healed ever so slowly, and reached for a strength that she had been gifted by her own mother. It was getting warmer, and she was desperate for a change in season that marked more distance from a day in July that had brought her so much shame.

※

'Hey, is that mine?' Henry packed his bag for work, and he glanced and saw her as she stood watching him, as if behind glass, her hands gripping a cup of coffee. 'You look tired. Dazed.' They'd slept together a few times since he'd arrived back, and he noticed a sadness in the way she kissed him, or a confusion, almost. But she'd not been sleeping well, and he assumed she was also still annoyed about the fact that he'd been away so long.

She blinked and forced herself to focus. 'So, I was thinking of taking Slava to the Avon today. For a picnic. Sit on the banks and relax for a bit.'

'Sounds good.' He zipped up his rucksack and looked up. 'Are you sure you want to do that?' He squinted. 'It'll be warm out today.'

'Just tired. I feel fine otherwise.' She sipped his coffee absentmindedly.

He grabbed the coffee out of her hands. 'If *that's* 'fine', I'd hate to see what 'ill' looks like.' He gulped a mouthful. 'Thanks for drinking my coffee by the way.'

He handed it back, then left quickly, jumping on his bicycle for the long ride into work.

'Mama.' Slava padded out into the kitchen in her thin nightdress, soft matted hair full of sleep.

'Hey! So,' Julia crouched down to her daughter's height. 'We need to pack some things with us because we're taking the bus to the river for some adventure today.'

'Mama will we see ducks? Can we feed them?'

'Sure, love.'

After breakfast, Julia scraped a few of Henry's shirts and trousers off the washboard and wrung them out in the sunlight, pinning them to the delicate line that was attached to two wooden posts, stretching horizontally across the garden. Then she dressed Slava in a light cotton dress that she had sewed a little while ago, a thick pinafore that always survived play, a hat, shoes, and enough bits of food in the straw bag for the journey.

At the very end of the road they lived on, past all the farmhouses, there was a small, winding path that rose up to lead to a main dirt road that cars and buses would use to get into the main town of Stratford. They found the stop, and waited for it expectantly, pleased at how soon it arrived. It was a beige-painted tin animal, with convenient pram hooks for mothers with children to board without issue. All sorted, they settled into the generous leather seats—Slava by the window, Julia beside. Slava played a curious game of What Is That and Who Are Those People, and it was a curious conditioning of sorts: travelling so much and so often, her young mind was now conditioned to make an adventure of it all, a game.

As soon as the dust rose around them and the bus jerked and rumbled to a start, Julia felt cold and her forehead damp in mild panic. *I forgot something*, she looked around her, patting the pockets of her dress. She looked in her bag. *Tissues, money, sweets, lipstick, food. That's it, yes?* She looked at Slava, who was now on her knees, clinging to the seat and peering over at the gentleman behind her. She scanned her little body. *Her hair was tied, she had the clothes that she needed.* She had a knot, a subtle dread, like she'd left something behind, though maybe it was exhaustion. Distraction. It unnerved her.

'Sit down, Slava. Seats are for bottoms, not for feet.' Distracted, she held Slava's arm too tightly, her sudden frustration making her react to everything.

The bus lurched over unfamiliar and rough patches of gravel, making everyone on the bus grab their stomachs. 'Oh, honestly this is very unpleasant, my breakfast feels like it's swimming.' Slava erupted in giggles.

'Oh, Mama. I'm hungry, Mama. Do you have anything to eat?' Julia rummaged through her bag and found some water crackers. She took one for herself and gave a few to Slava. Her stomach ached.

After what felt like a year-long (45 minutes, but oh how they dragged on) trip, seven stops as usual, the wheels squealed to a stop, and everyone stood up, grabbing various coats and cardigans and bags. Slava raced ahead and stood at the front excitedly. 'Mama! We're here let's go let's go! Mama!' The sun was bright in the sky and the air smelled sweet.

Julia smiled. She needed this.

And then she felt a strange lurch in her stomach again, only this time it wasn't from the bus ride, and suddenly her food was rising in an uncontrollable tide and the acid in her throat was the first to come out. The vomit came embarrassingly quickly, right between her feet. She bowed her head partly in shame and partly to make sure her dress wouldn't stain. Slava looked on, mouth agape. 'Oh no…'

She felt a hand on her shoulder, felt like a man's. 'You alright, madam?'

'Oh, sorry. I'm so sorry.' She didn't dare look up and see faces watching her in disgust. She stared at the ground, the glistening, vulgar patch in front of her framed by pale red dust. Wiping her hand across her lips, and then on her skirt, she walked around the mess and pulled Slava's entire body up and over it, made no eye contact, and walked ahead. *I've forgotten something.* It lingered, that thought.

She saw the river glisten before they got there, through the slender trees that were planted along the perimeter. The road they walked on was busy with people and cars, but manageable. It was an easy walk. 10 minutes, with clearly marked signs saying where the park was. The banks were lined not only with trees, but also flat grassy patches dotted with benches all along the way, and it was the perfect spot for the two of them to burn the hours of the day.

'Here!' Slava picked a spot next to another family: a husband and wife and a small baby. They looked wealthy, in the sense that their clothes were pressed and cut in a clean and modern way, the jewelry tasteful and the baby looking immaculate. Julia nodded a quiet hello and then looked down at her own dress, that she had sewn for herself, from a pattern that she had found in something called Australian Home Journal that displayed drawings of slim women with carefully positioned hair and long eyelashes, wearing perfectly acceptable dresses that every woman should. Julia's was a light blue cotton with a pattern of small red rosebuds, tied at the waist, with cuffed sleeves leading up to a v-shaped collar. In comparison, it was plain, and she didn't look like these women, and so the couple nodded and turned away in response mumbling something about 'another immigrant'.

The grass stretched along the length of the river like a green ribbon, people dotted on and around it on days similar to theirs, she imagined. They placed their belongings on a spot that Slava had picked and settled for the day.

Julia took her shoes off, watching Slava run up ahead to the playground to the right of her, and leaned back on her elbows, looked up at the sky, and let herself heal. And slowly, her need to remember dissipated, and her breath languished in a stillness. .

❧

'Oh god, not again.'

It was two days later, and Julia was walking past the pavilion in the park, watching Slava eat ice cream, when the nausea hit her. She doubled over, clutching her stomach, hoping no one would notice. People walked by, and it was busy, which hopefully meant that she could be inconspicuous as she ran over to a tree, the vomit spilling from her mouth and hitting its base.

Slava was watching, distractedly. 'Wait a minute, Slava. Just wait there, I'm not feeling well,' She gestured weakly with a hand, the other one propping herself up.

She sat down helplessly, looking up at the sky. It was blue. Irritatingly blue and perfect and serene. *What the hell is going on*, she thought, distractedly watching as Slava stood knock-kneed, ice cream dripping down her fingers. Julia felt her forehead: it was cold and hot at the same time. She hadn't eaten anything this morning, so she couldn't understand why her stomach had tried to empty itself.

She looked over and saw a woman walking past the pavilion: She had a straw hat and sunglasses, white gloves, and a dress that looked expensive, the silky floral-patterned fabric resting importantly over her pregnant belly. She was beautiful and walked ever so lightly in her ladylike navy heels. A silk dress would feel lovely on her skin, and she imagined it would be cool to the touch and caught the breeze easily.

And then a curious thing happened: that understanding and admission when something important is once forgotten and suddenly remembered, that understanding that is alternately cold and warm all at once, and when breath becomes fast and shallow. Julia new exactly what it was, because it had happened to her three times before.

She had been too distracted recently to notice, but now was feverishly recounting the times that she'd slept with Henry, and then the time with Iliya, and oh god it all became too much for her to keep her balance. She sat down on a clean patch of grass and spent the next hour watching Slava only casually, as she tried to understand what it was that was happening to her.

'I'm so sorry' she looked down, her eyes focusing on the dark blue cotton of the dress resting on the part of her that held the truth.

Slava walked up to her and sat down next to her and put her head on her shoulder.

Julia padded her swollen eyes, the redness increasingly fading. 'Oh Slava, I really don't feel well. My head hurts, my stomach is funny, my heart—' She stopped herself short of saying *my heart hurts*, as Slava would've picked up on something a bit more serious.

'My heart is filled with happiness that you had your ice cream and now it's all over your dress and your face!' She distracted with disproportionate joy and laughter through the tears. Slava erupted into giggles. In a daze, Julia reached for her and placed her on her lap. She looked at her ruddy cheeks, leaner than they were when she was a baby, her watery blue eyes hovering in wait for something magical. *Maybe there is a reason for all this. And who's to say it will survive, anyway. But maybe it will.*

'Right.' She wobbled her legs underneath Slava and she pitched to the side, rolling over in a squeal. 'I think we should probably make a move.' She started to walk, slowly, waiting for Slava to catch up. She felt like walking for miles. She didn't want to go home— not out of fear, but out of a pure desire to make something unknown more solid, more understandable. She watched people pass her by as she held onto her daughter, and as she saw them and thought that everyone had their own thoughts in their head that others would never know, she thought that it might be for the best that certain truths are best left unspoken for a time. And immediately after she resolved that *that* was the way to think, she asked Slava what her favorite flavor of ice cream was, and what she would like for dinner, and then she told her she loved her as they boarded the bus home.

What had been then, was a lifetime ago, Julia thought as she grabbed fistfuls of weeds by the front door as she left the house that evening. When she looked down, she smiled with a sadness that had never entirely dissipated, even after seven years: she had worn Maria's shoes today. It was the only thing she had left of her past— a memory of love, of sisterhood. Julia kissed the tips of her fingers and padded the faded leather. 'You would like it here, Marioshka,' and turned towards the open sky, her cheeks reddening in the thin sunlight.

The smoke from burning cane sugar billowed in thick piles that sat across the horizon whilst Julia walked, her thin shirt rising gently with the breeze, and in the pocket of her skirts, a rosary rattled softly. She felt comfort in knowing that as soon as the black clouds turned to grey and then white, Henry would be home shortly thereafter, and his lips would taste of burnt sugar and his handsome, lean face would have a dusting of soot. Their daughter was napping when Julia had left, her small, sweaty body tangled in the bed sheets in the room that she'd now lived for the last two years.

The starlings were murmuring in the sky above the green and yellow fields as she proceeded towards the wooden fences at the perimeter of the farm, a basket by her side, the small white farmhouse shrinking in the distance behind her. In the past, there would be four of them— she and her siblings— all on a field like this, crisp wheat matted flat under their bodies lying and observing the sky, and now, only Julia remained with the memory.

Another house to the left, similar to theirs, a distance down the gravel and weed-strewn path, was Iliya and Elina's, and it sat empty. Iliya was working in the fields with Henry, and Elina was finishing her day at the bookshop. Elina had become a good friend to her, and Julia reminded herself that she would need to see her soon — sometimes a burden is easier when it is shared.

Julia kept on, until she reached the pens, the cows like dots of pepper on the pasture in front of her. *Ck ck ck* her tongue rolled at the back of her mouth and clicked against her back teeth. *Ck ck ck* and one by one, they looked up, shivering and swatting tails, nickering their greeting. 'Eh eh eyy', Julia murmured to a brown heifer with white socks and a white star on her forehead. She patted its flank. 'My beauty,' She whispered, burying her head into its neck.

'Look at the way they listen to you,' Henry spoke, his voice gravelly, suddenly appearing around the corner of the house with a pitchfork, as he watched Julia, the cows moving towards his wife as she stood by them, changing their feed and giving them fresh water, fresh milk in a bucket at her feet. Fresh milk was a comfort that she'd had as a child: it was warm and sweet and thick, and she still craved it daily.

'Hey! Wasn't expecting you.' Julia smiled, standing up to greet him, her feet nervously knocking into the basket of eggs beside. His presence had always unsettled her, and now, it was because she needed so speak to him.

'A welcome surprise?' Henry leaned the pitchfork against the fence and lit a cigarette, his lean body curved as the flame sputtered, then straightening as he looked across at her. He was dashing, she thought, the afternoon light settling around him, his hair dark, his thick lips parting in a wide smile. *I owe you the truth*, she thought. But at his smile, the impulse vanished.

'Of course, it is' Her cheeks rose as she smiled. 'Better than a kick in the knee, my Baba used to say.' They both laughed.

'I see you're busy with company.'

'My friends, all of them!' Julia replied, a smile lighting her face as she spread out her arms. 'They keep me very entertained.' She wiped an arm across her brow.

Henry laughed, and then a sooty cough caught his throat. 'I think you're the one that keeps them entertained.'

Julia sat down gently on a bale of hay, gathering her skirts, watching lazily as Henry hovered around the animals. He patted the brown flank of one of the cows. 'Slava alright?' He looked back at the house in the distance.

'She needed a little rest. She ran me ragged today.' She wondered if he was scanning her face. She wondered if he knew already.

'Ah, well. Takes after her father.' He walked over to her and sat down next to Julia, the hay bale sagging under his weight.

'Strange, isn't it.' The smoke curled around him and hovered as he spoke.

'What?'

'Us. Here.'

'Oh, I don't know.' She looked at him. 'Feels familiar.'

'What does?'

She gestured at their bodies, sat so close. 'This.'

He smiled, and exhaled smoke, placing a hand on her leg. 'We've only been here a short while.' He straightened his shoulders. 'But maybe it's because we no longer have fear in our shadow.'

'Yes, no more looking over our shoulders.' Julia sighed. 'No more pain.'

Henry coughed and looked down at his scarred hands. 'I feel very old for my twenty-eight years. And we may always be looking over our shoulders, I have a feeling.' He ran a hand through his hair and left it resting on his head. 'I just want this feeling to leave me.'

Julia glanced at him and her breath caught. 'What feeling?'

'Like there will always be yet another thing. Another worry.' He looked squarely at Julia. 'Unsettling.'

'Maybe you will always feel that way, in one way or another.' Julia looked at his profile. He was noble, his face was sharp and contemplative, but the shadows under his eyes defined him for as long as she'd known him. 'Your father?' she whispered.

Henry nodded, looking down. 'It's the past. It should stay in the past.'

'Ah, well. That's the shame, Hironimus. Ghosts don't have a preference of time.'

Henry stretched his head back, breathing deeply, releasing the spirit of his father. The skies were darkening, and the smoke had cleared into a thin veil, exposing a thin line of muted orange as the sun set.

'I feel safe here.' Julia folded her hands across her chest and nodded, looking across and saw the quiet farmhouses lit with a faint glow, just like theirs, small and insignificant in the distance, underneath the blanket of the Australian sky. 'Maybe the ground won't move under my feet again.' She took off Maria's shoes and dug her toes into the dirt. 'It feels good.' She was trying to convince herself; she was trying to hide a secret, and it was imperceptible even to her own husband.

'We are too small for it,' Henry nodded. 'Our little lives.'

'This big, what they call, 'dust bowl'.' She leaned against him, her small body fitting into the crook of his side, a puzzle piece. 'But maybe I think I understand it now.'

'Understand what, exactly? The dust on our faces?'

'Yes. The dust. The reason. Why we are here.' Julia pointed at their house. 'I mean, we have Slava, and we have time now. And hopefully, well—' she pushed her elbow into his arm gently. '—we can create a life here.'

'Ah. I see where this is going.' Henry looked at the sky with a wry smile and felt for Julia's hand. 'Do you want more?'

Julia hung her head, placing her palm on her stomach, and running it across gently.

Henry's eyes rested on her face. 'What if it doesn't work?'

Julia placed a hand on his arm and looked at him resolutely. 'But what if it *does* work? And then we'll look back and realize that some broken things just need a bit more time to fix.' She shrugged, smiling. She felt broken, and confused, and yet here was a man that loved her, that stood by her. *Now. She would tell him now.*

She stood up and moved in front of him, putting her hands on his shoulders. 'Henry…' She paused, and held her breath. And then told him the truth. The truth about where she was now, and not about what the past had done to her. 'I'm pregnant.'

The words came out quickly and unceremoniously, and she looked over his shoulder at the fields behind him. Sometimes not seeing someone's face helped dissipate the news; made it less traumatic, more manageable. She turned her face back to look at him.

'Okay.' He stood up and put his hands in his pockets, his cigarette firmly in the corner of his mouth, and scanned her face hesitantly for the confirmation of truth. 'You're sure.'

'Well, I've been really ill the past week,' She sighed, 'and then today I realized that I hadn't bled for a month or so…' She drifted off, hating that she couldn't give him any more of an explanation. Men liked a reason. A solution. She had neither.

'Well, then.' He ran his fingers through his hair tentatively. His voice was charged. 'What about a doctor? Why don't you just confirm it for a doctor before you worry. Or celebrate. We have lost before, so…'

'Yes, but what if? What if I really am?' She scratched her head absentmindedly and shrugged.

He leaned forward and brought his large square hand to the side of her face, stroking it quietly. 'It means we have to have more chickens. And more celebratory dinners with friends, to share the good news.'

He put his arm around her and stamped out his cigarette. 'You act as if this is terrible. We are not broken. You are not broken.' He squeezed her to his side.

'*You* look broken, though.' Julia laughed. 'Broken and thin, like they've scraped you off the cross.'

'Well, then. That's probably because I am desperate for some food.'

'No more rations to live off of, at least,' Julia shook her head in relief. 'I have no idea how we keep surviving this life.'

'I don't think it's a good idea to count our blessings yet. It feels like only last week that we were in Germany, praying for miracles.' Henry sighed. 'And yet, here we are. With a miracle.'

Julia nodded. 'Come, let's go in. Our memories are the making of us, it seems.' Julia lifted her basket, the eggs delicately scraping next to each other. 'Besides, it's time to wake up Slava.' They walked back together, and Julia felt for his hand, lacing her fingers through his.

The last hint of sun left the sky, and the animals slowly settled their warm bodies close to one another, quiet secrets between them.

> ➤

When the house was quiet that evening and everyone slept heavily, Julia watched from the small window by their bed, in the bedroom, as the dull orange glow of the fires in the fields that day filtered out. It reminded her of the gold icons of Ukrainian churches: glistening metal portraits, melancholy and silent, glowing as if lit from within. A mile's walk from the farm in Lviv, there was a church full of them in every corner. The church was all wooden, held together with without a single nail, like a puzzle of architecture. It had three carved, tall wooden pillars that to her, as a little girl, felt like they would possibly be the gates to heaven. She felt small in that church, yet never lonely. She remembered the heaviness of the incense surrounding her; clouds of it emanating from hidden corners. The icons would wink through the smoke, watching her, winking at her, watching her. The murmurs and chants of solemn prayers would fill the small space and vibrate through her small body as she prayed.

She heard movement from the other room and heard Henry's footsteps come up behind her. He positioned himself beside her and put his hand on her stomach tenderly.

 'Listen. It won't be easy.'

 'I know,' she nodded, wishing she could say more.

16

Marta, a kind neighbor that lived in a house down the path in the opposite direction of Iliya and Elina, had agreed to look after Slava one morning, as Julia readied herself to get to the bus. She'd spent the better part of the morning doubled over in the outhouse, her face flushed, expelling bile, for she hadn't eaten yet. She'd deposited Slava with her battered toy and then slipped away quickly walking back to the house willing herself to keep the contents of her stomach inside her. *You look absolutely awful,* Marta had said to her as she waved her thanks and left her holding Slava's hand.

As she walked, Julia thought of how she had met Marta, and it was a moment that divided a day into two parts: happiness and grief. Marta was an older woman, childless, that had until recently been married, but was now a widow that kept to her house and sewed intricate embroidery to sell at the weekly market in Stratford. She was generous and kind, and had been beautiful once, but her grief mapped her face in soft lines. Peter, her husband, had been working in the cane fields and had suffered a devastating heart attack that killed him instantly. Henry had delivered the news to her as he'd arrived home that evening and walked over to see her. *It's Peter, Marta, I'm so sorry*, he'd said, his face implying exactly what she understood to be true, standing at her doorway as if delivering the milk, and he had caught her as she collapsed in her grief. They all seemed connected now, in a kind of thin understanding of sorrow.

Julia took the bus into Stratford. Her handbag had her identity card, some money, an apple and tissues. The bus clattered ungracefully along the road, as she looked out the window not having any inkling as to what she would do when she arrived at the hospital.

The bus slowed its approach and positioned itself in front of the main doors at the front of an imposing tall brick building, with a white wooden porch wrapping itself around the front. There were a few nurses stood outside smoking, crisp white uniforms like paper cutouts against the red of the facade. Julia walked in clutching her handbag too tight, her heels too loud against the steps.

'Hello, can I help you madam?' the woman at the desk had a friendly round face, glasses slightly too big, making her appearance entirely more approachable than her tone.

'Yes, I would like to see a doctor please.'

'Why, exactly? What's the problem?'

'Oh, well, I think I may be pregnant.'

'Alright, please have a seat,' She handed her a piece of paper and a pen. 'Fill this out will you, and give it back to me.'

And then it was over: it took 25 minutes. She walked in, was handed a cup with a lid on it, went to the bathroom, came back out and handed the nurse the yellow liquid. It reminded her of Neumarkt. And Acerra. And Bonegilla. And then she walked back out in the dust, waiting for someone to confirm or deny what she knew almost positively to be true.

🕊

'Oh look, nice to see you here,' she heard him say, and she immediately recognized the voice and her heart sank as if into ice water.

Julia was standing, waiting for the bus and checking her watch, steadying herself by staring at a point on the ground. When he spoke, she looked up and there they were: he and Elina with her arm linked through his, walking towards her. Her instinct was to run, but to where? Her face lost its color. She needed to come home, and it would look highly unnatural for her to leave suddenly as they approached. Besides, the people waiting alongside her already heard Iliya address her, so she kept up the facade and parted her lips into a wide smile.

They stopped next to her, and Elina leaned forward to place a kiss on both cheeks.

'Julia, how lovely to see you here. Where are you off to?'

Julia smiled, her insides in knots. 'Oh, just home. Needed to do a bit of shopping.'

Iliya leaned in. 'What, no hello for me,' and kissed her on the cheek, offering a wide smile and a wink. He pulled out a packet of cigarettes. They were fresh. There was a black line of dirt lining the tips of his nails.

Elina's eyes searched her husband's face, and then glanced at the bag near Julia's feet.

'Didn't come away with much, then?'

Julia's cheeks reddened. 'Oh, no, I needed… well, it was just…' she watched as Elina studied her, and Julia panicked. 'I was at the doctor.'

'Oh dear, I hope nothing serious.' Elina's eyes widened. Iliya smoked and listened calmly.

'No, of course not. Just a cold.' Julia moved the wave of her hair closer to her jaw, covering the fresh pink scar.

'Well, let me know if you need anything of course,' Elina placed a hand on her shoulder.

'Yes, anything at all,' Iliya nodded, another smile appearing behind the veil of smoke. To everyone else he looked charming, rakish and handsome. She nodded uncomfortably. Elina looked at him, and then at Julia, her
lips pursed.

'Haven't seen Henry in a while, since I moved to another group. Shame. More money for me, though.' As he inhaled, he looked at her as if examining a statue, and then slowly let the smoke dissipate in her direction. 'Maybe I should invite myself to dinner soon.' He smiled, and she felt her stomach turn.

'I thought you came to see Henry just the other night,' Elina looked at him, adjusting the handbag on her arm.

'Oh well, yes, but such a short meeting,' he replied, directly at Elina, and then looked over at Julia. 'We should all do dinner again soon.' They both looked at Julia, and it took every ounce of her frayed energy to respond with, 'Yes, of course, that would be nice.' Her stomach lurched and she swallowed hard.

A woman tapped her on the shoulder suddenly, and Julia very nearly jumped out of her skin. 'The bus just pulled up ma'am.'

Julia turned back to Iliya and Elina, waved goodbye, and boarded. The smile was still on his lips as he turned with Elina and kept walking on.

Julia wondered if she feared him, or for her friendship with Elina, or the revelation of the truth. Or all three.

❧

  Seven days passed, and then ten, and then sixteen. And in that period, everything felt as if nothing had changed, apart from the fact that Julia had begun smoking her husband's cigarettes carelessly, the tobacco fibers constantly on the tip of her tongue.

  This particular morning, she held one in her hand, the ash falling like confetti at her feet. She watched, sat on the steps, as Slava played in the fields to the front, her feet dirty and her green dress hidden in the tall grass. It was Saturday, and the afternoon light was soft and yellow, and she could see the hills rise far beyond, before they dropped towards the sea in the distance.

  In her other hand, was a letter.

  Henry had gone into town, to meet someone that was interested in contracting him out in a cutting group for extra money. It was common for cutting gangs to—despite the long hours and hard conditions—want to earn even more money than they were, with private companies. The money was more than they could've made anywhere else so far.

  She inhaled deeply; her fingertips hot with the ever-shrinking cigarette. She saw him down the path, approaching her, his body growing taller as he walked. His lean shoulders belied his exhaustion. They sloped and softened and shifted with each step.

  He stopped at the bottom of the stairs and saw what she held in her hand.

  She waved the letter like a flag. 'Well, here we are.'

'Okay, okay.. well?'

'Here.'

He opened it. *Pregnant.* Big, black lettering. *Ten weeks.*

  And then he was back in Germany, watching as the girl he barely knew tearfully told him how scared she was that they would bring a child into a war. And he felt fearful, though he didn't tell her, which is why he walked away. And he feared that he would resent that decision, and that he would grow distant like his father, and raise a child that didn't love him, and yet, here he was, with a golden-haired child that slept in his embrace, and a woman he loved. And now he stood before the same scared girl, and they'd been given another chance to try again. And maybe they could. And now there was no war, but he still felt fearful, though he didn't tell her now.

'Let's see what happens,' he shrugged, and smiled at her.

Julia's neck and face flushed, and she immediately felt the compulsion, the ache, to tell him finally; to tell him everything, about why this had happened, and how. But the reality was that he wanted this child as badly as she did, and the truth would forever extinguish the hope that arose from his words.

She blinked, and a tear fell quietly. 'Yes, let's see.'

17

April 1949

The line of blood started it all.

Julia lifted her skirt up, and like a scarlet thread, it slowly progressed down her thigh, and though it scared her because of her prior miscarriages, she knew it was different because her waters followed after. She had been trying to clear the table after breakfast, but a familiar ache had been distracting her: her back radiated with a consistent tightness, the lower part of her stomach muscles pushed in a kind of familiar rhythm, back and forth and down. She had done this once before now, it would happen today. She clung to anything to steady herself: chairs, bed frames, the kitchen table with breakfast plates clattering as she pitched herself forward with a coming contraction.

She breathed. It was suddenly quiet. She turned to walk towards her husband, and it was then that she felt it: a burning, like a rope being pulled through her back, dividing every tissue of her abdomen on its way through the other side. She doubled over and gripped a chair, its back shaking from her effort. 'Hironimus.' Her voice was insistent and flat. 'This is wrong.'

As she called for him, his name catching in her throat, she heard him in the other room with Slava. She had been in their lives for seven years now, and they had hoped and tried for more children, but the luck had run out until nine months ago. Still a young family with so much to look forward to. And now this. 'A miracle, finally', Henry called it, his face overcome with relief at the news.

'Papa! Look at that!' Her joyful twittering mixed with his low laughter, and their voices echoed in the thin farmhouse as if it were just another day, books and toys and pencils strewn across the floor, drawings of giant eyes and round faces atop spindly legs on sheets of paper that would eventually be torn and discarded. A life in one room as it was, a life that would begin in another. And when the bright burst of new pain came again, she became uneasy and unsure, and became nauseated.

'Henry. Can you ask Marta to help look after Slava? 'It's… just…' The words drowned in a fresh burst of pain in her stomach and back. Her face went white. She worried that it would end up a failure, like so many others before it.

Her husband finally walked in, hands in his pockets, as if he were waiting for the train. Henry was the calm one. Some may say cold, others would say controlled. She searched his face for strength. She looked down and just before another surge of pain, she noticed that one of his socks had a hole in the toe, and she would remember that detail more than anything else in that moment, for some reason— probably because it was a little thing. A little thing that could unravel over time.

'Hey, hey…' he said softly and came closer and his hands reached out and rested on her shoulders as he saw that she was pale and staring and though he was prepared for her to ask him something, he wasn't sure what, and he felt immediately insecure of how to respond. She looked different than she had the other time, with Slava.

'Tell Marta. And then take me to the hospital. I need a doctor.'

'Why not Elina? I'm sure she'd— '

Julia shot him a look. 'No. Not Elina. Just… because…' she searched her thoughts. 'It would be better to have someone older, maybe. Or she's probably working.' She stiffened and groaned softly. 'Just please ask Marta.'

She clutched her belly and took slow, steady breaths. In the pause between the pain she shuffled slowly to the bedroom, stopping occasionally to use the wall as support. She reached the dressing table (the dressing table he'd bought for her in Germany, shortly after they'd married) and sat, leaning forward on her elbows and folding her hands behind her head, legs spread onto the chair and belly comfortably in between.

When she was alone, it felt better. Important things are sometimes better accomplished alone, her mother used to say.

The room was quiet, and the smell of soap and coffee clung to the air. She noticed the bed hadn't been made, and his shirt lay on the floor beside her— the one that he'd slept in-- discarded from his body as if he'd vanished abruptly, leaving a soft shell. She picked it up and held it to her cheek and buried her face in it: it was still faintly warm to the touch. She still found joy in these small things, and these things were important in a marriage.

꩜

Henry padded urgently down the path that cut through the tall, dry grass to the house three doors down. The earth hugged his shoes as his lanky body loped along. He was surprised at how protective he felt over someone. This woman that he'd grown to love. Marriage was never what he'd wanted or didn't think he even deserved (let alone love, for love was not an economical use of a man's time, his father had always said). And yet, he knew (as if he'd known it always) that their path had taken them to the
right place: here, in Stratford, newly married with a baby on one hip, and another life on the brink of arrival. They hadn't thought, or planned, how to survive in the barren fields, surrounded by winds and rain, in a mill town that had a layer of dust on its doorstep, but they had given it a go.

This, he thought, was what he'd done for them, and more recently, after Julia had announced the pregnancy, he had worked harder than he'd ever had before. He had been contracted out to a private group of cutters, earning more money, which in turn lead to thoughts of eventually moving the family to Sydney, once their time had been served here. His felt a warm sense of duty, and love, as he imagined his young family in a warm, solid house sat within view of the ocean. He put his hands in his pockets and his face broke into a smile.

꩜

He took a breath, and then knocked. 'Marta.' His voice was hoarse and certain. 'I need help. Julia needs help.' 'Marta. Can you hear me?'

There was a shuffling and what sounded like a wooden handle being dropped on the floor and then a drawer being opening, and then a groan, footsteps coming closer still, and then she appeared, in a black dressing gown with faded red poppies on it, her dark eyes heavy, as if a light had been shut off.

'Oh. Henry. What can I do for you?' She rustled for a pack of cigarettes in her pocket, pulling one out and holding it, acting confused as to what she needed to do next. She was missing something. It was still early, and Henry was embarrassed that he had intruded.

'Marta, do you mind if I bring Slava to your house this morning? Julia is starting to feel contractions and she's—' he paused, letting fear escape his facade '— she's worried. She needs to get to the hospital.'

Her eyes widened a bit, and then composed themselves again. She fingered the other pocket of her gown: 'Yes, fine, bring her.' She had always hated children, but Slava was manageable.

'Yes, okay, thank you very much, she'll be over shortly? Thank you, Marta.'

'Fine.' With Marta, things were always 'fine'. She withdrew her husband's Zippo and sparked it sadly as she closed the door.

❧

'Henry?' Julia called from the bedroom as he came back in.

'Yes, yes, Marta is fine to take her.'

'All right well can you get her ready? I'm just here.' She gripped the dressing table and sat immobile.

Slava's voice rang out like bells. 'Mama! Mama!' She bounded across the floor, the untreated floorboards creaking beneath her feet.

'Oh rabbit,' Julia murmured as the toddler flapped at her legs. 'Papa will get you dressed,' and she turned her little body away. 'Henry, can you please…?' Her mind had already wandered to the things she had to do that morning, the things that would be forgotten shortly.

'Mama, but I'm hungry!'

'Marta has milk and bread,' Julia answered, her breath hissing in focused energy as she watched Henry coax Slava's legs into tights and then a green cotton dress.

'Mama?'

'Mmm?'

'Mama, love you.' She covered Julia's cheek with a wet kiss and patted her belly. 'Sweet baby, in there.'

'Yes, yes, okay go. Go with Papa.'

Julia dug her fingernails inside her closed fist as she heard him speak to Slava. Their voices faded the farther they got, and she felt the sharpness of betrayal. He'd tried his very best in the kind of situation that he'd never been able to adjust to, and she felt sorry that she had led him away from a secret that would change both of their lives. She heard him as he assured Slava that yes, they'd go to Marta's, and that yes, they could take a few buns with them and that Mama would be fine she just needed to see a doctor because she felt unwell and that the baby was coming. It was all coming out monotone, and here she was, sat in a chair in the other room, disconnected from it all.

Another contraction came and tasted metal on her tongue, and then an acidic tightness radiated throughout her abdomen, sending her forward in a dry retch, saliva glistening at the corners of her mouth. She suddenly felt a hand on her back, and she silently realized how much she needed her husband, and how good he was, despite it all, and how foolish she had been. She winced in regret; she winced in apology. They were connected, yet neither realized it.

'Julia, come. Are you able to make it to the car?'

Another wave of pain, her jaw tightened, and she grabbed his hand.

'Help me, Henry.' Her voice broke, and she cleared it. 'Would be a shame to have the baby in a car.'

'I'm sure worse has happened.'

So much worse.

'Just get me there. I will be okay.' And she felt his hand circle her waist, the weight of his arm pushing her forward.

The pale grey walls and oval windows of the old hospital dwarfed her swollen frame, and his lean one, as she bent over her knees in a wooden chair and he paced the room at its perimeter. From the outside, the tall, solid wood and brick building perched amongst tall trees and an attractive white porch encircled its entire perimeter. The inside, however, smelled of antiseptic and fresh cotton, and the floors were hard, so every footstep echoed like a tiny explosion in the room. She had spent so many days and months and moments brooding on her guilt, her complacency, but now she felt helpless.

Julia winced and groaned, looking down at her stomach her hands circling its largeness, feeling like the only person there, despite there being roughly 20 women in the room all with the same look of concern, wringing their hands and biting the corners of their lips. She wanted her mother. And then another contraction, the gold of her wedding band glinting in the dusty light of the room.

'Julia?' She and Henry looked up and saw them: a man, tall, with glasses that were too small for his round, creamy face, and a nurse with beige, greying hair stood beside him, plain and quiet, both dressed in crisp white and blue uniforms. 'Please let's have you come with us now.' She saw that they noticed the dried blood on her leg as she stood up and she hesitated, looking around the room. She was unsure. Her instinct was to run, without knowing where. Her legs stayed rooted to the floor, her fists clenched. *Protect Your Child*, a yellowed poster shouted from its place on the wall. *Lithiated Soda!* and *Smart Mums Smoke Camels*. None of this made sense to her.

'Madam?' *But the room smelled of bleach.*
'Julia.' *Her dress had a hole in it.*
'*JULIA.*'

Henry's eyes were dark behind the thin curtain of cigarette smoke separating them both. He had been pacing the floor and then leaning against the wall, pausing only to light a cigarette and now snap her back into the room where she sat, confused.

A faint smile flit across her face. 'Happy Birthday, you know.'

The corner of Henry's mouth lifted in a wry smile. 'Thank you for my present. You really know how to surprise me,' he said, and nodded for her to turn around and get going.

Julia stood and retreated towards the hall, meekly sandwiched in the middle of her two guides in white coats that would possibly be stained with her blood, her breath coming in short bursts to mitigate the pain. Three serious figures walked down a long stretch of polished, hard floor that seemed to split off into thousands of little doors, all hiding private stories narrated by soft voices that weren't for her to understand. Hers would be the second to last one, a white bed with starched pillows at the head, perching on a metal frame that creaked as she sat on it. Nothing felt comfortable, and then the contractions came again, and she gripped the frame and kneaded the mattress. They held her but she shifted constantly: she crouched and squatted, sat and rocked forward and moaned, bent over the edge of the bed, she climbed on all fours and begged the pain to stop. There were hands gripping her arms to stop her from moving and then she felt them shift her to the bed to lie still with her knees bent; it made her anxious. Something felt too urgent, too heavy. There seemed to be many more figures appearing through the doorway and spreading into the room; hushed voices and heads leaning towards one another in confidence and urgency and then a holding her arm still as she felt a needle in her arm and then saw a mask hovering to be placed over her mouth. And then a wonderful lightness lifted her away and loosened her jaw and the even the skin on her eyelids settled as she listened to pieces of conversation.

'…breech, they could move more but the heartbeats have slowed…'

'…a section, possibly avoided, however…'

'…manual manipulation…?'

'…no, need her awake, during…'

'… both heartbeats have stabilized…'

'Madam, I'm going to go ahead and put my hands inside to reposition the baby, alright?'

Julia nodded, her mind disconnected from their words, and her body disconnected from her. Their mouths and motions became softer and more distant as a medicine seeped into her body and her mind slowed its pace. She felt a vague sense of release in her chest—as if it were cracking open— with a pulling sensation further down, as if her body was spilt neatly in half. The lights were soft, and the faces seemed friendly, and she wanted in that moment to float above it all for a little while, gently brushing against the ceiling and watching the scene below as they moved her limbs and placed their gloved hands inside her. She imagined very vividly that she could then slip through the cracks and lines of broken plaster and float even higher and meet with the vapor of the clouds and the damp branches of the trees embracing the late summer sky. She would see the dust roads of Stratford, and the roar of the Barron Falls, then the bustle of Cairns glittering like a jewel on the edge of the Coral sea, and then the horizon would appear and she would drift farther away until both the sea and sky met in the blackness of night and her world would evaporate entirely and she, like gossamer, would disintegrate, piece by piece.

'Madam, we need you to push now.' Their voices were urgent, their hands were on her belly and her legs. Julia stiffened her arms, clasped the sides of her bed as if floating on a raft at sea, and closed her eyes. The remnants of nothingness were still there as she held her breath and pushed through her chest and back and belly and legs. Her eyes felt wet underneath her lashes. She rested against the pillow. And now again, another push, another two. A breath. And then another, and yet another, and then, her body felt suddenly empty of air and deflated, and a nurse held a small, doughy, white-coated baby covered in blood. She sighed and her back and arms collapsed in exhaustion and back onto the bed.

'Madam, wait. You'll need to push again in a second. Here comes the next one, you're doing very well.'

Another one. 'Sorry? I'm not sure what you mean.' Her blue eyes flashed. She was confused. 'I'm sorry, I don't understand.' her voice rose, breathless in alarm, as she'd not anticipated anything but a child, one child, inside her. She looked across to the nurse, the doctor, the faces masked in cotton masks and smiling eyes.

The nurse chuckled and placed a hand on Julia's thigh. 'Madam, you're having twins. Two babies, how incredibly blessed you are! But now we need to help the other one out. Push *now*.'

She held her breath. *Twins.*

A whimper caught in her throat, and she closed her eyes, her body aching. Three, two, one, breathe. And again. Her heartbeat was in her ears. And again. Gently, Julia, they reminded. With each space of breath in between, her mind looped from one thought to the next: she wondered what Henry was doing, and if their daughter had gone to bed peacefully, and whether the air smelled of rain and if the orchids had pushed through the soil; she wondered what the world was doing right at this very minute, because it would instantly change in the moments after; the present and past intertwining and colliding in chaos.

The cries sounded the same, like an echo of each other, ripples on water. Julia lay back on the pillow as one of the nurses wiped the blood off her legs and the other held two small bundles. Through the halo of her medicine, she saw two round faces, both the same, and her first worry was that she wouldn't be able to tell the difference between them. Their skin was like folded dough, like the 'babka' her mother used to make for Easter. Twins. She had made two of the same, and although she had been one of five siblings, and Henry was one of three, there had been no twins in either family. This should feel like a blessing, surely? What moments are these, that test the heart.

Julia smiled softly and felt a kind of ache overtaking her as they took them away, snuffling and snorting in the nurse's arms. Her body lay flat. Dehydrated. Wanting. And who told you to do this, her mother would say, gripping her face with dry, thick hands. Who told you? *I chose this,* she whispered. *This is my redemption.*

Darkness settled on the empty room, the ping of machines accompanying the distant rattle of metal trays and soft voices and curtains being opened and closed on the stories held within the halls. Footsteps clicked upon the thin tile floors, louder with each step towards her room and white figures stood in her doorway and filtered away as she drifted off to sleep.

The next day, Henry stopped in to see Julia, as he wasn't allowed the night before, as Julia was in recovery and asleep.

'Madam, your husband is here to see you.' A nurse opened the door carrying two bundles in each arm and handed them to Julia as Henry approached. The room felt instantly warmer.

'They told me. I can't believe it. Twins. A boy and a girl.' He walked over softly, smiling, his eyes creasing as he approached the bed to look down at the little faces scrunched under tiny knitted hats. 'Oh, Julia. I honestly don't know what to say. It's a little bit terrifying and wonderful.'

'I know.' She watched as he reached for them and she placed each delicately in his arms. 'But you have a son.' Her heart beat swiftly at the thought of a child in the image of Henry.

'What a life, eh?' He leaned his head back with a throaty laugh, his eyes wet and shining.

'Well, God has blessed us with a large family. Maybe a bit larger than we expected.'

He chuckled softly. 'God has a strange sense of humor, that's for sure. For years, nothing and now *this*.' He swayed back and forth as the babies gurgled in his arms, their mouths searching. 'What do you think about names?'

'What about Lesia? And Maksim?'

Henry squinted, pausing to think. 'Lesia, *from God*. And Maksim. A leader. A strong son of mine.' He nodded and smiled, kissing the doughy faces. 'Yes.'

'Henry, we have three healthy children now. *Three*. And look at the heartache that we'd had so long ago.' A surge of positivity and adrenaline coursed through her.

Henry placed them back in her arms and watched as she settled them and began to feed.

'Julia, I need to get back to work.' He kissed her softly on the forehead and walked a few steps, and then turned, looking at Julia for a moment. He tapped his chest pocket and retrieved a cigarette, a sigh escaping his lips.

Julia wondered, then, if she could ever tell him, but he looked happy, and she realized that he could be happy. They could be.

And then he walked through the door with the grace of a breeze.

18

August 1952

Two years rolled on without consequence as the family adjusted to the newness. The days, hours, weeks, minutes and months passed in an intangible recklessness and a delicious fever. Henry would come home and read to the twins nightly, as they curled up against his body in the small bed, their tiny hands and feet exploring his shirt, listening to his voice resonate. It was all a heady mix that Julia loved and felt consumed by, and it diminished much of her guilt.

Their lives had changed and stayed the same, equally, though Julia's relationship with Elina was now colored with a cool distance. Julia buried her secret in the deepest recesses of her mind, but every time she saw Elina, or Iliya, and pretended that life was as it should be, and they all moved around each other at polite dinners and smiled greetings, she grieved the loss of that friendship. Elina, for her part, graciously stepped back, assuming that Julia was overwhelmed with the twins. But she suspected something was amiss, and she observed from a distance, for a time.

By the following summer, Lesia's hair had grown thick and fast: it was a shade darker than Slava's, like a dimmed sunbeam, and it was soft, clinging in short, shining whisps to her neck, not long enough to be blown too wild by the wind. She had a small round birthmark next to her lip, and it was as dark her eyes: an almost black brown that contrasted beautifully with her light hair. Maksim's hair was dark and thick and was the color of milky chocolate; Julia would routinely run her fingers through it as she fed him, looking as his eyes slowly changed from the blue at birth. Julia wondered if they'd be hazel, like her sister's had been. Whilst Lesia was lean, Maksim was wide, and his head was large. Lesia needed constant affection, where her brother eschewed it. Lesia cried out to be held most of the day, whilst Maksim was observant and still.

They played constantly and their laughter had become her music, and Julia covered them constantly with affection, peppering their faces and their hands with kisses. Their life together simmered with abandon and hope, and Julia fully claimed them as her own and felt that nothing had, or would, come between them; her heart swelled as the marks of her pain faded and she held their warm bodies to her own. She healed in her love for them.

Henry was working more than usual, and he had told Julia of his thoughts on Sydney, but in her focused bliss and exhaustion as a new mother she had placed that in the recesses of her mind. The air between them, the four walls that surrounded them, felt safe, and the burdens that Henry had carried before were released from his shoulders and he carried the love of his children as the grateful father he was. It felt like the patterns in their behavior had found a happy rhythm, and so Julia indulged in the new life that had been thrust upon them. She had started taking Slava to a small school in Stratford a few times a week, now that she was older, which left the days for her to spend with the twins.

This morning, she'd been at the park with them, after dropping off Slava at a local play school. The day was clear, and it bled its peacefulness into the afternoon. She took out a book that she had found at home and brought with her: it was her accountancy and mathematics book, with a pale blue cover, and had survived the years-long journey from her school days. These were two classes that Julia had excelled in. She remembered the classroom as white, bare walls, shining wood floors, windows with limited views and that caked with snow in the winter. She remembered sitting across from her best friend, Sofia, and remembered her hair: always in a sharp bun, a white ribbon tied around it.

She thumbed a cracked yellowed page: the ink had faded almost completely, scrawled in a hurried hand:

Started business-- capital 100,000
Capital (100,000) + Liabilities (0) = Assets (cash = 100,000)
Bought furniture 25, 000
Solution?
Capital (100,000) + Liabilities (0) = Assets (Cash = 75,000 + Furniture = 25,000)
Bought goods for cash 20, 000
Capital (100, 000) + Liabilities (0) = Assets (Cash = 55,000 + Furniture = 25,000 + Goods = 20,000
Brought goods from Mr. Nelson on credit $5,000
Solution???
Capital (100, 000) + Liabilities (Nelson = 5,000) = Assets (Cash = 55,000 + Furniture = 25,000 + Goods = 25,000

She remembered she had once seen an accounting machine; the teacher had brought it to show the class. It fascinated her: it was like a strange, heavy stony grey beast sat atop the main desk, spattered with seemingly hundreds of pale-colored keys, uniformly spaced apart. It had purpose. She liked that it had purpose. It made her want to have purpose. She smiled, closing the book. It felt good to see the parts of her that had been hidden for so long.

Along the river there was a small gazebo that had been built before the war: it was a cream-colored hexagonal structure with slim pieces of wood laced together and all converging into a pointed roof. There were small benches on each of the six sides within and was big enough to hold groups of people relaxing by the river and taking in the view. Occasionally, there was a wedding party that took pictures there, and Julia always liked seeing a gathering like that, for the dresses alone.

It was there today, on one of the benches, that she saw him, though she wasn't sure at first, and then wondered if it actually was, or if it was her imagination that was reeling. And then she looked again, and confirmed that it *was*, and saw him smoking with a few friends, sitting in the same languid pose that she remembered, arm draped on the back of someone's shoulders. There were two women with him, dressed nicely, and three other men.

They had probably been out to lunch, or perhaps were just setting off somewhere. Julia looked away, aware that she'd been staring, and turned her attention back onto the twins. She watched them distractedly, only half paying attention as they sat at her feet. She turned again to look, and she regretted it instantly, for Iliya saw her, trapped her gaze, and waved. She watched as he turned back to his group, motioned that he would be right back to them and started walking over, and Julia cursed that she'd even looked, and wondered how quickly she could leave without creating any drama.

'Well! Look who it is…' he smiled as he approached, nothing remarkable about his face, just incredibly familiar. 'Can I sit down? Is it just you?' The strength in the knowledge of what he had done, and that she would never admit to what had happened to her, emanated in a kind of smugness that could easily be mistaken as confidence. He had that power, and they both knew it.

'No. Please go away.' She stumbled over her words and tried to stifle the urge to scream or run, she couldn't decide which.

He crouched down next to her and rested his arms on his thighs. 'I'm about to go off to lunch with a few friends, but I thought I'd say hello.' He looked over to the group. They had been casually watching them. He waved. 'Henry probably knows them, some of the men worked with him. We're waiting for Elina to join us. How's the family?'

She wasn't looking at him, so he had a few indulgent moments to scan the side of her face; her hair was plaited loosely and hung down her neck, the buttons of her dress were silvery and neat, all done up and containing her modesty. Her wool coat that had always been too big now perched on her shoulders delicately, like a cape. She turned to him, breaking his gaze. 'Please leave me alone.' Her cheeks were crimson, and he leaned into her, and from afar, someone could say that these two people looked extremely comfortable in each other's presence.

Lesia toddled up, found Julia's leg and clung to it, her lips wet on her knee. Maksim was sitting next to her and started whimpering for a feed.

'Time changes things, doesn't it?' He rocked back on his heels, staring at her a bit too long, and then reached for Maksim's head, attempting to stroke his soft hair.

Julia picked him up and moved him to the other side, hissing *don't touch him* only loud enough for the two of them. 'Many things change.'

'Yes. Shame, all that.'—he waved his hand in her direction glibly.

'Don't.' Julia's face burned with anger. 'Have you no shame for what you did?'

The side of his mouth lifted. 'Do *you*? For opening your legs to another man?'

Julia's face burned and her eyes raged. 'How dare you.' She bounced Maksim on her lap in direct contrast to the subject matter, to entertain him so he couldn't sense the tension, but also to avoid feeding him in front of a man that had seen her breast before.

'Life happens, sometimes. Desperate times, where we are.' He stroked the side of her face with his index finger.

'Get the hell away from me,' she hissed.

He laughed. 'Don't worry. We are leaving anyway.' He looked down at his hands. 'Or maybe just me. I cannot bear to stay in this shit hole any longer.' He looked at Julia and winked. 'Shame, really. I began to like it here.' He leaned forward and kissed the side of her face briefly. Before she could recoil, the moment was witnessed by another person who had walked over to the group by the pavilion and had watched the scene play out, only a minute before, and whose suspicions had now been confirmed.

Julia rolled her body away finally and looked up at him.

'Either way,' he stood up, and then stopped. 'Nice to see you again.' He smiled, and she remembered that smile, because it had been familiar, and now it destroyed her in so many miniscule ways, and an anger erupted inside her as he walked away, and then he inserted himself back into his group seamlessly, and they all moved together, their laughter dissipating down the road.

That moment kept hanging over her, the weight of panic looming on her chest, knowing that she had a part of her past that was indefinable. It existed, he existed, that night broke her and pieced her back together; she was unable to erase it.

She started packing up the pieces of the day into her bag, in a daze, not really aware of what she was doing, unaware that her world would soon be scattered in many pieces, like leaves on the wind that she now felt on her skin.

19

'Julia, come inside, please.'

She heard Henry's voice call her from inside the house, and there was something in the tone of it that made her hairs stand on her arm. The air felt quiet. It waited for something.

It was Saturday. Slava had been outside that morning, helping her mother weed the small garden at the back of the house, her hands caked in dirt, fistfuls of dandelions at her side. The twins were playing in one corner, on a flattened patch of brown grass, with some brightly-colored plastic toys had been brought over by one of the neighbors, they were happily engrossed and the laundry had been hung up and was fluttering in the breeze like the sail of a heeling boat. The sky was grey.

She looked up, the wind making her eyes stream. 'Wait just a minute, I have to finish.'

She saw his face appear in the window and scan the perimeter of the garden. 'No, you don't. They will be fine.'

She turned back to Slava. 'Wait here, I have to speak to your father. Look after Lesia and Maks.' Slava watched her leave, she watched her all the time, and listened always, and Julia knew it. Julia didn't turn back, and walked towards the front of the house, praying for a swift end to whatever mood was approaching.

When she walked in, Henry was leaning against the table in the kitchen, staring past her, and then at her. He was silent. His eyes were knowing. She looked back at the garden. The children would be alright.

'Yes, what?' Her hands were on her hips, trying to gauge his mood.

She felt a bit exposed, standing that way. She waited.

'So, you know what I heard?' he asked her, and she knew he didn't want her to finish.

She took the bait. 'No. What?'

'I heard that I married a whore.' He carefully lit a cigarette, letting *whore* hang in the air between them. He inhaled slowly, and then exhaled. 'Apparently.'

And all of a sudden, Julia felt like she was choking.

'Oh, right, sure,' Julia admonished and snapped herself out of her daze, though her thoughts were already a few steps ahead, searching. 'And where, exactly, is this from?'

'A friend.'

'Well. Some friend.'

'I trust them.'

'Obviously.'

'Well?'

The staccato of the words stopped abruptly, and Julia felt anger approach her chest, in fiery defense.

'Wait, wait.' Julia threw her hands up and closed her eyes as if to stop an army's approach. 'You have no idea what you're talking about and this 'friend' of yours is terribly mistaken.'

'Mmm, right.' He leaned forward, his palms gripping the table. 'So, how should we talk about this, then? Are you going to tell me, and will it be a lie? Or should I tell you what I heard, and you can respond? Either way, it's going to be damn painful for the both of us.'

She crossed her arms. 'Go ahead. Go ahead and tell me this ridiculousness.'

'So,' he paused. He gathered his words. 'I was told that you were with someone the other evening. Were you?'

'Which day? Who??' She chose her words carefully.

'You didn't answer my question. Were. You. With. Someone.'

'Well, it's a bit vague, isn't it? I've seen people, yes.'

'Julia,' He leaned his palms on the table, gritting his teeth. 'The thing that makes me sad here, is that I'm opening a door for you. I'm giving you the option to tell me what's going on—'

'No, actually,' Julia interrupted, placing her hands on her hips. 'You're not. If you remember, you just called me a whore.'

He kept talking.

'—and you're not being honest with me. So, fine. I'll tell you what I know. I know that someone told me they saw you in the park last week. Very comfortable, apparently, with you and the children. And that you apparently like to have a little meeting with that person, if I'm not around.'

'STOP saying someone! *Someone, someone, someone,* you know you're just trying to make me angry is that it?! What do you want me to tell you to make you happy?' Her heart felt like it belonged to someone else in that moment, it felt foreign and pale and cold, like the center of her chest had a hole in it and she was about to crumble to the floor.

'Go ahead. Lie to me.' Henry looked at her with a distant sympathy, as if he didn't understand who she was, but felt incredibly sorry for her.

'Who, then?' he was almost irritatingly calm in his demeanor.

'Who, what? What do you mean?'

'The other night, when I obviously wasn't here, and in the park. What's going on?'

She looked down. She'd forgotten to sweep the floor earlier. Specks of flour gathered around her toes. 'That's not what happened,' she whispered, almost inaudibly and in a daze.

'Excuse me?'

Her face was ashen as the memories of that night came flooding back. 'You're talking about Iliya, aren't you?'

'Well, then. You're having an affair.'

'No, no. That's not true.'

'What was he doing with you in the park?'

The park. How would Henry know about the park. And then it dawned on her. *Elina.* 'He came over to me. I didn't want to talk to him. He was trying to tell me—'

'That he's upset that he can't have you? He can take you, for all I care.'

'Henry stop, let me explain—'

'Obviously you slept with him.'

She hesitated, and he saw it as admission. 'No.'

'When did it happen?'

'I said *no*, didn't you hear me?'

'You're lying.'

Julia let herself feel angry. 'You've already made up your mind, Henry, and it leaves no room for me to tell the truth.'

'*When* did you start with this man,' he hissed, pointing at her face. 'Tell me.'

She covered her ears with her hands, pleading. 'Stop. Please stop.'

He was standing a foot away from her, not letting her back away. He grabbed her and shook her violently.

She wrenched herself away and reached for the door, launching herself outside and into the light, the empty fields around her. She stopped, knowing he'd follow her, and she didn't know what to say. The less she said now, the easier it would be, she realized. It's a funny thing, truth. It can be more destructive than a lie.

And then she panicked as she looked back at all the times she had lied to him, and she felt her stomach lurch and a nausea erupt in the center of her.

She heard his footsteps behind her, and she turned around.

'Henry, please,' her voice was withered, raspy. 'I can't fix it; I can't undo what happened.'

'You still haven't told me when it happened.'

'Why do you have to know?'

'Fresh pain, Julia.' He spat. 'For both of us. So I can see you humiliated.'

Her thoughts spun. *Do you remember that I told you that Slava had bashed into me? Do you remember? And when I told you I was pregnant? Do you understand now?*

'July.'

'It's October. *This* past July?'

'Last…July.' Her stare was unflinching, a tear still caught in the corner of her eye. 'Last year. It was that one time.'

He moved towards her, and then stopped. She thought it might be because he could forgive her. *That one time.* She walked to him. The leaves battled each other in the wind above their heads.

'That was over a year ago.'

'Yes.'

He looked back at the house and heard laughter. He turned back to her and she knew he'd counted. He'd calculated. She couldn't stop herself; she had been released from her guilt, and shame, and anger had been bottled inside for far too long and began to set fire to the air around them. 'Yes, after that, I found out I was pregnant. And it didn't make me want them any less. I wanted them because we couldn't have any of our own and my *God* you wanted them too, and you loved them just as much as I did, so what does it matter, please, what does it matter now… there is nothing to forgive, Henry.'

  Henry's face lost its color. The realization that his children were most likely not his own was devastating. Catastrophic. Incendiary. Heartbreaking. The words set off a chain of anger and disappointment in him that he had only once felt: for his father.

  In the hours that followed the revelation, Henry chose (because it was the easier option and presented less difficulty navigating emotional obstacles that were the complicated results of an assault) not to believe his wife, and instead, began to convince himself that he was a betrayed by the one person he trusted. And the arguing possessed both of them in a kind of bottomless mire: Henry needing to believe that she had been unfaithful, and Julia needing him to accept that she had been assaulted, and to release the past of its pain.

🐦

'No, are *you* hearing me at all?' They were standing in the front of the house, the argument spilling out by the road, as Henry had started to leave to go anywhere but here. His world had been spun too far out of his reach and he was flailing. She had asked him if he was listening to her, and he had turned around to face her, walking towards her, a shaking index finger pointed at her face. 'Are *you* understanding *me*?? You slept with someone almost two years ago, and now you're saying that he raped you. And, guess what: those two sleeping children in that house, my house, those two children that I have loved, and wanted and held in my arms—' 'his voice broke at each admission— 'are they yours? Yes. Are they mine? I don't know. I don't *know*. *I don't know*. Do you have *any* idea what that feels like for me?' The tears threatened.

  'But…'

  'I don't know whether to be angry, or sad, or shout, or break apart everything I own, or take Slava— *my* child, I'll have you know-- of this house and leave you to your misery.'

She grew cold, staring at Henry, not really seeing him, hearing words coming and yet feeling like there was a transparent wall between them.

'So, what if they are Iliya's?'

Henry reached his arms to the heavens, dropping them down again in exhaustion. 'Stop saying his *name*!'

'Why can't they be ours now? They're here now. We've made a home for them.'

'You're asking me to love children that are not my own!'

'But you love them.'

'There are plenty of others who would love these children. I can't fathom raising children that are not my own blood.' He looked across at the house where they now were, the boy and the girl that were strangers to him, and yet his heart broke and yearned for them.

'But *we* do. We have, wanted them. They are innocent in all of this, why would you punish them? Or me for that matter?'

He was shaking and walked over to the car and punched the metal with the meat of his fist, his arms tightening as he pressed down on the hood. 'Are you mad? You're asking me a question when, after almost *two years* with the belief that they were mine, the truth is that they're most likely not, and you tell me he raped you, and how am I to believe you when you had said nothing, *nothing*, for so long. Why?! Why did you not trust me enough to tell me! I loved you and love you still, and you had no faith in me.'

'But I was scared and I'm telling you now,' she pleaded, wondering if he would back down; if she could actually get him to believe her. 'You have to believe that it's the truth.'

'I don't think *you* even know the truth anymore, Julia.'

'Please just listen to me—'

'— honestly, I can't. This is madness. You're actually asking me to take care of another man's children? Absolutely not.'

He wouldn't change course, and his voice had become a kind of still that felt too conclusive, so she pointed at the very weakest spot to see if she could break him open again. 'Well, then, you didn't love them really, did you.'

And oh, God, his anger flooded the space between them when she'd said those words. She meant them, and he knew it, and it broke his heart with more power than his father ever did (though he would never tell her that) and so when his palm came across her cheek, she'd expected it. She knew to brace herself when she saw his eyes widen and his hand lift. She clenched her jaw, her lips soft and closed, as his open palm connected to her skin; the sting and fire erupted like an explosion, repeated in burning waves, her eyes closed and tearing underneath. He had never raised a hand to her, and now he felt sick at the thought.

He bent his head, shoulders dropping, hurting for what he did and what she had done to him. Her eyes remained closed, and she became the center of where she was, pretended that it was all revolving around her. As long as she stood still, anything could happen; planets could revolve, the sun could rise and set, the children could play, and the world could go on perfectly fine without her.

'You have a choice, Julia.'

She stayed quiet, unprepared as to what he would say.

He looked up at her. 'Give them away, or I'm leaving.'

'What?' Her eyes widened.

His jaw pulsed as he set his teeth. 'That's right. Give them up. Or I'm taking Slava with me. Out of here.'

Julia shook her head. 'Give them away? That's impossible.'

'There are plenty of families that are childless. They can have these... children.' He stopped himself from saying *bastards*. His heart felt as if it were splintering into shards, there was too much for him to process.

Julia felt her skin grow cold, the hair on her arms standing, her heart falling to the bottoms of her feet, breaking at each corner inside her body. Impossible.

'No. *No no no no*, you cannot make me do that.' Her voice strained through her throat as she spoke, she wanted to wail. 'No. You're just saying that out of anger. You have to stay calm; you have to believe...'

'--What choice do you give me, Julia? *WHAT. CHOICE.*' Henry's voice cut through the air around them.

'...that you can love them still.'

Henry clenched his fist and his entire body shook. 'I *did* love them. I still *do* love them. And yet you tell me they weren't mine. Can't you even understand what that *feels like*? Can you see how my entire world has burned in front of my eyes? What truth can I believe now? What am I supposed to do?'

'You cannot make me give away my children, the ones that we have loved, no no...' Her voice began to rise, her lungs bursting as her breathing became erratic. '*Our* children. Please, please,' she pleaded, and dropped her head into her palms, still speaking softly. 'Oh God, Henry. Please, oh God what have I done to us...' She began to sob uncontrollably, an animal-like sound coming from her; a keening from her exquisite, unhinged pain.

He was torn: the woman standing in front of him was the woman he loved, but the betrayal, the secret, the unknown story that his children now were a part of. It was all too much for him to take, and so he turned away, though he wanted to hold her, but the pain was too severe, the cut too deep. He felt powerless.

Suddenly the door opened, and Slava ran out, gold hair shining in the sunlight, dress billowing in the wind. 'Mama! Papa! Stop shouting!' She began to cry, running towards them. 'Why are you fighting??'

Julia held her breath to stop from crying, and was grateful for Slava's body running towards her, pushing into the side of hers as she clung to her.

Henry looked over at Julia sharply, in admonishment, gesturing with a hand. 'You see? This is what you've created.'

'Oh, my love. I'm so sorry,' Julia ignored his comment and spoke with an unwavering voice, though she was wounded beyond repair now. She knelt down, wiping the tears from Slava's cheeks. 'Don't worry, everything is alright.'

'Slava,' Henry interrupted. 'Why don't you come with me— 'Julia's heart went cold and she stood up, clutching the child's small hand. '— for some ice cream. Would you like that? We can pretend it's your birthday again.'

Julia released her breath slowly, grateful. Everything suddenly felt unpredictable.

'Yes, Papa! Yes!' her eyes shone, and she smiled brightly. 'Can we go now?'

'Yes, now.' He held out his hand, and Slava grabbed it excitedly.

'Will Mama come with us? And Lesia and Maks?'

His eyes moved from Slava's face to Julia's, and back to Slava's. 'Mama needs to stay here.'

'Okay.' Slava skipped as they started to walk. 'Papa?'

'Yes, rabbit.'

'I love you.'

He couldn't reply, the tears streaming down his cheeks. The pain of his choices would be his alone to bear, his father had warned him of it.

Julia raced back to the house, her feet creating tufts of dust as she hit the ground. She ran to the garden, picking up Lesia and placing her on one hip, and then Maksim on the other, sobbing. She knew she had one last option, and she walked deftly down the familiar path, past their house, hundreds of feet ahead, her body small against the backdrop of the sugar smoke and pale fields and blue sky, to a farmhouse that had become so familiar to her.

When she arrived, she pounded on the door, breathless. 'Iliya? *Iliya,*' her voice was strident. 'Open the door.'

Silence. She knew he would be home, so she waited, the twins gurgling at her side. She held them to her suddenly, desperately, each time she felt their skin or heard their voice, tears threatened to weaken her anger. She felt fire in her chest.

'God damn it, open the door.' She used the ball of her foot to hit the bottom of the wooden frame.

He appeared in the doorway and opened it. 'Well, come in. This is a nice--'

Julia flew past him into the center of the front room, placing the twins on the floor by her feet. She put her hands up. 'Spare me the welcome.' Her face burned with anger. 'I need your help.'

By the time he and Slava reached Stratford, Henry's breathing had become more even. He tapped his chest pocket and withdrew a cigarette as they walked, clamping it in the corner of his mouth and wiping the sweat off his brow. Once lit, he sighed and looked down at his daughter. He was grateful that she was at the age where she held his hand often; he needed to feel her cool hand in his, especially today.

When they approached the ice cream shop on Griffin Street, just before the promenade Slava asked for an ice cream, which Henry happily obliged. She chose a sugar cone of sweet vanilla with a cherry on top, and after Henry paid, he took her to sit on a bench facing the Avon. The ice cream glistened as she licked it, her legs swinging happily a few inches off the ground. He watched as families wandered together in the crisp afternoon sun and heard children's laughter in the playground just beyond.

'Papa, why didn't you get one?' Slava frowned, moving her hair off her cheek with a sticky finger.

Henry took a drag on his cigarette and looked at the water, the sunlight scattering on the ripples like diamonds. 'I wasn't hungry.'

'Because of the fight? Because of you and Mama?' She licked her fingers as the ice cream melted onto them.

'No, not really.'

'Why were you shouting?' Slava squinted at the view and looked over her shoulder to the park where a few children played. She turned back disinterested and bit the edge of the ice cream. 'I don't like it when you shout.'

'I know, rabbit.' Henry's eyes filled with tears, and he looked away as he wiped them off quickly.

He turned back and smiled. 'Life can be tricky, I guess.' He shrugged and looked down at Slava studying his face.

'Is Mama okay? She was crying. And you were angry.'

'Yes.' He cleared his throat. 'We are okay.'

'Because you love each other.'

In that moment, Henry saw memories that had would lose their meaning, like tarnished keepsakes: Maksim sitting for hours on the kitchen floor with Lesia, pencils in hand, drawing in bold strokes and pointing. He giggles as Julia sits behind him, clapping at his progress, and he reaches for Henry; Slava with her sister, helping brush her hair after a bath, their soft skin and nightdresses in his arms as he embraces them before bed; Maksim sat on his lap, pointing at drawings in a fairytale, saying 'Papa' when he sees a prince, and 'Mama' when he sees a princess; Lesia asleep next to him, the moonlight in her blonde hair and across her round cheeks.

Henry watched Slava eat the last of her ice cream and didn't reply. He stroked her soft hair and remained silent, a storm of images swirling around him.

Iliya closed the door behind him and turned to Julia. 'What help do you need, exactly?'

'Henry knows. He *knows.*' Her lips quivered as she spoke, and she clenched her teeth.

Iliya dragged a chair to sit down in, the metal scraping the floor. 'Well then.'

'But he doesn't understand what happened, and now--'

'What do you mean, what *happened*?'

'He doesn't know the truth, Iliya, and he's going to leave me and take Slava--'

Iliya leaned back in his chair. 'What truth?'

Julia stamped her foot. 'LISTEN, will you. I am going to lose my entire family, my life,'-- she gestured to the twins-- 'if you don't tell him what happened. Otherwise, I have to admit adultery to him, and lose the two children that you see in front of you. I can't let him do that, you have to tell him the truth. Please let me keep my children, *all* of them.' Her face creased in her anguish. 'Please, Iliya.'

Iliya looked down at the twins, crawling on the floor happily. He looked up at Julia. 'Why would he give away...'

The both of them stared at one another and in the quiet, Iliya suddenly understood.

He stubbed out his cigarette and held his hands up, laughing wryly. 'Listen, this is not my mess to clean up. Your truth is what you believe it to be. And besides, I'm not interested in ruining my marriage and my work- and for what? To solve your unhappy marriage that is in crisis?' He walked over and stood in front of her, her face now contorted in her helplessness. He wiped her cheek, and felt the scar on her jaw, now dark pink as she cried. 'Besides,' he whispered softly and leaned forward; breath hot on her cheek. 'Who would believe you?'

Julia clung to his arms, disgusted at what she touched, yet pleading for what could be saved. '*Please please,* Iliya. Please...' she hung her head and kept repeating the word *please.*

The door swung open, and Julia and Iliya turned to face Elina, her face stony with anger.

'What the hell is going on? What is *she* doing here?' Elina dropped her handbag on the floor, her eyes wide, surveying. She looked down at the doughy twins sat on her floor. 'What in Christ is happening?'

Iliya smiled, and patted Julia on the shoulder. 'Poor woman has lost it a bit. Very unhappy with her husband.' Julia was too tired to glare at him and instead, looked at the woman that she'd once loved as a friend.

'I don't care what she's lost, I want her out of here.' She shrugged off her dress coat. 'And *you* can take your hands off her.'

Iliya raised up his hands and backed away. Julia wiped her eyes with her arm. She nodded, and now realized it had been Elina. Elina had been Henry's 'friend' that had brought her life to a crashing end. 'Please, Elina, just listen.'

Elina walked over to Julia and stood in front of her, her full length towering a head above Julia. Iliya watched the scene, arms folded. 'No, *you* listen. I don't care for your games.' Her voice needled and pierced as she spoke. 'You *poor* thing, your husband makes you unhappy, you're a lonely, pathetic orphan,'-- she grabbed Julia's shoulders and craned down-- 'and you look to my husband to save you. To give you comfort. Did you enjoy it? Did you?' Julia grabbed the hands that held her. 'Elina, stop, that's not what--'

'And now, you've ruined a marriage-'

Iliya shook his head. 'Elina, that's enough. She's apparently going to lose her children...' Elina shot him a withering look, and he raised his hands. 'Alright, alright. I'm just...'

Elina turned to Julia. 'Wait a minute.' She stepped back. 'Why? Why the twins?'

Julia spoke quickly while she had the chance. 'Elina, Henry is forcing me to give them away...' She looked over at Iliya, who wasn't showing the least bit of concern about anything that she would say. She was powerless. No one would believe her. 'He thinks that Iliya and I...'

Elina raised her hand to Julia, and everyone went quiet. The quiet settled as the three of them looked at one another. Elina looked down at the twins, and then at her husband, and covered her mouth, her eyes widening and cheeks trembling. Her hands started to shake as she pointed at Julia. 'I cannot bear the sight of you. The both of you.' Her head shook from side to side, slowly, and she walked up to Julia again, her face and neck erupting in bright red flashes of anger, her eyes full of hurt. 'Congratulations. You have ruined a friendship, and now a family. Your very own family. You have destroyed it completely. And now you have to live with it all, for the rest of your days. And for what, exactly? A moment of misunderstood kindness? Pity?'

'It wasn't that,' Julia whispered.

Elina cocked her head to the side. 'What did you say?'

Julia looked directly at Elina, suddenly angry, her voice clear. 'It wasn't kindness or pity, Elina. Your husband isn't capable of any of it.' Julia's body tensed at her own words; they undid whatever pieces that had healed so long ago and obliterated them fully.

Elina's palm cracked across Julia's cheek, turning it crimson. Elina walked over to the twins and kneeled, touching their soft, warm heads. 'Well done, my friend, what an example of a mother you are.' She stood up again and looked at Julia. 'Those poor babies, it breaks my heart.' Her face softened for a second and then snapped back into place, as she pointed to the door. 'You can get out.'

Julia swallowed her sobs and crouched next to her babies, her arms shaking as she lifted Lesia first, and then Maksim, their happy faces searching hers. She turned, Elina and Iliya's faces watching her, the wall of their bodies standing firm.

'The truth, Elina.' Julia said softly. 'If only you could see the truth. Maybe you will allow me that one day.'

Elina walked past her and opened the door, gesturing to the outside with an open palm.

Julia walked home quietly, her grief unbearable, her sobs uninhibited as her body looked small and worn against the blanket of sky beyond her.

She had lost.

20

Julia hadn't slept, and barely ate. Henry disengaged from her, from the twins, as they reached for him, not understanding why he would peel their fingers off his legs, not pick them up when they needed him. Julia watched her family as if a voyeur— one that was not allowed to belong— with a grief that had descended over her entire life, as if a sticky film on a forgotten painting, or a glass that was slowly cracking, its fissures about to break and explode and disintegrate.

A part of her had died once already with one man, and now she would die a slow death with another, as he forced her hand. Would she survive this? Would her children? Would her marriage? In the darkest of nights, she wished for nothing else but an end, but her saving grace was their daughter, and there was now a reason why they called her 'Glory', and Julia reminded herself of the fact that she would, in fact, have to carry on with this life. Without them.

❧

The morning was warm and quiet, the twins still asleep. Henry had left early to go for a walk, crept out without a word, which she was grateful for. She padded into her room and stood in the doorway, staring at the small bed in the corner with the two sleeping babies. Lesia's hair was matted on the mattress from sweat. Maksim's cheeks were lined from his blanket clutched so firmly to his face. The breaths were slow and even. These are the things she would remember, though they would fade over time. A childhood only captured in photographs and stories, existing ever so briefly.

Julia's fingers curled around a cup of slightly lukewarm tea, thinking about what she had, in the last weeks, decided. In her other hand she was holding a thin, small spoon, stirring the liquid in circles, around and again, the pattern comforting, as if she was tracing the line of her thoughts and reaching the same conclusion, over and over again. She had not put milk in the tea this time, and as a result, she saw the lines of her face reflected in the liquid briefly, before disappearing again and again.

The trip to the courthouse was silent. They'd taken the train into Stratford, side-by-side sat in resentment and heartbreak. Julia had taken Slava across the road to Marta's, and then asked another neighbor, Olya, to look after Lesia and Maksim. She felt completely bereft at what would happen soon, but ultimately, the choice was made. In order to save her marriage and keep her family intact, she had to make the ultimate sacrifice.

The courthouse was small, white, set on a patch of grass dotted with two benches out front. It was formal and plain, and as they strode in through the door, Julia felt the heaviness of her footsteps as they clacked loudly on the floor.

'Yes? Do you have an appointment?' The secretary was pale and blonde, her straight, shining hair pulled back in a bun at her neck, her cheeks flushed as if she had just run back into the room, embarrassed.

'Yes, we're here to sign a declaration, the consent to adoption order. We called a week ago.' Henry tapped his fingers on the counter, Julia stood with her arms in front, holding her bag. Numb.

'Name?'

'Rudnick.'

'Yes, I see you here. Have a seat, Mr. Bennett will be with you in a few minutes.'

In the minutes as they sat in the waiting room, Julia was confronted with panic. *I don't know English very well, how do I know what to say? What do I do?* She looked over at Henry, he was standing at the window, looking past the town, towards the sky, towards the fields that had turned gold in the dense summer heat.

Joseph Bennett was a man with greying hair and limited knowledge in how a suit should fit a man's body properly. His round face was accentuated with jowls on either side, and his tawny hair was thinning and almost entirely absent at the crown, due to a very poor diet. His career in family law had seen him though 20 years of adoptions, and this case didn't seem at all unique, as the family were migrants, and he expected as much with people who had little intelligence to know when to stop having children. He was the sort of man to declare *it's not like they have any other entertainment for themselves, dear lord. Leave the thinking to the rest of us*, over dinner with friends, holding his crystal glass of wine in his fine little hands. And so today, he would meet his new clients, and go through the extremely tedious process of rehoming their children.

Julia saw him walk through the door, holding a folder of documents, and she searched his face, wondering if he would listen to her. 'Nice to meet you both, I'm Joseph Bennett, I'll be helping you with your declaration', he held out his hand. Henry shook it and followed him as he ushered them both into his office.

Henry started speaking as Bennett shut the door. 'We don't speak English very well, sorry, so you need to explain to us where we put our names. My wife,' he pointed at Julia with vague interest, 'She's worse. Tell her what to do please.'

'Mr. Rudnick, I understand your concerns, but not to worry, I'll help guide you towards the best solution for you and your wife. Now, do you understand what you're here to do?'

'Yes, we have two children we need adopted.'

Bennett nodded, turned to Julia. 'Madam, do you understand, is this why you're here?'

'Yes.'

'Okay, well, the first thing we have to do,'—he shuffled the papers around on his desk and found a white form, fed it into his typewriter—' is fill out this declaration, it's a statement that you need to sign, telling me the details that led you to decide to adopt your children out to a new family. This won't take long.' Bennett leaned forward, folded his hands on the desk.

'So. What is the reason, for my records?'

'My wife got pregnant with children that are someone else's. These are not my children, I'm not their father.' Every word felt labored, but Henry steeled himself at each one.

Bennett swallowed abruptly at the admission, and then looked over at Julia, and wondered if the words this man uttered were correct, for he'd never heard of such a thing, though similar things have probably happened in the world. 'Is this a fact?'

'Would you believe me if I told you the truth? That he forced himself on me?'

The men looked at each other, and the power of the truth and the freedom of the words that she'd wanted to say for what seemed like most of her life--even if they didn't believe her-- crashed through the room and created a deafening silence.

Julia's eyes glistened. 'Would you listen?'

'Madam, I hardly— '

'What about understanding what happened to me? Can I tell you what happened?'

'Madam. Is there a police report?'

'No.'

'Well, if this man assaulted you, as you say,' Bennett looked over at Henry and saw nothing but a stony face, so he looked back at Julia. "Then surely you would have reported it?'

Henry spoke first.

'No.'

Bennett stayed silent.

The keys clicked, spelling out black letters: 'Julia', and then, 'wife of Henry Rudnick'.

'So. When did you commit adultery?' *And despite her freedom in that moment, she was trapped again.*

'July. 2 years ago.'

'And, who was he?'

Iliya.

Henry answered for her. 'Iliya Dalevich. He worked with me; he was a cane cutter.'

'Is he aware?'

'No.'

'And where is he now?'

Julia spoke this time. 'I don't know.'

Okay, that's fine. And then what happened?' Click-clack, the keys swept along with the dialogue.

Julia held her breath and then slowly let it out. She could answer one of two ways: the truth, which was entirely useless here, or go along with the story that her husband told. She pressed her fists onto her thighs and reopened the scar.

'He… well.' *Slowly. Wrong story. Try again.* 'We slept together.' *Keep with the lie. The truth won't help you now.* She looked down. 'Then, I found out I was pregnant. I told my husband the truth in August this year.' *That's it. Well done.*

'So, let me get this correct,' Bennett stopped typing, resting his fingers on the black keys. 'You committed adultery with a man, became pregnant and then had the twins, telling your husband that they were his?' He cleared his throat and looked at her. His face resembled a man that was watching a very dull movie.

'Am I correct?'

'Yes, I didn't know if they were or not.'

He began typing again. 'Well, were you having, ahem, relations with your husband at the time as well?'

Henry interrupted and shifted in his chair. 'Is that necessary?'

'Yes, sir, I'm afraid it is, to see the possibility of there being a different alternative to this case.'

Henry lit a cigarette and looked at Julia and then back at Bennett. 'No.'

She was shocked. He was punishing her and felt it as if he had dug a cold knife slowly into her heart. He was lying. She looked at Bennett, imploringly. 'But we *were*.'

'Hmm. See, I do think, madam, that a man would remember these things quite well,' he smirked. 'And to be fair, your memory is a bit sullied with, let's say'-- he motioned to the paperwork, and then to her-- 'what you were *preoccupied* with.' He continued typing. 'Regardless, it's safe to say that your adultery is a punishable offense to your marriage regardless.' Bennett shook his head, and whether it was in admonishment or disbelief, Julia wasn't sure. She felt invisible.

'So, you told your husband and you and your husband decided that the only choice was to put your two, possibly illegitimate children, up for adoption. Yes?'

They both nodded.

'Have you considered the possibility of raising these children as your own?'

'I already told you, no.' His heart had changed. It had built a layer of distrust around it, and it firmly stood in self-preservation, unwavering. If he didn't utter these words calmly and detach, he would break. 'This is our decision.'

Bennett turned to Julia. 'Is this correct?'

Julia felt her chest grow cold and tight. 'Yes. What my husband says is correct.'

Two sheets of paper spooled out of the typewriter, heavy with black words and dates and spaces to sign. Bennett handed them pens. He pointed at a final declaration that Julia and Henry had to sign, a simple date and confirmation of the decision made:

QUEENSLAND
STATE CHILDREN DEPARTMENT

I, THE UNDERSIGNED <u>Julia Rudnick</u>, OF STRATFORD NEAR CAIRNS, BEING THE MOTHER OF THE INFANT, HEREBY STATE THAT I UNDERSTAND THE NATURE AND THE EFFECT OF THE ADOPTION ORDER FOR WHICH THIS APPLICATION IS MADE; AND THAT IN PARTICULAR I UNDERSTAND THAT THE EFFECT OF THE ORDER WILL DEPRIVE ME OF MY PARENTAL RIGHTS; AND I HEREBY CONSENT TO THE MAKING OF AN ADOPTION ORDER IN FAVOR OF ANY APPLICANT APPROVED BY THE DIRECTOR, STATE CHILDREN DEPARTMENT. IN WITNESS WHEREOF I HAVE SIGNED THIS CONSENT ON THE 15TH DAY OF NOVEMBER, 1951.

Henry signed his without issue. She waited; her fingers hot as she clutched the pen. 'I, ah, what does this mean?' Her eyes looked up from the paper, searching Bennett's. One possible moment of understanding. One possible explanation, reason or purpose that could help her find the clarity that she desperately wanted. Her hand hovered.

'Mrs. Rudnick, you are agreeing to an adoption, because as you have declared, you have committed adultery and your husband said he would forgive you if you gave up the children that he, and you, suspect aren't his. In signing this, you are agreeing that you will leave this in the hands of the state, and the state will decide for you whom will have your children. You are agreeing that you will not have any rights as a parent to the children you are giving up.' He clarified. 'You can't go back through this door once it's closed, do you understand?'

She looked down at the paper, a thin black line waiting for her pen to rest, and then looked over at Henry; he was looking towards the middle of the room, at no one, casually staring past her, cold and indifferent.

And then the slow destruction of her world finally began as she touched the pen to paper, her fingers shaking as she carved her name with solid dark lines. She was being told the worst thing a mother could ever hear, a pain that wasn't even remotely imaginable by even the wildest scope of thought: that she was unworthy of the children that she had wanted and loved.

They left the courthouse as they arrived: in silence.

In the weeks immediately following, Julia and Henry played the placid family game. Moments revolved and grew around the suppurating silence of a broken marriage; the trust was irretrievable, and as much as Julia reached, Henry drew back, walked away. She would catch him staring at the family, wondering if he'd still leave. Silences were only interrupted by young voices, a sometimes-painful reminder that what was true now, would soon be so different.

In the days she had with her little family, Julia tried to ignore the inevitability that there was probably a couple, young and married, who were at this moment, signing white pieces of paper in front of someone like Mr. Bennett. They would be smiling at each other, She would be dressed in a pale blue jacket and skirt, her hair done nicely but not too primly. Her husband would be leaning towards her, talking to her about the decision that they would be making. *Are you okay with this? Should we go through with it? Yes,* she would say. *I love you, and this would be a blessing for us,* is what she would say. This would all be happening at the same time Julia would be dressing

Lesia in a dress that she made for her; Maksim would be in his shirt and trousers, his light brown hair swept to the side, blue eyes searching. It would all be happening as if in a slower, parallel life: this woman in her blue suit would be clutching her handbag, happily in conversation with someone official and lean, watching her husband shake another man's hand, an agreement in place for their future. Sometimes Julia would sit next to Slava and they would both watch Maksim and Lesia as if memorizing their faces.

'Slava, I need to tell you something.' Julia was sat on the bed folding laundry distractedly. Folding, refolding, forgetting what she was doing.

'Yes?' She responded, looking up from her drawing, then back down. She was drawing a woman with yellow hair and a big red smile, holding a baby.

'What, Mama?'

'Slava, you know how Lesia and Maksim are here with us?'

'Yes.'

'Well, they will be going on a trip soon.'

'Can I come?'

'No, it's just for Maksim and Lesia. They'll be going on a trip with a man and a lady, they are nice people and they'll look after them for a while.'

'Why?'

'Because,' She ran her fingers through her hair, words failing her. 'Because, it will help us. Papa and I decided it would be for the best.' She got up from the bed, walked out of the room. 'For the best,' She murmured quietly, to no one in particular.

'Mama?'

'Yes, Slava.'

'Will it be okay?'

'Of course.'

'Will they have a good time?'

'Yes.'

'Will the people be kind?'

Oh, she hoped. 'Yes.'

She walked out to see the twins on the floor of the main room, with books, laughing and teasing, their hands mimicking the each other's like shadows. It was a scene that was too painful to watch, too beautiful to walk away from.

A few days later, a letter arrived in the post, stamped with the insignia of *The Office of Joseph Bennett*, addressed to *Mr. and Mrs. Henry Rudnick*. She ripped it open, and there in black ink was an appointment for them:

Dear Sir and Madam:
This letter is to advise you that there has been an appointed day for you both to come to the <u>Townsville Receiving Depot</u> to sign the adoption declaration, and for your children, Maksim and Lesia, to be placed in welfare before they are assigned to their adoptive family.
Please bring both children to the courthouse at 1pm, as well as any medical records, a few items of clothing and any personal possessions that they may require.
Sincerely,
<u>*Joseph Bennett*</u>
Solicitor

She was holding the letter delicately, as if it were a rare jewel, or a bomb. Her insides felt as if they had been scraped out. Hollow and lifeless. There were no tears, for it felt too great of a flood to pick at. She had, in fact, destroyed her family, and she had ten days to fill her time without any temptation of taking her own life, though wouldn't that be selfish. Evenings would be the worst, she knew. Every day the minutes would count down to her sentence, every minute lost was one less of seeing her children clutch at their well-worn blankets; every day was one less of smelling their skin when she held them. This was irreversible, and any other words that could possibly describe it, and the most extraordinary, consuming pain she had ever felt in her life; so much so, that she had almost entirely gone numb to it.

Ten days crawled at a slow pace; some moments felt too protracted, and yet others felt unsatisfying in their brevity. Ten days spent wondering how she would cope without them, ten days spent wondering whether she had done the right thing and whether she could eventually cope with Henry leaving her, because, it was possible. This love, this guilt, tore at her like a fresh wound, over and over again, until there was no blood left.

21

Six weeks had passed, and now, Julia had run out of time.

It was humid for November, and the first thing she wanted to do that morning was the mundane, and it was as if she was discovering old memories, memorizing them, and then erasing them resolutely, preparing for a new version of the future: clearing the sink with empty cups, rubbing out the stains left from breakfast, and the clothes that still needed hanging on the line. She was still a mother, after all, and would always be one, and this to her was a kind of comfort.

She checked every room and folded the sheets tightly on the bed and ran her fingers over the dust that had collected on the dressers.

She walked outside into the fog that was lifting from the warm rains that morning, and walked to the back of the house, and rung out the clothes that had been left there the night before, the ones that she'd forgotten about.

She swept the steps and walked over to the chickens, throwing their feed in sandy bursts at them.

She walked over to the cows and filled their troughs with water. She scanned the garden to see if there were any vegetables ready to pick, and a few soft ruby-colored tomatoes were ready, so she thumbed them off their stalks and carried them in her skirts back to the house.

꩜

After breakfast, Maksim and Lesia came running towards her as she sat outside, careering their bodies around the edge of a chair, narrowly missing the table, and falling into Julia's side. Slava padded out after them. Julia was folding clothes into a bag, putting favorite books on top. She felt Maksim's warm little arms around her own, and she looked into his searching eyes. 'Where's your sister, mmm?' She looked across the garden as Lesia placed a ring of daisies around her head. 'Mama, look!' Slava shouted as she stood behind Lesia. She whispered in her ear and then the two of them began to sing. Maksim giggled and ran over to be with them.

Julia watched as their arms stretched wide, a song on their lips that she taught them, the Ukrainian words and melody surrounding the air around them, the sunlight on their faces. Julia murmured 'yes, well done' and smiled, as her shaking hands placed the children's last few toys into a canvas bag. They were still playing, their hands linked together, when Julia stood. She watched as Slava brushed the hair from Lesia's face, and that moment withered whatever was left of Julia's insides.

'We must leave soon, yes?' Julia announced to them.

'Mama?' Maksim pointed. 'Sad?' Slava followed his gaze. She was 6 now, and she observed her world keenly. The children padded over to her.

Julia crouched down and stroked his face. 'No, sweetheart. Not sad tears,' Julia cleared her throat. 'Happy ones. Too much love,' she smiled weakly.

Slava placed her hand on Julia's shoulder. 'Mama, what's wrong?'

Julia wiped her face with the back of her hand and moved forward to Maksim and Lesia. 'It's time to go on your little trip, sweetheart.'

'Oh, a picnic?' Lesia clapped excitedly.

Maksim looked up at Slava and back at Julia. 'A picnic? Mama, with you?'

'No, not with me.'

'What do you mean, Mama?' Slava frowned.

'Papa and I have people we know who will take you two on a little trip and you will stay with them…'

'— For how long?' Slava interrupted.

Julia couldn't answer. Lesia reached out for her arm and Maksim stood, distracted by the bag that Julia held next to her. 'I have your toys in here,' Julia patted the bag. 'And you will have lots of fun because these are good people.' Her chest felt heavy as she said it, because the truth was, she could only hope they were.

Julia stood up, and the twins placed their hands in her own. 'Come, let's make you a little lunch and then we'll go, yes?'

Slava looked back at the garden and ran back to grab the daisy crown and followed them inside. 'Mama?'

Julia turned around, letting go of the twins. 'Yes, rabbit.'

'Where are Lesia and Maksim going?'

'They'll stay with a nice family for a while.'

'But…'

'Can you put a dress on, please? You're going to Marta's.'

Slava paused, frowning, waiting for more of an explanation.

'Please do as I say.' Julia bit her lip: her curt tone wasn't for Slava, it was for the guilt. 'Thank you' she called out to her when she walked off.

After lunch, Henry took Slava to Marta's house, which was not too far from Elina and Iliya's house, and that knowledge levelled Julia with fresh pain and humiliation. Marta would surely know what had happened, and Elina more than likely told her.

Julia brought the canvas bag to the front door. She had packed a blanket, a small wooden cross, their favorite few pieces of clothing, a toy and a Ukrainian story book. She looked back at the two children walking towards her, walking towards the open door that would lead away from the house, towards the path, towards the car, towards the courthouse and through an entirely different door. One by one, they all walked down the steps, followed by Henry holding the bag, followed by Julia, as she shut the door behind her.

﹅

The black writing on the placard said Townsville State Department of Child Welfare. The building was as wide as it was tall, white boarded, with the roof extending not a bit too high in three separate points. The path curved gently towards the door, surrounded by green grass on either side and fences at the border of the property. It was expansive and lent itself to be friendly and warm, despite circumstance. She wondered what the house was like on the inside, what the children were like and what ages they were, what languages they spoke.

Walking towards it, Julia felt a sick panic in the center of her chest.

She looked behind her quickly and searched for somewhere to run, a path leading somewhere, anywhere, else. It was lunacy, she knew she'd make a spectacle of herself and Henry would probably have her arrested or worse, taken away from the family entirely. She watched Henry walk ahead, bags in hand, saw his footsteps; they were purposeful, unlike hers. He had a reason to be there, but did she? She wasn't sure anymore. Maybe her life was not made to have them in it, their beds, the extra food and money needed for them, maybe it was all superfluous; maybe giving them up to someone else was the ultimate selfless act, for them to be safe, to be looked after. She stood in between the twins, their hair tickling her thighs as they clung to her. She smiled. 'Come. Let's go in.'

At the door, the Australian lilt echoed in the rooms within. Henry went in first, she followed after.

They stood up from their chairs, a woman dressed in a simple green linen jacket and skirt, her dark blonde hair cascading in waves down to her shoulders, and shoes that were polished leather, and were probably bought new. A man stood next to her, a few inches taller, dark hair that had been doused with a pomade, combed to the side. Dark trousers, white shirt, tie. Bennett stood behind his desk.

'Hello, I'm Gordon, from welfare…'

'…and my name is Sarah. We work for the state and will be taking the children to their temporary home before they are formally adopted.' She stretched her hand out. Her skin felt soft, cold; thinly stretched around her delicate fingers, like a doll. They scanned Julia and the twins.

Julia nodded, clutching the children to her legs. As if feeling her hesitation, they responded by grabbing her skirt nervously, peering from behind it. 'Mama, carry.' Arms outstretched, waiting. Julia's instinct battled with what was expected of her. She felt an entire room watching her. She bent down and picked up Lesia, her body melting so perfectly into hers, like a thumbprint into dough. Maksim held onto her other leg.

'Here.' Julia shifted Lesia off her hip and slid her down to the floor, holding her small hand. She watched as this Sarah woman knelt down and touched Lesia on the arm. She bristled.

'Hi there, sweet girl. Are you excited to come and stay here, and play for a while?'

Lesia, confused, looked up at Julia and reached for her. 'Mama? Going?'

'No,' the word rode the crest of her sigh. 'No, Lesia, you and Maksim are going with these nice people.' She took her hand and gently guided it towards Sarah. Henry stood back and watched.

'Yes, your mummy is right, little one.' Sarah stood up and uttered every word as if it would break. 'You and your brother are coming to stay here. It'll be very fun, and you'll meet so many other children. Is that okay?'

Gordon spoke next, hurrying it along. 'Thanks Sarah, but it's a bit tricky, with the whole--' and he spoke this out of the side of his mouth '-- English language thing,' his palms made helpless shapes in the air. 'You know, it's a bit hard on all of them.' Julia looked at him and he forced a smile as she scowled. She knew enough English to know when someone was being distasteful.

'Ahh, yes, sure, this is all new to me.' Sarah folded her arms, and then dropped them quickly. Apologetically.

Bennett came forward. 'Mr. and Mrs. Rudnick, you've signed and dated the required forms here... the children will be brought to a temporary housing facility for children their age, where there will be a settling in period, and the official adoption will be more than likely two or so months in the future. At that time, we will also reissue you a new birth certificate to register Lesia and Maksim's new birth names. Does that all sound acceptable to you?'

Julia and Henry both nodded in agreement, and then Julia sensed the end of the meeting looming, so she reached out to Sarah, despite every cell of herself not wanting to.

'Miss—' She touched her arm, and then gestured towards the twins behind her—'it's okay, I will get them ready.' She stepped back and crouched down, holding the twins on each side of her, wrapping both arms around their tiny waists, her head in between theirs as she smelled their sugary skin.

She looked at their faces and hungrily memorized them: the new freckles that had recently scattered on the bridge of Maksim's nose, the dark blonde hairs that changed to white at Lesia's temples. The long eyelashes that had shone through suspended tears in the moments where she'd needed her. Julia raised her hand and placed her son's palm in hers, and it was a fraction of the size, so small and fat and unlined, like fresh dough.

Lesia's arm snaked around Julia's neck, and it felt so thin, like cold porcelain. In that moment, she saw them as they would be, without her: she saw them at 5, as their legs lengthened, and their cheeks hollowed slowly. And then at 10, as their hair thickened and lengthened, and they discovered newfound strength in their small limbs. At 15, when they would try and heal from broken hearts, and find joy in burgeoning love stories. And even at 20, when their bodies would find their grace and discover a world of their own.

She saw their entire, changing, vivid lives in that moment, and she indulged it and was broken by it, and it took every ounce of whatever strength she had left in the very bones of her not to collapse in absolute grief. She would do that later, alone. Grief was a thing that was always better when managed alone, her mother had told her.

'Be kind', she whispered, and then 'I love you,' as she backed away, but they both began to cry and fell into her arms. It was the hardest thing she had ever done in her life, letting go of them. She couldn't imagine that it would be the last time she would see their faces or say the words that comforted them. The thought was incomprehensible to her.

Sarah appeared by her side, and a door then opened to a different room, one that was behind Bennett's desk that she hadn't noticed before, and as Gordon held it open, Sarah took both twins by the hands and led them away.

'Mam*aaa*!' Lesia let out a protracted cry as she turned and saw that her mother wasn't walking with them.

'Please don't take my babies,' she mouthed silently, her tears collecting on her lips as she spoke, her body shaking in anguish, rooted to the spot, Lesia's eyes connecting to hers for the last time as the door closed.

꙳

Julia was unaware that she'd been standing there for five solid minutes, her face and neck slick with tears; she had sobbed silently, her hands in fists at her side, the sounds catching in her throat as her body tensed. She finally became aware that once Sarah and Gordon left, Henry had gone to the car, so the only person in the room with her was a young secretary tidying up files and gathering paperwork. Julia had seen when they'd first arrived.

Julia had been deconstructed in her shame, and left to gather herself, alone. She picked up her handbag absentmindedly and tried to find her coat, realized that she hadn't taken one, and so she stood, not understanding what to do with herself, or where to go. And then the only words she could muster were the ones that meant she might preserve some hope. She spoke, her voice fragile. 'Hello, miss?'

The girl turned, not a hair out of place, her glasses perched on her nose.

'I... I am the...' Julia stammered, not sure how to begin.

'I know who you are, I logged the appointment,' she replied, her eyes quizzical. 'Can I help you?'

'Can I write to them?'

'To whom?'

'My children.'

'I'm not sure that's not allowed, because firstly, they don't have a permanent home yet, and won't for a while, and secondly, the adoption is closed, and only after a certain age would they be allowed to look for you, and even then, only if their adoptive parents would allow it.' It was a list of hurdles that she presented, and Julia hung her head.

'Ah. Okay,' she shuddered as she caught her breath and the tears gathered in her eyes again. And then, the woman approached, and Julia saw she was young, probably no more than 21, and her eyes were kind, and her hair was more careless seen up close, wild wisps of it touching her thin neck and delicate shoulders. She reminded Julia of her sister.

'Listen, give it some time.' She then paused, looked past Julia through the doorway, and then back at her. 'Wait a moment.' And she walked over to Bennett's desk, opening a drawer and taking out a pen and paper and scrawling down letters and numbers. 'I'm probably not supposed to do this, but here.' She pressed a bit of paper into Julia's hand and looked intently at her. 'This is the address of where they'll be going, as there is an older couple that has been waiting for two children for over a year now. You could write, but I would wait for a while. And maybe one day...' the woman shrugged delicately, letting the small hope linger.

Without looking down, Julia placed it in her handbag and closed it. 'I'm so sorry,' she murmured. 'So sorry...my babies...'

'—no, I understand,' the woman interrupted, and paused as if to say something else; as if she too had had a broken heart that had been left to heal somehow. And then she changed, her face stiffening as she walked back out of the office, her stride with a purpose, holding the files that proved to anyone who'd possibly seen her, that she'd been so busy with her work that she spent a little while longer making sure it was all done properly.

Julia nodded, and turned on her heels and slowly walked towards the door, and she noticed that her handbag had nail marks pressed into the worn cream leather. And in that handbag, she remembered that she'd brought the twins' original birth certificates with her, not knowing whether Bennett needed it or not, but he hadn't because he had requested copies from the hospital, so they were still there, folded into two small squares, next to an address, invisible to everyone but her.

22

Melbourne

The radio in the kitchen crackled briefly with a weather bulletin, something about *Cairns* and *flood warning* as Irene turned the knob and found a station with classical music, before feeding the lamb roast in the oven and heading upstairs to the bathroom.

She washed her hands, wiping them on a towel that was folded neatly in the corner of the bathroom, and one by one, took down her hair from its nested bun, watching as it unfolded and dropped past her shoulders. She put each pin carefully in a glass box, and ran her fingers from temple to nape, her scalp aching from the past few days' happenings. She looked at her face—her eyes were tired, but the black of her lashes and the powder on her cheeks were all still in place; there had been no tears. She wondered if there would be, one day, but for now, all she felt was grateful.

She undid the clasp on her watch and set it down, walking down the hallway, and saw Bill standing in the doorway of the small bedroom opposite their own.

'Hey.' She joined him and folded her arms across her chest. She watched, contentedly, as the two children in front of them explored their space, fat arms out, eyes wide, toddling unsteadily as they reached for things they had never seen before: the unfamiliar beds, the soft, cool, pillows, squealing at the beautifully painted toys' they touched these new objects to see how they lived in this world, and what their place was.

Their beds were separate, both solid wood frames, the sheets and pillows decorated in whites and pale yellows, embroidered with ducklings.

There was a noble wooden rocking horse in the corner, positioned as if it had waited its whole life to be ridden. There was a small wardrobe up against the wall full of lovely clothes, and books laid out on the dresser that sat underneath the window, with two stuffed rabbits on either side of the pile.

'Mama?' Said the girl as she stood by the rocking horse, her fingers entwined in its yarn mane. Her eyes were searching Irene's-- she wasn't calling for her but another. 'Mama.'

'Yes, Roslyn? What do you need, sweetheart?'

Confused at the name, the girl wandered over to her brother who was standing unsteadily at the window, pointing. She grabbed his body to steady herself and then placed a little hand on the window, the fields beyond her winking in the sunlight.

'Mama, mama' she murmured softly, eyes searching.

Irene turned to Bill and saw water in his eyes, soft regret etched in his face.

She smiled and grabbed his forearm, squeezing it gently. 'Bill. Listen. We'll be alright, sweetheart. They'll understand that their life started when we found them, and that's all they'll ever have to know.'

'I realize that, honey. But God, what a crazy thing, this.' He ran a hand through his hair and looked over at Irene. 'We have kids now. A boy and a girl. They were someone's and now they're *ours*.' He looked over at her. 'Will they be alright?'

Irene smiled stiffly; a deep breath lodged in her chest. 'Why wouldn't they be?'

'Well, there's a mother out there. We don't know her story. Will we? Will they, ever?' He nodded to the twins, sat on the floor, playing with a few wooden blocks. 'I mean, am I right to even bring it up?'

'Why do they need to know her story?'

Ed shrugged. 'Because they might want to know where they came from, one day.'

Irene frowned. 'Are you regretting this?'

'No, of course not, honey. We're so lucky. I'm just thinking out loud, is all.'

Irene patted him on the back and linked her arm through his. 'I know. I guess we'll have to play it by ear, really. They didn't come from the best of backgrounds, really.'

'How do you know?'

'An immigrant family— sugarcane farmers. Not exactly the most stable environment.'

'Sure, I guess.' Ed smiled as Roslyn looked up at him, showing him a book that she'd found. 'Do you think they were happy?'

'I don't know. I assume so. But we could drive ourselves crazy second guessing this. The most important thing is that we can love them, and take care of them, and tell them that we wanted them so much, that God granted our wish.'

Ed leaned his head towards Irene and kissed her on the cheek. 'You're right. They'll be happy.'

She looked up at him, her eyes resolute. 'Of course, they will be, we'll always make sure of it. There won't be a reason to look back. Only forward.' She smoothed her hair, and a thin gold bracelet gleamed on her wrist.

'One idea, though.'

'Yes?'

'We should leave something for them. After we're gone.'

Irene frowned. 'Maybe. We have a long time before we need to discuss that.'

Bill nodded. He felt it was the right thing to do, and he knew Irene would soften over time.

'Right. Let's get the table set for dinner, yes?'

And before he could respond, she walked away, the hallway echoing with her footsteps, the children's laughter behind her.

23

Stratford, May 1953

The storm warnings had come over the radio for the last week, but in their kitchen, Slava was bursting with excitement, her hands expressive and flying, just like Julia's used to, when she was little. She didn't know, and didn't care, what a 'cyclone' was.

'Mama, at school today I read out loud to the class from my book. And the teacher clapped at how well I *eee-nun--see-ayted*!' Slava took her tie off and partially unzipped her wool pinafore, her short bob bouncing along with her energetic fidgeting. 'Ach, these uniforms are *so* itchy!' She proceeded to fully unzip the pinafore and throw it to the side, along with her tie. The January day had been warm, and yet the school required it, and it unnerved her no end. 'There!' She stood triumphantly in her underwear and a white short sleeve shirt, her fists aloft. 'Much better!'

'Go and play outside, there's no reason for you to be in the house.' Her voice was tired, and her wrists ached as she rolled dough, and prepared the carrots for dinner later. Her morning was spent doing accounts at a small bank in Stratford, a part time job that she'd started once Slava started school full time. It had been a pleasant distraction and the last several years passed her by quietly, though she felt more tired than she ever had.

Julia heard a wooden toy clatter to the floor in Slava's room, and she spoke before she could stop herself. 'Maks— '. She caught her breath as she felt a stinging in the center of her stomach. Still, even now, their names came to her so easily. She couldn't help but hear remnants of their voices in the house, echoes of their footsteps down the stairs, blades of grass scattered on the floor from their daily adventures. They would be forgetting now: forgetting how to curl their tongue to utter the language that they had been brought up to speak, forgetting Julia's songs and the rhythm of her voice as they fell asleep. And though she tried her hardest to remember, her memories of them were slowly fading, and their voices would echo uncomfortably in her ear, like a stranger's.

'Ah, and again they say the same thing,' Julia sighed, and turned the radio down, a carrot rolling away from her grip. It had been reporting for days about the storm and she'd heard enough. The first one was bad enough: four years ago, before the twins (she often used their births as a kind of marker in her life) and shortly after they had had settled into their house, the winds arrived, howling and lopping the tops off the trees, rains piercing the earth like nails. She had never experienced destruction to this degree (oh, it wasn't nearly as bad as the storm a few years back, they'd tell here later on, as if to make her feel even remotely better). She felt confused and insecure, watching it all unfold as little Slava clung to her skirts and called out for her too many times for a reassurance that she didn't have. It was one of the very first times that she'd questioned the purpose of their life together; she had seen a life that was foreign to her, a language that wasn't explained and a world that she had no rulebooks for, and she was meant to proceed, unaided. That was the first seed of resentment planted, and it had flourished intensely.

'Hey, Hank, would'ya help us out with these here boards?'
The steel clang of the bells erupted in the distance, and it didn't announce a celebration, for no one was at the church for joy, or for mourning. It was empty, and the echo was to warn of the weather to arrive. Everyone that was able, had left their houses that afternoon to prepare, to shield and secure from winds and rain, and to encourage that this was

nothing unheard of. Henry was in town that morning and the warning bells had pealed just as he was approached by the butcher.

'Yeah, sure Al.' Henry cringed. 'Give me a minute.' No amount of reminding people would help, not even after four years of living in Stratford: the iteration of his given name had taken many forms, and so it was a useless cause: no one ever bothered to learn to say his name correctly. There was always a 'do you have a shorter name, buddy' thrown around since their arrival those many years ago. Almost immediately, he'd been christened with a new, easier, name, which would help him fit with the group of laborers in the cane fields. He considered them all a boring, provincial collection of busybodies, but he reluctantly accepted it, for this was a lesson in humility, though the gossip would travel that it quite curious that a loving mother would punish her child with a name as ridiculous as 'Hironimus', and 'Henry' was ever so formal, so 'Hank' it was.

He raised a few thin planks of wood upright, a hammer and nails jangling in the leather pouch that hung over his cotton trousers. It was almost useless, this preparation, because the farmhouses were sparse in material to begin with: thin pieces of driftwood reinforcing door frames, thick tape across windows, and moving crockery and furniture to recessed corners of their farm. It was all they could do, really, and pray that the destruction would be minimal. The last years had seen Henry successfully earning enough money to buy more land around their house, and they'd developed it into a bigger farm, and it reminded them of home. A few more cows, goats, and feral cats that lingered and languished on the porch. The expanse of it all connected Henry and Julia with a thin thread, but it was enough, and now they'd met enough people that they would have the help if they needed it, and a bit of the burden was lifted. They'd arrived here so naive and hopeful, off a steamship from war, like artifacts from a building that was destroyed, and now, it was a life that made sense to them finally, despite the pain at the edges. Earlier, he had looked back and saw Julia holding Slava's hand and carrying a basket with her other one, Slava filling it with eggs that she had collected, and his heart felt a little less of the anguish that he had privately endured.

'I have never asked you, actually—.' Henry embraced a pile of thick brown parcel paper that had just been shoved into his arms. '— about your name.'

'Mine?' Al's eyes that were perpetually half-lidded, as if he'd just woken up, or the sun had always been too bright for him. He stared at Henry as if a strange smell had been put in front of him, and ran his palm across his shirt, marking it with dirt.

'Yes. Is it short for anything?'

'Well,' The man scratched his head and paused, as if no one had ever asked him this before, and he was sure no one would again. 'Albert. But my mum called me that, and only when I was bein' a right old pain.' He smiled at another memory. 'My dad always called me Al, come to think of it.'

'It was my mother that called me by a shorter name., she'd always liked *Henry*. My father called me Hironimus.'

'I thought your name was Henry.'

'That's my shorter name.'

'Oh, that's right. You told me you had a big long name but god, that's a hard one to say. Do ya mind that I say *Hank* ?'

And maybe Henry didn't after all, he thought. Maybe Al had asked Henry for help because he knew he was good for something, and although he probably thought of him as the immigrant with the pretty, sad, wife and the tearaway blond girl, maybe this was a way that they fit him onto the page of their lives, in faint pencil script; this could be the way he would be understood if only for a short while.

Henry looped rough twine under his elbow and back toward and across his palm to make an oval, again and again and again until he could put it all over his shoulder. 'Albert, I don't mind.'

Al caught the joke and laughed, clapping him on the back. 'Let's get a beer.' And the two men walked off, the oval shape of sweat soaking through the backs of their shirts.

➤

'Mama?' Slava grabbed at her hip and embraced her. 'Walk with me when I'm on your leg, that's funny, I like when you do that.'

'Oh, kitten, you're too heavy and I have to prepare dinner. Ask your father.'

'He's working outside. He doesn't like me bothering him and messing things, he says. I get in trouble.' Her bright blue eyes were apologetic. She wondered if he resented the image of his daughter, sometimes: the blonde child with silvery blue eyes that looked nothing like him, or his wife. They were dark and she was light. She represented something unknown to him.

'Mama?'

'Yes?'

'I love you.'

She looked down at the now tall, bright thing at her side, and returned to the carrots.

The house was quiet because Henry had left, as he usually did after dinner. The sky that night had turned dark unusually early, and Julia was busy sitting with Slava, whispering the flourishing ends of a fairy tale.

His solitary ritual began the same way each night: around nine o'clock, he'd check his shirt pocket, feeling for the soft packet of cigarettes, and then roll up the sleeves of his shirt as he walked out the screen door to the small square of land out front a stone's throw away from the cane fields. The wooden and glass structure was only as high as he was tall, and it had been there when they first arrived at the house. It was abandoned and had overgrown, dehydrated weeds, but it was just enough to house something all his own. What would you use this for, Julia had asked. Orchids, he had replied, and then began a small collection that he retrieved from a florist in Stratford, who in turn had traveled to Fiji to procure them from an orchid farm.

Tonight, his hands hovered tender and large over their thin skeletons; lips and spurs never attaching to the soot on his fingertips, his eyes languid and worshipful over each curve. A chipped tumbler held the dregs of his vodka and balanced timidly on the edge of a short wooden stool beside him. He'd thrown that stool across the room in a fit of anger a few months ago and had tried to repair the legs, but he hadn't done it very well, so it wobbled.

'You have yet to fix that,' Julia pointed out, leaning against the frame. She had been watching him for a while now, and he hadn't noticed.

'Yes, I'm aware.'

'Okay, well,' she stopped, wanting to say something else of purpose. 'What's the use in a broken thing?'

His jaw went rigid. He looked up at Julia and plucked the back of his shirt, moon shapes of sweat marking his armpits. 'I'll fix it, I'm aware.' He prodded it with his hand. 'It's still useful.'

She watched as a tin-framed lamp cast a tall silhouette of his bent frame against the glass panels of the greenhouse.

'How long will you be?'

'Does it matter?' The corner of his mouth flattened into his cheek. 'To you, I mean. Does it matter?' He leaned on his knee and waited, examining her face. It was plain and drawn, and he imagined what she had accomplished this evening: he imagined that she had quietly swept the floor after dinner, he imagined that she had wiped the back of her wet hands on the front panel of her skirt, and smoothed her hair back off of the neck that he had touched so often. He imagined her to be the girl he'd seen, that one day when he'd projected a future memory of her, as all men and women do. He looked at her now and felt a sour taste sat at the back of his throat. So much had changed, though he loved her still, but his anger hovered faintly above him like a moving cloud, following him, setting the rains on him when he thought of the past. He lit another cigarette and turned back.

Julia rubbed her palm with the opposite thumb, watching the shadows battle the creamy yellow lamplight. 'Things matter, yes.' She shrugged her shoulders. 'Maybe, only to me.' They both kept a polite distance from the other. Politeness was survival.

He stood up, misting a petal— it was the darkest red, the color of clotted blood— watching as the water settled and veiled.

Julia pursed her lips at his silence.

'I'm going to bed.' Julia looked up and felt the heaviness of the air. The farmlands were peaceful and deserted. She turned on her heel, her skirts kicking at the back of her knee as she walked into the night.

Not long after, as he closed the glass door behind him and the lamplight had flickered its end, he drew on the last of his cigarette. He stood in the dark, feeling the air change direction; beneath the layers of his skin, underneath his clothes, he felt it. He speculated, as he sometimes did when he saw the house from this distance (a dark, small thing lit from within) he wasn't sure he could have been anything in particular in his life, but he could survive it, survive all of it, and wasn't that the point? Love wasn't the thing that he could understand. Perseverance was. And maybe within perseverance is a commitment to loving someone.

He stepped forward, taking a quick look back at the orchids, protected in their small, dark space, and walked towards the house. His footsteps heavy in his battered and torn boots, he finished the last of his cigarette, the embers dying in the ground as he crushed out the final spark. The winds picked up momentum, and he only vaguely noticed the glass shudder in response to the increasing winds.

—

She thought she was dreaming, when the howling started. It wasn't even dawn yet, and Julia sat bolt upright in bed, quickly realizing that she was definitely not dreaming. The wind was whipping around the house, slamming against the shutters, forcing the trees to bend and huddle and beg. The family had weathered wet season successfully before, but this was different. It was angry and inhospitable and relentless in its pursuit to destroy. She ran into the kitchen and tried to switch on a radio. Static. She checked the phone line. Dead. Henry was still asleep. She debated waking him as it was so early. So, she went back to bed and prayed for it to stop.

It didn't.

—

5:45am. Something hit the house, it sounded like a piece of wood. Then on the other side, a cracking sound. More wind, higher pitched sounds and moaning, like an animal dying. She got out of bed again, and this time Henry started to stir. She padded to the kitchen and looked out the window. Sheets and sheets of grey, horizontal rain, the sky threateningly dark and furious. 'Henry!' She hissed as she ran back into their room. 'HENRY!'

'What, what is it? Why are you panicking?'

'There's a storm out there, it's bad. I don't know what's happening.'

He ran out with her to the window. 'Ahh God damn it, the fields will be flooded soon.' He ran back to get dressed in anything he could find. 'Check the animals!' he shouted back.

Julia threw on a coat and boots and opened the door carefully, forcing her way outside. The winds were extraordinary; She felt like she could be lifted off so easily, her arms and legs tethered to nothing and everything all at once. She made it outside, clutching the side of the house as the winds howled, running against the rains and into the pens to check on the cows and chickens. She cupped her hands around her mouth and called, shrieked, shouted, and waited for sounds of reply. She kept walking, each footstep lifting off before she could plant it. And then she found them all, huddled together, matted chocolate and white hides, lying in a corner of the pen lamenting. The goats in the next pen, bleating their distress, a strange dog howling underneath the house, cats mewing their discontent, their protection in the form of something that could very easily kill them. She didn't know what to do, and she watched them helpless. She needed Henry to guide her.

She ran back to see him surveying the damage on one outside of the house, soaked through, there was an honesty in his face that she recognized from long ago. 'I'm going in, the animals seem to be fine, but even if they weren't, there's nothing we can do.'

'Okay, go in. Make sure Slava's room is secure.'

'How?'

'Just... I don't know! Take things off shelves, get her on the ground, just *go!*' Henry ran to herd the animals to somewhere safe and disappeared from view.

᠅

7:30am. Slava had been up for an hour already, the wind coming in through the rooms with unrelenting force. 'Mama! Papa!' She was sat in the middle of the room, by the door, shaking, huddling under blankets as Julia ran in. 'What's happening?!'

'Wet season... just more wet than usual I guess,' Julia joked feebly and walked towards her. And just then, a loud cracking sound interrupted her, and she veered to the window and saw a tree split in half as if by an otherworldly force and fall to the ground. *Henry*. She ran back outside, shouting for him, her voice suffocated by the winds, every breath drawn out of her. She finally heard him faintly, and saw him in the driving rain, a small body moving across, eerily bright. She stood resolutely, gripping the side of the door, letting the wind whip her hair, the weight of her dress increasing as the hem absorbed millions of drops of warm rain.

'Mama? What's happening?' Slava sat huddled under their blankets still.

'It's fine, Papa is sorting it out. It's fine.' She turned back into the house, and then heard him clattering up the steps. He pushed through the door, breathless.

'Jesus Christ, it's bad out there. It's as if the world has been stamped flat.' A crack then silenced them all, louder this time, and it came from the left side of the house, as if the sky had imploded. Then a howl against the window, pushing in. She looked over at him and saw him reach for her. 'Julia, down. Get down!' And not a moment after he reached her, she crouched over Slava and he embraced them both, a pile on the floor, just as the window cracked in half and shattered completely, sending shards of wet glass and pouring rain into the middle of the room. They waited. Slava was crying.

'Shhhh…. shhhhh,' Julia whispered. 'Stay quiet.' Just then, another aggressive gust of wind bellowed through the other window, crossing through the center of the house and lifting it up, an invisible hand unlatching the entire house and setting it back down like a toy onto the earth.

'Uhm', Slava whimpered, her nails digging into Julia's arm.

'It'll pass, Slava. Be patient.'

It took until late that afternoon for the winds to stop and the rains to slow, and it was only then, when people were safe to venture delicately out of their houses, that the devastation began to surface. It was oddly peaceful. Julia and Henry stood outside the house, speechless at how much flooding there was. The first two steps leading up to their house were submerged. The sugar cane drooped inches from the ground. There was no electricity for miles. It was a wasteland.

'How am I supposed to fix this?' He sat down on the top step, lighting a cigarette. 'How the *hell* am I supposed to see past this? *This?*' He waved his hand at the scene in front of him.

He walked down the stairs, stopping at the second one, his toes hitting the water. He stood, looking down, trapped for the time being by his own country. He understood the feeling. He looked across, to his left. He'd hoped against hope that the greenhouse would be intact. Julia joined him, and placed her arm through his, and they scanned the land: thin panes of glass and pieces of metal lying like a battered corpse on the ground. Pieces of pottery lay strewn across the ground like confetti, and underneath all of it, black-purple petals crushed underneath. The mixture of soil and the perfume of the crushed flowers on the flat earth combined to create a metallic, iron-rich fragrance; if it was a funeral, he would have wept.

24

April 1954

The greenhouse hadn't been rebuilt even a year later, and they were still finding bits of glass and gnarled pieces of steel that had been carried by the winds as far as the trees at the perimeter of the farm. They had gathered much of the carcass of wood and metal from various parts of the farm and had given it to the town to use for scraps. The town itself was still healing, and shops were slowly, delicately, coming to life as if recovering from an illness. The flatlands had been erased, and the farmhouses had been emptied.

None of the animals had survived, so they used what they could from the flesh and buried the rest. Julia wore trousers and a short sleeve shirt today, as she dug in the garden, planting new seeds. Slava was sat in her underwear next to her, the heat of the day on their backs.

'Mama,' Slava sunk her tiny hand into the dirt and removed a worm. 'Do you think Papa is sad?'

'About what, sweetheart?' Julia couldn't face a question about the twins, and she set her teeth in anticipation.'

'The little ones.'

'What little ones?'

'The flowers.'

The greenhouse. 'Oh, you mean the purple flowers?'

'Yes. Those. He was always in that little house with the little 'ones', the little flowers.'

Julia sat back on her calves; her knees folded underneath her. 'Those were his orchids, yes.' She looked across at the land that was empty now. 'He worked hard protecting them.'

'He loved them.'

Julia smiled at her daughter. 'He did.' She looked across at the empty farmhouse. 'He loved them very much.'

'Will he get more?'

Julia began to dig again, her tears wetting the soil. 'No, sweetheart. We won't be getting any more.' She looked over at Slava. 'Hey,' she whispered conspiratorially.

Slava squinted in the sun. 'Yes, Mama?'

Julia hooked a finger and Slava leaned closer to her. Julia suddenly wrapped her in her arms and nuzzled her neck. And Slava erupted in giggles as the soil sprinkled off of Julia's hands onto her sunlit hair.

That evening the family had celebrated Henry's birthday, and Julia remembered what that meant. Her heart freshly ached, as if they'd been gone only minutes, and it was then, after the sticky sweetness of cake had faded and the coffee had been poured and Slava was asleep, that she knew she couldn't do this anymore. Not here. Not anywhere, really, but having the constant reminder of ghosts that never returned, it was too much for her now. The cyclone had been an ending and a new beginning, yes, but the emptiness was still there. Old memories living in the walls that surrounded her.

Julia leaned over the table and watched him as he sipped his coffee. She knew him well enough now to know that his thoughts wheeled in his head.

'Henry. What are you thinking about?'

He put his cup down and it rattled into the saucer. He spun it slowly with a finger. 'We spent a year rebuilding this farm.'

'I know. It's getting better, slowly.' She wondered where this would go.

Henry stood up. The room where they'd been through so much, the house where they never seemed to stray far from, the pain and the arguments and the memories of love lost and gained; it suddenly occurred to him that he'd grown accustomed to it. He tapped his chest pocket and slowly reached for a cigarette. They had grown accustomed to life as it was, here, reinventing the story in the same spot.

'I have an idea.' He snapped his lighter shut, and flicked it open again.

Julia held her breath. She wasn't sure what he would say all of a sudden and she braced herself as if she would fall into the sea.

'I don't think the journey for us ends here.'

Julia slowly let out her breath. 'You're talking as if we're dying.'

He placed his hands in his pockets and walked slowly around the room, a skeptical laugh at his throat. 'Granite.'

'What?'

He stopped pacing and faced Julia. 'You told me once I was made of granite. And you are made of dreams. Rebirth.'

Julia warmed at the memory, but it saddened her. So much had happened since then, and she wasn't sure she believed it now. 'Yes, I remember. But what does that mean?'

'It means that we have to keep going. I don't think we're meant to be here.'

'Why?'

'Well, most importantly, because there's literally nothing left here. My work has been rebuilding this farm, and not earning as much money as I could be. We are living off of what we have saved and there won't be much left unless we change course.'

Julia folded her arms. 'What are you suggesting?'

'We move.'

Julia rested her arms on her head and then raised them up, pleading. 'Our entire life has been about moving!' She dropped her hands on the table. 'Where?'

'I've been thinking for the past two years about Sydney. I've been planning. Meeting with people. Seeing where the opportunities lie. We need to earn money, and we can't do it here anymore. Sydney has jobs for people like us, I don't necessarily care what it is, but it will be a sight better than cutting cane for 18 hours a day. It's a city, we can rent a small place like we did in Germany.'

Julia shot him a skeptical look.

Henry walked over and sat down. 'It will be temporary. But cities are where the opportunities are. We have to move with the tide.'

Julia groaned, and reached over for his cigarette, which both shocked Henry and connected him to her briefly. She inhaled on it and gave it back to him. 'And isn't that the way, for us, Henry.' The smoke rippled out of her mouth. 'Isn't that how we survive. The leopard that changes his spots for his world.'

Henry lit a fresh cigarette, searching her face. 'God knows we've made a meal out of the misfortune of last two years.'

Julia stood up and walked over to the window by the door. She saw so little of what had been. 'When will we come back to ourselves, I wonder.'

'When the time is right for us to.' Henry tapped fresh ashes into the tray beside him. 'But we can never get back to who we were. Life doesn't work that way. We learn more about who we are when we look ahead.'

Later that night, after Henry had retired to bed, Julia remembered again that it was his birthday, their birthday. Soon, this house would be empty, deserted of the lives that they had created, and she would be gone, and so she decided that she could write. She would write to them finally, and she would see them if only for a second.

She scanned the shelf behind her for a piece of paper and then saw it: the faded book that she had read to them so many times, about the lost mitten and the family of animals that had burst it at the seams. She opened it and wistfully shuffled the edges in her fingertips, stopping on something inside: two pressed wildflowers that they'd picked for her only a year ago, and that she'd casually promised to keep but then actually did. She'd forgotten about this, and it flooded her memory with their faces and their voices and their laughter. She ran her fingers over the small dried husks and flat petals and was grateful for the discovery, as she placed it back on the shelf and began to write, her tears staining the paper.

Once she finished, she folded it and walked over to her bedroom. Henry was already asleep, the deep sound of his breathing filling the quiet room. She padded to the dresser and opened a drawer, knocking over her handbag in the process. She turned but saw that he didn't stir. She picked up the handbag to replace it and saw the contents of it had spilled, and as she picked them up, she saw a small piece of paper with delicate and even handwriting. It was an address in Melbourne. Her heartbeat quickened and her face flushed. She'd forgotten that she'd kept this too, and immediately returned it to her handbag with the letter beside it, and snapped it shut.

　　　　　　　　　　　　🕊

It was a week later when Julia walked solemnly down a quiet street in Melbourne, her pockets now empty, her throat tight, her hands trembling. She had been so close. She had almost seen their faces.

She had heard their laughter; she had seen the house. She knew they were happy without her, and it was a small comfort. But it would be the last time her footsteps would take her anywhere near them. The tide was receding under her feet again, but this time, she would be different. This time, she would lock away a part of herself. And with each mile that took her back to Stratford, each road that she walked, each frame of landscape that passed by her window seat on the bus— she would grow stronger still, until this memory healed into a faded scar, like the one on her face.

Just before she arrived at the bus stop, she passed by a stone with heavy red-painted wooden doors, worshipers filing in slowly for service. She looked at the engraved plaque. St. Maria Goretti Immaculate Church. She said a silent prayer that someday, she would find them, and kept walking.

　　　　　　　　　　　　🕊

Over the next year, the family had resettled in Sydney— they had found space in a hostel in the center of town, and Henry began to work for a wealthy property developer, collecting rent from tenement buildings down by the docks. Though the work was menial and occasionally hostile, he was the only one in the group of migrant workers who insisted on wearing a suit, as if he could see more for himself than this. It was a pleasing arrogance that caught the eye of the developer, and over time, he kept a watchful eye on this tall, dark-eyed man who kept to himself and didn't talk much.

Over the course of several months, he developed a liking for Henry, and would call him into his office for a quick chat, finding more about who he was and where he had come from, and what family he had. It was on one of those occasions that he told Henry about his cousin in New York.

'You haven't ever been, I assume.' the man lit up a fat cigar and unbuttoned his jacket, revealing a silk waistcoat. He had a paunch that matched the roughness of his face, and fat fingers that splayed out, a thumb hooked into his pocket.

'No sir, I have not.' Henry sat uneasily.

The man cleared his throat. 'I sometimes forget that you're a Uke, a spillover from the war.'

Henry was used to these kinds of conversations. They didn't matter to him anymore.

'Reason is, I think there's something about you.' He chewed on the end of the cigar. 'Something that I think I could use you for.'

'And what would that be?'

'Work. You and a load of other immigrants that have gusto. Fire. Mettle.'

'I'm not sure what you mean.'

The man leaned forward. 'New York. I have a cousin who has a few buildings in the city. A part of the city, anyway, called Brooklyn. He'll need people like you.' He lit the end of his cigar again, took a few puffs, and leaned back.

Henry was interested. 'What kind of work?'

'Oh, very wonderful and amazing. Job of a lifetime.' The man smiled, knowingly overselling it, his bald head glistening as he sat behind his oak desk. 'Beautiful buildings that need work and managing. He needs me to ship over a whole load of you to him, and he'll sponsor it. God knows both of us are rich enough, and there are too many of you here, crawling around as it is. Australia needs a bit of a clean out.' He stared at Henry. 'Well?'

Henry flattened his mustache with his fingers, his breath even. 'Where would we live?'

'Tenement housing. Everywhere, there are people dropping off boats over there, like little ants, getting work. It's the American Dream, son.' The man was only ten years older than Henry but looked and acted as if he'd stumbled into money and grabbed it all voraciously. Greedily. 'What do you say?'

Henry closed his eyes and wondered if this decision would finally be the one to destabilize him. Or maybe it was the one that would build him back up again.

25

Julia stood at the side of a pale, white, steel ship painted with huge black letters **ORSOVA**, Sydney harbor surrounding her and countless others waiting to board. Black smoke poured out of the top of the ship like a boiling kettle, simmering, waiting for its owner to claim it. Spires of metal protruding into the sky, life rafts secured up at the top, tugboats tethered to its side. It all felt too familiar. She turned to watch as office buildings stood tall and watchful, rooted in their places, an unchanging landscape to her constantly changing one. Though it was so large, the ship projected a kind of submissiveness: it was tied to the docks, on both sides, with giant ropes the width of two of her legs, if not more. It looked strangely submissive, this incredibly grandiose beast. It sat and waited for them all.

She held Slava's hand, gripped it tightly as if reassuring herself that this was all real, all right, all supposed to happen. Slava stood still, her recently bobbed hair glossy and thick underneath a hat. Her dress was thick, layered with a sweater and coat in preparation for the unknown weather changes. They were all ready to board, Henry had already given over all of their possessions and they'd signed the passenger list.

In comparison, it was a more comfortable journey than the passage to Australia. *Leaving is nicer, it seems*, she thought romantically. There was talk of fresh food and music and rooms that have quaint portholes to watch the world go by. She didn't know what Henry had paid for, and what they could afford, and she was careful in her expectations.

'Three weeks or so, they say,' a woman leaned towards Julia, clutching a pamphlet and fanning her face. And Julia assessed her, as women do, quickly and surreptitiously: she had tight red curls gathered underneath a small cream-colored pillbox hat with lace edges and wore a dress that cinched at her waist and was the buttery color of late-autumn sunflowers. She smelled extraordinary, like musty roses and lilies, and hanging off her thin wrist was an impractically small beige handbag. 'Good gracious, three infernal weeks stuck on this thing. Well. At least there's decent food.'

'Mmm. Yes, three weeks.' Julia nodded, immediately chastising herself for speaking to this woman. The woman smiled, her claret-red lips revealing teeth that hadn't touched a drop of wine or smoked a single cigarette. 'So. America as well, then?' Julia was taken aback by the light conversation, and she smoothed her hair.

'Sorry?'

'America. You are *going* there, yes?' her words were deliberately slow, but it was imperceptible to Julia.

'Ah. America. Yes,' she nodded a few too many times, and then once she said it out loud, it felt real, as if a missing brick in a wall had been found. Julia was too conscious of her own thoughts to hear that the woman had whispered something about 'infernal immigrants' before she moved aside.

᠉

One of the first things Julia noticed when they boarded was that there were soft lounge chairs. And tables with smooth wooden corners. And oddly shaped glass ashtrays. And crisp, white napkins on tablecloth-draped tables in the main dining area. It was as if someone had poured the contents of a wealthy man's house straight into the belly of a ship. She was staring, amazed that such a thing existed.

'Madam, please keep going, tourist class is down below,' a steward sniveled and interrupted her thoughts, though he didn't realize she'd knowingly been holding up the line.

'This, it's all so wonderful,' she gestured. She'd never seen anything so grand that made her feel so insignificant.

'First class, madam', he responded, staring at her as if he'd smelled something awful.

'Mmm. Yes. Yes of course,' and deliberately, slowly, walked in the direction he'd pointed towards. She had learned to stand tall in the face of ignorance.

'You did that on purpose,' Henry admonished with laughter in his eyes.

'Of course, I did.'

The family finally reached the lower level, and then it was onward to find their cabin: past the toilet room, past the hall with the hot machinery spitting steam, past many crowded other cabins with families and couples and around the corner from another set of rooms, this time used for the storage of medical equipment. And then a small oval door, and they saw what their space for the next many weeks would be: a small room decorated in green and yellow plaid cotton fabric and brown tones. There was a small wooden dresser that was secured to the wall, a sink and cabinet, and two beds, one on top of the other, in bunk-fashion. There was one toilet and one shower, and they were down the hall, and were communal.

They dropped their bags in a heap and tried to remember where the dining hall was, which now, looking back, seemed a gargantuan journey. 'Christ. *Davai*, Slava, come with me,' Julia grabbed her hand. 'Let's have a look around.' As she left the cabin, she turned to see Henry leaning against the tiniest porthole, half the size of his head.

'Do you want to come with us?'

'No. You go. I can meet you later.'

The ship felt like a small city, teeming with people dressed in immaculate silks and hats with grosgrain ribbons, men in suits carrying leather briefcases; it all felt as if she were in a dream, or part of a large theater, and background players were the ones that looked like Julia: plain cotton dresses and sensible shoes, hair tied back and faces slightly reddened from exercise, or fresh air. Slava was in awe of it all, walking the decks with her parents, their hair whipping across their faces, listening to stories about this big city called New York that they would arrive in, and the new lives that would unfold for them.

In the weeks ahead, Julia would find time for reflection, and search for quiet moments where she was alone. The pages of her life had been scattered, but she felt that someday she would find the missing ones and stitch the story back together again— there was still hope there. It wasn't just because she had kept the birth certificates. Henry had reminded her that she was made of dreams. And when the breezes combined with the water to cool the air surrounding her face, she looked at the sea and sky as they pursed the horizons together. And she finally almost felt whole again.

Motherland

*Like billowing clouds, like the incessant gurgle of the brook,
the longing of the spirit can never be stilled.*

— Hildegard von Bingen

Part III
New York
1954-1981

26

New York

It was the 21st of April, and Henry had forgotten her birthday by five days, so Julia hadn't at all expected him to walk through the door home brandishing two wrapped packages under his arm.

The weather had been grey, and the sky had opened up, and the city pavements were flooded with hurried footsteps of people heading back home to dinners and musty hallways and rain pelting the windows. He placed his umbrella by the heavy door and took off his felt tweed fedora that he was almost never without. He shrugged off his overcoat, hooked it on the back of the door, and remembered to turn the three metal latches to lock it, as well as the one above that slid into the top of the frame. Sometimes he forgot how strange it was, to lock a door more than once, but this was New York, and he'd seen enough doors kicked off their hinges to remember.

Twenty years had passed since the steamship docked in San Francisco. Twenty years since they boarded a train that seemed to take months, and where Slava had suffered with a poorly stomach due to incredibly suspect food, and where their journey finally ended as the train pulled into Pennsylvania Station. Almost immediately to them the smell in the air was of steel and exhaust fumes, along with horns, voices crowds of people and children sitting on stoops and playing games in the street.

The family found a small two-bedroom tenement apartment, on

East 71st street on the corner of 1st, in an area called Lenox Hill ('but there are no hills, Henry! Madness.'). It was on the street, which was odd, to them anyway. There was no garden, there were only wide expanses of concrete surrounding doorsteps. The apartment was in the basement ('Henry, are we supposed to live underground?? Who lives like this?') and they soon found out that their landlord, Jeffy, hated children. He made Slava scream every time she saw him: he had the blackest skin she had ever seen ('like *molasses*, Mama'), and his face was covered in small, round and hard scars. He was short and loud and had thick curly hair piled on top of his head and wore orange trousers that were wide at the bottom and had an unusually long index finger that he used when he emphasized his words. 'I. Don'. Want. Crazy. Chil'ren.' He would bellow and then laugh, in a thick Jamaican accent. It gave Slava nightmares. It was only over the course of many months that she would learn of Jeffy's own dark story, that he told her in quiet moments: Jeffy's grandmother and grandfather had been slaves, and he explained what slaves were, and then and his own mother had married a white man and when he'd been born, his own father had rejected him and put out cigarettes on his face, and as a result he spent his entire life feeling a specific kind of anger at the world, and felt lonely in a city that was teeming with bodies.

 New York was full of colors and shapes and towers of concrete and brick, streets that scattered their capillaries of rubble and noise and life, and rats and sewers that steamed through the streets and subways that smelled faintly of urine and roasted peanuts, but it was beautiful in its own grotesque way. Julia had traveled from farmland and storms, open skies and animals (and insects) afoot, to a city that smelled like the color grey. It was wonderful and shocking and unnerving and incomprehensibly narrow. She enrolled Slava in a small school down the road, on 69th and 2nd, and it wasn't an easy transition for her. Slava spoke very little English, tinged with an Australian lilt, and her long blonde hair fell down her back, so she wore it in a plait wrapped in a circle on top of her head. She was indefinable and misplaced, which was seen as 'weird' by most of her peers. Slava's name was purposefully mispronounced as 'Slave', or 'Saliva', and these trials made her strong, but not without many tears. Julia had accepted a job at William H. Fisk Insurance Company: a neo-gothic monster of a building with a facade that looked like an overuse of architectural styles on South William street, as an assistant, and she enjoyed it, because it was the same, every day, and that monotony was comfortable to her. People found her likeable and hard-working, and they endeared themselves to this small, dark-haired woman who had kind, sad eyes and always kept a small photograph of what looked to be her parents, in her desk drawer. She arrived not a minute later than 9, and sometimes a minute before, and spoke very little, as her broken English was still an obstacle for her, though no one minded very much.

'Happy Birthday.' Henry handed her two boxes: one small one, wrapped neatly in gold paper, and one rectangular one, wrapped in red. His face was beautifully expectant.

She looked up from her sewing. 'Bit late, no?' Slava was out with friends and had left an array of clothes on the fabric couch. Their tights had holes in them, and they weren't going to fix themselves, so she'd been sitting with her stockinged legs, Indian style, carefully mending them.

'I know I know, but better than never.' He sat down next to her.

'Well, thank you.' She meant it. "That's sweet. But I didn't really ask for anything.'

'Yes, but I always hear you when we walk down Fifth and you stop and stare through the windows.' He took her sewing and placed it on a cushion and replaced it with the gifts. 'Open them.'

She looked at him with tenderness, a bit like a child, and gently undid the smaller parcel, her fingers weary from working all day. He watched her cautiously, ever so slightly wary but connected. 'I wasn't sure what you'd like, but I know you well enough that when I saw this, I thought it would suit you.'

The gold paper revealed a navy rectangular container, and in it was a bracelet: glittering strands of marcasite soldered into silver, strands as delicate as cobwebs, linked to each other and wrapped around oval pieces of flat, shining onyx. Black mirrors, six of them, surrounding her wrist as lightly as flower petals.

'Henry, my God. I love it. Where on earth did you find something like this?'

'Luckily there are a lot of little antique shops down by one of the buildings I manage down in Brooklyn, you know, by Prospect?' The owner showed me this, said it was made in Poland. I'm glad you like it.' His speech was unsentimental and somehow warm at the same time.

'I do, oh I do.' She started to open the second box, the larger of the two. 'And… this? Can't think what this might be.'

Before she even saw what was within, the paper seemed soaked with the smell of gardenia, lilacs and lilies; comforting and familiar. It smelled of wet grass and wildflowers and summers spent without care. It smelled of childhood. The red paper revealed a box on the inside, pale pink, the profile of a woman's face etched on the front.

'What? You bought me perfume?'

'Yes. You love flowers, always moan that there aren't enough in the house, that you don't have a garden to grow them, and we don't have the money...'-- he paused, as if to say something else, but then continued. '-- and, well, I thought it would be a good memory for you, though I didn't do it *all* myself, the woman behind the counter had to help me, and oh it was a *process*, let me tell you.'

She laughed at the thought of Henry's height darkening a glass underlit counter, opposite an immaculately groomed woman with shining hair and high heels, testing fragrances. Dark and light. 'Well, the effort was worth it.'

He remembered her this way, her hair falling forward, still long, but now with a dusting of silver strands underneath and by her forehead. 'When I first saw you, in Lviv-- I mean, I may be wrong here-- but I think you were carrying a basket of them?'

'What?? No, you're an idiot. It was a basket of washing probably.'

'Well, sorry! Either way, this is your gift.' And he took his shoes off and walked to the kitchen to wash his hands and light the stove to make tea for them both. 'When is Slava coming back?' he called out over his shoulder.

'She is out with her friends, leave her alone. She is not a child anymore.'

Henry walked back, rolling up his sleeves. 'Still a child in my mind's eye,' he sighed, sitting down heavily on the chair opposite Julia.

By the time Slava was on the precipice of her twenties, Julia and Henry had carved out a steady life for themselves in New York. Using some money that he had saved from his time in Australia, and now in Manhattan, he bought his own rental building in Brooklyn. It was welfare housing and although it was going to be hard, he knew how to manage a piece of run-down real estate. Phone calls in the middle of the night to fix persistent leaks, heating that had gone off, brown outs: this was his role. A doctor to a building. He would drive hours round trip, and still get up in the morning to see Slava off to school. It was his, his own world of his own making; it all rested on his shoulders and not on the shoulders of a man in a high castle. His pride was put on a shelf whilst he kept his family safe and cared for. His life hadn't changed so much, he realized. He had gone from working until his back broke in the blistering sun and torrential rain, to working in basements at all hours of the night and day.

And like the crumbling insides of these buildings, the couple spent this time repairing the damage that had almost been catastrophic to their marriage. The memories of Iliya had faded almost entirely, like a dream upon waking. The pain of separation from Lesia and Maksim ceased to wake her up nightly; had ceased to be the distraction and sadness it used to be and developed into more of a resigned sorrow. It lingered like a bruise, but it was manageable. They would be so different now, she thought so many times to comfort herself, children no longer, and the few letters that she had sent were returned, a red stamp declaring INCORRECT ADDRESS, so she slowly stopped writing them. Life had gotten too busy to worry about things she could not change.

Occasionally, she and Henry would drive out of the city and leave Slava at home, the two of them seeking an escape just with one another. The long drives ended on narrowing roads out east, on Long Island, the one that caught their eye was Glen Cove, close to the shore in a quiet community of houses and connected villages with gardens and parks, and a line of sand along the shore that looked out to Long Island Sound. It was an easy drive: a long, straight road, endless and quiet, the blue horizon and salty air encouraging them towards a simpler existence. They rarely spoke on the journey, but not out of any anger, now—it was only because they craved the stillness.

Tonight, Julia and Henry had drinks planned with friends at a bar in the East Village, and Julia realized that he had forgotten.

'You're sitting there like a lump, when we have to get ready.' She put her sewing down on the table next to where she sat.

Henry unbuttoned his shirt and stroked his stubbled chin. 'Oh, I forgot.'

'Well, we have time.' Julia stood up. 'But this— 'she gestured to his plaid shirt and trousers stained with bleach and confetti-like marks of paint '— is not acceptable at The Orchidea.'

Henry leaned his head back on the couch and sighed. 'How do you have the energy.'

Julia held her hand out. 'I learn from the best. Come now let's make a drink. I can wear my birthday present.' She smiled as he pushed himself up and walked to the bedroom, her hand prodding him as he went, laughing as she did.

Slava knocked softly at first, and then unlocked the door, her dress touching the frame softly. 'Mama? You here?'

The house was quiet as she walked through the door, turned on the light, and threw her keys on the telephone table. She shut the door behind her and wondered if her parents had left already. 'Mama? I need those earrings that you promised I could wear. Hello?' She shrugged her coat off and laid it on the sofa.

The house was silent: rooms quiet, neat as a pin, the bookshelves messy with papers and stories and little boxes of trinkets that her parents had collected over the years. She walked through the kitchen in her green silk dress, the bias cut of the hem catching on her heel. Her blonde hair was up and twisted into a bun, and a thin gold necklace sunk into the hollow at the base of her neck, glittering in the light as she moved. Two glasses of wine were on the counter and a cigarette had been stubbed out. She walked through the small dining room with the embroidered tablecloth and the cracked sideboard heaving under stacks of china that they only used at Christmas and Easter, and then down the hallway towards the bedroom, the smell of lilies hinting at her mother's recent absence.

A few times a year Henry and Julia were invited to attend small social gatherings, through the Ukrainian diaspora in the city. There was a small, but very close-knit community in the village and occasionally couples would meet in restaurants or bars and dress in grand nods to the era: jackets cut slim and lapels too wide and drinks inevitably too strong. And with Henry being overworked, it was a welcome escape. This particular evening, Slava was invited to join them, but had requested a pair of earrings, which Julia had left out for her, in case they would meet her at dinner instead of at the apartment.

She found what she had been looking for: the tiniest green emeralds given to her mother for Christmas from her father. They lay on the small table right next to her side of the bed, and Slava placed them gently into her ears, fastening the back.

As she turned to leave, her heel pierced something that was sticking out from under the bed. She looked down and saw the corners of two pieces of paper, thin and old, like the leaves of an ancient book. She unpicked them from her heel and placed them on the bedside table. She looked at the thin watch on her wrist, in a daze. She was late.

As she left the room, the fold undid slightly and the black lettering of QUEENSLAND, AUSTRALIA peeked out from the top. The room echoed with the sound of the door closing.

That evening the Orchidea glittered and swayed, the strains of music filtering through the air from the live band as people danced together and milled about in corners drinking and smoking. Laughter and conversations peppered the room, bouncing from wall to wall, with Ukrainian words and stories lacing together like an ornate tapestry.

Across a white–dressed table adorned with luxuriously thin dinnerware and wine bottles, Slava watched her mother. She watched as she leaned forward in conversations, smiling at a friend, gesturing to Henry, playing the role of wife and companion, hostess and lover. Her father had his arm around her mother, and she saw how rigid her body became sometimes, under his gaze. It fascinated her. Her mother's earrings were delicate gold hoops, her dress was a dark green, darker still in the folds of the silk that wrapped around her and embraced her shape. The small windows of the wine glasses and candle holders and vases altered her face as she moved, different perspectives and colors, the light playing it delicately, beautifully.

'Slava, you're miles away, are you feeling alright?' Andrij, an older family friend that had known her for five years, leaned forward, the lapels on his suit jacket shining in opposition to the matte material of the body, his reddish hair matching his cheeks that had flushed with alcohol.

'Yes, fine. Just thinking.'

'You think too much.' Andrij winked at her. 'About Emilian?'

Slava blushed violently. 'Stop it!'

'So, where is he?'

'Working.' She smiled. 'I didn't want to subject him to the Ukrainian chaos and binge-drinking.' Andrij chuckled and slapped his thighs. 'Well! Isn't that the truth! But that's part of our charm.' He put a hand on her shoulder. 'Speaking of. Need a drink?'

Slava played with the gold beading on her clutch absentmindedly. It was her mother's that she'd borrowed. Gold glass beading on cream colored silk. 'Actually, no. Just tonic water. With lemon.'

Andrij's mouth fell open, mocking her. 'What?? Since when do you not have a drink in your hand?'

'Oh, stop it.' Slava had nothing else she could offer. 'Just not feeling myself, that's all.'

'I'll drink your share, don't worry. Be right back.'

When Andrij walked off, Slava saw her mother sit down, whispering confidences to an older woman, quite possibly a friend, as her father walked off.

'Mama…' Slava called across the table, reaching for the silver case of cigarettes at the center of the table and the lighter beside it, but then remembered herself, and left it there.

Julia turned to her. 'Yes, what is it?'

Slava shook her head, knowing that she didn't need to tell her yet. It wasn't the right time. It was never the right time, with her mother; her subtle distance encouraged Slava to have built a wall over the years. 'Nothing, nothing.'

'Here you go.' Andrij sat down next to her and Slava took a sip.

'Right. Care to dance with an old friend?'

Andrij nodded, and took her by the hand, leading her to the dance floor.

🕊

Julia watched as Slava left the table and suspected that she'd had something on her mind. She thought better of pursuing it. Sometimes, it was better to let things work themselves out, in time.

Irena broke the silence. 'Smile, Julia! Such a serious face!' Irena pointed the camera at the table, shouting at the others to lean in. Henry was standing to the side. Julia leaned forward in her chair and laugh-smiled to the camera as she posed, her thoughts on an old ache that had stirred up inside her.

27

New York, 1978

'Christ, that woman will always confuse me.'
Slava threw her keys down on the only piece of furniture in their rented apartment: a small bookshelf that she and her boyfriend Emilian had found on tenth street, in front of the charity shop that always smelled of cat piss. We should definitely take it, he'd told her, we got our apartment cheap because we said *unfurnished*. He'd seen the skepticism in her blue eyes and feared the worst; she wasn't the best at masking her true feelings. But she gave in, and here they were, in a dank basement with one window that looked out at feet hurrying along the sidewalk, and a piece of wood that they used for keys, eating their dinner on, and storage for old university textbooks.

She kicked the door closed with her heel and peeled off her running shoes. 'Em? Are you here?'

Silence.

She pulled off the elastic band that had carried her hair on her run, and the thick blonde mess of it all tumbled out, half dry, half matted and dark underneath from sweat. She ran her fingers through it and opened the refrigerator as footsteps approached from the small room next to the bed.

'Hey- I thought I heard some rage and figured that was you, or maybe a highly neurotic burglar.' She laughed and turned to the familiar lilt of his voice: Emilian was carrying a few books in one hand, and a pencil behind his ear, and he raised his eyebrows comically. 'Emilian Morris at your service for all your emotional needs. I just came out of my cage. You need me?'

Their studio apartment had come with a strange closet-type space that you couldn't turn around in, and Emiilan used as a makeshift office to study for his Series 7. *Sounds like a group of viral infections*, Slava had said when they first met, and he immediately wanted to know more about this girl with the strange name and the humorless voice. She was light, and he was dark, and yet their personalities were the opposite: she had a personality that held things close, almost cold, and he had a voice that was perpetually at the end of a joke. It was the thing that she'd immediately liked about him when they'd met in— of all places— the public library, where his loud voice and tendency to easy laughter was entirely provocative.

He patted her on the small of her back as he moved around her to place his coffee cup in the sink and his books beside it. 'Breakfast? I can make a mean fried egg and bacon.'

Slava grimaced and closed the refrigerator. 'Oh god no, don't even. I don't feel well.' She leaned over the sink, turned on the tap, and palmed some water into her mouth.

'What? You always rave about my poor man breakfast.'

'I can't.' Her stomach lurched and she muffled a burp. 'Besides, I'm meeting Alex in an hour.'

Emilian feigned anger. 'Who is this Alex, and do I have to kill him?'

'You're such a dummy. *Alexandra*. She's only been out to dinner with us about 50 times.'

'Ahh yes. The one who has a thing for true crime documentaries and good tequila.'

'Yes, that's the one.'

'I like her style.' Emilian put a bagel in the toaster. 'I thought you were off today.'

Slava faltered. *That's right*, she thought. *She'd told him that.* 'Well…'

'Research?'

Slava took the cue. 'Yep. She has the latest labs for the Acute Phase Reactants…'

Emilian put up a hand. 'Whoah. Stop. You had me at 'labs'. *No* idea what you're talking about, oh smart one.'

Slava smiled. 'Did you know, that the amount of protein— '

He leaned over and tried to kiss her. She moved.

'— means that there can be acute…'

'You're cute.'

Slava flushed. 'Stop it.' her voice was coy. 'I'm very important.'

'Yes. I have a damn smart girlfriend scientist. The best. I'm very proud of that fact.' He reached around her and locked his arms behind her. 'Fact is, I can't follow because all I know is Latin text in giant books that I probably will never understand.'

'But you look good in a suit.'

'Well, that's true.'

She leaned her body towards him and placed her palms on his chest, sinking into his warmth. She saw the things she loved most as his face drew near: the green flecks in the hazel of his eyes, the freckles spattered across the bridge of his nose, and the reddish-brown mop of thick curls that were always gently unruly.

'And if I ever get arrested, I'm almost positive I'd hire you.'

'Nice.' He kissed her and let go, walking back towards the small room. 'Listen, do me a favor. Don't try and be a burglar, because you'd be a pretty bad one, judging from your entrance earlier.'

Slava rolled her eyes and took off her hoodie, revealing a sweaty t-shirt underneath. 'Why would we have a burglar? We live in a place that has one piece of furniture.' She looked around and pointed to the corner of the room. 'Oh, and a bed.'

'Beds are very valuable,'

She took off her socks and then remembered that her mother had called earlier. 'Argh. Totally forgot.'

'What now?'

'Oh, forget it.'

'Okay okay, I'll bite. Let it out.' He leaned back against the counter, careful not to break off the piece of yellow formica that he'd superglued earlier. 'What's got you annoyed?'

'My mother.'

'Why am I not surprised. She's a tough one. A year in, and barely remembers my name and that we live together, but yeah, she's lovely.' Emilian lifted a corner of his mouth.

'Yeah, well, she wants us to come for tea, and when she talks, it means she's planning something, or, I don't know. Who knows. She's a bit strange sometimes.'

'When?'

She shrugged. 'Eventually, she said. Could be in a week, or a month. Time to her is immaterial, apparently. She exists in a bubble.'

'My mother is like that. Maybe it's the Eastern European streak.'

'Your mother is Hungarian, and your father is Irish. That's a *whole* other set of issues.' Slava mocked.

'I know! Maybe she's pregnant.' Emilian offered, trying to lighten her mood. Slava was quick to anger, but she let go easily, and he knew the times that he could encourage her to. But in that moment, he saw Slava's face shift and the blue in her eyes darkened. He came towards her. 'Oh, c'mon. It was a joke. I didn't— '

And then suddenly, she came back to him. 'Science can't even be *that* weird,' she laughed. 'You're such a loon.'

Emilian softened. 'But really, though, your dad is fine, she's perfectly healthy, what could it possibly be?'

'I don't know.' She walked to the bed, exactly six steps from the kitchen, and sat down, facing him. 'I'd like to say that it's a puppy but I'm too tired to try out your jokes.'

Emilian smiled at the effort, though he knew that something else was bothering her. There had been a simmering in her eyes recently, like the energy of a locked door. He knew better than to prod.

Slava pulled off her jogging bottoms. 'Right. We have an hour and a bit before I have to leave.' She looked up at Emilian. 'What do you say we make the most of our second piece of furniture?' And then she took off her t-shirt, and leaned her face towards his, and they spoke of nothing else.

🕊

Slava walked through the door of the aptly named *Coffee Pot* on the corner of 7th Avenue and 10th street, satisfied that Emilian believed her lie. The glass-muffled traffic surged noisily outside as she scanned the room and then she saw her at a table in the corner, sitting straight, winding the thin watch on her wrist.

Her mother looked regal, in a camel dress coat, her hair tied back in a high bun, revealing sharp cheekbones and bright eyes. It was easy to forget who she was: a woman with a proud spine and a cool distance in the way she carried herself. It was beautiful, and Slava wished she'd observed it more when she was younger.

She slipped her shoulder bag off and sat down heavily, shrugging her jacket off onto the back of the chair. The coffee machines squealed and steamed in the far corner of the room and the air smelled of cinnamon and sugar.

'I'm late, Mama.'

Julia didn't offer a reaction, and only checked her watch. 'Yes, I am aware. 25 minutes late.' She motioned for a waiter to come over.

'No, more like a week.'

There was a hint of a smile, and then Julia leaned forward lacing her fingers together, eyes hopeful. 'Are you sure?'

'I'm never late. But then again, this could be a false alarm. I just thought I'd tell you.'

Julia waited a bit, and then nodded. 'Well. Have you told Emilian?'

'No. I didn't want to start the ball rolling on that particular path.'

The waiter came over with menus. Slava raised a hand. 'Oh, I can't. Do you have any tea?' He nodded.

Julia smiled. 'Two please, thank you. With honey on the side.' When he walked off, she continued. 'I am not sure of all these 'balls and paths', but you must think about this. Sometimes, it doesn't happen, but if it does, what a miracle.'

'Oh God, Mama,' Slava snorted. 'You're always so negative despite attempting optimism.'

Julia nodded. 'That may be so, but all I am saying is be prepared either way. Life is funny.'

'You always strike me as so wary, nervous.' Slava folded and unfolded the napkin in front of her. 'It's like you're afraid to be bold, but you're also hard as nails.'

Julia didn't respond. 'You'd need to get your apartment ready.'

'Hang on, slow down. You mean our closet space under the ground? Yeah, well, our lease is up soon and who the hell knows where we'll move after that.'

Julia reached for her daughter. 'Don't you want children yet? Have you thought about it?'

Slava softened. 'Well, not *really*. In an ideal world? No, not right now. I'd imagine that I'd be more ready than I am right now. Besides, there are options. I mean, an abortion wouldn't be ideal, but— '

Julia's face flushed and her voice rose. 'Shhh! Don't ever say anything like that! That's disgraceful.'

'Mama, calm down.' Slava looked around, embarrassed for them. She was grateful the place was half empty. 'Stop freaking out. I never said I would *get* one, but hey, welcome to 1974.'

Slava watched as Julia became visibly agitated, and when the tea was brought there was silence for a good five minutes as the women sat in their own thoughts. Slava stirred the honey into her cup, the spoon scraping the porcelain.

'Mama— '

'Slava, don't. What you said is incredibly upsetting to me. You would be lucky to have a child. Incredibly blessed.' Julia became almost possessive of Slava's news, as if it were her own.

'I know this, of course. But I also have a right to choose now.'

'Choices are dangerous.' Julia's eyes shone.

'Choices are good. It means you have freedom.'

'No, Slava. You're wrong. One choice could change your entire life.'

Slava had seen this before, her mother had a darkness to her that rarely came out, but when it did, it seeped slowly, as if it were an uncontrollable fire; smoke leaking out of a locked room. Today, it was more than she'd ever seen. She wanted to push her further, but instead, she reached across and gripped her mother's hand.

'Mama, hear me out. I just wanted to tell you— '

'Why?' Julia interrupted. 'Why would you tell me about something that you're not sure about?'

'Because you're my mother.'

Julia took a napkin and dabbed the corners of her eyes. 'I know, *sertseh*. I'm sorry. I never got to tell my own mother these things, that's probably why. There's no need for so much emotion.'

Slava sensed the lie, but she left it. Julia composed herself and locked the darkness away again. 'Thank you for telling me, no matter what happens.'

The same waiter appeared carrying a pad and pencil and two menus. 'Would you like anything else?'

'Milk, please,' Julia replied, and smiled at her daughter, the pain dissipating. 'For both of us.'

※

Later that afternoon, Emilian was out and Slava walked through the empty apartment, slowly discarding one shoe, then the other, then her bag and finally her coat. She walked into the bathroom and stood in front of the small mirror, spotted with toothpaste flicks from morning routines. She had six a mere six months to finish her master's, had a steady job at Sloane Kettering, and Emilian had been promised a position at Smith Barney, working for his mentor from college. They had very little, but it was everything to them.

There was a large part of her childhood that Slava didn't remember, and things that her mother had never told her. 'Such a long time ago, how could I remember,' she would say often. She'd been shown faded photographs of her smiling face in fields and farmhouses, tucked into the arms of her mother and father, but her own memories remained blank. And her mother never talked of the past, as if she'd moved on to another life when they'd arrived on the concrete paths of Manhattan. She'd lived a hard life, Slava assumed, and that was just the immigrant story. Keeping the past tucked away.

She walked out of the bathroom and over to the bed, where they had been, only six hours before. She lay down and placed a hand on her stomach slowly moving it across the thin material of her blouse and back again, her thoughts growing quiet as she fell asleep to the sound of the rain hitting the street just above her.

※

It would be a week later that her period would come, and the tests would show that it was, in fact, a disappearing moment, and as Slava stood in the shower and reinserted herself back into her life, she felt she'd accomplished something that she'd never done before: she had revealed a little bit of the woman that sat across from her.

28

'We are moving', Julia announced a month later as she put her embroidery on her lap. The threads lay in a clump on her knees: black, cranberry red and kelly green. It was going to be a bouquet of poppies. Two other pairs of eyes were staring at her, and then Slava turned to Emilian and cocked her eyebrow. *See? I told you. Ridiculous.*

'What?' It was Saturday, the tea had been poured, Slava was arranging folders of lab results on the floor in front of her, the insignia of Sloane-Kettering Hospital branded on the top of each; she was inundated with work more and more lately because labs never shut on the weekends and now she had been promoted to supervisor. Emilian sat behind her on the couch; his place was still a spectator. She was looking at her mother in disbelief. 'But why? You love the city.'

Julia smiled. 'Our life, Papa's and mine, it's always been so busy. Not once have we stopped working, but we're getting older now… he is 54, after all. He comes home like he used to: tired and covered in dirt. He never says 'no' to what anyone wants from him.' She took a sip of hot tea and placed it back onto the coffee table.

'Well, you can't just move and… well, do you have a plan? Everyone needs a plan.' She leaned back on Emilian's legs and folded her arms across her chest.

'Oh, Slava. Such focus. You remember how you used to shout at me *Vava do it* when you were 5?'

Slava blushed in embarrassment. 'Not really.'

Julia continued. 'Yes, there is a plan. You know the building that

Papa bought on President Street a few years ago?'

'Yes, the one that was a dump.'

'Well, over time, there have been a lot of buildings that have been bought on that street and done up really nicely: painted and renovated and the original brick restored.'

'So, what does that have to do with Papa?'

'A few weeks ago, a couple of developers approached Papa when he was working and told him that they'd be interested in buying the rental off him.'

'Holy God!'

The clinking of keys and the turning of the look interrupted them. Henry was home. He lumbered in, his frame appearing in the door.

'Oh, Emilian. Slava.' He took his hat off and hooked it on the back of the door. 'What was that ungodly screeching? Was that you?'

'Yes, Papa. Mama just told me about the house in Brooklyn.'

He peeled off his jacket and sat down heavily, nodding a hello to Emilian. 'Well, they seem very interested, which is strange. But I guess the area will become popular maybe? I don't know these kinds of things. But I'll take good money if it's offered. I've worked my bones raw in that building.'

'What money, then?'

'They offered four times what Papa paid for it', Julia interrupted proudly.

'She's talking to me, Julia', he admonished with a sigh. 'Yes, it was four times.' He turned to Julia. 'Always money with you.' Emilian and Slava shifted their bodies uncomfortably.

'Don't be argumentative just because you're exhausted, Henry. I'm glad it's a lot of money, and yes, it makes me happy to know that you're rewarded for hard work just like *every other* reasonably-minded husband.' She waved her hand towards him. 'You can't just fix pipes and grow orchids your whole life and expect that to be okay, now can you.' As soon as she said the words, she regretted them.

Henry stood up. 'You're lucky I respect you that little bit not to dive into an argument. I don't have the energy for it.' He walked down the hallway towards the bedroom, and everyone heard a shuffling of papers and a drawer opening. Julia's face went white.

'Henry,' she said loudly. 'What are you looking for?'

'Something I found the other day.'

Julia stood up as Henry walked back into the room clutching a file with several pieces of paper in it. She sat back down and smoothed her blouse, the color returning to her face. Slava had watched her the entire time.

'Look,' Henry offered to Slava, and winked at her. 'Your mother likes a good number.' Julia rolled her eyes.

'Here we go again. Please, be nice, both of you.' Slava took the papers and looked through them and showed Emilian. She shot a look at Julia. "Wow. Well, all the little comments aside, this is a good thing. Will you go through with it you think?'

Julia still stung from their words. 'Yes, yes, of course he'll take the money. We'll use it to find a place out in Long Island, where there's a nice little community.'

'Ah. Where you and Papa disappear to sometimes?'

'Mmm. Glen Cove. It has a little main street with shops, a cinema, a beach, a lovely church, and plenty of space. It's what they call 'new development', and it seems to have a lot of potential for us. Somewhere we can breathe a bit.'

'What will happen to this place?' Slava looked at the embroidered cushions on the couch and smoothed the faded oriental rug where she sat. 'There's so much history here.'

'Well, that's good that you like it, as Papa and I decided that you can have it.'

Slava's eyes widened and looked over at Emilian. 'Mrs. Rudnick, we couldn't possibly— '

'— And what should we do with it then?' Julia interrupted. 'Sell it to a stranger? Besides, we have already bought it from the owner of this building, years ago.' Julia smiled. 'We saved, and we bought it to have in the family.'

Henry folded his arms across his chest and cocked an eyebrow. 'Isn't your lease coming up soon?'

'Yes, sir,' Emilian answered. 'But with all due respect we couldn't—'

'Too late,' Julia interrupted, clapping her palms together to end the thought. 'It's for you. It's history, as you said.' She looked over at Slava. 'And you can't rent if you have children.'

Slava rolled her eyes and laughed. 'Not again, Mama.'

Emilian looked at her and winked and looked at Julia. 'I keep *telling* her.'

Julia frowned. 'Marriage first. Do it properly.'

'Oh, like everything you both have done is so proper,' Slava snorted, shuffling her papers together and standing up.

Julia blushed; her face lost its smile. 'Anyway, there you have it. That is our news.'

'Thanks, Mama.' Slava embraced her mother tightly. She always noticed how her body stiffened ever so slightly. She never understood it. Slava kissed her father on his leathery cheeks and waited for Emilian at the door as she put her coat on— it was one that her mother had given her: brown suede with white, red and green yarn woven in a flower pattern all along the edges of the sleeves and the bottom hem. It had been made in Ukraine by a friend of the family. It was history. They, and now Emilian, and this apartment, all of it was now her home.

30

Despite having brought only a bookshelf, a bed, and a mirror, the apartment still hadn't been settled yet, there were carboard boxes and packing tape and dishes that hadn't found a place to live yet. Her hands trailed over the dark wood of the hallway: her mother had left a few paintings hanging delicately, some wood etchings by Ukrainian artists that Slava knew nothing about. There were volumes of Pushkin, old maps, encyclopedias that she used to use for school, dust had collected on their spines. She was home.

Her parents had left them a few pieces of furniture and took the rest to Glen Cove in six separate trips, the process taking most of a weekend. Slava looked around, the lazy Sunday light flooding the windows of the living room, the shadow of the fire escape creating a pattern on the floor. The dark walls held so many old memories of their arrival in New York: the tenants that roamed the hallways and gathered on the stoop below, in the summer heat; the radiators spitting and popping during the winters that frosted the window panes; the blare of sirens that they got used to so quickly, and seemed comforted by over time.

'Do we want to keep these?' Emilian strode out of the kitchen with an armful of embroidered napkins.

'Yeah, let's just put them in a cupboard somewhere.'

'We'll never use them though.'

'Did I ever tell you that my mother made some of those?'

He looked at the pile of material in his arms. 'Um, no?' He cocked an eyebrow at Slava. 'In her spare time? Sitting around and stitching red poppies?'

Slava smiled sadly. 'No. In the war.'

Emilian flattened his lips. 'Oh. Sorry.'

'Don't worry.'

'She doesn't talk much about any of that,' Emilian responded, folding each napkin gently and placing it into a box. 'Do you ever ask her?'

Slava shrugged, walking over to the small phone table by the door with a stack of letters on it. 'I try to, but she shuts down. She once told me *no one will ever know the real me* and I found that really sad.'

'Yeah, that's weird.'

Slava fingered each letter absentmindedly, her thoughts elsewhere. 'Well, I don't know. I mean, it *was* a war.' She stopped on one letter, addressed to Julia Rudnick. 'Too many painful memories I guess.'

'Yeah, I get it.' Emilian folded the lip of the box and pushed it aside. 'What else you got for me?'

Slava ripped the edge of the envelope and reached inside. 'This is for my mother. From...'-- she turned it back to the front and read the sender's address-- 'Townsville State Department.'

'There you go!' Emilian slapped his knee. 'She's on the run from the government!' He laughed and stood up, walking past her into the living room, and opening a window. 'I'm getting married into the Ukrainian mafia.'

Slava looked up, blushing. 'Excuse me now? What is this marriage you speak of?' She raised the hand that held the paper and pointed to her ring finger. 'I don't see a ring on there?'

Emilian tapped his nose. 'Working on it.'

'Stop it, you're such a weirdo.' Slava rolled her eyes and unfolded the paper: it was a news article, the headline read ANNOUNCEMENTS OF BIRTHS, MARRIAGES, AND DEATHS, and then a handful of black and white squares with images and words.

'What is it?'

'Something about births, marriages, deaths, in an Australian newspaper.'

'Nothing else?'

'Nope.'

'It's a sign from God.' She looked over at Emilian sat on the windowsill; he was looking through an old photo album. 'We should put our marriage in the paper.'

Slava chuckled and walked towards the phone. 'Honestly, some days I wonder about you...'

Her mother picked up on the second ring. 'Slava?'

'Hi Mama.'

'Everything alright? How's the apartment?'

'Everything is fine, it's still a mess,' Slava glanced at Emilian 'partly due to my lazy almost-fiancé in the corner over there...' Emilian stretched his face into comedy shock and winked.

'What??'

'Never mind,' Slava raised the paper and looked at it. 'Listen, someone sent something to this address, for you.'

'Oh? Who?'

'Well, the envelope says it's from the 'Townsville Welfare Office.'

Silence.

'Mama?'

'Sorry, go on, yes... and what was it?'

'Well, it's a bit strange,' Slava flipped it over in her hands, and back again, scanning it. 'It's just a newspaper clipping of births, marriages and deaths, dated...' Slava squinted at the top of the page '... June fifteenth, nineteen-seventy-nine. So, from a few months ago.' There was silence again, and Slava only heard her breathing. 'Mama? Should I send it to you?'

'No, no. That's alright.'

'You sure?'

'Yes, absolutely. Probably a case of mistaken identity or something. You can throw it away.

'Alright.'

Slava was about to ask her something else, but her mother had already replaced the receiver.

'Hey, everything alright?' Emilian walked up to her, a pile of books in his hand.

'Sure,' Slava responded, looking through him. 'Yeah.' She placed the clipping in the envelope, and then in a file, and placed it on the shelf. She had always been good at listening to her instinct.

30

Melbourne, 1980

Ed had gotten the phone call before, and felt obliged to listen, though he knew what she was going to say before she said it, and knew the inflections of her voice as they hinted at her state of mind. Siblings were strange that way, twins probably even more so; they read each other like books. He tucked the phone onto his shoulder and trapped it with his ear, waiting patiently for her to continue.

'I don't know, maybe I'm being too sensitive, but I'm so,'—her voice hesitated on the other side of the mobile, and Ed knew why. '—I guess nervous, maybe, about it all, I mean do you think any of this is a good idea? I mean, it's Mum and Dad's stuff, won't it be really emotional? I don't think I can handle it.' The tempo of her voice was halting, fractured, holding up an invisible barrier to rational thought or reason in its staccato moments. 'They'd only been sick for such a short time. This is just…' her voice tapered off.

'I know, Roz. I know. But we can't start backtracking here. We agreed to sell the house, after all of this happened. And it won't happen overnight, either. Let's just take our time.' Roslyn had called him this afternoon, as she had done once a week for the past six months after the funeral, to grieve, to talk, to tell him the details of her anxiety about it all and share the shock of what had happened. This was a big deal, of course, and it was only natural that the act of preserving the past would be denying the future. They'd both decided, soon after their parents' death, to start dividing up history— a life that their parents had protected for them, and now she would rather that they stick their heads in the sand and ignore it all. He understood it, it was painful for both of them. But there was no question in his mind that this was what they needed right now.

His fingers ached from holding the phone and it had grown hot at his ear. 'Roz. I've already told you; you've got to relax with all this. I mean, you're the lawyer for goodness' sake. Get your pragmatic brain on. It'll be fine— '

'Will it though? I mean seriously. I'm an estate lawyer for *other* people. Not for *my* family. What if'—'

'What if what? We find out our parents had really bad taste in furniture? We already knew that.'

Helen opened the door just then placing her keys on the table, a bag of shopping sagging in the crook of her elbow. Ed covered the receiver and mouthed *Roz again*, and she nodded and mouthed *just let her get it out* in response and walked off.

'Listen,' he continued, 'just let me handle it and I'll let you know. It may not come to much, to be honest, so who knows, it may be something interesting at the least.'

'Helen's there isn't she.'

'Yeah, why.'

'You went quiet for a second. You think I'm being nuts. Your wife has much more time for me than you do these days.'

'Well, that's a given.' He laughed and ran his fingers across the keyboard distractedly and stared at the wallpaper on his computer screen. It was a black and white photograph of the Kakadu National Park taken at a distance, with a little girl in the foreground, holding the hand of her parent, hair loose the side of her face visible as she looked up, wondering. He'd taken this when he'd been on an assignment for the Melbourne Parks Authority. He'd shot an entire series of landscape photos and had been about to leave when he saw two figures, in conversation: a parent and a child, wandering without purpose. And it struck him as if a remembered dream, and he immediately took a few shots, grateful that he'd captured the moment for himself.

'Anyway. I'll see you at the house in a few months, alright? The buyers are giving us time to go through and take what we need, and I have an assignment I need to finish up first. Do something to take your mind off it, because you're going to crack in half. I mean, I understand how you feel, but one day, when this is all settled and the paperwork is sorted out, we can figure out the house. And let's make it a good day.' Roz was never good at being patient, even as a child. She'd always been willful and insistent, and Ed was the pragmatist. Where she was emotional and reactive, he was patient and thorough. They had always been opposites, but very close and protective of each other; their parents had always commented that they were the best kind of puzzle pieces: all angles and curves that fit together well, though occasionally a bit forced in their partnership with each other.

She laughed easily now, and he pictured her immediately, the husky, familiar voice perfectly congruous with her greying blonde hair and dark eyes that had always been so wild and wary. 'Okay, fine. I'll talk to you soon, yeah?'

'Yep. No worries.'

Ed hung up and placed the phone on the desk, quickly skimmed over the last of his edit, and then walked outside to sit alone on the porch. He'd built it himself almost immediately after he and Helen first bought the property in Trinity Park, because it was a wide and open and easily lent itself to soft light, in with its windows on every side. It sat at the end of a road perched on a hill with views down to the small crescent beach, and the lush green trails of Earl Hill Summit, well-worn by a stream of constant hikers determined in their exploration, towards the sides and back. But for its expanse, it was limited in space outside, and Ed had always craved, insisted on really, views of the sky and a bit of the sea.

The inside was representative of the plain outside: clean and modern, with pale wood floors and whitewashed and old furniture, greens and blues and greys dominating the choice of paint colors and soft furnishings. At every turn, the walls around him displayed something new: contemporary aboriginal paintings done in black and red, with lines and circles and thousands of small dots scattered within and around; sunlit, undulating plains dehydrated in the blistering sun; black and white photographs taken by his parents, from his travels to Fiji as a child; the photos of Ed and Helen posing somewhere exotic, having accomplished an adventure; the family photographs that were left to him and his sister after their mother--and then soon after, their father--had died.

Ed loved stories, and his parents had encouraged his appreciation of cultures and wonder, which is probably why he had stayed where he had been raised, and sought his studies at a college in Melbourne to become a travel photographer (though in recent years he had started consulting, as the plane journeys and had become too much of a chore now that he was a much older man). He'd made a healthy career out of seeing worlds through a lens and meeting people that he'd never see again, though in the recesses of his memory he knew, and felt, that he had one more story to search for. But how, he thought, would he ever find it. And what would that mean for him and his wife and maybe his children one day, and would he regret seeking it? He had never been able to answer that.

The rains hovered in the distance and the air felt luxuriously heavy; at any moment, the storm would begin. He would have to close the shutters in the bedrooms, he thought; the last time he didn't, the rain had coated the floor and ruined a thick stack of paper that he'd left on his desk. A year of documentation, paperwork and filings about his parents' lives, any information that pertained to their work and their personal assets and information, correspondence with various banks and trusts and work colleagues—all of it had been soaked through and had taken a month to dry, and underneath was a pile of discarded papers that needed to be fed into the shredder.

He stood up to go back inside, when he saw the dust plume delicately in the distance and then heard the small car pull up at the bottom of the drive. He heard the door squeak open, then heard it shut again, and willed himself to wait for the car to retreat again, before he walked down to the mailbox.

The rain started upon his ascent back to the house, gently at first then harder, coating his greying hair just as he managed to get back inside, and he sat down to look through it all: two catalogues advertising outdoor gear, a magazine about photography, and a white envelope with typed black letters on the front, addressed to his parents, forwarded to him. The return address read: Queensland Government, Department of Communities, Child Safety and Disability Services.

'Ed?' Helen called out from upstairs.

'Yeah?' He held the envelope in his hand, poised to open it.

'Can you check the closet in the master bedroom? The hinges have come off again, sorry.'

He groaned. 'Yep, coming.'

He placed the pieces of mail on the edge of the desk and walked off, not noticing as it all fell to the floor into the pile of shredding.

31

Glen Cove, 1980

On one of their trips to Glen Cove, Henry saw a FOR SALE sign beside a small building: a yellow, one-level complex with 10 rooms nest to a 100-foot long beach. It didn't take long for both Henry and Julia to both realize that this was the investment that they had been looking for, something to keep their minds occupied and their money working. Within days, they'd put in an offer and became the new owners. It needed a lot of repair work, cosmetic mostly, the docks needed fixing and the units needed cleaning… but it was theirs.

In the very beginning, the couple decided that Henry would move upstate full time and Julia would continue with her job at Fisk. She'd had a stable job that treated her well, and she couldn't just leave it overnight. She needed time. Every weekend, she and Slava would both take the bus from Penn Station and travel the hour and a half across the city, over the bridge and into Glen Cove, with Henry picking them up at the station. It was something she looked forward to every week: it was their project that they shared. It brought them forward towards a goal. It was stabilizing.

❧

It was September 1976, and an Indian summer had gently settled on the water. Green and gold speckled the trees and hinted of autumn, but the air still felt deliciously warm. It was a battle of seasons; the push of colder weather and the pull of long days and nights were the sun didn't set too early. The heat, however, guaranteed business, and that pleased Henry. He ran the building not as he used to in Brooklyn, but rather with calm intention: he saw the usefulness of each fragment of the property, he saw the value that it could bring. The days were long and there were so many things he had to take care of, but this was home.

A few months prior, Julia had decided to give up her job and move upstate full time. Slava helped her pack up the 71st street flat without much ceremony and Julia moved to the motel to live there full time. It was the last bus ride that she would take, the familiar streets that she'd walked so often, giving way to wide stretches of road and skies unburdened by looming skyscrapers. She knew she'd never return.

This particular Saturday felt quiet. Henry was laying down another coat of varnish on the docks to winterize them; the winters by the lake were occasionally sharp and insidious, despite the beauty it brought. The wood expanded and contracted like a beating heart, and cracks would form over time. It was best to protect it as much as possible. The rhythm was comforting back and forth, the brush forward and back, against the lapping of the water against the beach.

He heard footsteps and looked up; Julia was walking towards him with a cup of coffee.

'Is that mine?' he rubbed the sweat from his brow with his forearm.

'No. Did you want one?'

'Never mind.' He put his brush down and reached for his cigarettes. 'Well, hopefully, this will stay strong,' he drew on his cigarette. 'Not sure, but worth a try anyway.' He exhaled.

'Yes, looks good, although the color is a bit off. Maybe a lighter color next time? A bit too dark.'

'Okay, give me the instruction manual next time, then, eh?'

'Ach, sorry, should've just said it was fine.'

'Yes.'

'So, Slava called, she and Emilian are driving up later today after she gets a few last things out of 71st, maybe we can all have a nice dinner?'

'Sure, fine, we'll have a dinner. When she gets here, ask her to come out, she'll need to help with a few things.' He stubbed out his cigarette and started painting.

'Alright. Did you want coffee?'
'Yes. Cream and five sugars.'

That evening, the oval wooden table was set with simple china, embroidered napkins and crystal tumblers. A few candles helped magnify the two small table lamps in the corners of the room. Julia was in the kitchen, her apron tied loosely around her, sipping a small glass of wine, navigating the steam emanating from the roast pork she took out just minutes before.

'Mama, do you need help?' Slava walked in first, a fitted black turtleneck hugging her body, her blonde hair scraped back in one long braid that looped around itself at the top. Emilian followed behind her to say hello, and then retreated to the other room to stand with Henry.

Julia swept her arm in front of Slava to direct her, deftly instructing her, as her mother had done with her when she was young. The moment wasn't lost on Slava, she watched her mother—the salty streaks in her dark hair more prominent than ever— as she seasoned and grabbed handfuls of ingredients and mashed and chopped and stirred and kneaded.

'How do you remember all this, without a book?' She helpfully stirred, watching Julia season the vegetables. 'My mother taught me,' she replied, 'and I'm teaching you. Although I probably haven't taught you as much as I could.'

'You're doing it now, though. That's what counts.'

Henry asked Slava about work, Emilian asked Henry about the new house, and Julia spoke little, though her preference was to observe often and engage and watch the people she loved as they moved and smiled and connected. When she did speak, she asked Slava and Emilian if they'd get married one day or had considered children at least.

Slava rolled her eyes. 'No, Mama. Not now. Too busy.'

Julia pushed a bit more. 'Don't you want to have children one day?'

Emilian interrupted, forcing levity into the subject. 'Hey, I hope I get a say in this?' Henry laughed but said nothing and watched as the women bristled.

'Listen Mama, I'm not lonely for children, and I don't, *we* don't, feel the need. What's the point?'

'Of course, yes, that's not what I meant, that you're lonely or bored, you know that.' She looked over at Emilian and smiled and felt a pang of her own past. 'You're just getting older now, so…'

'Come on, I'm 35. Em is 37. That's hardly *that* old.'

'I'd already had *you* when I was 26.'

'Children aren't everything.'

'Ah, but you're wrong. They are. Work isn't.'

'Well,' Slava leaned back from the table, her cheeks flushed from the interrogation and the wine and the gaze of her parents. 'Maybe I don't want to have children.'

'Don't, they're trouble.' Henry interjected, and Emilian laughed, and raised his glass to the comment.

Julia's tone became insistent. 'Oh please. Slava was fine. More than one was a--' Henry looked at Julia and she caught his eye. She had forgotten herself. '-- *would* be troublesome, I imagine.' He looked away again.

'I'll figure it out, Mama.' Slava had heard the change in her mother's voice and she understood then that her father knew. It made her incredibly sad. 'Besides, my life is too full.'

'With what, exactly?' Henry challenged.

'Work, I *said*. Em is studying to be a lawyer. We both want to travel. I want to do things that you and Mama never did.'

'Oh, we did more than you would ever do in one lifetime.'

'Like keep running from country to country and argue with each other all the time? That's what you call 'enough'? And then you ask me if I want to get married and have children?'

'You know what', Henry dug his fingers into the table and leaned forward. 'You have absolutely *no* idea what we've been through.'

'Henry, you're being a bit sensitive—' Julia interrupted, protecting Slava from reaching a depth she wasn't prepared for.

Slava stood up. 'Are you kidding? My whole life I've seen you both tear at each other because of some anger, or things that you don't want to say to each other,' she felt Julia's hand on her arm, urging her to stop. 'Don't you think I feel it, how you speak to Mama? How you both try so hard to ignore the things that make you so angry?'

Henry watched, immobile, as Slava pushed the chair to the dining table and put her coat on. 'But it's okay. We all have our ways. But please, please don't ask me about marriage or children because I don't think I've been shown the best example sometimes,' she said, as her eyes welled for her mother, and for things that she had wanted to say for so long, but never dared.

Emilian stood up, addressing Julia first. 'Very sorry. Thank you—' he turned to Henry now '— both, for a great evening, but I'm going to go with Slava.' And walked out after her.

Slava walked, and then ran, out into the dark, towards the car, because she suddenly knew she couldn't stay: the things she said would leave lasting marks, fresh lashes of pain on all of them, and she knew too much as it was. She wiped her eyes with her sleeve and rolled down the window, breathing the night in, and waited as Emilian opened the driver's side door and started the engine. He looked over at her, and all she could say was 'Just go. Please let's just go.'

And then the screen door to the motel opened, and a rectangle of light from inside the house illuminated the driveway.

'Slava, stop. Wait.' Henry's footsteps lumbered forward in a slow, serious pace, his hands in his pockets. She watched him, not knowing what he would do. Would he shout at her? Would he disown her? Would he tell her that she had failed? Would he push her away? She couldn't bear any of the outcomes, she didn't have any energy left. She felt broken.

Emilian clutched the steering wheel and watched as Henry grabbed the door and crouched down, his head on his hands, framed in the open window. 'Slava, I'm sorry. Sometimes I don't think I'm the father you needed,' he whispered. Tears stained his cheeks: she knew this because it was a clear night, and the moon shone on his face.

She rested her hands on his. She stared at this man, her father, and realized it was the first time he'd told her he loved her, and she wondered if she would ever hear it again.

32

1981

Three years had passed, and it was now September, and the end of the season, and Henry and Slava had both helped a few neighbors untie their boats from the dock that afternoon. Some pleasantries were shared, a few 'have a great autumn', and then quiet finally. The water lapped the shore, and Henry told his daughter that he was tired, and that he wanted a change.

'Well, no one can do the same thing forever, that's not realistic is it, maybe time to try something new,' Slava stood up from where she had been sitting on the docks.

'Slava,' Henry sat back in his chair and drew on his cigarette. 'not even something new can interest me now, I don't think. I have invested my money in property, and I feel that my body is aging like those buildings.'

He lazily watched the silhouettes of powerboats in the distance. The sky was turning pink, and the clouds reflected a pale sunset as they flit across. It was a nice luxury, watching the close of a day: he didn't remember seeing any when he was on the other side of the world, or with his father, or during his days smelling of sugar in the fields. Or maybe he had, he'd just forgotten.

Uncharacteristically for the family, they had created Slava, a child that was something of an optimist, something that initially had irritated Henry. He didn't understand how someone could be so naïve, but he wanted to see what she had in mind. 'So, what're you thinking, then?'

'Not sure. I'm guessing the area is so popular that someone might want a piece of it?'

'Not a bad idea. But if I sell, I can't just sit around.'

'True, but this place is just too big.'

Henry sighed deeply. 'I know. I just can't keep going. I've done the work on this place for years, mostly on my own. My life has been about maintenance and detail: long hours, little time for rest. Sweat and blood.' He looked down at his shirt, pale grey plaid stained from varnish. His stomach softly protruded over his belt, and his breath was labored and contained a slight wheeze. 'Maybe something smaller. I'd hate to completely stop.'

'So, you're going to keep going in this property business?' She dragged over a white plastic chair from the beach and sat down.

'Probably. I like it. I like taking care of something and seeing the pleasure that people get out of something I've done. You know, I'm not the smartest man—'

'Ha!' Slava interrupted. 'Who are you kidding? You may not show it off, but you're pretty solid company amongst idiots.'

Henry nodded. 'Not sure that's saying much, but good point,' He winked. 'I know how to work hard. 'My hands—he lifted them up, weathered and worn, their square shape in stark contrast to the orange sky— they've only known work. I can slow down, but I don't think I can stop yet. And someday, once I feel that I can stop, then I will. I think I have my father's 'fight' in me. So do you,' he elbowed his daughter gently. His affection for her had grown little by little since that explosion one night, and though it didn't change exponentially, they both noticed it, and were grateful for it.

'Yes, but there's something to be said for finding peace sometimes, though.'

Henry stood up. 'Right. Let's not get all soft. My whiskey is waiting, and let's pray your mother didn't burn the dinner—otherwise I'll have to go back to that bar again at midnight…you know the one? Lone Bull? Just down the road by Capri motel. They have the best pastrami sandwiches…', he mused as they walked up the slope.

After he'd put the lake house on the market, Henry was surprised that the offer came so quickly, though he had been looking at new properties already. It was January 1980, and he'd had a buyer knock on his door, wondering if he'd be willing to sell.

'Twice the money, Julia.' He piled the sugar into his black coffee, reaching for the cream as he stirred. 'It's a good offer,' he coughed suddenly, slapping his chest to be rid of it.

'Really?' She sat down at the table in the front office. 'But it's January. Why now?'

He reached into his shirt pocket for a cigarette. 'Well, think about it. Someone wants to get ready for the summer season, so they can probably buy it for less than they would if it was summer. Plus, it's still more money than we paid for it anyway.' The smoke veiled his face temporarily and he pushed it away. 'Don't you want to have a smaller place to take care of? We're in pushing 60 now, for God's sake, do we want to break our backs making people's beds for the rest of our years?'

'Not a bad idea.'

'I know it is.'

'You always manage to land on your feet, husband.'

'It's a special talent.'

'No, your arrogance is.'

'Listen, why don't we go for a drive, I'll show you what I found.'

'What? You already found something?'

He was already putting on his coat. 'Come on.'

🕊

FOR SALE: 5 UNITS
INTERESTED? PLEASE CONTACT 212-668-7409

'What do you think?' Henry had turned the car off of Route 9N, the main road that cut straight through the village, and spotted this sign, not one minute down Birch Avenue, painted crudely in white letters on a big piece of plywood, nailed to a post. They'd been driving 20 minutes in either direction out of Glen Cove, looking for new properties. 'Let's go have a look.' As they slowed down, Julia looked around: to the right and left there were meager, small clapboard houses with rickety-fenced borders. Driveways with log piles in the corners frosted with snow, metal post boxes that needed paint. It was quiet, as if everyone had abandoned their houses in favor of somewhere better. Huge green evergreens with thick snowy branches dominated the skyline: she'd traded New York skyscrapers for towering, leafy guardians. The heavy green and the smell of pine was almost oppressive.

He stopped the car. 'It's over here- look', he pointed to his left. Two small gravelly paths, well-worn by cars, led about 100 feet in, separated by a small mound of grass trapped in snow, and a sickly tree.

On one side, there was what looked like a small grey one-bedroom bungalow unit, and on the other, a series of three grey connected units, each with their own set of wooden stairs. There was a main 'house' at the front, with long and flat concrete steps leading up to the wooden porch and screen door. 5 separate metal post boxes guarded the front. There was no sign, and a small truck was parked towards the back of the property.

'Meh,' Julia shrugged her shoulders. 'Looks like beggars live here,' She pointed at the units. 'And the color! Grey? Like a dead mouse.'

Henry rolled his eyes and reached his arm towards here, clasping her arm tenderly, resting it there. 'Julia, see it for what it is: it's small and manageable and can make us a bit of money in our old age.'

She looked over at him. 'Can't we sell and just find a house to live in, find somewhere and just *live*?' Her head had become too crowded it seemed. She hadn't been sleeping well and her hands ached often lately. She craved a home where time slowed down and the pace was less busy.

'And do what, exactly? Wait to die?' He leaned back and grabbed the wheel again. 'No thank you. God has given my body many more years, and I want to do something with what I've been given.'

'Fine, let's have a look if you're going to be so stubborn about it.' He shifted gears and slowly pulled the car in the drive and told Julia to stay whilst he looked for the owner.

'Henry!' She shouted out of the open window. 'I'm going for a walk, just down the road, I don't want to sit in here.' She grabbed her purse, wrapped her coat around her and pulled her wool hat down, and watched as he waved her off. She knew he wouldn't be very long, once he made up his mind about something, it stuck.

Her boots sounded crisp on the snowy gravel, the heel giving off a muffled crackle as she walked. She'd left her hair loose today, the curlers from last night creating thick waves that hugged her neck and shoulders and peeped out of her hat in small collections of grey and brown. The road was straight and plain, and the houses on either side were few and far between. The ones that were there, were simple family bungalows with unkempt gardens and broken fences out front. *I would change that*, she thought. *No need for fences. Everything needs space*, she mused. She passed someone walking their dog. She tried to glance through open windows as she progressed, tried to see what was happening behind the curtains, tried to hear voices. She wondered if she would walk this road often. She saw a rectangular brown and orange sign to her right: *Gage Rd*. Just as she started to turn back on her heel, she saw it directly across: *Evergreen Cemetery*. It was surrounded by a heavy, dark-grey steel fence: the kind of fencing that reminded her of Germany, during the war. It was imposing and formal, a strange contrast to the lushness and quiet within. It made her think of her parents, who were more than likely dead now. She looked up, the blue sky as crisp and cold as blue glass. She inhaled and closed her eyes. 'Mama. Mama…' She whispered, as her eyes filled with tears. 'Where have I ended up? What am I meant to do now, so much has changed.'

As if answering, the car trundled up, crunching the road beside her. 'Get in,' Henry leaned over, opening her door. 'We're about to have a new little project.'

During next few days, as they came to look at the property and came up with a list of things that needed working on, Henry and Julia saw a For Sale sign on a little gravel road that led to nowhere, called Cooper Street. There was a house there that had come up for sale: it was positioned on the very end of that gravel road and sat atop a small hill by the entrance to a bramble-covered path and was a stone's throw from the very center of town. It was as if someone had placed it, patted it down, and left it for them to discover.

It had white clapboard siding, a black roof, and five concrete steps that led up to the yellow door. It had a carpeted basement and an upper floor, three small bedrooms, two bathrooms, and a wide wooden porch that protruded in the back, over the half-acre garden that sloped down into an open field. The center of town had shop fronts and busy roads, and beaches that filled with children and families in the summer, but this small road afforded them a piece of the home that they had left behind so long ago. A footprint that stayed on the earth for a time. Julia fell in love with it as soon as she saw it. Henry felt deeply happy that the two of them could see themselves living there, and with the money they'd made on Treasure Cove, they could afford to buy the Birch Avenue property to rent out and buy this for themselves to live.

     Over the rest of that year, half of their days were spent at the larger property to develop for rental: it was solid, built on a skeleton of hardy foundations, but there was a lot of work. There was paintwork to be done, the roofs needed completely new tiles, the bathrooms had accumulated a significant amount of mold in various corners and drains, and the drives needed paving. Towards the Spring, when the work was almost complete, Henry, Julia and Slava together sawed, shaped and painted a large wooden sign out of heavy timber, and carved the silhouette of a pine tree on the front, with heavy coats of dark green and brown letters underneath, spelling out *SOSONKA*. The day they staked it into the ground, Henry smiled as he looked up. 'Our little 'evergreen'. It fits.'

     Half of their time, or Julia's time, really, was spent at the house on Cooper Street. She spent hours elbow-deep in the garden, though it was comparatively small to the one from her childhood. It was potent however, regardless of size; the tinny taste of soil on her tongue as she breathed, the hydrangeas huddled in the corner of the fence, by the peonies, overpowering everything with perfume. The gooseberries and currants ran rampant along the near side, competing for space, their thorny branches daring anyone to pick them. Sweet red tomatoes clung to the vines in the middle, and there were yellow zucchini flowers and carrots peeking up on the left-hand side. The garden was at the bottom of a sloping green, the porch above it where she would sit in front of sliding glass doors that led into the living room and dining room.

     She could walk nine paces in either direction to reach newly planted beds shaded by a pear tree, which was more than enough space for her to have a days' worth of work at her feet. A pile of compost had been created in the far corner, and as she walked towards the end of the property, she could see through the metal fencing an open field and would lace her fingers through it, staring through the metal as she had done in Germany, to a world beyond her reach— this time, her gaze landed on small houses dotted just beyond, with gardens of their own, and a small school.

The inside of the house was warm and comfortable: the front room had pale green carpet and was surrounded by windows all the way around. The previous owners had left some furniture behind, which was useful, as they'd been spending money furnishing Sosonka. There was a long metal desk along the left wall, three drawers on each side with thin pull-handles. A rotary phone and a Yellow Pages sat on the surface. Above the desk were built-in shelves that had— even over such a short period of time— accumulated books that they'd brought with them from, and out of, various countries: *Taras Shevchenko, Zakhar Berkut, Kobzar and Haidamaky, Unordnung und frühes Leid, The Magic Pudding*, among others.

The inner rooms were dark, with dark tile and pale brown carpet: the kitchen to the left, overlooked the street, and the living area on the right, overlooked the garden below. There was a stone fireplace with framed pictures of family, a crucifix hanging above overlooking it all. The dining room was further on, an oval wooden table in the center surrounded by eight chairs. On the right of the table, up against the wall, was a collection of china that had been painted with poppies and *vyshyvanka* patterns. These had been a gift from Jeffy when Julia and Henry had moved out of New York, and they thought of him often. Down the hallway from the living area were four small bedrooms: two on the left overlooking the street, two on the right overlooking the garden, with a main bathroom at the end. Julia and Henry had decided to take the bedroom on the right, it had pale blue carpet, a dressing area and table with a mirror, and a sizeable closet. It also had a door that directly accessed the porch in back.

She walked in towards the living area and opened the door to the basement. There was a washing machine below, a wet bar and a storage room that led to the garage. It was more than enough space for them, but it was perfect for guests and family to come and stay. She walked downstairs, turning on the light. She immediately turned back and walked up, closing the door behind her. She didn't understand basements. It was a waste, and it made her feel uncomfortable in some way.

The doorbell rang, voices called through the door before Julia even opened it. 'Hey!! We're tired! Open it!' It was Slava and Henry.

Henry moved passed her once he could, smelling of sweat and paint.

He dropped his various bags, brushes and paint-splattered bandana on the green carpet as Slava moved in behind him. 'We've been at Birch all day. I need a drink, both of us do, and not that fizzy Cola nonsense.'

'Alright, alright...' She moved past him and walked up the step into the kitchen. 'Just leave any dirty clothes in that room, I have enough to do than to worry about getting paint out of the carpet.' She turned to Slava. 'Are you staying? Should I make dinner?'

'No, Mama, I can't. I need to go straight back to the city tonight, as I have a meeting tomorrow morning.'

'Lab technicians have meetings?' her father teased.

'Oh, god, not this again.'

'Just get your drinks and get in the house already,' Julia scolded and walked back into the kitchen, stifling a smirk.

That evening, there was dinner, and wine for the parents and water for Slava, and conversations about politics. And then later Henry poured himself whiskey and explained his philosophy about how the government was corrupt, Slava interjected her theories about how women in the workplace were undervalued and underpaid. Henry defended his position on how the government would never allow immigrants a fair stake in any country they reside, and Julia listened, and watched. She watched her daughter, a daughter both of them hadn't given much time to understand, hold her own against a dominant personality like her own father. Henry labored to get across his points now, for he was too tired to be as clever as he once was and with many years of drinking and eating to excess, he'd grown tired.

'Ay, come on with all the heavy!' Julia exclaimed. She looked at Henry, his eyes growing heavy. 'Look at him,' Julia gestured. 'Slava, you need to get on the road, and we need to go to bed.'

Slava stood up and came over to her father and put her hand on his broad, rounded shoulder. 'Papa, I need to go in a minute. It's 7:30, and I need to drive for three hours.'

'I'll walk you out.' Henry stood up, reaching into his shirt pocket for a cigarette as they both walked down the front steps and then towards the car parked in the driveway behind the house to say their goodbyes. The pair stood next to each other for a brief second: the five-and-a-half-foot girl next to the six-foot-three tall old man. She elbowed him gently in the arm. 'Papa, you shouldn't smoke so much. It's bad for you.' He smiled. 'Ahh, Slava.

Don't worry about me. Get back to your important work.' He winked at her.

Slava slipped into the car and looked back as Henry walked up the steps towards the porch. 'Julia, leave the basement door open,' she heard him say. 'You know I like when doors are left open. Closed doors are bad omens.' And then he turned back, smiled, and walked inside.

꩜

After Slava had left, Julia and Henry moved with a contentedness that could be described as monotony: she had washed and tidied the dinner plates away, one by one, and then dried the glasses, as he sat on his favorite chair outside on the porch, the cool night air on his face. The porch jutted out just enough that when he sat, he could only see sky. He watched as the smoke from his cigarette drew a silver line from his fingers, reaching for the navy summer night, dissipating peacefully.

Julia opened the door and leaned against the frame, drying her hands on her apron. 'Need some company?'

He reached over and pulled an extra chair to him, the sound wood on wood creating his invitation.

Julia walked over, untying the knot behind her back, dropping the apron on the floor, and sat down. She leaned her head back and looked up at the sky. 'It's lovely and quiet here, in this spot.' She pointed across. 'Even at night, you can't see the garden, but it's there. Waiting. And then beyond… the fields beyond.'

Henry nodded. 'Home.' He meant it in ways that Julia didn't realize.

'Yes. Finally.'

'I wonder, occasionally.'

'About what?' It was unlike Henry to reminisce, or become nostalgic about the past, so Julia was curious.

'About the paths we've taken to arrive here.' He raised his hand and passed it through the air in front of him. 'Like stars, moving along the sky.'

'They were all hard, in so many ways. But we wouldn't have arrived here without them.'

Henry nodded. 'Regrets?' He looked over at Julia, her face bathed in the half light of a waning moon.

She smiled and looked at him. 'Don't we all. But nothing that breaks my dreams.' She saw that his eyes shone with tears, or maybe it was a trick of the moonlight.

Julia locked her fingers together, as if clasped in lazy prayer. 'You?'

He looked back at the night sky, and watched as the cigarette he held burnt out, the embers turning increasingly black. 'Nothing that breaks granite.' He exhaled a final plume of smoke. 'Besides, if I had any, they are something that God and I will have to discuss one day.'

His other hand reached for hers, and they both finished their evening in silence.

33

The night was still. Which was why, when Julia woke, she thought she was dreaming. It sounded like the beginning of a storm. Muffled. Troubled.

'What was that?' she didn't move her head off her pillow and sleepily waited for a response. When she heard nothing, she assumed she'd been dreaming and started to fall asleep again.

There was little wind that evening, and she could still see the moon as it hung in wait for the dawn: thin, silvery slices through the folds of the curtains. She'd heard a kind of thin forced wheeze, then heavier, guttural, and it had woken her. She wasn't sure if it was the house settling. It could possibly be; it was always settling, and there were occasionally small animals in the garden.

The silence was more than that, though: she'd recall later that it carried with it absolutely no life. It was hollow. She opened her eyes again and listened. Nothing.

She closed her eyes, the relief of being half-asleep and hearing nothing, except for the wind shuddering through the trees. She'd never known him not to snore, so this felt wonderfully luxurious.

Five minutes later, she opened them again as if she remembered something, for something had suddenly changed.

She turned over to face him, her hand reached out for his chest. No sound. She shook him a little. 'Henry. Hey.' He was stiff, the skin underneath his shirt felt unyielding. She listened to his breath. Nothing. 'Henry. *Henry answer me.*' She sat up and shook him with both hands, and then she knew, and slid off the bed and turned on the light as she ran through her bedroom down the small hallway, her nightgown flying behind her ankles, the glut of material irritating her for some reason, her grey hair wild around her face. She jerked open the door to the front room and reached the phone, dialing frantically. She'd memorized her number by heart.

'Oh Jesus. Oh Jesus, help me,' she repeated as she waited for an answer.

'Hello— '

'Slava, Slava help me...' She was gasping for air and hysterical. '... help me... it's Papa, he's... I can't... I heard a sound, I don't remember... I tried to wake him... Slava... what do I do...' her voice heaved and broke and sobbed and did the thing that voices do when no words come out, only sharp intakes of breath and heavy exhales.

Julia heard Emilian's concern in the background, and then Slava's. 'Mama calm. Wait. What—'

'I can't wake him, what do I do, oh Slava,' She wailed on the line, her voice broken.

'Mama— what happened?!'

'I don't know, Slava, I don't— 'Julia's felt as if she were drowning.

'Is he breathing?'

'Slava, I *don't know!* I think so, but I can't tell.'

'Okay, fine, call 911. Now. Do it. Call me when you've done it. Hang up. Dial 911. Do you understand? 9-1-1.'

'Yes.' The dial tone rang in her ear. She was alone. She didn't remember dialing the numbers, she didn't remember what Henry was wearing, she didn't remember how many men arrived at their house, the blue and red colors painting the sky like silent fireworks. She didn't remember how they got Henry onto a stretcher, she didn't remember if she cried, and how she looked, and if they'd had an argument the night before and what they'd said to each other before they went to bed. All she remembered was that his body had lost its spirit next to hers, and she'd felt it and it made her feel a loneliness that crippled her.

Glens Falls Hospital, they said. She remembered that too. She didn't ask if she could go with them. She was in her nightgown. It wouldn't be appropriate, she thought, soberly and completely irrationally.

She remembered when they shut the door. She remembered

watching the red lights fade down the road, wink feebly from a distance, and then disappear into blackness. She saw a neighbor's window light go off, as if they'd been watching the entire time. She turned the house lights off, erasing her silhouette from anyone's view. She leaned against the closed door and felt her body slowly disintegrate, her legs gave way until she sat on the floor, rocking forwards, her head in her hands.

Henry.
Oh God, Henry.
Slava.
Oh, she remembered. *Call Slava.*

'Mama?' it didn't even ring fully before she answered the phone. 'Where is he, what's happening?' Julia heard Emilian in the background, concern in his voice.

'Slava, they took him—' her breath became labored again. '—took him to the hospital. The one on St. Andrews. I can't drive, I don't know how to drive—' tears fell down her cheeks, the receiver wet as she spoke. '—How have I never learned how to drive??'

'Mama, listen…'
'Shouldn't I go now? How do I get there?'
'Stop. Listen.'

'Okay.' She sounded small. Slava listened patiently as Julia swallowed her sobs and tried to breathe. She was drowning.

'There's nothing you can do there right now, so we'll drive over, fast as we can, and we'll take you to the hospital. Is that alright? Just try and stay calm. It'll be okay.'

'Okay.'
'Mama. You'll be okay.'
'Will I? Oh Slava. Please hurry.' And she put the phone down.

She was alone. The house felt like it would swallow her whole, her thin body felt invisible against the weight of his presence in this house. He was still here, and yet, he was gone.

She went into the kitchen and searched the cupboards blindly, found the tea, and set it next to the kettle. Then she withdrew the milk from the refrigerator. She took a teaspoon and dipped it into a pot of honey and watched it coat the bowl with a thin golden sheen and then slide slowly off it and back down into the pot. It was a ritual that her mother used to do with her. *Troshky, troshky davai. Bit by bit, let yourself feel.* Moments and memories lived in simple actions, but there was no one to witness it now, apart from her, in an empty house, sipping tea from a honeyed spoon like she'd done when she was a child. It was the only memory she could recall then, and it brought her some comfort, as her tears fell.

꧁꧂

The early morning sky was still a pale navy, and yet the entrance to the hospital was as bright as if it were already noon, bright as the sun. There were EMTs standing to the side, surrounded by rings of smoke. Emilian and Slava were by her side as they parked the car and led her to the entrance. Emilian and Slava had exchanged a private look to each other, *you go with her, I'll stay here,* and Julia was grateful that it would be only her and Slava walking together.

'Mama, this way,' Slava motioned, seeing that her mother was distracted.

'Ah, okay.' She was blinded by what was ahead, not only by the lights but by what was happening. She had no idea what to expect: it was a childlike reaction to something serious; she was oblivious to the world around her, only the world that existed in her head. She was still in her nightgown and coat. Slava had brought a bag with some clothes for her to change into, but she didn't care.

They stopped at reception and Slava spoke. 'Henry Rudnick? Which room?'

'Oh sure, yeah, Rood-nick' the woman casually flipped through a chart. Americans don't know how to trill their r's, Slava thought. 'Room 3F, on the Intensive Care floor, he was sent there from the Neurodiagnostics department. You have to sign this and—'

'What did the scans say, then?' Slava interrupted and snatched her pen and scribbled her name without looking down.

'You'll have to talk to Doctor Lee ma'am, he'll be on the third floor.'

'Thanks,' she shot back. They had already started towards the elevator.

The Intensive Care Unit was almost reverent in its construction. Smooth, sterile white floors as if no one had ever stepped on them before. The walls were the same color, with pale wood paneling placed every 5 feet or so, to break up the monotone. Pictures of flowers and landscapes and happy, healthy people were framed, mocking anyone's pain with saccharine smiles.

    Slava saw a doctor walking towards them, a clipboard under his arm. 'I need to speak to Dr. Lee, where's Doctor Lee?' The man stopped, placed a hand on her shoulder. 'Dr. Lee will be right with you, I'll tell him you're looking for him, who are you here to see?'

    'Henry, Rudnick, 3F they said.'

    'There,'—he gestured down the hallway—'on your right, one of the last ones.'

    As they walked, they saw each room had small, wire-laced 'windows': as if thin, incompetent barriers to see what was within. But anyone could still see, and it did nothing bought obstruct the view that people needed, of loved ones losing their battles.

    3F

    PATIENT: Henry RUDNIC

    'Can't even spell his goddamn name right,' Slava sighed.

    She heard footsteps and saw Emilian walking down the hallway, his crisp jacket and worn jeans a comfort in the sterile, grey hallway.

    Emilian touched her arm, and he felt her muscles suddenly go slack at knowing he was there. He smiled softly as she looked at him. 'I just wanted to tell you that I'm here. I couldn't just leave you both here, I felt like I could be helpful maybe. But you probably need to do this the way *you* need, so I'll be here—' he pointed at a molded plastic bench bolted to the wall in the hallway, with thin padding on each seat, magazines beside it, '—in my very own, luxurious lounge chair.'

    They both laughed in the thin way that only happens when you grieve, and Slava was grateful for it.

    'Do you want coffee? You haven't eaten anything. You need to look after yourself.' He winked, stroking her arm.

    'No, I'm fine.' She smiled at his reference, kissed him, and turned back to face the door.

    It was silent. And then, it was as if the ground softened under their feet. Julia inhaled sharply when she saw Henry, and whispered *Bozshe miliy, moya lyubov. Oh God, there is my love.*

    'Henry...' She pressed her hands and forehead up against the glass, helpless, her tears wetting the window. 'Slava can I go in? I need to see him.'

Slava backed away.

Julia opened the door quietly, as if not to wake him from a deep sleep or stir the plastic tubes from their metal hangers. He was covered in starched white sheets and grey felted blankets, his hands flat on the bed beside his body, eyes and mouth closed. His chest moved artificially, clear plastic snaking around his arms and his face and in his nose, all connected to constantly beeping machines. Numbers and lights flashed on two separate screens and an IV stand hovered limply, feeding yellow-tinted fluid. It was like a white curtain delivering the final act of a play. Serene. Sad. Final.

She saw a small metal chair, pulled it to his bedside and sat down, her two delicate hands covering his one wide one. Their wedding rings collided as their hands met. '*Znova, do mene.*' 'Henry, come back to me,' she whispered. She laid her head down next to his hand and felt warmth. He was still here. So, she waited for a response. She waited for his eyes to open and for him to say *my little Julia*. She had waited for Maria this way, forty years ago.

Only the machines spoke in clicks and flutters and metallic whines.

'Henry, I can't do this without you here, you know.' Julia dried her eyes. 'Look at the state of me, I'm in a damn nightgown,' she laughed. 'It would really embarrass you if you saw me right now.' She stroked his hand and turned it over and saw that his callouses had softened. His hands had been so worn and toughened, the skin split and repaired so often, and now, as he had wished, he had slowed his pace. His body had started its recovery. Or, at least part of him had, she mused sadly.

'None of this makes any sense. Here we are, finally at a place where we can stay. And have peace. No more turning back. Just like we wanted.' She struggled to keep her voice even. 'Please don't leave now. Not yet.'

The sun broke through the window, followed swiftly by a cloud. She suddenly felt someone next to her. It was Slava. 'Mama let's just be with him, that's what he needs right now. Talk to him, because he's still here. We don't know what will happen. Just pray. All we can do is pray.' She pulled a chair over to sit down next to her.

The door opened, and a short balding man with a round, smooth face stood there, holding a clipboard. His tie was undone, as if he'd just finished a long shift. 'Ma'am, are you the daughter?' Slava nodded and walked over to him as he stuck out his hand. 'I'm Dr. Lee.' He gestured to the door. 'Let's speak in my office. I'd like to talk about your father.'

Slava looked back at her mother, still holding Henry's hand, still in the same spot. 'Mama?'

Julia nodded. 'Yes. Go. I will be here.'

Slava clenched her fists and felt like pacing the floor, but she was sat rooted to her spot. 'Mark, I'm aware of what a brain aneurysm is, I worked in a hospital as a clinician.'

Dr. Lee's office was decorated in the typical style: various certificates in frames on the wall, three shelves with thick medical textbooks, anatomy encyclopedias, leather-bound journals, a light box for x-rays, and a few awards. But there were things that said much more about who Dr. Lee was: a metal tray on the desk that held envelopes and forms and file folders with neon tabs stuck to the sides, a stress ball, three unfinished cups of coffee, and a few pictures with children in them, as well as colorful drawings stuck to the wall with scotch tape.

Dr. Lee's name was Mark, and that's what Slava called him now, for airs and graces disappeared in this kind of conversation. Mark was trying to explain to Slava that her father's brain had exploded, but in medical terms. He was using a metal pointer to describe the mass on the x-ray. Slava was looking at a drawing of a cartoon mouse on the wall when he'd done that. She didn't need a diagram.

Mark was patient. He'd dealt with many versions of grief and pain before.

'Well, the aneurysm contributed to a subarachnoid hemorrhage. It was so severe, that it makes me think it was happening over a long period of time, just hadn't been diagnosed.'

'Like a ticking— '

'Time bomb. Yes.' Mark nodded and leaned back in his chair as if they were having the most natural of conversations, and not about a man who was dying in the other room. 'What was his lifestyle like? Did he smoke?'

'Yes. All his life.'

'Did he have a healthy diet?'

Slava offered a weary laugh. 'If you can call inches of butter on his bread, and coffee white with heavy cream and plenty of sugar in it, and alcohol-fueled card games at midnight... healthy?' She wiped a tear off her cheek and cleared her throat. It felt like dry, broken glass. 'What about his other scans, what did they show? Reception, or rather the nurse who was sitting at reception, told us that he'd been in the neurosciences unit.'

Mark picked up the chart that had been attached to Henry's door. 'Well, it says here that when he was admitted, his blood pressure reading was 200 systolic over 105 diastolic...'

His blood was bubbling like a pot of boiling water, basically. 'Jesus Christ,' she whispered.

'Yes. There was extensive bleeding on the brain, and the current scans show no activity at all.' His face was sympathetic. 'No change from before.'

'So, the respirator is breathing for him, basically. But what about the rest of him?'

He put the charts down and leaned forward. 'His brain shows no activity, but his heart is extraordinarily strong, considering what condition he was in when he got here. It could very easily keep going for days, weeks, or it could stop within hours. His brain, however, is... well...'

'Gone.' Slava hung her head.

'Yes. There are no electrical impulses being sent from his brain. The machines are helping him breathe, which obviously circulates oxygenated blood through the body, but the heart's intrinsic electrical system can keep the organ beating for a short while after a person becomes brain-dead — and some biological processes — including kidney and gastric functions — can continue for a week or so. Alternatively, the heart could just give up on its own.'

'Okay, so what do I need to do?'

'I'd say give yourselves time with him, and then you can decide if you want to keep him on machines, or...'

'...let him die with dignity, and no artificial means,' Slava interrupted.

'Yes, that's a way of putting it.'

'Thank you.'

Mark walked back around his desk and sat on the edge, folding his hands on his thighs. 'I'm really so sorry.' He stood up and walked towards the door. 'If you need time in here, just take whatever you need. Or ask me anything. Do you need me to bring your mother in?'

'No,' Slava shook her head. 'I'll go back in a minute.'

He nodded and walked off, Slava watching his white lab coat dust the sides of the door frame and turn the corner.

Slava listened to the quiet of the room, and heard the noise of the hospital behind her, as if a thick fog had settled. Her father, the man that seemed to be the strongest, tenacious man she had ever met, had lost his fight; his mind had given up. And yet his heart refused to let go.

Glen Cove spread out in a spill of land that had was connected by green spaces and winding roads that worked their way towards the Long Island Sound. You could see it all on a clear day, standing at the perfect height, or sat on their favorite bench by the beach, watching the water lap the sand. Julia saw it all now, through the hospital window and felt as if she were standing on the precipice of something unfamiliar. The feeling merged with a distant memory: of arriving at the western edge of Australia with Henry, looking out at the edge of a ship and seeing nothing but water at their feet and the long edge of a country that she'd never eyes on before. The difference was, that she was now alone, and the cry of seagulls were replaced with the whine of machines.

Julia felt certain areas of her body light up, whilst the rest stayed disconnected: she was conscious of her breath, as if she had to focus to remember to breathe; her ankles hurt, but her feet and legs felt numb; her fingertips felt cold; she'd been grinding her teeth apparently because her jaw now ached. She walked over to the chair that she'd just left, and moved it closer to Henry's bed, up at his head.

She leaned forward, her face a couple inches from him and scanned his skin: it was pale and sunken, the dark circles under his eyes not as pronounced as they had once been, probably an effect of the machined oxygen coursing through his lungs. His hair was brushed back. *When had it turned so silvery? How had she missed that?* she thought. His lips were soft and flat, relaxed underneath the cannula under his nose that was taped to both cheeks. She couldn't remember the last time she'd looked at him so closely, so acutely aware of the texture of his face, the shadow of his eyelashes, the way his hair lay, the soft fuzz that had grown on the edges of his ears. It was the way a child would look at its parents: intently, faces up close, digesting and imprinting it all. Adults, they just don't. She spied a few freckles under his right eye, and saw the grey in his eyebrows, still as full and pronounced as they were when she'd met him.

She delicately followed the map of his face with her finger, creating a permanent mark on her memory. She followed the lines on his forehead, the shape of his hairline, his jaw, chin and neck. She laid her palm on his head, similar to what she imagined she would do with her own daughter when she was ill. 'Henry', She whispered. 'Henry, what's happened to you,' she asked, as she placed her hand in his limp one. She smiled at how big it still was, compared to her own. It felt heavy and lifeless and unnatural, and she'd hoped that by holding it she could warm it slightly.

She felt a hand on her shoulder. Slava pulled up a chair and sat next to her.

'You know,' She spoke without looking at Slava, tracing her finger around his wedding band, 'I never thought he'd stop. I thought he'd live forever, or at least until he'd learn to slow down and spend time doing the things he loved.'

'I know, Mama. I always thought the same.' Slava leaned forward and rolled the IV drip to the side. The click and whirr of the ventilator responded. 'It was too much for you both. Too much work, too much worry, maybe.' She moved her hair off her shoulder, the blonde streaks bright against the blue of her sweater.

'He would be so disappointed with this,' Julia gestured to the room. "*Dai Bozshe, for God's Sake*, look at me now', he'd say. "Look at this useless body doing nothing but lying around!" A laugh escaped as she blinked away tears. 'So undignified, this end, for someone like him. And now what do we do?'

Slava rested her hand on Julia's arm. They let the silence in, the weight of the day. The minutes drifted as they sat in their own thoughts.

Julia turned to Slava. 'Do you need a minute with him, rabbit?'

Slava weakened at the childhood nickname that she hadn't heard in years. Her mother had carried a distance with her for so long, and this one little word revealed an incredible amount. 'Yes, Mama. She turned and saw that Emilian was still there, keeping quiet vigil, reading a book. 'Emilian can help you get some coffee.' She helped her up and led her to the door.

It was many minutes before Slava spoke. At first, she felt embarrassed that she had nothing to say, and no plan with how to say it. Her father had always called her a 'planner'. *You always need a reason for things. You probably get that from me.* She was in a room that felt like a vacuum. It could have been hours that she'd been sitting there, or it could have been seconds. Nothing mattered.

She leaned back in her chair. 'Papa, can I tell you something?'

The machines whirred.

'I wish I knew more about you and Mama. I wish I knew more about what happened to her, to you, to your lives. I get a sense that I wasn't ever told much, just the things at the surface. It created distance; like I'd missed something important.' She shifted in her chair at the admission. 'Emilian always told me that it would get there. I would know more, just like everyone does when they get older. You know, parents ending up looking like regular people, doing their best.' A sigh escaped. 'But we never got there, you and I.'

A beep from the machine prompted her to glance at the monitor, but it was nothing urgent.

'I haven't asked Mama about her life. Maybe I will, I don't know. I feel like with this happening, you here, I need to take that opportunity. Get to know her, I guess.' Slava rested both hands in front of her stomach, fingers laced together. 'Maybe that's something that as a wife and a mother and a woman you just, you bury things and solve them slowly on your own. Not letting people in. Maybe that's what you do for your children. For your husband. For your family. You lock things away so you can love each other the best way you can.' Her throat caught. 'Papa, you loved each other. I don't remember anything much about Australia, but I remember the love.'

Please talk to me. Just one word.

Slava shifted her feet softly, like a child. 'I remember anger too. Especially as I got older. But all you needed to say to each other was *I love you*. It's not that hard.'

She looked up at him and pulled her hair down onto her shoulder, twirling it around her finger as she'd done when she was little. She was a daughter who was losing a father and telling him all the things that she'd never been able to. She'd just needed more time: more time to learn about who he was, more time to tell him who she was. So, she told him now, because she knew she would always do the same for the baby growing inside her— she would tell her everything.

'Papa, I love you' she whispered, and her chest crackled as she began to sob.

'I'm so sorry for the things that I've never said to you and for the moments we never got a chance to share. I'm sorry for not being the daughter that listened and behaved and made you chase me around the house when I was naughty,' she laughed through her tears. 'I'm sorry I never took walks with you and asked you what your favorite season was, or your favorite piece of music.' She pressed on her cheeks to dry the tears. 'I'm sorry that we didn't hug, or kiss or show each other anything but expectation. I know it was always understood, but we could have said it more.' The bedsheet was wet, her face swollen as she leaned on her hands on the metal rail beside his bed.

She turned her head to the side and her eyes became distant at the beginning of a memory. 'Papa, do you remember that day that I walked into the greenhouse and you were angry at me because you were worried that I would break something, but then I watched you, and I listened. Mama told me that was the day you told me about the orchids. You told me how to care for them and how to raise them and how to protect them.'

She stood up, the shadows of the afternoon filtering into the room, creating glittering shapes of the bits of dust in the air. She leaned over and kissed his forehead, like a mother to a child, lingering to imprint the feel of his skin on her memory. '*Ya tebe lyublyu*, Papa. I love you. Thank you for being my father.' She felt her stomach again. Only she and Emilian knew their secret, and now her father would. 'I wish you could have met your grandchild.'

The machines beeped and hummed.

When she left the room, she saw the name on the door again. RUDNIC. She reached over to his chart, withdrew a black pen and quickly drew a K at the end. 'There you go,' she smirked and wiped a tear away. 'You would've wanted me to do that.'

That evening as the streets grew dark and quiet and the bright lights of the hospital shone, Emilian, Julia and Slava maintained a vigil in his room or in the hallway. Slava had explained to Julia as plainly as possible that the man they had loved was dying, and Julia had known, despite the words breaking her heart. She had felt it in the air around him, in the room she had seen him in, even the night where she couldn't wake him up. Her strength was in knowing, and in the decision she knew she had to make soon.

Nurses drifted in and out at regular intervals, checking on vital signs. Sometimes the family were together, but oftentimes apart, one of them grabbing coffee or water or something to eat. Julia prayed at his side with a fist of rosary, and Slava paced, or watched her mother through the glass, wondering who the girl was that had lost the man she had loved.

'Hey, do you want to go home for a bit, for a little sleep, and then come back?' Emilian looked as tired as Slava suspected she was, but she hadn't looked in a mirror all day. He was her mirror.

'Yeah, probably. We can stay at my mother's, if that's okay?'

Emilian nodded in response.

Slava looked through the glass. Her mother was still praying. 'She'd be there all night if she could.'

'She won't go willingly.'

Slava shrugged and opened the door to the room.

'Mama?' She walked over and saw her mother's face. She looked as if she was in a dream, her eyes staring and tired.

'Yes? Any news for Papa?'

Slava shook her head. 'Listen, I think we should go home to rest a little, and then we can come back later, or tomorrow? You need to have some sleep.'

'Can I stay here?'

'No, Mama. They'll take good care of him, don't worry.'

Julia nodded trustingly. 'Can you leave me? I'll be ready in a minute.'

Slava nodded and walked out, softly closing the door behind her.

Julia stood up and walked over to the window again. The sky was the kind of blue that was lit from within, not the kind of night that was black as pitch and had no depth. She could see cottony white clouds, the scattered stars, and the red light of a plane, winking in the distance. Further still, she saw the faint warm lights of houses that lined the shore. Not far from those houses was their own. *Hers,* now. They had settled their life in it together, piece by piece, and they were happy. She would be surrounded by memories of him, and it would fill the space without him there. She grabbed her right hand, spun her wedding ring round and round in a type of meditation. Forty years of seeing someone's life burn bright. And now, snuffed out.

She turned to look at him and the sight of his peaceful face made her lips tremble. Tears fell. 'Henry, you know, you weren't the easiest person. But then, neither was I. We suffered greatly, you and I, so many broken pieces that we couldn't put back together,' she tilted her head to the side. 'But we had each other. And that was enough.' There was forgiveness in her voice.

She walked over to him and sat down, taking his hand in hers, the touch of him still so comforting and safe. 'I will miss you' she whispered, for 'love' was too great a word to bear out loud. And as her lips touched his cheek, she watched his eyes, in the fleeting hope that he would respond with just a single movement.

The next morning, the sun dangled in the sky and a dark pink ribbon of cloud stretched across the horizon. Shops opened their doors and reversed their 'closed' signs, people carried their morning coffees to work, waves lapped the shore, and the sound of birdsong crept over the winds. In the small house on Cooper Slava slept in Emilian's arms, their secret safe and warm inside her, and Julia slept heavily in the other room, clutching Henry's pillow to her body.

The world was welcoming a new day with simmering activity. But in Henry Rudnick's room, a man who had lived a life that had been vast and complicated and loud, the machines finally fell silent.

34

On the afternoon of the funeral, the grey stone church stood lonely against the weather, its stained glass muted. The cold rain ran in rivulets against the dark cars that collected on the road, the sky was an opaque grey. As they sat in the car in front of the church, at a distance behind the hearse, Julia rested her face on the window and looked out. They'd been there together, she and Henry, for an occasional Sunday morning mass. It was an easy walk from their house, a straight smooth gravel road and then a left past the cemetery. They'd come here together even today, but she would leave alone.

'Mama, are you ready?' Slava undid the seatbelt that had nested itself under her protruding belly and turned to Julia. She saw her mother gazing at the church, the car windows spattered with rain.

'My mother used to tell me that death is simple.' Her voice broke. 'It doesn't care for ceremony.' Julia's face remained facing the church, recalling this memory in a trance. Slava watched her mother as she grieved, and reached over to Emilian in the driver's seat, finding his hand and squeezing it as Julia continued. 'Death does not care of wind, or rain, or sun, for nothing matters when the time comes to meet with God.' She wiped a tear from her cheek and looked down. 'Yes, I'm ready.'

Julia watched as people streamed into the church, the heavy, ornate wooden doors held open by two priests (one Ukrainian, one English). Some she recognized, many she didn't. Word had spread in the city, and then farther still to anyone that had known Henry, that a great spirit had dimmed, and his obituary was the flag for mourning: for immigrants, for

Ukrainians, for people that had survived journey, and for those that hadn't. It was a celebration of his life, and a grieving for it.

People were huddled and whispering in groups: somber black suits, and dresses adorned with red wooden beads and embroidered flowers, smells of hairspray and rose-tinged perfumes combining with heavy colognes. *Surely funerals should be private,* thought Julia. *People are only here to mourn their own loss, and eat the food carefully laid out for them.* Her anger was misplaced, but it was normal. Her husband had created a community of spirits, and his sudden absence in their lives unsettled them.

Julia and Slava walked, slowly, Emilian trailing respectfully beside them, behind the heavy coffin as it was brought into the church and laid at the front, white flowers trailing on the corners of the altar and down the sides. Before the service, the casket was opened, and lines of people solemnly walked up to it, pressing their palms on the shining mahogany and saying silent prayers. Julia was last, and she watched slowly as his face appeared to her as she walked up. He was as she remembered him in the hospital yet took comfort that there were no machines chained to his body. He was peaceful, there was no pain of the flesh, no presence in him now. He was gone. She turned where she stood, and saw a sea of people sat behind her, as far back as the door to the church, and even lining the back walls. Young and old, people that had traveled distances to be here, people that lived around the corner and had never said but a few words.

The two priests began, one holding an overly ornate icon of a gold Jesus lamenting his fate on the cross, quietly reciting the hymns of St Henry Damascene, both chanting in monotone Gregorian voices. The beatitudes followed, all the while the three metal chains of the *kadylo*, the incense burner held by the priests, clanged and shook, releasing frankincense in heavy clouds, incensing the body. It was intensely cathartic and heart-rending, the repetition and the smells creating a frenzy of melancholy worship. Then, the beginning of *Vichnaya Pamyat*, the hypnotic and dark funeral song, blessing the dead.

'In the name of the father and son and holy ghost, with God's almighty blessing…' one of the priests began, in a deep booming voice cutting through the silence, '…shall this soul see his eternal reward.' He held the notes, the walls reverberating with a sound that was almost inhuman. 'Peace will now be granted unto your soul, with Christ and the Holy Mother of God residing on their thrones beside you as you enter the gates of heaven.' His voice rose within the minor notes of the song, the force almost withdrawing the blackness of the day and releasing a ghost. The congregation began their response, the various harmonies filling the space:

'In the name of the father, son and holy ghost, may your memory live on, live on in our hearts, through our lives, may your memory be an eternal reminder to the souls you have left behind on this earth, a reminder that God will be waiting for us… may your memory live eternally, may you find the peace that your soul has longed for. And now, Slava would like to sing *Zhuravli*, will everyone please rise.' And then Slava stood up and walked to the front of the church, her hand resting on her belly, her heels echoing in the space, and she saw her mother nodding at her to go on. She reached the front and turned around in her somber black dress that she had bought just for this occasion and would never wear again. She whispered *Papa, I miss you* to herself, and through her tears she began to sing the opening notes of her father's favorite song:

> *Do you hear, my brother, my friend?*
> *The cranes departing, with silvery wings aloft*
> *Their voices calling out, as they cross the sea…*

Her voice lifted and echoed amongst the silent, cold walls of the room, and then a few voices joined her, slowly, and then more still-- baritones and tenors and altos, men and women's voices joining together-- as it was a song that they had all heard as children and felt deeply. The far corners of Julia's life finally connected in their collective mourning and their memories of Henry collided with their own realization: that death was the final freedom that he had spent his entire life searching for. It seemed a sea of faces, not a single one dry, sang for the loss of a man that had lived a long life in too short a time.

At the end of the service, as people streamed back out and black umbrellas unfurled against the sky and moved towards the cars, Julia sat on her own, a lonely figure in the front pew, thinking about what was left of her life. She looked around at the saints preserved in stained glass, and at the gold pots of incense in the corner, their chains hanging loosely on the floor. The only sound in the room was of her breath, long and steady, and the settling of the walls. Julia placed her jacket on her shoulders and took the small bag next to her as she stood up and walked to the casket, and then kneeled in front of it and looked in at Henry's face, and then down to his hands that were placed one on top of the other. She saw that the mortician had left his wedding ring on. 'I will come back to you one day,' she whispered, and quickly stood up, clasping her hands in prayer. The ring was his promise to her. And she would never take it off. When she stood up, she reached for a large bag that she had placed by her feet, and from it she withdrew a fedora, the one he had always worn, and placed it delicately by his side.

The coming days blended into one another like watercolors, the plates had been scraped and the glasses washed, once everyone had gone and the last bit of food had been covered and put away, once the bedrooms had been emptied of guests and the last light in the house had been turned off, Julia sat down in a house that was extraordinarily quiet. She was alone, and felt it like a sodden dress, or the pull of gravity.

She was still wearing her dress: thin black silk that had long sleeves, a high neck and a hem that delicately hugged her knees as she walked. She had barely slept: the phone had been ringing relentlessly, the well-wishers had been at her doorstep offering food and sentiment. For the first time in days, she'd finally captured a quiet minute. She was sitting on the old worn couch in the living area, arms at her sides, her bare feet sinking into the dark brown pile carpet. The wood-framed pictures above the stone fireplace smiled placidly at no one in particular. There was no dominant voice in the house. The moon-faced grandfather clock clicked its arm past midnight. Julia observed that, part from the few extra plates and glasses from well-wishers, the house was exactly as she had left it when it happened; the day that Henry died. His flannel shirts still hung in the bedroom closet; his favorite slippers were by the door. It was better that way, or at least, for the time being. Tonight, Julia sat and closed her eyes, attempting to sleep somewhere that wasn't in a room where she still felt him. As she drifted off, she felt the hairs on her arms raise and the temperature drop, imperceptibly. She opened her eyes.

I probably left the door open, or a window, she thought, wondering where the draft was coming from. She looked towards the door to the front room.

It was closed. To the right, the windows were shut. To her left, at the door to the basement. It was closed. *I'm just tired*, she resolved, leaning her head back and shutting her eyes.

Shhh

One of the things that she'd learned to live with, when they moved to Cooper Street, was that the door to the basement was slightly too tall for the height of the carpet pile beneath it, so as it closed, it always made a recognizable sound, like someone raising their finger to their lips and saying

Shhh

She opened her eyes and stayed very still, as if in a dream not of her own making. As she slowly turned her head left, the door moved, ever so gently open, as if a child was entering, or a breeze finding its way through. She blinked hard, but it was still apparent that she wasn't dreaming. And then a ribbon of cold air traveled from her left shoulder, across her chest, then to her right shoulder, down her arm, and was gone. And then the warmth of the room embraced her, and she knew that he'd finally left.

A month after the funeral, Slava moved back to the city for an indefinite period of time, waiting for their new arrival. She and Emilian's jobs had no leniency for time away, and they had both used all of their compassionate leave, so she and Emilian said their goodbyes to Julia and promised to come up on Saturdays to see her, and maybe occasionally during the week as well.

After their daughter was born, they helped Julia sell her share in the apartment building on President Street as well as the building in Glen Cove, the money from it a healthy sum that would sustain Julia comfortably for a little while at least, before her social security afforded that little bit extra in the remaining years of her life.

It could be said that loss lives within us and around us, comfortably. Like a scar, or a separation from a loved one, we don't survive it, or erase it, but rather, place it permanently in a part of our daily lives that learns to accept and be grateful for what it teaches us; it enriches us with a sense of identity to the past; an attachment to a memory of someone, or something, affecting us profoundly. Julia had lost her siblings, her parents, she had given up two children and gave two more to God, and she had now buried her husband. But loss cannot exist without love, and so with time, Julia discovered the beauty in the melancholy again.

The contentedness in the solitary walks she took to see Henry was rivalled only by the joy spent in her garden: Julia would spend most of her days wrist-deep in the dark earth of the tidy garden, wedding band winking, her now longer, whiter hair tied loosely by her neck and covered with a cotton scarf to shield her eyes from the sun, her knees resting by explosions of hydrangeas and marigolds. She didn't look over her shoulder anymore to see Henry to walk through the wooden gate, though she had for the first few years after he'd gone. His presence diminished gradually, and now, twenty years later, Julia only spoke of him occasionally with Slava, or in her nightly prayers, sometimes leafing through several pictures of him that she kept on her nightstand.

This particular evening, after she'd had dinner at the long table that now only had one place setting, she ran a bath and indulged in it-- her body so still and her thoughts so deep, that the water looked as if made of glass. As the water cooled, she realized why her thoughts consumed her: it was Henry's birthday. She removed the plug and watched as the water cycloned towards the drain, and once the bath was empty, she stood up and retrieved a towel from the back of the door. She wrapped herself in a thin blue robe and looked in the mirror to survey her age: the heavy blue in her eyes, that had once been described by Henry as 'like the sea before a storm', had lightened, and there were dark spots on her forehead and cheeks, marking all the years the sun had chased her. Her nose, once sharp and Roman, had softened slightly, and the lines of Venus on her neck were deeply etched into her thin skin.

She walked out of the bathroom and towards the closet and stood on the very tips of her toes to retrieve a large, rectangular wooden box crudely engraved with sunflowers, which she brought back to the bed with her skin still slightly damp. It was light in weight, but the contents had sat heavy in it for years. She sat down on the bed, cross-legged, as she used to when she was younger, and opened it to reveal two folded pieces of paper, permanently creased into quarters, hidden memories from so long ago. Beside them was a stack of unopened letters that had been returned to her, each with a stamp bearing the words *RETURN TO SENDER-INCORRECT ADDRESS*.

She took both pieces of paper out and opened them, scanning the information. They would be fifty years old. She had missed an entire lifetime. She glanced over at the letters and realized it was pointless to search for answers now. She would stop wondering how their arms felt around her. She would stop wondering if they'd ever asked for her, longed for her, if they'd longed for her to sing to them. For so long, her heart had filled with the unrelenting hope of seeing their faces again, and so she held onto withering evidence as proof: proof that they did, in fact, happen, and that they loved her once, and she them. But fifty years can pass by in oppressively long minutes, or vast floods of seconds vanishing in a single drop. Time doesn't deliberate, doesn't debate age or circumstance. It spins the world on its axel, and the world has no choice but to turn, and as a result, the desire for one single thing disappears, due to lack of time, lack of energy, or even lack of hope. And the acceptance of this can mean the beginning of a different story.

 Julia took each sealed envelope, without ceremony or emotion, slowly tore them in half, and then into quarters, one by one, until there was a pile of paper at her feet that resembled nothing but ink and empty words. She placed them all on the floor by her bed, and then she took the two remaining memories and placed them on the nightstand, no longer hidden from view, and withdrew the pale blue rosary that her mother had given her, placing it in the pocket of her robe, and walked out of the bedroom. She proceeded down the narrow hallway, stopping in the kitchen briefly to shut off the small lamp by the window, and then past the grandfather clock, towards the door to the porch. She walked outside and down the ten wooden steps towards the garden, the bright moonlight stretched its silvery light across the perimeter of the garden and out into the fields where it faded. She stood, alone, her eyes reflecting what little light there was left, looking out across the dark fields, as she had done so many times in countries that she would no longer see again.

 When she closed her eyes and felt her feet sink into the soft grass, she remembered again that it was Henry's birthday, and what that meant.

Motherland

Therefore, I say to you, her sins, which are many, are forgiven, for she loved much.

Luke 7:47-48

Motherland

Part IV

2011-2015

35

Glen Cove

'Why do you still wear it,' the cashier asked as she placed a handful of marigolds in the shallow box that Julia held. 'I mean, after so long, you know?'

Julia smiled. She had seen Alice every week for as long as she and Henry had lived there, which wasn't that long, now that he had gone. Alice was young and pale, with wide green eyes and a halo of red curls that were always gathered into a ponytail. She had always been kind, always interested. She had always said *Hello Julia* and waved, whenever she saw her walk down the path past the shop, towards the beach, heading home. She always asked questions. It made Julia smile, and reminded her of when she was that age.

Julia looked down at the worn gold of her wedding band. 'Love persists, I think,' she moved the flowers aside to make room for a few packets of seeds. 'within the things that force you to remember.' She looked up. 'Photographs, letters, jewelry. Little things can mean everything.'

Alice pressed the keys of the cash register and took the money from Julia. 'I think I'd be super messed up if my Mom died. It's just her and me, you know. After my Dad left.' She rolled a piece of gum in her cheek and sighed. 'Can't even think about it.'

Julia retrieved her change and lifted the small box to leave. 'You would be very surprised at what the heart can endure if it has to.' And she walked home.

In the twenty years after Henry's death, and after nearly an entire life of constant upheaval, Julia's life began to settle, like the earth after a seismic shift. She knew her life would eventually end here, in the spot where Henry left her, and the only journey she was interested in was a small one: the daily visits to see the place where he was laid to rest. And today, on the day after his birthday, she needed it more than ever, to lift the burden of a heavy heart.

This morning was similar to all the others before it: she dressed in trousers and a sweater for the invigorating weather, for it was bright sun but also brisk enough to redden her cheeks with an intense scarlet. She parted the thin curtains to reveal the view of the horizon beyond the garden, she smoothed the bedsheets, stacked the pillows, and smoothed the sheets. She arranged her perfumes in a line of various shaped atomizers on her dressing table and hung her robe in the closet and closed the door. She made her favorite tea, black with raw honey, and stood looking through the window above the sink that looked out onto the front of the house, and as it steeped, she found the thick gloves and the small, rusted trowel that she'd always kept in the drawer by the door-- the one that kept all the remnants and tools and odd bits of a house that had had a story once-- and placed them in the oversized pocket of her thick parka that she'd left hanging on a chair by the hallway. What's the use in keeping broken things, Henry had often remarked to her as she would unearth strange metal clasps and knobs and old keys, and she would reply that nothing was ever fully broken; everything had a purpose.

She slipped on the pair of boots that she always wore, even in summer, and locked the front door, leaving instead through her bedroom and the sliding door that led to the porch and down the stairs. She stayed for a few minutes to indulge in the view in front of her: the pines and oak trees standing in a line across the distance, with the small humps of mountains farther still behind them, their tops hidden by the feet of the hovering clouds.

Down the stairs then, and left onto the gravel mile from the house, straight past the small craggy trails that lead to the woods, and then right, down the street where the dogwoods bloomed and carpeted the path with white. Past the pines that hovered at the stone gates of the church, past the small hotel with a new name that they used to own, and then down the road towards the cemetery walled in by a plain iron fence and mounds of overfertilized grass.

Before she would walk in, she would look for the pale pink wildflowers that she she'd seen once before and never again, though she vaguely remembered something called a waxflower. And anyway, there were usually many others hiding in the abandoned lot across the road, in the bramble overgrowth: bluebells, dog violets, ground ivy, and foxglove. She would pick them, and then, clutching the offerings in her hand, follow a wide footpath that curled around the perimeter and then towards the middle, leading her to a four-foot tall rectangle of dark granite, engraved with a byzantine cross hovering over black letters:

Hironimus (Henry) Rudnick
Beloved father and husband
1919-1978

She knelt down and placed the flowers in front, noticing that a few weeds had grown at the base of the stone.

'Henry, today has been a good day.' She took her wool hat off and brushed aside strands of tangled white hair hanging in front of her face. She spoke softly, as if to a friend. 'Slava was here the other day, helping me organize some of your things. She had a daughter. Lyuba. You would love her little face, dark like yours, with a birthmark on her cheek like a star. When she comes back to work, they said they would promote her to senior technician in the neonatal department, which has something to do with taking care of babies, she had to explain to me. She is taking care of babies.' Julia's eyes creased; her smile flooded her face. 'I wonder sometimes, about my babies. I pray for them. I know you did to, when you were still here.' She sifted some dead leaves from the side of the headstone and traced the letters of his name with an arthritic finger. 'Slava is also helping me sort out your will. Or lack of one.' She sighed. 'I wonder if this was a way for you to keep me busy?' Her lips rose at the corners. 'I wonder if, had you stayed, you would have started doing things differently? Smoking less? Working less? Would you have been happy?'

She paused, and answered for herself, the admission of love much easier when the dead had no answer. 'We were happy, Henry. I know it. Despite it all. We tried our best.' The uncertainty in her voice was met with her own confirmation of the past; the hindsight to her life was truthful, and it lent itself to a kind of peaceful acceptance.

Her knees ached, and she removed her gloves and placed her palms on the ground to shift her weight.

She moved to a tender spot in the earth where she knelt, left of the headstone, and her palm sunk slightly further and it felt as if he had given her permission. In her right pocket, she withdrew the trowel and placed it in front of her. In the left pocket, she withdrew two pieces of paper, and closed her hand around them, and with her other hand she pierced the soil through the grass until the handle almost disappeared.

She began to open up a bit of the earth and looked at the small, folded pieces of paper in her hand. *Burying the past.* The soil waited for her decision, like an open wound; she wondered if she could place them inside. But she realized that it would be letting them go a second time, so she placed them back in her pocket, and slowly her hands gradually covered the open earth: dark moist granules soft on her hands, spilling off, back to where they belonged.

Julia stood up, her gloves in one hand and trowel in the other, and walked away, leaving only the imprint of her knees on the ground in front of Henry's name, forever imprinted in granite.

She walked the long path out of the cemetery--past the fences that bordered small gardens, past the paths that disappeared into thick woods, past the stone church that lay in wait for another marriage or funeral, past the small grocery store that had only just opened its doors and past the post office around the corner. Her patient steps took her along the familiar gravel road that narrowed gradually towards the small white house on the hill; the house with the yellow door, where hope still lived even still though life had been unkind, and where a widow with a secret had lost so many things she'd loved.

That evening, after Julia ran a bath and dressed for bed, she walked over to the coat she had laid on the chair by the door, and withdrew the birth certificates, wiping the soil off gently. She then took an old, thin cotton skirt that she had worn in her days in Australia and hadn't worn since, and within the battered and worn cotton lining, she sewed the folded pieces of paper inside. It was a peculiar habit that remained, from years of wars and secrets kept.

She replaced the skirt on the hanger, the rails scraping as she pushed it to the back of the closet and closed the door.

36

Melbourne, Australia

The spire of the stone church pierced the cornflower blue of the sky that morning, and the hymns of the parishioners died down as the service ended. Slowly, the heavy, red- painted doors opened and a rainbow of silk skirts, pale shirts and ordinary trousers flooded the steps as everyone left, waving their hellos and goodbyes and shaking the hand of the priest as he stood nodding. It was Sunday, and the inside of the church would be quiet soon, resting in the air that had been filled with incense and perfume just moments ago.

In one of the empty, dark, pews sat a woman with her head bowed. Her neck was thin, her shoulders broad and delicate. Regal. Her body was tall, her grey-blonde hair scraped back and up, a single braid circling her head like a halo. She held a prayer book on her lap.

The echoes of leather shoes rang out crisply as the priest walked down to the woman, his form silhouetted by the light of the church's open door. He collected prayer books along the way and stopped as he reached her. He sat in the pew in front of her. She raised her head in greeting her eyes wet as she smiled. 'Hello, father.'

'Hello again.' He nodded to the altar behind him, resplendent in white linens in front of the intricate stained glass. 'Third time this week. How are you keeping?'

'Alright. As much as I can be, really.' The priest cocked his head sympathetically. 'Death is never a stranger for long, in this life. How long has it been now?'

'Six months, just about.'

'Still feels as if he could walk through the door, then?'

She smiled. 'Yes.'

'Do you have your daughter to help you manage for the time being?'

'Yes. she has been wonderful, really, she and her husband. And I have my friends to lean on, it's not that I need any help.' She reached into her pocket and withdrew a handkerchief, dabbing her eyes. It had been her husband's, and still smelled of his cologne.

The priest leaned in, sensing something unspoken. 'I know you well enough now to know that your churchgoing isn't entirely related to Walter's death. You have always been a pragmatic woman. Never wavering. There is something else.'

She looked up. 'Yes.'

He nodded. 'Is it something that we've discussed in the confessional?'

She looked back down.

The priest crossed his legs, placing his hands on his black robes. 'The past can harm or heal, but the truth always heals a broken heart.' He watched as the woman stayed silent.

'Do you think it's time?'

The woman handed the prayer book to him and looked up, placing the handkerchief in her pocket. 'I'm not sure I can.'

'This has been a heaviness in your heart for as long as I have known you, and that's an easy twenty years.' He sighed. 'Did Walter know?'

'No,' she replied softly. 'I never told him, and never told Irena. Only you.'

'Do you think you can live with this any longer?'

'No. I don't think I can.'

The priest stood up and placed his hand on her shoulder. 'We teach our children never to run away from the truth. We teach them to face it.'

The woman stood up, smoothing her skirt and straightening her trench coat. 'I fear that I will not be forgiven for the years that I have waited.' They both began walking towards the entrance, the light flooding the space around them. The priest stopped and turned to her.

'Elina, all you can do is hope. Forgiveness lives within hope.'

After the service, Elina walked slowly on the sidewalk towards home, her mahogany cane helping her navigate the hard ground. Her linen trench coat swayed behind her and her cotton skirt peeked out from under it. A rosary glistened on her neck over her cream blouse as she walked, the sun hitting its facets proudly. She was grateful that the church had not been too crowded, the small moments of peace that existed between the stone walls and the echoed hymns.

The sermon this morning was about forgiveness, which is why she lingered after everyone's footsteps had receded. As she sat on the hard-wooden pew, her hands folded in prayer, she remembered a face from her past that she had thought about her entire life, but that featured more prominently in her thoughts, prayers, and dreams lately now that her husband was long gone. He had never known of her past, and now it seems the past had been catching up to her.

When she approached her house, she stepped onto the porch and unlocked the heavy door and felt the cool breeze from the front room spread across her face and her arms as she took her coat off. She hung her coat on the door, slipped her shoes off, and placed her cane against the wall that was covered in photos. As she walked down the narrow hallway to the kitchen, she touched every single one of them: ones of her husband, of the both of them on their wedding day, and of his parents, long gone. There were photos of Irena as a child, and then as an adolescent, then an adult, and also plates with red and black vishyvanka patterns displayed on wire hooks, and wood carvings of sparrows and wheat fields perched on the high shelves. Time had passed considerably.

Elina walked into the warm and bright kitchen, past a small metal table with a chair and a telephone, set the water to boil, and then walked through into the dining room and then up the stairs to the bedroom, where she sat down on the bed, the lace patterned white quilt sagging underneath her. She reached over and looked at a small picture in a silver frame, and it made her smile as she ran her fingers along the glass. The small face of the toddler grinned happily in her mother's embrace, people milling on the boardwalk behind them on that summer's day. Elina remembered that day with her daughter as if it were yesterday.

She placed the picture in her lap as she slowly unbraided her hair and let it fall. Her eyes filled with tears, the weight of the past flooding her heart, the memories of so many moments that had gone terribly wrong. And what now, she thought. What could she say now?

She put the picture back in its place on the table, and walked back downstairs to the kitchen, taking the kettle off the stove.

When the tea sat and the water became darker, she sat down next to the telephone pressing the numbers tentatively and lifting the receiver to her ear.

'Hello my love... Yes, yes I'm fine. You? ... yes, yes... I was calling because, I was wondering...I will need you to use your computer for me. ...Yes... yes, I know I should learn, but I have you. Why?'

Elina paused.

'... I was wondering if you could help me find an old friend.'

37

Glen Cove

When the phone rang, Julia didn't hear it at first, as she had just slipped into a beautiful dream. She was standing in a field, barefoot, the crisp spines of wheat bending between her toes. The air was mildly scented, sweet and familiar, but she couldn't place it for certain. It reminded her of someone.

The sky was wide and the lightest shade of pink she had ever seen, the yellow of the sun mixing to create a warmth that settled on her skin like dew. Her feet stayed still, and yet her eyes saw perfectly across the field as if she was walking across it, and then suddenly her vision changed and rose and she could see the field as if it rested beneath her, and then her hands reached out and skimmed across the tops of the trees, above and towards the dark, meandering river and then back down its length to turn around and return, as the crane flies.

Her hair was dark again, and long, and it had been taken out of its plaits, as she used to do as a child before bed; the waves of it moving in the slight breeze like heavy silks. She looked down. Her dress was blue and soft cotton, and she recognized it only when she saw Henry in the distance, watching her; for it was her wedding dress. He was holding something on either side, his arms stretched down and slightly away from his sides, each hand clasping and attached to, what was it, she couldn't see yet-- so she moved closer, curious, the square of his shoulders and the length of his body clearer at each step. And then she was there, looking at him, indulging in the heavy dark brown of his eyes, the way his cheeks protruded and rose as he smiled, the way his lips flattened underneath his moustache and his dark hair flopped lazily to the side, and the way the lines around his eyes proudly decorated the sides of his face. There was no smoke, no sugar, only the solid warmth of his body as he stood underneath her gaze. Oh, she loved him still, and their lives had fallen together and apart and back together again, and that was the point of love— the falling together again.

She lowered her eyes, remembering that he was holding something in each hand, and it was then that she saw them: one small hand in each of his large square ones, their bodies clinging to his legs, giggling as they looked up at her. He let go of them and she knelt down as they fell into her, slowly, burying their heads into her as she kissed their soft faces and smelled their warm skin. *My babies, my babies,* she repeated over and over again, her voice breaking, incapable of containing the flood that she had bottled for so long and so her veins untied and let love in, and she looked up at Henry and she saw his eyes, the tears collecting in his dark eyes. She was grateful, and though forgiveness was never something he had asked for, she knew now that he had kept it, there, in the locked place where grief resides with love and loss. For they were the same, their hearts. They had loved and lost and grieved in parallel, and it was only now that she understood.

The phone rang again. And again.

Julia opened her eyes and squinted at the clock by the bed. It read *11:35*. She turned the knob on the light, and it flooded the room, as she covered her eyes with her hand and placed the receiver to her ear. 'Hello?'

There was an intake of breath on the other end. And then silence.

'Hello? Who is there? Slava?'

'Julia?' The woman's voice was thin. Reedy. It sounded like sand coated in honey. It was vaguely familiar. 'Hello?' she said again. 'Julia, is that you?'

'Who is this.'

'Please don't hang up when I tell you.'

'What?' Julia frowned. 'Who is this?'

'It's... it's Elina.'

Julia felt her heart grow cold. Her hands began to shake. She squeezed the receiver as if it were the only thing that would keep her tethered to this world, and it would soon melt in her grip. 'Why are you calling me.' She hissed.

'Wait. Please listen.'

'Just like you listened to me. How dare you.' With her other hand, Julia gripped the bed sheets and pulled them to her. 'Why would I entertain anything that you say?'

'Because I needed to tell you something. Something important. Please don't hang up.'

She could so easily end the conversation. She could place the receiver down and never answer it again. But Elina's voice had ignited something inside her, and she wasn't entirely sure if it would be pain or joy, or both. So, she listened.

'I honestly don't know what to say to you, Elina.'

'Then don't say anything. Hear me out.'

'Fine.'

Elina took a breath. 'I'll start from the beginning. And I promise you, you will be glad you listened.'

38

She repeated it over and over in her head, but it was as loud as if she were shouting.

Mine. His. Ours. They were ours.

'No. This is impossible.' Julia's thoughts ran in circles in her head, her chest felt on fire, and her hands shook as she listened to Elina's voice, not wanting the truth to settle.

'They were yours, Julia. They were always yours,' Elina spoke, her voice breaking with tears. 'I am so sorry…I didn't even realize it until I became pregnant. And then, I was too scared to reveal any of it to anyone.' She repeated it over and over again. It was a bomb detonating with the fresh smell of fire and metal.

Julia had been listening, her eyes wide, body as still as a statue. At points in the conversation, she stood up and told Elina to stop and wait, because she needed to catch her breath. She paced, she walked out of the room softly, shaking her head, tears falling, and then would come back to her voice, asked her to continue, and then asked her to stop again. This went on for three hours, until the entire story was revealed. She had told Elina about the assault, and Elina had finally told her the truth.

They had been Henry's. Her entire life had changed course because of an assumption. An unknown. And now she had to come to terms with it.

'Elina, I can't begin to explain to you the amount of life I have lost,' Julia whispered, tangling her fingers in the phone cord over and over. 'I'm not sure I needed to hear this now, did I?'

'Of course, you did. You had been wronged your entire life because of a lie. And I was a part of it. I couldn't live a life knowing that I had this secret.'

'What good does it do me now, Elina. You are doing this to ease your own guilt, maybe.' There was anger in her voice.

'I know you feel so much anger and sadness right now, Julia, but you have to understand that I did this because I knew that I might be able to help you. To give you something, *anything*, after so many years.'

'Elina, it's too much, I don't even know where to begin. What do I do? Or say?' She sighed. 'Why now?'

'Because we are mothers. And our children need to know our stories.' She paused. 'Why don't I help you?'

'How?'

'I am in Australia still. Do you have anything that could find them?'

'No. I only kept their birth certificates.'

'Alright, well, that may help. Can you send them to me if I give you my address?'

Julia hesitated.

'Julia, you can trust me.'

'Yes, but that's all I have. I have nothing else.'

'Think. Are you certain?'

Julia looked around her room, nothing was out of place, she knew the contents of every drawer, practically. 'Hang on,' she replied and placed the receiver on her bed. She walked out of her bedroom into the dining room, and stood, looking at the pictures on the walls, the sideboard groaning with old china plates and heirlooms. She walked downstairs into the basement and switched on the light, and saw chairs stacked on top of one another, dress bags hanging on a clothing rail, boxes labelled 'Henry', and 'House things', and 'Paperwork'. She turned to leave and saw a box in the corner, next to an old doll house that had a layer of dust on its red-painted shutters. The box said 'Slava' on it, and it reminded Julia of the time she'd moved into the apartment on 71st street and Julia had moved to Glen Cove with some of Slava's things, prompting Henry to laugh that a mother and daughter always had a complicated connection.

Slava.

Upon reaching her bedroom again, she picked up the phone. 'Elina,' she was breathless. 'Are you still there?'

'Yes, of course. Did you find anything?'

'No, but I know how to find it. Please can you give me your number and I will call you back tomorrow?'

※

Slava felt the mobile buzzing in her shoulder bag as she unlocked the door. She picked it up and saw it was her mother.

'Hello, Mama, hang on a minute.' She walked in and placed the bag on the table and kicked off her shoes. Emilian walked into the room, taking his glasses off and placing a kiss on her cheek and closed the door behind her. He had been working, and his fingers were stained with graphite. 'It's my mother,' Slava whispered, holding her hand over the mouthpiece.

Emilian moved her hand from it. 'Hello Julia, how're you?' he said loudly, smiling, taking Slava's jacket from her as she unzipped it. He asked Slava if she needed him, she shook her head, and so she continued. 'So, what's going on?'

'Hello sweetheart, can I please ask you to do something for me? It's important.'

'Sure.'

'I need to ask you a strange question.'

'I'm used to those, Mama.'

Julia laughed. 'Do you remember a long time ago, when you moved into the apartment with Emilian?'

'Of course.'

'And you found a letter that was sent to me?'

'Wait, the one I called you about? The weird one?'

'Yes, yes.'

'Did you keep it at all?' Julia's voice sounded apologetic suddenly. 'Don't worry if not, it's fine, I just...'

Slava was already walking towards the study. 'Funny. And here you've always told me that I'm too curious or sentimental.' She stood on tiptoe and reached for a folder. 'Hang on.' She held the phone with her shoulder and opened the file. It was full of old drawings, pictures, ticket stubs, notes and a torn, thin envelope with the newspaper clipping inside.

She returned the phone to her ear as she looked at it.

'Yes, I still have it.'

Julia sighed. 'Alright, thank you. Can you please read out to me the address on the front of the envelope?'

'Yes, sure, but why...'

'-- don't ask, I'll explain later.'

After she hung up, Slava scanned the newspaper clipping and the envelope. Emilian walked in. 'Everything okay? What's the drama?'

'No drama. Just my mother being herself,' she smiled, and folded it all into her pocket, replacing the folder back on the shelf.

Julia walked over to her closet, slowly moving the racks of clothes to the side, the sound of metal and soft cotton under her fingertips. On the last hanger, she stopped, lifting it up to her eyes, seeing how the blue and red material had faded to pale pink and grey. Small threads hung loose from the seams, and a button was missing.

She brought it to the bed and fanned it out, lifting up the inside lining, running her hands up along the inside until her fingers felt the extra stitches and small square lump. She turned the skirt inside out and with a fingernail gingerly unpicked the stitches, one by one, revealing the papers inside. She lifted them out and held them to her heart briefly, pressing them onto her chest, before walking downstairs and placing them in an envelope. Before she sealed it, she took a framed picture off the shelf and removed it from the frame. Hidden inside the back panel was a faded, silvery picture— of Julia with all three of her children. It was the only one she had.

She hoped Elina could find them; she couldn't bear losing them twice.

39

One month later

The taxi left, the dust and gravel scattering behind its wheels, and Elina stood at the door of the welfare office. She checked the contents of her purse, and she had the two weathered birth certificates in her hand, and a picture that had been sent with them. She smiled at the face looking outwardly, with bright eyes and dark hair. She wondered what Julia looked like now and imagined that the hope in the face of her youth would come back to her, if she'd lost it long ago.

The room was quiet, with scratchy chairs and metal legs, baskets with old magazines in them and a plastic drinks dispenser in the corner. There was a young couple sat in the corner, waiting, looking through a magazine and whispering tenderly to each other. Behind the polished desk was a secretary, her straight brown hair curtained over her white shirt. She was checking her phone, tapping it lightly, leaning back in her chair.

'Hello, Miss?' Elina leaned closer to the desk.

'Morning, how can I help you?'

'I'm here to see Mr. Bennett.'

'Who?'

'The owner, or partner rather, of this place…' Elina's index finger made the shape of a circle in the air. 'Is he still working here?'

'Oh, gosh, no. He retired about fifteen years ago.'

'Ah.' Elina's face showed defeat.

'Can I help you with anything maybe?'

'Well, possibly. I am looking to find two people.'

'Are they related to you?'

'No. But I knew their mother.'

'I don't really have access to information like that, really, but maybe I can get someone else to help you?' The woman picked up the phone and held it to her hear with her shoulder. 'Hang on,' she raised a finger.

Elina walked over to a chair and sat down, holding her purse in her lap, both hands clutching it. The wool of the seat padding felt hard under her skirt, and she pinched the silk of her shirt and fanned it delicately, grateful for the cool air on her skin. She looked out the window and saw the neon signs displayed above shops, bright yellows and reds and greens, and wondered when it had happened that the world had become so different.

The click of heels on the floor grew louder as a woman approached, dressed in matching trousers and jacket, thin wire glasses perched on her nose, her curly hair undone and hanging to her shoulders. She walked over to Elina. 'Hello, I'm Katherine, and you are?'

Elina stood up. 'My name is Elina.'

'Hello Elina, why don't you come with me to my office, and we can chat about what you need, yes?'

Elina sat down in a leather chair while Katherine closed the door and walked back behind her desk. 'So, how can I help you?' She clasped her hands and leaned forward.

'I need your help finding two people.'

'Yes, Andrea told me that much. I'll see what I can do.'

Elina set her handbag next to her chair and undid her coat slightly. 'Well, my friend has had a terrible thing happen to her, and only I can make this right.'

Katherine held her hand up. 'Wait, does this involve some kind of police investigation?'

'No, no. You see, she was forced to give up her children in 1952.'

'Yes, there were a lot of adoptions at that time, sure.'

'But she was led to believe that they were the result of an assault. Which is why she was forced to give them up. Her husband thought they weren't his.'

'Why didn't she report the assault?'

Elina raised her eyebrows. 'It's only in recent years that women are starting to be believed. And she felt guilty that she had contributed to this assault somehow.

'How do you know all this?'

'Because it was my husband, at the time, who had assaulted her.' Elina looked across to the window at the blue sky over the Stratford skyline. 'It was something that I had suspected, but never believed, because I had been envious of the fact that she could have children. And it was reason for me to assume that what he told me was true.'

'What did he tell you?'

'That she had come onto him and started an affair.' Elina looked back at Katherine. 'So, I told her husband. '

Katherine moved her chair back to stand up. 'I'm not really sure where I come into all of this, to be honest...'

Elina raised her hand. 'Wait. Please.'

Katherine sat back down.

'You see, when I told her husband, I can only assume that he calculated back to when the affair happened, and then he, and my friend, both realized that the twins that she had given birth to almost two years ago, were a result of this assault.'

Katherine nodded, urging her to continue.

Elina shrugged. 'She came to me, to ask me for help, she begged me to hear the truth of what happened, and I couldn't. I threw her out of my house.' She stared at her hands. 'She lost everything.'

Katherine sighed. 'I appreciate that you need me, but I don't really know what I'm supposed to do here.'

Elina continued, ignoring the question. 'I always thought it was me. I always thought I couldn't have children. I thought they *were* his children, don't you see.'

'I'm not following.'

Elina reached down for her handbag and unsnapped it, reaching inside and retrieving two worn birth certificates, holding them in her hand as she spoke. 'He had always faulted me for the fact that we were barren. We had never been able to have children. I just accepted that it was me, and when I saw those children and thought that they'd been a result of their 'affair', it broke me. It broke my trust, and my friendship.' She shook the papers in her hand. 'But I was able to have a child. My daughter. I remarried, and then I knew.' She placed the papers on the desk. 'Then I knew that those children were, in fact, her own.' Elina's eyes filled with tears and she reached for a tissue from a box on the desk. 'She had to give up her own children. And I couldn't live with that knowledge anymore.'

Katherine sat quietly, her mouth slightly open, and ran her palms over her eyes, shaking her head. 'Elina. If you want me to release closed adoption records, I can't. What if the adoptive parents are unwilling? And even if they're not around anymore, I can't guarantee that these children are in Australia anymore.' She looked sympathetically at Elina. 'I understand your friend's tragedy, and it's heart-breaking, but I can't release this kind of information.'

Elina leaned forward. 'Katherine, please.' She pushed the papers towards her.

Katherine sighed and looked down, unfolding the pages delicately.

REGISTRATION OF BIRTHS, DEATHS AND MARRIAGES REGULATIONS

BIRTH CERTIFICATE

Child
Family name   Rudnick
Christian or given name Maksim
Sex   Male
Date of Birth   April 1949
Place of Birth   Stratford, Cairns

Mother
Family name   Rudnick
Maiden family name   Mishik
Christian or given name Julia
Occupation   Wife
Age   26
Place of Birth   Lviv, Ukraine

Father
Family name   Rudnick

Christian or given name	Hironimus
Occupation	Farmer
Age	30
Place of Birth	Stryi, Ukraine

Marriage of Parents
Date of Marriage	1942
Place of Marriage	Germany

She switched her gaze to the other, her hands turning cold, her eyes widening.

BIRTH CERTIFICATE

Child
Family name	Rudnick
Christian or given name	Lesia
Sex	Female
Date of Birth	April 1949
Place of Birth	Stratford, Cairns

Mother
Family name	Rudnick
Maiden family name	Mishik
Christian or given name	Julia
Occupation	Wife
Age	26
Place of Birth	Lviv, Ukraine

Father
Family name	Rudnick
Christian or given name	Hironimus
Occupation	Farmer
Age	30
Place of Birth	Stryi, Ukraine

Marriage of Parents	
Date of Marriage	1942
Place of Marriage	Germany

Katherine placed the papers back on her desk and folded her hands, smiling. Elina saw tears in her eyes.

'Elina.'

'Yes?'

'Did Andrea tell you anything about me?'

Julia frowned. 'No, why? She only told me that you would be in charge of something like this.'

'No, of course. Well, when I graduated high school in 1950, I came to work here. As a secretary.' Katherine's voice was even, but expectant, the words hovering in her mouth.

Elina opened her handbag again and withdrew the photograph, handing it to Katherine. 'That is my friend. Julia.'

Katherine held it, wiping a tear from the corner of her eye. 'Yes, I know,' she nodded. 'I remember. I sent her a newspaper clipping from Australia years ago. I had always remembered her, and I managed to find her last known address in New York. The newspaper clipping was of one of the twins' marriage announcements.' She shook her head in disbelief. 'It's extraordinary, this story.'

She gave the photo back to Elina. 'Give me a week, would it be alright for you to come back? I hope to have what you need by then.'

Elina let out a breath, knowing that she was now part of the story of her friend's life. This was forgiveness.

She nodded gratefully. 'Thank you.'

40

Glen Cove

The sky was a milky gray and the snow had begun to fall as Slava fiddled with the knob on the car radio. The traffic was slow, and she wanted something to listen to that wasn't Christmas music. Another swipe of the metal blade across the glass revealed the pink undertones of the sky. She loved this kind of weather in the late afternoon: the air sat heavy and comfortable on her skin and it smelled of sweet, humid cold. The windshield wipers slowly and rhythmically swept the flecks of snow and she finally settled on an inoffensive radio station, with no talking and music that had no words.

    Emilian wasn't with her, he was at work, and their daughter Misha was at college. He encouraged her to do this thing alone, because important things were always done alone, he'd said. So today, she resolved to see her mother: the woman who may have held something back from everyone yet had somehow never diminished any bit of her strength. *Come over, sweetheart* she had said. *I'd love to chat with you about something.* She never just 'chatted.'

    She'd pulled the car up to the house just in time for the snow to finish settling, walked into the house, shutting the faded yellow door behind her. The heat of the front room made her cold cheeks sting. 'Mama?' Julia heard her voice and walked out from the kitchen to meet her. She'd left the door unlocked that afternoon, expecting her.

    'Ey, don't get snow all over.' She wiped her hands on her apron and undid the knot at the back. Her grey hair was dusted with flour from

Christmas preparations, and she rolled up her sleeves, her thin fingers still graceful despite her age. She took Slava's coat as she peeled it off, and looked past her, expecting someone else. 'Is Emilian not with you?'

'No, he has work.'

'On a Saturday?'

'Money never sleeps, especially not in the city.'

'I thought he was— '

'— a secretary?' Slava laughed, her newly bobbed hair settling down as she took her hat off. 'It's been so long, Mama, how do you not remember what he does?'

'Oh, Slava, look. You brought the snow in.' Julia sighed and picked up fingerfuls of slush but shook them off, giving up.

'It's snow, Mama. It'll melt. I'm not five.' She took off her gloves, her thin gold wedding band feeling too tight on her cold, swollen fingers.

'True. You were much worse, then.' Julia chuckled and shook her head. 'So much worse.'

Slava placed her gloves on a wicker chair next to the door. 'He's the secretary of a wall street firm, by the way.'

'See?' Julia pointed at her. 'I said. Secretary.'

'Never mind. Anyway, listen, I—'

'Wine? Come, it's cold in here.' Julia interrupted. Slava saw she had a purpose.

She followed her mother through the door and stepped into the warm, dark kitchen and then past the tall grandfather clock that stood opposite the dining room and sat down at the oval oak table where they had all once been together. The tablecloth was folded over on one side only, and delicate china was set aside, along with napkins and sprigs of holly and poppies made into a *vinok* wreath that Slava used to wear on her head as a child in Christmases past.

The kitchen smelled of onions and oil and minced sauerkraut, and the kitchen counter was swollen with plates of *kutya*, and *pyrohy*, and stuffed cabbage leaves, *holubtsi*. She imagined her mother pinching the soft edges of the dough, and delicately spooning the molasses over the barley, the poppyseeds glittering underneath, black and sticky. It didn't seem to matter how much she had lost, or how distant she had been, there was a softness to her now, and a warm, that was beautiful.

Julia moved past her and removed two glasses from the antique sideboard that held the vyshyvanka-patterned china and more black and red embroidered napkins. One of the glasses was chipped slightly. She took out a handful of napkins and added them to the already rising pile, reminding herself to press them later.

'How is my little Lyuba?' Julia loved saying her name. Short for *Lyubov*. Love.

Slava smirked. 'Not so little anymore. A tall girl with strong legs and blonde hair. *Shandar*. Whirlwind.'

Julia wagged a finger. 'Just like her mother. It's good for you to have the child you need, not the child you want.'

'Ahh, so you need me, do you?' Slava smiled.

'Ha!' Julia pinched the stem of the wine glass and rolled it between her fingers. 'More than you probably know.' It was an admission that lit the room for a second.

'Do you ever use any of that?' Slava asked, gesturing to the glass-filled cabinet. 'I mean, it's not like there will be lots of people here for Christmas, just Em and I and you.'

Julia looked at Slava. 'Why do you call him that?'

'What. Em?'

'Yes. His name is Emilian. You should use it. It's beautiful.'

'Well, it's affectionate, I guess. Didn't you call Papa by something short?'

Julia remembered that occasionally she'd use *Hirko* instead of Henry or even Hironimus, and it had bothered him each time she did, for in Ukrainian it meant *bitter*. She smiled at the memory but chose not to reveal it, for it was something that she didn't need anyone dissecting. It was her small thing to keep about her husband. 'Yes, sure. You know, my parents had softer names for themselves.'

'Oh? You never told me that.'

'Yes.' Julia smiled, remembering the sweet way they would call to each other. 'My mother called my father 'Kolya', and my father would call my mother 'Anushka'.

'So, then you understand. I like 'Em'.'

'You know what is short for Emilian? Not Em.'

'What is it?'

'Milo.' Julia felt a sting in her eyes as she said it.

'Oh.' For a second, Slava though it unwise to pick at old wounds this evening, but maybe her mother was ready.

Slava pointed to the cabinet. 'Why not sell most of it?'

'What, all these old things? Who would want them? They have stories in them.' Julia withdrew a small oval platter that displayed yellow bunches of wheat all gathered with red ribbon, painted against a pale blue sky. 'This, for example. Papa had this made for me in New York, you know his friend Roman that worked at Bachinsky's deli on 9th street?'

'God, that place. Everyone in there was Ukrainian, and also, the restaurant across the street too— '

'Veselka.'

'That's the one. Anyway, sorry. Roman. The one with the lazy eye?'

Julia laughed and remembered Slava as a child in the company of this man, confused as to which eye to speak to, so she'd developed a habit of looking at a spot in the middle of his forehead. 'Yes, him.'

'He painted?'

'Yes. He would do it to remember.'

'Remember what?'

'Home.'

She returned it and withdrew a teacup, small and thin enough to crack if placed on the table too energetically. It was white, thin as glass, with a sheer blue line across the top, and a rose engraved on the bottom. 'And this, this I was given by Helen, the woman who let us live with her in Germany.'

'I get it. Memories.'

'I choose to think of them as stories. It's easier to say stories, because it's as if it happened to someone else.' Julia went into the kitchen and checked the stove and covered the resting dough with a thick tea towel, and then reached for a bottle of wine, half empty, and brought it to the table. She poured, a drop of red liquid catching on the chip at the top, like it had pierced soft skin, and sat down.

Julia took a sip and looked across at her daughter. 'So.'

'Yes, what?'

'I need to tell you something.'

'Sure.' Slava fingered the corner of an embroidered napkin; the stitches were blood red.

'So, not too long after Papa died, you and I were going through the paperwork with the lawyer and figuring out the will and the money and house, and, well, there was a lot of stuff to go through.'

'I know,' Slava sighed. 'I didn't understand any of it, it was horrible to have to see Papa as if he'd existed only on paper.'

'Yes, it was hard. But we got through it. And, anyway.'

Slava reached over and rested her hand on Julia's, because she thought it would help. Julia's eyes searched her daughter's. 'I wanted to wait until after he died, one day, to tell you something about my life. And I honestly didn't think I'd have the courage to, but something happened the other day that made me realize how important the truth is.'

'Okay. What about?'

'From when I was much younger. Something that we've never talked about.'

Julia watched Slava's face change. 'I know, Mama. You have always kept something inside, and I never could see what it was.'

Julia's face flushed in embarrassment. 'I'm sorry. It's just that life is complicated enough without adding so much more to it. Our plates have been full.'

Julia smiled sadly, her hands running across the smooth wood of the dining table.

Slava leaned in. 'So, when, exactly, when we moved to the city?'

Julia ran her finger along the edge of the wine glass, and then down the stem. 'No. Australia.'

Julia cleared her throat and walked over to the kitchen. Slava watched her through the separation between the cupboards and the center island. She saw as she rested her hands on the counter underneath the small window, her head hung forward, her head lit by the light above her, like a halo.

'Mama?'

Julia walked back towards the dining table and sat down.

'Papa and I moved to Australia with nothing and built everything for ourselves. We had a farm, a life, and you. But that wasn't enough. We wanted more, and we tried for more children.'

'Well, I am *more* than enough for one child,' Slava smiled.

Julia laughed. 'That may be true, but I came from a large family. And I had lost them all. It was lonely for me, the wife of a man who worked his hands raw. I wanted the noise of a large family, sat around a table, like the memories of my childhood.'

'Did you try?'

'We did. So many times. Each time my body refused it.'

'Oh, Mama. I'm sorry.'

'It's okay,' Julia moved a lock of hair off her face. 'And anyway, God had different plans for us. You see, there was a couple that we were friends with, that we lived not too far from, and the man in the couple, worked for Henry,' Julia couldn't bear to say his name out loud. 'And the wife, her name was Elina, and she became my friend.'

'At least you had someone there when Papa wasn't, right?'

'Well. Yes.' Julia poured a splash of wine into her glass and stared at it. 'It was a friendship that was lost, in the end.'

'Why?'

Julia looked at Slava and searched her face. What could she tell her? How could she reveal things about herself that had stayed dark for so long? She was a sister. A lie had been easier, and now the truth was bubbling underneath the surface, the layers had been skimmed from the top. 'Because of a lie.'

41

Melbourne

The cardboard boxes huddled in the corner, in the dusty corners of the white rooms. They filled with old books and papers, and the furniture stood in corners exactly as they had done for fifty years, or maybe even more. There was a hint of grey ash in the fireplace that hadn't been used for years, the dining table had a sheet over it, and in the kitchen, the cupboards were bare and only bore the scratches from tin cans and the smell of a few old spice jars.

The windows were raised to let the air in, and Ed was on the second floor, in their old bedroom. Roz was downstairs, sat on the floor, a glass of wine perched on a stack of books as she perused old files and photo albums. Their parents' lives were now in boxes labeled 'Xmas', 'Kids', 'School', and 'House'.

'Ed, there is a lot 'a stuff to go through here, honestly.' She took another sip and surveyed the room. 'It's all interesting for sure, but why don't we just ask some guy to come over with a truck and put it all in a storage container?'

Ed's footsteps slowly navigated the stairs as he came back down, his arms full of a small desk clock, a table lamp, and an old leash. He set the pile down on the floor next to Roz. 'Take it as a trip down memory lane, eh?' He picked up the bright red leash with a gold clasp, too small for a normal sized dog. 'Oh, God, speaking of memory lane. Do you remember this? Remember old Barry?'

'Jesus,' Roz let out a throaty giggle. 'You were so hell bent on Mum and Dad getting you a pet that you took your stuffed badger and dragged it around on this leash.'

'I was 4, right? 5?' He turned the worn bit of leather in his hands. 'Where did I even find it?'

'Think we were in a toy store and it was on the mannequin dog in the window.' Roz pinched her eyes clear of the tears that her laughing had induced. 'God, but you were a weirdo.'

Ed threw the lead in an open box. 'That may be, but I was creative, no one can argue with that.'

Roslyn withdrew a wooden plaque with a gold statue of a man running, attached to it. 'Look at this! Ha!' She looked over at Ed with a crooked smile. 'What a treasure!'

Ed rolled his eyes. 'Right, you can stop that now, thanks.'

'I'm your sister, that's what I do.'

Roz walked up to him and waved the statue in front of his face. I'm going to leave it on the mantel for the new owners, they'd be very pleased, I'm sure.' She walked over and placed it on the mantel above the fireplace and smiled. 'Remember cozy nights in front of this thing?' she pointed at the coal-stained stone surrounding the iron grate. 'Probably why I've always liked winters.'

Ed called out from the other room 'Hey, can you go look in the kitchen and see what in there needs organizing? You can be nostalgic another time.' He reached into a toy box and lifted out its contents and placed them in a box, as she walked past him to the back of the house. 'Hopeless romantic,' he muttered, smiling.

It was early afternoon when the glass on the door resonated with a series of delicate knocks.

'Roz, are you expecting one of the lawyers? Or the owner?' Ed called out as he stood up.

'No, why?'

'No, don't worry,' he replied as he walked over to the door and opened it.

Motherland

Standing in front of him was a tall woman, in her seventies, carrying herself like a dancer, delicately holding a cane, eyes bright underneath silver hair in a braid circling her head.

'Hello there, how can I help you?' Ed smiled.

'Is this the Douglas residence?'

Ed detected a faint accent. 'Yes, well, this was our parents' house, but my sister and I are here just going through some things. Did you know them?' He liked the look of her and smiled again. She seemed kind.

'No. I knew your mother.'

'Oh, so you knew Irene.'

'No. Your mother.'

Ed laughed. Surely this old woman was a bit senile. 'Listen, Mrs....'

'-- Kashiuk. Elina Kashiuk.'

'.. Kashiuk. Right. I'm not sure whom you're referring to, but my mother, Irene, passed a few months ago, not long after my father.'

'I'm very sorry.'

'Thank you.'

Roslyn appeared at the door. 'Hello,' she smiled. 'Who's this?'

Ed gestured with an open hand. 'This, Mrs. Kashiuk, was a friend of Mum's.'

Roslyn extended a hand. 'Nice to meet you. How did you two know each other?'

Elina realized she would have to play along. She leaned on her cane a bit, her yellow skirts swaying delicately as she did. She gathered her jacket closer. 'May I come in and sit, if that's alright? I can tell you how I knew her. It's a bit of a long story.'

Ed looked at Roslyn, his eyebrows raised in a question. Roslyn shrugged in response, and Ed turned back to Elina. 'Sure,' he offered, pushing the door open wider and extending a hand to her. 'I'm sure that'd be fine.'

✦

It was only an hour later, and an entire life had been upended, in the warm room of a house that had contained an entire life. Now that life felt like a lie.

'This is ridiculous.' Ed walked into the kitchen, shaking his head. 'Roz, help me out here.' A clattering of plates interrupted the silence as Ed busied his hands.

Elina sat stiffly, looking at Roz, who was staring at her like she'd just witnessed a death. 'You can imagine this is all a bit shocking.' She laced her fingers together and undid them, and then laced them again. 'How do we know you're not lying? How do we know you're not some—' she paused '— I don't know, *crazy* lady that walked in from the street and got her memories confused?'

'I am not senile, if that's what you mean,' Elina's voice lilted delicately. 'And I am not trying to disrespect your parents' memory, of course.'

Ed walked back in, but didn't sit down, leaning against the mantle above the fireplace instead. 'Well, it feels like an odd convergence of events, to be honest.' He ran his hand over the wood, a layer of dust collecting on his fingertips. 'Our parents aren't here to explain, and there's nothing in their paperwork—' he gestured to the boxes in the room '— that says otherwise.' He looked at his sister. 'Roz and I have literally no memory of being with anyone other than these two people, and now you're trying to tell us that we have another mum, and she had to give us up because she thought we were someone else's, but it turns out that we were actually hers… I mean, it sounds like something you'd watch in a film.' He shrugged. 'I just can't see it.'

Roz watched the woman in front of her: the way she sat, the calm, cool demeanor, the way she carried herself even sat in a chair, the way her clothes hovered on her, beautifully still. Her eyes held a story. She was purposeful. She had intent, and energy, and Roz immediately knew that there was something there. She wasn't trying to sell them on something, and she wasn't in a haze, or influenced by anything apart from the truth. She hinted at a truth.

Ed continued. 'Roz, I know I'm the practical one here, but you're the lawyer brain. Anything you want to say?'

Roz ran both her hands through her hair and looked back at Ed. 'Well, we need some kind of proof.' She turned back to Elina. 'What you're saying is incredible, but we need something. Anything.'

Elina nodded, and removed her jacket, placing it on the arm of the chair. She leaned forward, picking up her handbag and placing it on her lap.

'I understand,' she began. 'Which is why…' she snapped open the metal ridge of the top, spreading the leather apart. She removed the papers and handed them to Roz. '… I brought these.'

Roz took them from her, and Ed walked up to stand next to her, removing a pair of silvery reading glasses, placing them on his nose.

'Oh my God.'

The siblings scanned the papers, handing the sheets back and forth between them, reading them again, pausing only to let out steady a steady stream of held breaths, and starting again. The sounds in the room were loud in their gravity: crisp paper, fingertips tracing the words. Elina watched, her face not in a smile, or in a frown, but settled on the scene that played out in front of her.

Roz looked up finally. 'Our names. How…'

'*Leh*-shya,' Elina pronounced slowly. 'It means, 'promised to God.'

Ed looked up from his birth certificate. 'And…'

'Mahk-*sim*.' Elina leaned back in her chair, as if someone had taken an invisible weight off her back. She looked at the man standing in front of her. 'It means 'the greatest miracle'. It was your father's suggestion.' Elina's eyes pricked with tears. 'He had always wanted a son.'

Ed walked over to the dining room, and came back with a chair, setting it down next to Roz. They formed a group of three, as if round a fire, listening to an old woman softly tell a tale.

'What was he like?'

'It would not be my place to tell you. But I can tell you that they both loved you.'

'But why, then,' Ed held the paper up. 'Why?'

'It was complicated then, for women. The time was such that we were seen in certain roles, certain boxes, I guess. And any doubt sent ripples through our lives, our marriages.' She paused, rubbing her hands together as if they ached. 'We had to endure. We had to hide our— what is that word… *insecurity* I guess— and sometimes survival meant sacrificing for the sake of the betterment of our lives. I realize that sounds very old, now.'

Roz sat back. 'Well, it was common back then, I guess, but it's still hard to believe.' She shook her head. 'It's unbelievable.'

'We had no choice.' Elina leaned forward. 'And many of us now can look back on our lives, and the paths we've had to take, and live with the decisions we made. We have to. Otherwise, it would drive us mad.' She settled back in her chair.

Roz looked at the paper in her hands. 'Wait a minute.' She looked at Elina. 'I never asked where you got this. And to be honest, I don't even need to know how you found this address, let's just focus on one thing at a time.' She rubbed her temples. 'So…'

'Julia sent it to me.'

Ed clapped his hand on his forehead. 'She's still alive.'

'Yes. And she remembers. She has, all this time. It was when I realized that it was my husband at the time that could not have children, once I had my daughter, I knew I had to tell her one day. The truth.'

'So, you spoke to her,' Roz interrupted, her eyes widening.

'Yes, and she sent me your birth certificates.' Elina reached into her handbag again and withdrew a photograph. 'She also sent me this.' Julia's face peered out from the small black and white square. Her features were muted. Faded. But her dark hair fell in waves over a white cotton dress that showed a protruding belly, her slim, bare arms exposed. She was standing in a field of tall grass, robust trees in the distance behind her next to a small, dilapidated house. She held a small child's hand. Both faces were looking at the unknown photographer, smiling.

'She's beautiful.' Roz inspected the photo closely, Ed leaning over her shoulder, waiting for his turn. She passed it to him, and she looked at Elina. 'That was us. She was pregnant with us.' The truth settled in her eyes as she realized the pain that that woman, her mother, had been keeping inside her in exactly that moment.

'Yes. It is the only picture she has of you both, and she hadn't told anyone she kept it.'

Ed took his glasses off his nose and fed them into his shirt pocket, wiping his eyes. 'Elina.'

'Yes, Maks—' she caught herself and smiled. 'Yes, Ed.'

'You probably know what I'm going to ask you next.' He looked over at Roz, and she nodded in response to a silent question, as siblings tend to do.

Elina waited.

'Do you think I could call her? Do you think that would be alright with her?'

Elina closed her eyes and wept for the friend that she had abandoned long ago, and felt Roz reach out for her hand and clasp it with a kindness and warmth that was unexpected.

42

'What do you mean?' Slava looked at the woman who had always been as true as rain. Despite her tendency to distance, she had always been quietly persistent, and had always said to her as a child, 'lies are more painful than the truth.' And now Slava looked at her face and saw a kind of pain that she didn't understand.

'I have been through so much, Slava,' Julia said with a sigh. 'I have been unlucky.'

Silence followed the word *unlucky*.

Slava wasn't sure what she was getting at, and all she could do was wait for more. More from the woman who had always said less was better. Safer.

Julia stood up and walked over to the hallway, and then stopped, and then turned back, as if she had lost her way, or her thoughts, or something had reminded her. She walked over to the porch window and moved the gossamer curtains to the side, revealing the sky settling after the snowfall.

The grandfather clock moaned a slow chime.

Julia walked back to the table, her hand on her chest, fingering the gold necklace that she had worn for as long as Slava remembered. She sat down heavily.

Slava saw Julia's face change, a sculpture being more defined by its softening corners, its cracks and edges. She saw survival. She saw love.

'I don't know how to start—'

'Just try. Anything.' Slava reached for her hand. Julia smiled and heard Henry's voice. *All we can do is try.*

'Slava, when we lived in Australia, we wanted more children. We had you, but it wasn't enough. We wanted a large family. I wanted one like the memories of my childhood: noisy, full of faces around the table.'

Slava nodded. 'Sure. I understand.'

'And well, we were unlucky for a time,' Julia continued. 'Until something happened.'

Slava shifted in her chair.

'It was so unfortunate. I—' Julia stopped and leaned her forehead into her open palm, her elbow on the table. '— he was a friend. Or so I thought he was.' She looked up at Slava, noticing that her face had grown pale, her eyes staring. 'I didn't know what to do.'

'Mama, were you— '

Julia lifted her hand. 'I don't want to hear that word.' She hung her head. 'I thought it was my fault. I thought I had welcomed the attention, I had enjoyed his company, and I didn't understand what went wrong that evening…'

Slava placed her other hand on her mothers, now covering it entirely. 'Did you tell anyone?'

'No, because your father and I were happy, then, despite the difficulty of our life there. We had built a life, and this one thing would have felt like a mark on it; a shadow that would hover over us forever.'

'Then, what did you do?'

'I let it disappear. I kept it as something that would go away. And yet—' Julia moved a lock of hair over her ear, revealing a silvery scar, no bigger than thumbnail. '— a mark remains.'

'Oh, God, Mama,' Slava shook her head in disbelief. I can't believe you had to carry that with you all these years.' Slava leaned back, letting out a breath. 'But I'm confused about what that has to do with the friendship, with…?'

'Elina.'

'Right. And she was…'

'This man's wife.'

'Jesus. Did she know?'

'She and I had become friends of course because Henry and I and she and that man, well, we had become friendly. She confided in me many things, and one thing was that she could not have children. That she suspected her body could not make any. I felt sad for her.'

'Of course, but this… attack, happened…'

'After we had become close,' Julia clarified. 'She didn't know.'

'So, if she didn't know, how was the friendship cut off?'

Julia tented her fingertips above the table. 'Well, that is part of what happened after. You see, another reason I could not tell anyone the truth was because I became pregnant.'

Slava inhaled sharply. 'What??'

Julia nodded, her face reddening. 'So, I told no one, and had to pretend that everything was at it should be.'

'What about Papa?'

'No one.'

'So, Papa had no idea that this happened? None of it?'

'No.'

'Oh god, Mama.' Slava stood up, rubbing her eyes and walking to the kitchen. 'I can't believe this is you.'

Julia looked over at her daughter, worried that she had said something wrong, her face contorted in panic. 'In what way? Oh no, Slava,, I'm so sorry, this is all too much…'

'— no, that's not what I meant. The fact that you had to endure this, this…' Slava threw her hands up. 'I don't even know what to call it.'

'I know,' Julia sighed. She patted the table, her clammy hands leaving a small imprint on the polished wood. 'Come. Sit.'

Slava came back, sat down, and leaned on her elbows, facing Julia. 'Okay,' she breathed. 'Tell me.'

'I had twins, Slava. A boy and a girl.' Julia's eyes filled. 'Maksim and Lesia. They were beautiful. Maksim was dark, Lesia was light. They were mirrors of one another, but also so different. Maksim was sweet and patient, Lesia was impulsive and fiery.' She wiped a tear from the corner of her eye. 'I loved them.'

Slava sat, staring in disbelief. *Twins. Dark and light.* It was as if someone was reading her a story about a life that she knew nothing about. And yet, it was a story from *her* life. 'I'm almost afraid to ask, but…' she placed her fingertips on her temples and closed her eyes. '… what happened to them?'

'Everything was alright, when they arrived. Papa was happy. He had his son, and he never thought he would have one. We had a loud little family, and it was all we wanted. Life became quiet. In a good way, after everything that we had lost in the war. We felt as if we had survived, finally; we had fixed what had been broken.'

Slava opened her eyes. 'Well, the obvious question is, since I don't remember having siblings…'

'— is what happened to them,' Julia nodded. 'Yes. Well, Elina's husband still lingered, and Elina had suspicions about me. And maybe it was the anger at him, or the fact that she could not have children, but our friendship faltered. And when she told Papa about what she suspected…'

'— that the man attacked you?'

'— no, that we were having an affair, our friendship broke.'

'And Papa believed her, and not you?'

'He was a proud man that feared many things. And he feared somehow that I was unhappy in my life with him. He never gave me a choice to explain. And the day that I tried to fight for the truth, he gave me a choice: he told me to choose him and you, or the twins.'

Slava clapped a hand over her mouth. 'And you chose us.'

'Yes. I had no choice. I had to give them away.' Julia's tears spilled freely now, dropping onto the table faster than she could wipe them off her cheeks. 'It was the hardest thing I have ever had to do in my life; it was, and still is, a pain that has never fully disappeared.'

'I can't imagine it.'

Slava thought Emilian, and then of their own daughter, now a young adult, with dark hair past her shoulders like Julia had as a girl, hazel eyes that are constantly shadowed by long lashes. She imagined her face as a child, and her chest tightened at the thought of leaving her behind. The idea of that kind of pain was unbearable.

'Where was I in all this?'

'You were young enough not to remember, or to understand. But old enough at the time to see a kind of sadness. But I want you to listen to something. The reason why I called you here.'

'Surely there can't be more,' Slava shook her head. 'That's impossible.'

'There is,' Julia smiled. 'And this is something that life has given me, a gift, that I can share with you, after all of this.'

'What is it?'

'I received a call from Elina a little while ago.'

'What? Seriously? Why? She's still alive?' Slava's voice popped with energy, unable to contain her questions.

'She called to tell me something in her life that would affect mine. But it might not be good news, I'm not sure. But she told me a truth. She wants to help me.'

Slava frowned. 'About what? With what?'

'Many years ago, after the twins were adopted and you and Papa and I moved to New York, she left her husband and remarried eventually, and lived a happy life with her new husband, and… daughter.'

Slava pushed her chair back and squinted her eyes. 'Wait. She adopted?'

Julia shook her head. 'No. She gave birth to a daughter.'

'But I thought she was…'

Julia looked up at the ceiling and closed her eyes, Fresh tears slid down her cheeks. 'So did I.'

Slava turned her head to the right, then to the left, as if trying to solve a riddle. She looked at her mother and drew in a breath.

'Oh my God.'

Julia covered her face with her hands. The grandfather clock struck eleven, the metal resonating after the muffled heaviness of the gong.

'God will never forgive me.' Julia's voice sounded like a child behind her hands.

Slava wiped the tears from her cheeks and walked around to her, kneeling as she unpeeled her mother's hands from her wet face. 'Mama, don't you see? You are loved. You have been found. He has already.'

✒

That night, as the clock struck midnight, and later still, with her head bowed, Julia began to tell her daughter the stories that she thought she'd forgotten, that had haunted her for so long. Through the tears that pooled in the hollow of her neck, she told her daughter of the children she had wanted and had given to God, and the two children that had helped her heart heal after a crime that had broken it so badly, and the love that she'd had for all of them and then lost so painfully, so cruelly. She told her daughter that it wasn't her father's fault, and that she had forgiven him for the pain that he had contributed to, for he had also carried it in his heart to the end of his days.

She told her daughter about how she felt about love: that it is a great and complicated tragedy of joy and pain, for hearts can be broken and fixed again through hope, and still they break, and she told her that she had stopped resenting her husband and forgave him for the pain that he'd secretly had to endure, for a father losing his children is too great a sadness to bear.

They talked for hours, until their throats were scraped dry and the tears had dried in tracks on their faces. She wrung her hands and clasped them with her daughter's and presented an unflinching grief that she had never allowed herself to feel fully.

That evening, they both fell asleep under night skies that were dark and quieted by snow, felled by an incredible truth: the lost can someday be found again.

43

Glen Cove

The bright green numbers on the clock flashed 1:30am as the phone rang and woke Julia immediately, as if she had waited every second of her sleep to be in that exact moment.

The phone stopped suddenly, and she thought that maybe she'd imagined it, so she waited, her body rigid.

It started ringing again, and she held her breath as she reached across for the phone.

It stopped before she could get to it, and she had a sense that whoever was on the line was either doubting they had the right number, or second guessing themselves, or even, that the line was faulty. She reached for the lamp and switched it on, and lay back in bed, waiting. Curious.

It rang again, and this time Julia retrieved it, and grabbed the receiver and sighed. 'Elina? Is it you?'

Static, and then a voice. 'Hello? Is this Julia?'

'Yes?'

The line crackled and then a voice emerged. 'Hello…' The voice sounded elderly, but clear.

'Yes…? She was losing patience.

'I don't really know how to say this,' he began, still timid.

'Listen, it's late, whoever you are, and if you're trying to sell me something, I'm not interested, thank you.' She was about to replace the receiver to a now curious Emilian when he said, '*Wait, please, Mama*' and then she knew.

She placed the phone to her ear again. 'Maksim?'

Timid laughter. 'It's Maksim, this is Maksim.' It was said in a rush, as if to ripping the tape off a parcel and revealing its contents. *Maksim*. it sounded strange, this name that should be familiar to her, because it was said without the thick tongue of the Slavic *k* and *m*, and so her initial reaction was confusion, along with wondering if this was real. She looked around at the dark room, and reached for the rosary by the bed, her fingers lightly finding the facets and then pressing them into the pads of her fingers. It was real.

She mouthed his name to herself, silently. *Maksim*. Both her hands held the receiver to her ear now, as she leaned forward and closed her eyes. She felt his small body on her lap as she had done so long ago, his warm arms around her waist, his dark hair against her chest as he slept.

Her throat caught as she inhaled. 'Oh my God, I cannot believe it's you. Is it you?'

'Yes, it's me.'

She saw the memories of her life like the pages of a book, fluttering to an end before it closed. She couldn't speak for fear of losing track of these memories that had been left cold for so long, now warming her entire body, and she wanted them, craved them, adjusted to them with fresh authority.

She covered her eyes with her other hand whilst she held the receiver tightly to her ear, as if in a state of panic, not wanting his words to disappear into the crackle of a broken line again, but also because she wanted to digest every soft morsel of this voice, *his* voice, the voice that she had only ever known when he was a child; she heard it there still, faintly, despite the gravel of age changing it. He was there. He had found her.

They spoke until they couldn't speak any more, Julia listening to her son tell her so much about his life, or at least whatever he could fit into the next few hours. He would ask if she needed to sleep, and she would encourage him to continue, the minutes and hours passing swiftly, until the first hints of light spread across the morning, like a watercolor painting. As they ended the phone call, Ed promised that he would call with his sister on the line next time. His sister. *Her daughter,* Julia thought. She placed the receiver down like a piece of glass that would break. She was in shock and spent the rest of that morning walking in a slow and cautious pace, finally sitting outside on the porch that she had once shared with Henry. She sighed and leaned her head back, her face ruddy with tears, the sun drying them slowly.

    The light, now. She felt the light come through, and smiled, a relief settling across her shoulders. She thought of her mother's words: *there is always hope left in a broken thing.*

44

2013

Autumn had settled in green and gold, on Glen Cove, and after landing 24 hours earlier, Ed and Roslyn had taken a walk through the quiet streets of the sleepy town, just as it was coming alive in the crisp morning. The houses and shops on the streets had small porches and peaked roofs, with manicured gardens and mailboxes with painted numbers on them. The postal workers were clutching their coffees and delivery men were starting their trucks to start their routes.

It was as if they'd taken a step back to someone else's life; an old memory that hinted at a sense of peace, a foothold in safety.

They walked out of town, on East Drive, past the pile of stone that represented an old monastery, past the park by the golf course, and found their way to Prybil Beach, a small spit of sand shaped like a crescent moon, with benches along the edge of the water.

Ed zipped his sportscoat against the chill and sat down. 'Wow. I can't believe we're here.' He looked over at Roslyn, who was clutching a scarf around her neck, the orange strip of sky reflected in her bright eyes. 'What're you thinking?'

'Honestly? I don't know.' She let out a sigh. 'This all seems a bit surreal.' She looked at Ed. 'If I was ever a smoker, maybe now would be the time to do it.' The corner of her mouth lifted.

'What did you tell Martin?'

'Everything. And both girls too. I told him that I needed to do this first, with you, and that if it goes well…'

'— Of course, it'll go well.'

'— You know what I mean. If it feels right, then we can all come and meet each other.'

Ed nodded and folded his arms. 'Fair point.'

'What did you say to Helen?'

'Same. But I mean… what could go wrong, here?'

'Do you think it erases our past? That's what it feels like.'

'In what way?'

'Well, not entirely, but you know, our life with Mum and Dad.'

'It made us who we were. And so will this.'

'In what way?'

'Well, isn't that the million-dollar question.' Ed chuckled. 'It's a story about who we were, then. We're the same people, still, but our lives went in different directions. And we had more than one mother who loved us. That's something pretty great.'

'What about our real father?' Roslyn clasped her hands in her lap tightly. 'I mean—' she stopped, her voice apologetic.

'No, I know what you meant. I mean, we *had* a father.' Ed shrugged. 'And now we have two. Or, *had*, anyway.'

'More than most.'

'I wonder what he would have been like,' Ed looked across at the Long Island Sound, the water lapping the shore.

'We'll learn about him through Julia. And pictures, I guess.'

'What do we call her?'

'What do you want to call her?'

Roslyn looked up at Ed and saw the brother that had been kind to her, and patient, if not sometimes distant and pragmatic. She saw a lifetime that now had so many new memories to uncover and layer, like the pages of a book settling, gusting air as it closed.

'Mama, I think.'

Ed nodded. The blue had overtaken the sky now, and the beach started to fill.

The room felt too small, suddenly. Maybe it was the curtains. Ed pressed his shirt down with his palm nervously and walked over to the window of the hotel room. He shifted the heavy curtains to the side, and stood with his hands in his pockets, scanning the parking lot's cars moving like silvery ants. Roslyn knocked at the door, and he walked over to let her in.

'You look nice,' she commented as she walked into the room, setting her handbag down on the desk next to the phone that was plastered with various numbers for room service, front desk, dialing-out, gym. She looked at her reflection and ran a hand through her hair and closed her lips to even out her lipstick. 'I look like shit.'

Ed was back at the window and looked back at his sister. 'You look fine, hon. You're just nervous.'

Roslyn gathered her thick hair in a fist and placed it on one shoulder. 'Maybe like this. Or a braid?' She pulled out a chair and sat down heavily, leaning back and clasping her hands together, her blouse billowing around her waist and her wrists. 'This is weird.' She looked over at Ed. 'Ed?'

'Yeah.'

'You okay?'

He pointed through the glass at a spot in the distance. 'Did you know that Glen Cove is considered the Gold Coast of the North Shore? Funny.'

'Oh, you mean that—'

'Yeah. Connections. Here we are, on the other side of the world from where we grew up, in a place that sounds so familiar.'

'Where, if I can ask, did you come up with that one?'

Ed turned around. 'Hotel pamphlets are great for that kind of stuff.' He looked at his watch. 'Ready?'

Roslyn shifted in her seat, the leatherette suddenly sticking to her bare legs. 'Sure.' It was a smile that was timid, and Ed felt for the hopeful for his sister. She seemed so little now.

❧

Slava stepped out of the car and walked around to the other side to help Julia slide out, lacing her arm through hers and closing the door. Julia straightened her back a handbag draped on her bent arm. Her trousers were a pale blue, the pink of her silk collar peeked out from underneath her thin jacket. She touched her hair lightly, a wave of white now streaked with gray, still as thick as it was when she was young. She placed her hand on Slava's, her wedding band catching the light. 'Slava…'

'Yes, Mama?' Slava pushed her sunglasses off her face, nesting them in her blonde hair.

'I am not sure I can do this.' Julia looked across at the familiar landscape of the town, and yet it felt strangely unfamiliar.

'Yes, you can.'

'How do you know?'

Slava squeezed her arm delicately, the fragile bone and soft skin underneath her fingers. 'Because you taught me. You taught me what it is to be strong, no matter what you see in front of you.' She scanned her mother's face. 'And the proof of that strength is waiting for you right now.'

Julia looked at her daughter, a relief spread across her face. She realized this wasn't her daughter anymore. She was a woman. A mother. A warrior for her family.

'Slava?'

'Yes, Mama.'

'Did I tell you enough that I am proud of you?'

Slava frowned. 'What?' Her mother was nervous, she knew that. But there was an openness in her words that felt different. Softer. 'What do you mean? Of course, I know you're proud of me.'

'No, that is not what I mean.' Julia leaned her face closer. 'Did I ever *tell* you how proud I am? And that I love you? Was I enough? Or did I miss too many moments?'

Slava's eyes filled, and she quickly dabbed the corners. 'Mama, I know. I know all of it. It's never too late to say it out loud.'

They began the walk slowly, across the lot, to the entrance, and then to the bank of elevators. Slava pressed the 'Up' button. When the gold doors spread open with a metal hiss, it revealed a wide mirror at the back. Both women stood as the door closed behind them, arms linked still, staring at their reflection. Julia, once dark, now light. Slava, still bright, her blue eyes against a strong face, her features sharpened by her age. Both women possessed strong shoulders and stood proudly, and Julia wondered how it was that her entire life had gone by without often acknowledging how beautiful Slava was, and how proud she was of her. She had kept her distance for so many years, and now they gathered in moments and memories in both of their faces.

'Mama,' Slava cocked her head to doors as they opened. 'This is us.'

The hallway was long, the carpet soft and firm under their shoes, the pattern heavy with black and orange diamond shapes, echoing the orange-tinted sconces dotted on the walls. Lilies sat in a glass vase on a telephone table halfway down the hall.

At the door, Slava looked at Julia. Her eyes were open, like a child's, simmering with energy and nervousness. She squeezed her arm. Julia nodded in response.

Slava rapped at the door and waited.
The door opened, and the first thing that Julia saw was light— the curtains were drawn, and a beautiful light flooded the room, hitting every corner. She squinted and walked through with Slava, the door closing behind them.

It was then that she saw them, standing side by side, by the window. At first, it was their silhouettes, the sun at their backs. Julia felt Slava's arm disconnect from her own, and she absentmindedly handed her handbag to hold.

Julia stepped closer, and they appeared. She saw Roslyn first, her wavy hair, with hints of red and gold, like strawberries, when she was a child. Her face creased in a smile as she saw the freckles that she used to count when she would put her to bed. She saw the proud nose and the wide shoulders. She was tall.

Julia looked across to Ed and inhaled sharply. The dark hair now with so much grey, the wide forehead, the flat lips and soft nose. The eyes that had shadows underneath them, that hinted of sadness. It was Henry. She saw Henry's face, and she knew. She knew that he had lost his own son, so long ago.

Ed withdrew two pieces of paper from his pocket. They were thin and yellowed, and Julia recognized them immediately, as he unfolded it. Her lip trembled as she heard him speak. 'These are ours. Yours.' Roslyn covered her mouth, her eyes creasing as the tears fell.

Her body shook as she walked to them, her head hung. 'Maksim. Lesia. My babies, oh my babies,' she whispered over and over again, the words that she had said when they had left her side so long ago. She felt their arms around her, and suddenly the world felt incredibly small and simple and right; Julia felt as if her heart had landed, and settled, into a place that she never imagined she could rest. It was all she had hoped for, and her entire body unfolded into their arms.

She stepped back to look at her children again, hungrily taking in every detail of their faces, and patted the tears from her face. She turned, extending her arm to Slava, who was standing to the side, observing the reunion, her hands clasped in front of her, eyes staring and filling with tears.

Sertseh, davai. Julia gestured for her to come over and looked back at Ed and Roslyn. 'I never thought I would ever say this...'

Julia placed her hand over her heart, her fingers splayed, wedding band glinting in the light, as if Henry was here in the room with her. Her eyes searched each of their faces as she realized all of her children were in one room. Together.

She turned to Slava and back to the twins.

'I want you to meet your sister.'

2018

Motherland

'Ready? Take my arm.' I watch as her cotton shirt shifts and rearranges itself when she rises slowly, sitting delicately on her skin; both thin to the touch. The room is cold, but she is radiating heat. Her bones, still solid, feel warm under my hands as she leans on my arm. Her fingers squeeze my flesh and she looks up at me, searching. She was little, only as tall as my shoulders now.

'When did you become so tall?' she smiles, her blue eyes wet., like a morning sea. 'You used to be so little, Mishka.' She reaches over to my hair and pinches the ends as they lay carelessly on my jacket. 'Your hair is dark, like chocolate. Mine used to be that dark.' She winces. 'It's so white now.' Her knotted fingers pat her hair gently, as if remembering what was once there; as if trying to conjure something.

'Life happens in a blink, Babchya,' I reply and lean my head towards her. 'It happens when you're busy with your exciting life.'

She wags a finger at me, scolding my words. 'Ha. My life didn't seem very exciting to me. Bez intrigi.' *Without excitement.* Her humility makes me smile.

She takes a step forward right alongside mine, and we walk in slow rhythm out of her room, down the airy grey corridor, past the nurses' desks with potted yellow flowers on them. One nurse smiles as she sees us pass; the plump, friendly one that sees me every afternoon, and comments that these visits are a gift. *She's had a hard life,* she tells me. *I know,* I always reply.

'This way,' I direct her.

'In the garden?' She squints, as if she'd never done this before. Memories always fade and return anew; they seem strange to her; she grasps at them with futile energy.

Motherland

'Yes. The garden.'

The green that surrounds our bench is robust and wide, not unlike her garden at Glen Cove, but the things that are missing are the marigolds, black-eyed susans, peonies. Colour and fire. The tart smell of the gooseberries freshly plucked and ready for canning, the redcurrants in their ruby glory standing tall and spreading out across the perimeter. blackberries, pears, breezes that bring the chernozem, the black earth, across the fields through the farmhouse windows where she'd once slept peacefully. She remembered that most, the colors of her early life coming back to her in waves of memory before disappearing again. That farm didn't exist anymore and hadn't for years. We would always have the same conversations, dipping in and out of the quiet, her fingers circling the now dull gold of her wedding ring, that she'd never taken off. *Oh, Mishka*, she would whisper almost inaudibly. *I miss Hirko*. I know you do, I'd reply. *He would be so proud of you, his little granddaughter*. And then she would drift to another memory. *I miss my brother*. Tell me about him, I'd say. And though I knew it all, I would always ask her to tell it to me. And she would. And her eyes would darken, and a mist would fall, as she remembered the fields, the cranes, and how she was taught to count the stars.

'Mishka.' she reaches over to set her hand on top of mine. Her skin seems as if its submerged in milk; its white and translucent.

'Yes, Babchya.'

'I want to tell you a story.'

I smile and hear a sigh of contentment surround her voice. 'Okay.'

'It was night when Marioshka and I left home; night was the best time for us to escape. It was the last time I saw my parents, Mishka.'

Her blue eyes mist as she looks across at the horizon, the breeze sitting softly on us, around us, reminding us how to find the words; life waits for quiet moments for the words to come.
And then her voice, as if whispering under the weight of the world, softly says, 'Mama', and I place my hand on hers.

And so, we begin again.

About this book

This story was inspired by my grandmother Yulia (I call her Babchya), and though I've had to take creative liberties with some of the scenes that play out in this novel (as well as change names), the book is largely true. Her escape from her home at 18, her survival in Germany, her meeting and loving my grandfather, their complicated life in Australia, and the assault that resulted in the forced adoption of her twins, and their life in New York… those events were all true, as well as the subsequent reunion where she finally saw the twins again. Sadly, my grandfather Hironimus never saw them after he and my grandmother left for New York, and he died when I was five years old. Though I imagine that he would have been overjoyed to see them flourish into wonderful adults, and I hope I managed to convey his presence in this book as I knew him to be from memory: a complicated man with a heart that was always trying to do the right thing.

The way this book came about was that a few years ago, my mother, Slava, received a phone call from Australia in the middle of the night from a man claiming to be her brother. This set into place a series of events, and a bit of research into adoption records and court filings, and emails from the twins to my mother that led to Babchya finally admitting what had happened to her. 'God will never forgive me' were the first words she uttered to my mother upon admission of the forced adoption, which led me straight into the process of finding out more of her life, and about Ukraine (I travelled there in 2018). I felt that the act of asking for unnecessary forgiveness— regardless of the depths of love a mother has for her children— was an extraordinary act of humility.

Babchya spent most of her life with the heavy regret and incredible guilt of leaving her children behind, and it shaped her life in a lot of ways. But in my research of immigrant displacement and family stories of that time, she was one of thousands of women whose fate was forced, and as a result, they'd kept secrets from their families because of the fear of feeling shame. I felt like it was my duty as a woman and as a mother to share how destructive that could be, but also that there is always resilience in the human spirit.

Soon after I published this book, and a week after her 96th birthday, Babchya quietly slipped away from us, on April 25th, 2020. My heart is broken for such a great light to be dimmed, and I miss her every single day, but I'm fortunate that she told me the stories of her life before they faded away. Even in her death, she inspires me every day to be a stronger woman, and to encourage others to tell their story. Her life, although unique to her, is still a universal story about love, loss, and motherhood, and about how important it is to learn about the path that someone takes to navigate their life; from the outside, it can look complicated and bleak, but despite it all, there is always hope.

Acknowledgements

I'm so thankful to all the agents, fellow authors, and community of wonderful people (both strangers and friends) who gave me such support and feedback during the journey of this book. It would have been so much harder to persevere if it hadn't been for each of you, at different times, urging me to write this story and to not give up. You connected so hugely to the themes in this book and made me realize that I had no choice but to write it all down, because it's so easy to forget such rich history.

I want to thank Nell, Elli, Sandra, Helen, Beci, Tess, Yvonne, Cecilia and Angie: the strong, loyal, and loving women in my life who always lend me their voices when I have trouble finding my own. Your generosity and love means more to me than I can ever express.

To my children: I wrote this for you. To know that I've added to your own family stories means everything to me. Babchya would be humbled to know that she will forever inhabit these pages for you.

Mamo and Tato, thank you for being my harshest critics and my loudest cheerleaders, and for encouraging me to never let anything get in my way.

And, never least, to Tom. You loving me so fiercely is the brightest light in my world. You always challenge me to be patient, to be true to myself, and to fight for what I love. I'm so grateful I found you.
.

Printed in Great Britain
by Amazon